To Everything a Time

ELEANOR WATKINS

malcolm down

PUBLISHING

'There is a time for everything, and a season for every activity under heaven:

> a time to be born and a time to die
> a time to plant and a time to uproot,
> a time to kill and a time to heal,
> a time to tear down and a time to build,
> a time to weep and a time to laugh,
> a time to mourn and a time to dance,
> a time to scatter stones and a time to gather them,
> a time to embrace and a time to refrain,
> a time to search and a time to give up,
> a time to keep and a time to throw away,
> a time to tear and a time to mend,
> a time to be silent and a time to speak,
> a time to love and a time to hate,
> a time for war, and a time for peace.'

Ecclesiastes3:1-8 (NIV)

Chapter One

Something is wrong with Adam. The memory of his haunted hazel eyes has stayed with me all morning.

Graham heaves a sigh when I try to explain to him at lunchtime.

"Haunted. What does that mean, exactly?"

Poor chap; he thinks I'm off on one of my flights of fancy again. I've been clearing away post-Christmas debris, and only had time to put together the very scratchiest of scratch meals. No chance of him fending for himself food-wise; his mother brought him up to believe that men do not do women's work. So he sits and scans the *Farmer's Weekly* while I put together my hastily improvised omelette. I'm wondering if he's becoming a little long-sighted; he seems to be holding the paper well away from him. Maybe I'll have to mention reading glasses to him at some point, but, right now, Adam occupies the forefront of my mind.

"It's just the look in his eyes," I say, sliding the cooked omelette onto a plate. "Kind of – pleading. Apprehensive. Full of foreboding. A nine-year-old shouldn't look like that."

Graham sighs again, rustles the paper, puts it down and picks up his knife and fork. "Maybe he's going down with some bug. They always do when they start back to school. I put it down to overheated classrooms."

"Yes, well, not everyone had your kind of Spartan upbringing. I don't think it's that, though. But there's definitely something. A mother can always tell."

He raises an eyebrow at me. "What were your New Year resolutions again?"

I know, I know. There were only two. To simplify my life and to worry less. I thought I was doing well with both for the first week or so of the New Year. I've tidied away all signs of Christmas festivities, and have the pine needles down the neck of my jumper to prove it. And

I've begun to reorganise the house, in my mind, at least. But the second resolution was a step too far for me.

Well, in for a penny, in for a pound.

"I'm worried about Michael too," I confess, sitting down with my own plate. "He came home in a filthy mood yesterday. He's been moody all over Christmas, but yesterday he had both Adam and Luke in tears within ten minutes of getting in."

And almost his mother too, though I don't speak this aloud.

Graham chews for a moment, swallows, takes a slurp of tea and then says "Hormones. He's a fifteen year old boy, for goodness' sake!"

"I know, but he used to be so lovely." He was, too, sunny-natured and sanguine; before he morphed into the morose stranger we now have living in the house. I'm sure something must have happened to precipitate the change, but of course it doesn't do to ask. I blink and turn my head to the window to stare out at the bare branches of the sycamore tree against a winter sky. It should be a brand-new sparkling new year, full of amazing possibilities, and instead, the feeling is grey, and lowering, and doom-laden, like the January day.

Then again, maybe it's my imagination working overtime again.

*

I don't suppose my life is any more complicated than anyone else's really and maybe some of the complications are of my own making. I seem to be on the run, at the beck and call of someone or other most of the time. If it's not the kids demanding clean socks/food/help with homework/food/driving to football or swimming or choir practice/ food, it's someone at church asking to help arrange this or that, or Graham needing errands run, or a friend or neighbour having some crisis. Graham says I should learn to say no, though of course never to him. It's not so easy.

I'm so thankful I married him, though. There were a couple of boyfriends before, semi-serious, but I'm glad God had Graham up his sleeve, so to speak. I look at him across the table, thick dark hair in need of a trim, grey-green eyes clear as spring water, and skin that tans easily. He's not all that tall, but muscular, with strong arms and shoulders. At a fairground once, years ago, I watched a group of young men trying to ring the bell with the hammer, none of them getting more than three-quarters of the way to the top. Graham did it first go. I felt I would burst with pride; my strong man. He's my rock, my stability, the one who keeps me, most of the time, from panicking, over-reacting and going off half cocked. And I still fancy him like mad.

I'm beginning to feel better. I think I'll give Graham the last of the chocolate gateau, which I thought I might eke out with a blob of squirty cream for tonight's dessert. I'm on my way to the fridge when the phone rings. It's my friend Jo, sounding flustered. Her dad's had a possible heart attack. She wants to go to see him tomorrow; could I possibly have her kids after school and to sleep over? Of course, I assure her and murmur a few encouraging words. News like that is always horrid.

Before I can sit down, the phone rings again. This time, I feel more than a slight flicker of alarm ,because it's Adam's teacher. Can I plan to come in a little early this afternoon as she'd like a word about Adam? No, it's not an accident or illness. No, she's sorry but she can't discuss it over the phone. She'll see me later this afternoon. Click!

I sink into my chair, stomach churning. "I knew it!"

Graham raises an eyebrow. "What now?"

"Adam." My voice sounds shaky. "Miss Cluny wants to talk to me about him after school. I knew something was wrong! I just knew it!"

Graham is far too nonchalant. "Don't go jumping to conclusions. Wait and see what it's about. Probably nothing much."

I want to scream at him. He doesn't seem worried at all. But then he never does. He always under-reacts, and that's partly why I overreact. Someone has to. I choke down my resentment and breathe deeply, in out. I won't panic, jump to conclusions or make a big fuss. I give myself a mental shake and tell myself to stay calm. He's probably right. He usually is.

But I feel suddenly deflated, like the bright balloons that glistened magically over the festive season and now sag limply, diminished bags of coloured rubber. The omelette seems tasteless and I'm having difficulty swallowing. The nagging worries have leapt into the forefront of my mind and turned into a dark foreboding. The New Year looks less promising than ever.

Time for an SOS prayer, of which I send up many these days.

Chapter Two

It's beautiful, where we live. Even in the dead of winter, before the first snowdrops have begun to push through last year's detritus, and there's mud underfoot, I love it with a passion. And even today, with the worry about Adam niggling at the back of my mind, I can't help taking a moment to pause on the steps before crossing the yard to the car. Bare trees throw a dark tracery of branches against a grey sky and there are black crows cawing and flapping in the tall oaks. Our farm perches on the side of a valley, with fields and woodland dropping gently away below. Opposite, on the other side of the valley, the farmland rises until it merges into blue misty hills that make up part of the towering Black Mountain range. The river runs through the valley, a shining silver ribbon twining its way from the hill farms to the rich red lowlands.

Some of my town friends pity me for living so far out in the wilds, others are envious. Me, I'm a country girl born and bred. I'd have it no other way. Even when the right heel of my best boot squishes into a noxious mixture of mud and tractor oil, as it just did. Drat! It's left a big mark on the camel-coloured suede. I took care with my appearance this afternoon to create a good impression with Miss Cluny and boost my confidence. Well, it's not the end of the world. Worse things happen in Siberia, which is one of my mother's sayings.

*

Kids are milling everywhere as I pull into the school car park. I didn't manage to get here more than a few minutes early, after all. My own two youngest approach across the tarmac, trailing bags, PE kit and lunchboxes. Adam has his coat slung on any old how and hanging unfastened from his shoulders, Luke's coat is half-zipped and his woolly hat is crammed on at a rakish angle. Luke's face breaks into the typical gap-toothed grin of an almost-seven-year old. He is always pleased to see me and never critical, unlike the other three, who regard me as falling far short of how the cool mum should present herself. Most

7

of the other mums seem younger than me, more elegant and better groomed, as many of them are career women and I'm a lady of leisure these days, according to Graham. The effect of my best stretch cords, suede jacket (faux), and long tasselled scarf, is somewhat marred by the large black smear on my right boot. I see Adam's eyes flicker over it.

"Tractor oil," I tell him. "Blame your father."

Adam isn't saying anything, eyeing me somewhat warily, sizing up the situation. He was a pretty baby, and will be a handsome young man one day, with a thatch of tawny hair and thick–lashed expressive grey/green eyes. At nine he's in the plain stage, all big front teeth in a face that hasn't quite caught up yet.

"You have to see Miss Cluny," he says accusingly. I wonder fleetingly whether other mothers' children address them in accusatory mode as often as mine do…

I get out and lock the car. "I know. What's it about?"

He shrugs, and scuffs his school shoes on the tarmac. There's a tense and anxious look about his eyes and the set of his shoulders. He and Luke trail back into school with me, swimming against the tide of departing mums and kids, and I leave them in reception while I go to Miss Cluny's room.

Judith Cluny is a nice friendly girl but today she looks serious. A cold chill goes down my spine and I decline her invitation to sit. There doesn't appear to be another adult–sized chair in the room anyway. She frowns and fiddles with the papers on her desk. Then she looks straight at me.

"I'll come right to the point. We're a little concerned about Adam." She clears her throat. "Is there – could there be – something at home – some situation – that's bothering him?"

What can she mean? Adam's obviously unhappy, but it can't be anything to do with his home life. Nothing has changed, other than the ordinary ups and downs of family life and the upheaval of Christmas festivities. He was a little mopey just before Christmas, but has been fine over the holidays. Just last weekend he was careering round the farm on his new trail bike, coming in mud–splattered and cheerful, kicking a football around with Michael, scrapping with Luke over the choosing of games for the play station, which was given to the boys as a joint present from my parents. It's only since term began that he's seemed troubled.

I say, in a voice that sounds uptight and defensive. "He's fine at home.

8

But he doesn't seem keen on school any more. I've no idea why."

Judith Cluny frowns and taps nervously on her desk with a pencil. She's younger than me by at least fifteen years and can't have had that much teaching experience. This might even be her first post. She says "Adam's been a very able pupil. Above average. And a well-behaved and well-adjusted one. Until just recently. Recently – there have been – incidents."

Dread clutches at my throat. I have refused a seat, but sit down now, on one of the child-sized chairs. I feel suddenly small and vulnerable, as though I'm a child myself again. Judith is clearly finding this difficult. She clears her throat, twiddles the pencil, pushes back a strand of blonde hair that's escaping its pony tail.

"I'm sorry, Mrs Harper, but Adam has been stealing. Not just once. Several times."

I'm suddenly on my feet again, indignant, angry. This is outrageous! My little tawny-haired Adam a thief? Never! How dare this inexperienced, wet-behind-the-ears slip of a girl even suggest such a thing!

Judith Cluny is taking control now. She repeats, kindly but firmly, "I'm sorry, Mrs Harper. This must come as a shock. But it's been proved. Some of the others missed articles – football stickers, sweets, pens – and these things have been found in Adam's drawer or his locker. Even in his sports bag. I found a missing badge there only yesterday."

My mind is reeling. I am in denial, big time. And I'm angry. But following hard on the heels of these emotions is another thought that makes me suddenly sick and cold. Twice or three times lately, entire six-packs of small chocolate bars have strangely vanished from the shelf in the cupboard where I keep special treats. And so has a brand new pack of felt-tips belonging to Luke.

It's unthinkable. But there's more. Judith Cluny has a look of compassion now.

"There's something else. Today, a very expensive pen went missing from my desk."

I am cold and shaky. "And?"

She shakes her head. "It hasn't shown up. But I thought you should be aware. Of the problem, and the need to get to the root of it."

I drive home, feeling sick and shaken, none of us talking. Adam wouldn't do such a petty thing as nicking stuff from his friends – would he? And as for stealing from his teacher – never! What was she thinking

9

of, anyway, bringing an expensive pen to school and leaving it lying about? I should have challenged her with that, if I'd thought of it in time, but it's too late now.

Luke begins to chatter but Adam is silent, his eyes huge and apprehensive, his over-large teeth biting his lower lip. My heart yearns over him. But I must speak to Graham before saying anything. I must not panic. I must not over-react. I must weigh up the situation before rushing in, that's what Graham would say. And he's right. I keep my eyes on the road and bide my time.

*

At supper time, Adam refuses his food, saying he doesn't feel well.

"Can I have his?" Michael is quick to ask.

For several years Michael and Lauren were about the same height, despite the two years between them in age. Then, around two years ago, Michael had a sudden huge growth spurt, and at fifteen is a tall, husky, blue-eyed giant. He is a bigger, blonder, younger version of his father, and he is perpetually hungry. It's a measure of comfort to my troubled soul that he's come home in a better mood today. Maybe I can cross him off my worry list.

"Go on, then," I say absently, and he slides the contents of Adam's plate onto his own.

Lauren looks primly disgusted and edges as far away as possible as though the two of them were contagious. She is going through a vegetarian, organic-only food phase and not a lot of that either. "That's *gross!*"

I am worried about Adam, my stomach clutched by the cold fear that comes when something is wrong with one of my brood. I surreptitiously feel his forehead as he leaves the table. He looks mournfully up at me. "I feel sick."

He does seem a bit warm. Maybe he's really ill. Other problems fade into insignificance as thoughts of meningitis, food poisoning, terrible unnamed viruses flood my mind. What do teachers know, anyway?

Adam makes no objection when I suggest early bed. He looks so small, pale and helpless lying there, all eyes and teeth. I tuck him in and say a quick prayer, my hand lightly on his tawny head.

"Thanks Mum." He sounds weak and pathetic, his long eyelashes fluttering. I have a sudden flicker of suspicion. Is all of this a little theatrical, a touch overdone?

I chide myself for unworthy doubts, my hand on the light switch.

"Night night, sweetheart."

"Mum?"

"Yes?"

"I don't have to go to school tomorrow, do I?"

His voice sounds stronger somehow. Maybe the Lord is answering prayer already. On the other hand –

"We'll see," I tell him, and switch off the light. I'd meant to have a quick frisk of his sports bag when he was in bed, but tonight he's taken it upstairs with him and placed it safely within arm's reach.

Chapter Three

Everyone has overslept. I fly round the house dispensing clean clothes and lunch boxes, my bare feet thrust into slippers, face unwashed, hair unbrushed. The boys like porridge, and I thank God for it as I stir a pot of the grey steaming stuff. At least they'll go off with something hot inside them on a cold winter morning.

Lauren has organic whole yoghurt with a spoonful of Manuka honey, which is wickedly expensive but acceptable to my daughter as it is produced from a particular shrub in New Zealand that never gets the least whiff of pesticide. I urge a hot cup of tea upon her, it looks as though snow might be about and she needs a hot drink inside her, at least, but she eschews my ordinary blend and makes herself a cup of something herbal and aromatic.

I marvel at the way any daughter of mine can be so beautiful and confident at thirteen. I was painfully shy at that age, had troublesome spots and greasy hair and I hated my legs because they were too short from the knee to the ankle. Lauren's skin is clear as alabaster and her hair would be a shining blonde waterfall if she hadn't gone and got her friend Paula to put in a purple streak last weekend. She wears the tiniest school skirt possible and thick black leggings on her long beautifully proportioned legs, with big black thick-soled boots. Her rucksack has a logo saying Music makes me High. She has a chunky black fleece, a big purple scarf and black fingerless mittens. She catches me looking at her and raises her eyebrows exaggeratedly. "What?"

"I was just thinking how nice you look."

She doesn't believe me. Standing by the Aga, hands clasped round her mug of tea, she eyes me critically in return. "Why don't you get yourself organised in the mornings, Mother? Like, you should see Paula's mum. She's dressed, her hair's done and her make-up on by eight every morning."

Bully for Paula's mum. I don't say it aloud though. It's a waste of time trying to pay my daughter a compliment these days. I dish out porridge in large dollops into the boys' bowls. Adam seems better; in fact he has a glow in his cheeks and looks positively cheerful. Evidently his indisposition has proved to be nothing much. Or God has answered prayer. Or is it that he feels possible trouble has been averted? Anyway, my heart is lightened. Graham and I will tackle the stealing problem later. Maybe it will all prove to be some huge mistake.

The big kids are in time for their bus for once, and nobody has forgotten their homework. We are almost at the Primary school when Luke suddenly pipes up from the back seat "Mum, Mum, *Mum*! I put that rubber spider from my Christmas stocking in my bag to show Cameron. And it's gone."

I feel my heart flip again but make light of it. "Never mind, sweetie. I expect you forgot. I'll look for it at home."

Adam's face in the mirror is nonchalant. Far too nonchalant, I have a sinking feeling in my middle. Something is wrong and I haven't a clue what's at the root of it. I sigh, wish the boys a good day as they climb out, and turn the car around to head home.

*

It's snowing a little by the time I get home, big feathery flakes that drift casually down as though they're not really serious about settling. I don't linger out of doors, though. Back inside, I run around, washing dishes, making beds, picking up and tidying up. It's almost eleven by the time I plonk down in the big cushioned rocking-chair by the Aga, cup of coffee beside me and Bible to hand. This is what I optimistically title my Quiet Time. Sometimes it happens. All too often I'm interrupted by the phone shrilling, doorbell ringing, a fertilizer delivery to sign for or Graham bursting in with some crisis situation. Today, he's repairing fences in one of the far fields and won't be home any time soon.

I notice though, that Ben has sneaked in from the cold and taken up a warm spot by the Aga. I've read a dog book that says Bassett Hounds are untrainable, and we have the living proof that it's true. We've never quite succeeded in house-training Ben; he remains a law unto himself. He regards me mournfully, face on the floor, ears fanned out around him, eyes rolled upwards with a piteous expression that appeals plaintively to my softer side.

It works. It's still snowing, on and off, and a keen North East wind has sprung up that blows the flakes horizontally. Ben has a sturdy kennel and we provide him with cosy padded dog beds and old duvets, all of which the fool dog insists on shredding into strips. We even bought him a smart warm red dog coat last winter and buckled him securely into it. He neatly removed it without any rips and buried it near the compost heap. He sighs deeply and rolls his eyes at me. I let him stay, and even share my Rich Tea biscuit with him. He's an old fellow now, I'd hate to be out in the cold today, and, hey, cleaning up the odd puddle is no big deal.

I'd meant to spend time this morning in serious prayer, 'storming the gates of heaven' on behalf of my Adam. His unhappiness surely calls for some serious intercession. I open my Bible to the words of St. Paul : *'Be joyful always, pray continually; give thanks in all circumstances, for this is God's will for you in Christ Jesus.'*

I close my eyes and let the words go in deep. The tension begins to drain away. I can safely put Adam into God's hands and leave him there. No problem is too big that we can't get through it with his help. I am inadequate, yes, but I have a God who is all–loving and all–powerful and I am rich in everything that matters.

The phone shrills. I jump, and Ben opens his eyes but does not lift his head.

"Alison. How are you?"

The sweet contralto tones are those of Caroline, our Vicar's wife. Now here, surely, is the opportunity to share my worries about Adam, to avail myself of the comfort and understanding of another Christian woman.

Instead, I feel my hackles rise and my defences go up.

"Fine, Caroline, thanks. And you?"

"Very well, thank you." A slight pause. "Just a possible small amendment to the agenda for February 5th."

I search my mind and find a blank. February 5th? That's two weeks away, isn't it? What is happening then? What agenda is this?

"The planning meeting for the Spring Fayre," says Caroline smoothly, with the faintest, faintest hint of rebuke at my hesitance. "You hadn't forgotten?"

"Of course not," I lie, and manage a little laugh. "February 5th, the Vicarage, yes?"

"Actually, no. There has to be a change of venue. In fact, that is why I'm calling. Unfortunately, the plumbers have chosen that day to install the new downstairs loo at the Vicarage. I couldn't quibble about the date; plumbers are so much in demand these days. So I'm wondering…"

I know what is coming before her honeyed tones inform me. Yes, I hear myself say; of course I can have the planning meeting up here at the farm. No, it's no trouble.

"February 5th, 2.30, okay?"

"Actually, its 2pm. I'll print out the agenda programmes, if that will help."

"Thank you so much." What am I thanking her for? I'm the one doing her the favour. I feel a simmering of resentment as we say our goodbyes. I wonder, unkindly and not for the first time, how a lovely man like our vicar Paul came to marry someone like Caroline.

*

It's just as well I'm getting on famously with my post-Christmas clean-up. I'm moving onward and upward. At lunch time I prevailed upon Graham to help me shift some of the big old pieces of furniture on the landing so I could clean behind.

"I'm doing a thorough job, because the planning committee will be here in a couple of weeks' time," I tell him.

"And are they planning to conduct an extensive hygiene inspection while they're here?

"Don't be silly. But they may need to use the upstairs toilet. Just shift the linen cupboard a foot or so out from the wall."

He does so with a very bad grace, sweating and huffing. "What have you got in here, the crown jewels?"

"Just sheets and blankets. Towels and things. They weigh heavy."

"Tell me about it." He straightens up and puts a hand to his back in an exaggerated way. "That's almost crippled me."

The phone rings, and he escapes downstairs, moving fast for a crippled person. I hear him talking machine parts with our local garage. Then the back door closes and he's gone.

I attack the dust and cobwebs. Our house is old and we share it with many non-human inmates. Mice scurry in the roof and wall cavities, squirrels sometimes find a space and squeeze in, thundering above our heads in hob-nailed boots. Mice and even squirrels I can stomach, rats make me squirm. You can tell a rat by the sound its tail makes dragging along behind.

There are insects of all kinds, earwigs and silverfish, flies dead and alive, and spiders. Lots of spiders. I see a big one now, scurrying out of a crack in the plaster and disappearing behind the skirting. That crack needs filling. I find some filler and apply it, hoping that no small

15

creatures are trapped behind. I'll need to let it dry before the cupboard is replaced.

*

My neighbour Sue has kindly offered to drop off my kids when she fetches her youngest from school this afternoon. But even without the school run the afternoon flies by.

I've finished the stairs and landing and am shaking out mops and dusters when Sue's muddy old truck pulls up. It's stopped snowing but the sky is grey and lowering and it's getting dark already. Even allowing for my two added to Sue's boy, the vehicle seems unusually full of children, with arms, legs and heads sticking out of windows.

When the doors burst open, they disgorge not only Adam and Luke, but also Jo's two boys Sam and William, clutching rucksacks.

"They said they were sleeping over at yours," explains Sue. "I said you hadn't mentioned it, but they were adamant. Is that okay?"

My hand flies to my mouth. Another thing that's slipped my mind. How could I have forgotten Jo's boys were coming? I haven't prepared beds, am not sure whether there's enough food.....

"Yes, of course," I say brightly. "Thanks for bringing them, Sue. Hi, you two."

Luke and Sam are already off upstairs, delighted to be having a sleepover.

Adam looks less pleased to be entertaining William, who's a year older and a lot huskier than himself. I resolve to have a word in his ear when I can get him alone. In the meantime, my mind flies to beds and supper. Luke's tiny room has bunk beds so that's no problem. There's a folding bed that can go in Adam's. I'm struggling with it when the door slams and the big kids are home.

Lauren passes by with her mobile clamped to her ear, acknowledging me with a dismissive wave that indicates she's not to be spoken to, and closes her door, continuing the conversation from within. Michael pauses in the doorway, removes his ipod and says, "Here, Mum, you're not getting that right. Let me." And in a few quick moves he has the bed unfolded and set up.

I rest for a moment, astonished and grateful that he's not only less surly but actually helpful. "Thanks, Michael."

He nonchalantly dusts off his hands. "No probs."

Lauren reappears, looking sniffily at the relocated linen cupboard.

"Why has that moved? And why are there so many children in this house?"

I answer both questions wearily, and add "I'd be really grateful if you two could help entertain them for a bit. Organise a game or something."

Lauren looks at me as though I've asked her to jump off the woodshed roof. But I'm pleasantly surprised again when Michael says "Ok Mum, no probs. Leave it to me."

The noise level is rising from downstairs. There's nothing like a multiplicity of small boys to create havoc in a formerly peaceful environment.

I don't know exactly how Michael does it, but he rounds them up, marshals them into his own room and organises some kind of game. Peace reigns. But not for long. I'm just telling myself that Michael is turning out all right after all when I find Adam at my elbow, belligerent and scowling. I sigh. "Why aren't you with the others?"

"I hate that game. William's good at it, but I'm not. I'm rubbish."

His head is down, his feet kicking at a frayed edge of carpet. It's no wonder my house has a lived-in appearance. I say automatically "Don't do that, sweetheart. And you're not rubbish. Did someone say that to you?"

"Everybody says it. I am. Even at football. I'm a rubbish player. I let in all the goals. I'm just a pile of – of – rubbish."

He is near to tears. This display of low self- esteem is beaming a ray of light into the foggy puzzlement I've been feeling about my middle son. If I only had a little time time, I'm sure I could get to the bottom of the whole thing. Is this the moment to bring up the matter of the stolen items?

There's a crash from Michael's room, followed by a small silence and then Luke's piping voice. "What's Mum going to say?"

At the moment, the phone downstairs begins to ring. No, now is definitely not the time.

*

I have managed to stretch the supplies to provide supper for two more, by dint of reducing everyone's sausage allowance and adding extra jacket potatoes and baked beans. The sausages are a tad overdone, but maybe nobody will notice.

"I like them burnt," says William gallantly, and I manage a wan smile. There's just enough apple crumble to go around if I pass on dessert.

All in all, I think I'm coping quite well. Until, later in the evening, I go to fetch a spare duvet from Michael's room. It's a tip. Having all those little boys in earlier didn't improve things at all. I pick up clothes, books, bags. There's a ring binder on the floor where someone could trip over it. It's Michael's collection of the Aircraft magazine he's taken for years. Since he was about eight years old he's been mad about planes. Now he's beginning to consider the RAF as a career. Graham seems both disappointed and relieved that his eldest may not want to follow him into farming. There's little future in agriculture these days. And we've long agreed that we'll encourage and support any career choices our children make.

I turn pages filled with glossy aircraft pictures and technical articles. Good old Michael. He was so helpful this afternoon, and in my more hopeful moments I see the makings of a fine young man.

And then I see the other publication, hidden away right in the centre of the aircraft binder. It's a soft–covered book entitled; *Your Relationship: things you need to know*, and has an illustration of a passionately kissing couple on the cover. I flick through the pages. The chapters have explicit titles: *Your questions about sex, Beginning a relationship, Staying safe, How do I tell if I'm pregnant?* and it has graphic illustrations and diagrams. I feel a flutter of alarm. This is a publication for young people, and of course all young people need information. It seems to be on the permissive side though, lacking the values we had hoped we were teaching our children. It's asking a lot to think that Michael would come to us with his questions, but even so...

I close the binder, my mind whirling. Is Michael thinking of starting a relationship?

He's only fifteen, for goodness sake! But they start young these days. Should I tackle him about it? He obviously feels uncomfortable about reading this because he's hidden the book. What can I say? Can I even look him in the eye?

Michael is downstairs with Graham, there's a match on with Man U playing and they are both supporters. Going downstairs, I hear Michael's voice roaring "Offside!" and think, he's only a child.

Later, when he's gone upstairs, I sit down beside my husband. I find I'm trembling. He eyes me casually, looks again, and says "What's the matter now?"

I tell him, tensely, what I've found. He listens. He's not saying anything. Has he heard a word I've said? Does he realise how serious this might be?

"What are we going to do?" I wail. "I told you something was wrong!" Graham is still silent. Then I see there's a twinkle in his eye. He leans over

18

and prods me gently in the ribs with a work-hardened finger. "Come on, drama queen. He's a fifteen year old boy wrestling with hormones, as I've said before. Just think back to that age. Weren't you curious? Didn't you read stuff? Did you always tell your parents everything?"

He's right, of course. As usual. My worries shrink back into perspective. My son is growing up, and he's growing up normal. He has mood changes, and that's normal too. It's something to thank God for.

Relief makes me quite light-headed. I kick off my shoes and put my feet in Grahams' lap and he massages my toes as we watch News Night together.

*

It's 10.30, and I'm tucked up in bed. Outside, in the chilly darkness, a barn-owl screeches, inside, the house is settling itself for the night, with creaks and squeaks and rustles. All four little boys are asleep. Streaks of light show under Michael's door and Lauren's, and Graham is downstairs watching a discussion programme, but I just couldn't have stayed on my feet any longer and almost fell asleep in the bath. I'd planned on talking about Adam to Graham when we're in bed, but I'll never hold out until he comes up. It will all have to wait until the morning.

The night sounds blur and dim in my ears. Some time later I half-imagine that I hear a sudden thud and exclamation of pain, but by then I am too far gone to do anything about it, or even to care.

Chapter Four

Sundays have changed in our house. There was always hassle, with breakfast, and putting the joint in the oven, and getting the right kids into the right clothes, and all of us to church more or less on time. But it's no longer a case of four little Harpers all in a row, in their Sunday best, all present and correct with Mum and Dad.

Now they're older it's even more stressful, if anything. The little boys are still obliged to attend, sometimes under duress. The other two go spasmodically, if they can be prised from their beds. Lauren goes to church as often as not, mostly because of the Youth Orchestra, where she plays flute and guitar and sometimes the keyboard, if our organist is away for some reason. She sings, too, in a sweet clear soprano, but we don't hear as much of that as we used to.

I sometimes think that it's only music that keeps Lauren, and therefore all of us, on something resembling an even keel. She's less keen on it these days, but music still means a lot to her. Michael used to play drums, but has lately hung up his drumsticks. I suspect they've both been convinced that performing in public (or at least in church), is not cool. Michael still comes to church sometimes, sitting in the back row with the other teenagers (all too few of them), and critically observing the proceedings rather than taking part.

Today, he's decided to come. Lauren isn't; she has a cold and remains a humped, sniffing mound under her duvet. Graham thinks he may be going down with a cold too. He sits, morose, on the bed, pulling on his socks and taking extra care with the right one.

I peer over his shoulder. The toes and part of the foot are an interesting mix of blacks and blues, shading to yellow in places. He sees me looking and grunts "Still darn painful." It's my fault he hurt his foot, for moving the linen cupboard and leaving it for him to walk into in the dark, and he doesn't let me forget it. It's four days ago now though, and I'm tired of feeling guilty.

"It looks much better," I say brightly. "The bruising's fading nicely."

He gives me a look. I see that very same look quite often these days on the face of his daughter.

*

This morning it's my turn for the class of four to sixes at Children's Church. The children I teach are called Little Tiddlers and I love them. Our church premises, as well as the vicarage, are being renovated, and my class has to use the basement kitchen. The kids sit demurely round a table while I tell the story of Moses and his deliverance from the basket in the bulrushes. Then we discuss the story. My aim is that they get a feeling of how precious, how valuable, each one of us is to God.

"So you see how God took care of baby Moses, by getting the princess to look after him, with his own mother helping," I tell them.

"And his sister," says Jessica, almost six.

"His sister, too," I agree. Jessica smiles smugly. She knows all about being a big sister. Or rather, aunt. She is the youngest of a family of much older brothers and sisters, the eldest of whom has a four-year-old, Rhys, who is in Little Tiddlers too. Jessica just loves being an aunt. She takes her responsibilities very seriously, and constantly admonishes Rhys to hurry up, sit down, stand up, put on his coat or take it off, stop yawning, grinning, frowning or picking his nose. Most things Rhys does meet with her disapproval, poor lad. She reminds him now to stop fiddling with the crayons.

"Not fiddling," mutters Rhys, who has developed something of a hangdog demeanour.

"You are fiddling!" she insists, with a toss of blonde pigtail.

I suggest that Rhys gives out the crayons and we will colour in our outline pictures of baby Moses, but Jessica objects to the proposal. There is nothing quite as bossy as a bossy little girl. "Rhys doesn't know all his colours yet," she tells me firmly.

Rhys has visibly brightened at the thought of distributing crayons. Now he droops again. I say, equally firmly "The colours don't matter. Just give some to everyone, Rhys, please."

Rhys doles out the crayons, more or less equally, colouring begins and peace reigns.

For a while. Then Jessica says "You're going over the lines, Rhys."

"I *like* going over the lines."

"But you're supposed to stay inside them. Not go over."

"I want to go over."

"Well, I said don't. And I know best, because I'm your aunt."

Rhys has had enough. He puts down his crayon and his cheeks go red. Then he hollers "I DON'T WANT YOU FOR MY ANT! I HATE ANTS!"

I rush to make peace. Jessica throws me an affronted look that says; Well, the ingratitude of it, after all I do for him! My sympathies are mostly with Rhys, I soothe them both, one huffy, the other tearful, and wonder if it might be a good time for Jessica to move up into Little Fish.

*

The last child is collected, and the basement kitchen is quiet. I gather up scattered crayons, books and papers, straighten the chairs. Starting up the stairs, I see a couple of pairs of legs in jeans drift by above on their way to the main entrance. It's Caroline and Paul's sixteen-year old daughter, Rebecca, and my Michael. They don't see me. Their heads are together and they're talking in low tones. I can't hear what they're discussing but neither of them is smiling and both their expressions can only be described as glum.

*

My parents are here for Sunday dinner. They live across the valley, almost opposite us, in the same farmhouse my brother and I grew up in. Except that there have been alterations since then. Unlike ours, their house has been fully modernised. It is tight-roofed, centrally heated, carpeted and nicely decorated. They have a gardener in once a week, to cut grass, trim hedges, weed and maintain.

My dad, Tom, farmed for many years. He now lets the land to neighbours, so, as my mum says, they enjoy the farming seasons and activities without having to do anything about it. But that doesn't mean my dad's retired. Oh no, he now runs a kind of export business, mostly on EBay, sourcing machine tools, buying and then selling them. He's doing very nicely too, thank you. His customers come from all around the world and are often here on buying trips. I have trouble remembering their names and home countries – there's Slawek from Poland, Carlos from Ecuador, Hanif from Kenya, Mikhail from Slovakia, and many others. My parents entertain them and in return are invited to visit. They've already been to some of the Eastern European countries and plan a visit to Trinidad next year. My dad has always been a quiet man and a hard worker, and he's turned out to be an astute businessman as well.

My mother, Emilia, is a remarkable woman too. She does not look her age, which is sixty-seven. Her hair is shiny and silvery, with some of the original dark blonde discreetly mixed in, cut in a chic bob. She's a little overweight but doesn't let it worry her; she knows what suits her and how to be up-to-date without looking ridiculous. Today she's wearing a long chocolate cord skirt, flaring out flatteringly at the hem, flat chocolate suede boots, a cream polo-neck under a sheepskin jacket. Lauren considers her well trendy. The boys think she's cool because (in order of importance) she understands football, she's computer literate, and she writes books. She's been writing for years, children's fiction mostly, reads voraciously, runs a prayer group for women, helps at a charity shop. And I should add that she's a nice person too. My husband lives in hope that the old saying about daughters turning into their mothers will turn out to be true. .

"Did you know," my mother remarks conversationally at the dinner table, "That before towns and communities appeared in the North American wilderness, there were such huge dense forests that a squirrel could travel the whole length of Pennsylvania without once touching the ground?"

My father rolls his eyes and passes her the broccoli. "Have some greens, dear."

The rest of us pause for a moment, pondering the information. This is a fact we hadn't known before.

"Is Pennsylvania big?" asks Adam, as the vegetable dishes begin to go round again. "As big as Wales?"

"Much bigger," says my mother.

"Moron," says Lauren, meaning her brother, not her grandmother.

"Why would a squirrel want to go all that way?" wonders Adam.

"Not a real squirrel, stupid," says Lauren.

"A pretend one?" asks Luke.

"A hypothetical one," says Lauren.

"Well done, Lauren," says my mother, and Lauren actually blushes and looks pleased. She is a different girl when my parents are around. Despite her cold, she got up for dinner and sits with us, declining the roast beef but accepting a roast potato, Yorkshire pudding and vegetables, with a splash of gravy.

My mother brings out the best in all of us. She is reading Annie Dillard just now, savouring and digesting and sharing nuggets of gold from the books. She has read all the authors I long to get into – Solzhenitsyn, Steinbeck, George Macdonald, G.K.Chesterton, and so on and so on. She always knows who is the current favourite for the Booker prize. Her house is full of books which she orders online or picks up second–hand in our local bookshops. My father has offered to buy her a Kindle, but she says she prefers real books. She is fascinated by everything – history, geography, the universe, flora, fauna, psychology, cause and effect, cultures, and most of all, people.

I long, more than anything, with the intensity of a needy child, to win my mum's approval, to make her proud of me. I can't imagine a world without her.

"Coming on the play–station, Gran?" asks Michael when the meal is over. She hesitates, not wanting to leave me to the big clear up, but my dad says quickly "Go on, Emmy, you know you want to. I'll do the washing up. Go and play."

I see a look pass between them, a look that holds within it a deep tolerance, affection, understanding, and something else I can't quite name, something which maybe belongs to them alone. They are comfortable and at peace with one another. I hope Graham and I will be like them when the years have passed. The whole tribe disappear up the stairs, and I soon hear squeaks and whoops and cheers. They all think their Gran is so cool, and don't want to miss a moment with her.

*

It's dark outside, and time for Mum and Dad to go home. They have a budgerigar and a cat to feed. Despite colds and sniffles, it's been a good, satisfying kind of day. No major fights broke out, no new and dreadful situation raised its head. This afternoon, Graham, Mum, Dad and I put on old coats and wellies and took a walk across the fields to look at Graham's winter corn. The landscape was wintry, snow still on the tops of the mountains and the air cold enough to turn our breaths into white steam. Returning, my mum takes me by the arm and points. There, under the big sycamores that fringe the edge of our yard, the first green spears of snowdrops are poking up from the dead brown leaves beneath. Already a hint of white flower is showing at the tip. "Spring isn't far away." says Mum. She says it every year when the snowdrops come.

As we go inside, my mum takes my arm again. We are alone in the utility, shedding coats and boots. "Alison, I wanted a word. Adam has a problem."

I hang up my old Barbour with a sinking heart. She's noticed. It must be that obvious. And I thought he'd seemed quite normal today. "I know. I'm really worried. I can't think what it's about."

"Oh, I know what it is," she says calmly. "He's being bullied. He told me."

I almost splutter. "He did?"

"Yes. When we had a moment alone earlier. He just came out with it. I think he wanted to tell someone. He says he hates school, because of a group of boys. They've been threatening him, maybe worse – I think he said something about Chinese Burns. He has to give them presents to make them leave him alone, kind of like protection money. So the poor little soul has been doing just that."

It's so obvious. How could I not have guessed – the missing sweets and small items. I should have worked it out long ago.

My mother is reading my thoughts. She pats my arm and says "Don't feel bad about it. He said he thought he'd look a wuss if he told anyone. He didn't want me to tell you and Graham. And especially not Michael and Lauren. But I thought something should be done."

Something certainly should. I am going to sort those bullies out, one way or another, sooner rather than later. Today has been a peaceful interlude, but very soon I must gird up my loins, so to speak, and go into battle, big time.

Chapter Five

It's been a miserable couple of weeks, in some ways. Lauren kindly passed on her cold to the rest of us, with the result that we sniffled, snuffled, sneezed and coughed our way through the days and often the nights, and batteries of Lemsip, Night Nurse, Day Nurse and various brands of cough syrup lined the kitchen counters. Graham's cold, predictably, turned out to be man–flu, though he soldiered on bravely as usual. Spartan upbringing notwithstanding, when he's ill he likes everyone to appreciate it. Mum and Dad have escaped so far, but every family with a child at school has suffered too. Luke's birthday party went ahead, to a cacophony of coughing and barking from his young guests, but they had a good time nonetheless, though their hostess was somewhat limp and washed–out at the end of it all.

The weather has been horrid too, day after day of lashing rain showers and gale–force winds, and nights of buffeting when the whole house seems to shake, rattle and roll. A couple of old apple trees blew down, and Graham has been busy with the chain saw. When the saw is in his hands he tends to get carried away, so he has felled a couple more rotting or dodgy trees, and the top of the near meadow is beginning to look like a lumber yard.

Today at last the gales have died down a little, and the valley is no longer obscured by sheets of driving rain. I can see that the river has burst its banks in several places along the valley bottom, there are wide stretches of standing water in some of the river meadows. Everything seems colourless and sodden. I think this must be my least favourite time of year.

Never mind, today at last I have time to take action on Adam's behalf. He and all, of them, missed a few days' school, but they're all back now, and I am on my way to do some reconnaissance work.

I haven't mentioned to Graham what I plan to do. He would call it snooping.

Maybe it was going a bit OTT to dress up in what can only be called camouflage gear. It's just a beige high–necked fleece and a pair of old khaki combats I wear for helping round the farm. I added the woolly hat and dark glasses in case either of the children or their friends happened to catch a glimpse of me and blow my cover.

The school building is 1970's, glass and brick, long and sprawling and beginning to look a little tired and dated. The grounds are wonderful though, a full half–acre of grass and tarmac, with a swimming pool and sports pitches. A grassy hill was incorporated in the layout, much loved by decades of little ones who have run up and down its sides. There are tall trees shielding the school and grounds from a road on one side and on the other, a public footpath leading to the main town car park. The branches of the beeches, oaks and sycamores are bare just now, but when spring comes will be covered with a cloak of new green to soften the strong protecting fence.

I park the car and skulk among the trees, noticing the tangle of undergrowing brambles that will produce blackberries later. The kids are beginning to emerge after their lunch, rending the air with the shrill clamour that could only come from a school playground. Several games of football are soon in progress. Little groups skitter off in all directions to begin various games of their own devising. I see Luke almost at once, he's neglected to put on his woolly hat and his coat is not zipped up. But he's cheerful and grinning, in the middle of a group of little boys. He's all right.

But where is Adam? I stand at the edge of the footpath, staying in the shelter of the bare sycamore trunks, peering around behind my dark glasses. He's not in any of the football games. Nor in any of the groups of two and three wandering about, laughing or arguing, scuffing their shoes on the tarmac.

Suddenly, I see my son. He's on his own, looking about him rather furtively. Then – oh, horrors! – he's coming this way, towards the fence and the sheltering trees.

I retreat several yards, staying as well concealed as I can. He's not looking my way. Where is he going? Is he trying to hide?

He's reached the fence and leans against it, his back to me. His shoulders are tense. I see two or three boys detach themselves from the main mass of children and come over. There's a muttered conversation – I'm just too far away to hear what's said. Then Adam's hands go into his pockets and he gives something to each of them. Someone laughs. Then one boy gives Adam a push – nothing much, just a warning shove, and they all saunter off towards the sports pitches. Adam goes with them. I keep my eye on him, and see another boy, Adam's friend Rob, come over and say something. I can't see Adam's face but he's relaxed now, the tension gone from his arms and shoulders. They're even joining in a football game with the bullies.

I've been holding my breath, and let it out in a long sigh. I actually brought a notebook and pencil with me, and I'm scribbling rapidly. I don't know any of the bully group, though I think I've seen the fair–haired one before. One was definitely the ringleader – a rather overweight, sandy–haired boy with light eyelashes. I saw his face clearly; saw the sneering expression as he held out his hand for the Mars bar. He was the one who shoved Adam. The other two seem to be more in the background, but I think I'd know them again. I'm writing down as accurate a description as I can of all three, collecting my evidence.

I'm still scribbling away, chewing my pencil and looking at the children and scribbling again, when I become aware that someone else is standing in the shelter of the trees. Several people have passed on the footpath, but this man is just standing there, also looking at the children – staring at them very intently, in fact.

I feel goose pimples rise on my arms and shoulders. What's he doing? How long has he been there? He's an ordinary looking guy – fortyish, dark hair cut short, blue jeans, bomber jacket, grey trainers. His hands are in his pockets and he's just standing and looking. Then he seems to sense my eyes on him and turns his head. I suddenly realise that, of the two of us, I'm the one who must cut the strangest figure. He says nothing, just looks at me, and then turns and walks away towards the car park.

I put my notebook away. My knees are a little wobbly and my glasses have misted up. I take them off. My hands are shaking a bit too. What was that man doing, standing carefully concealed at the edge of a playground and studying the children? How long had he been there? Is he some kind of weirdo? A pervert on the loose? Are the children quite safe behind their fence?

Should I report him? That's the question that worries me most as I pull off my silly woolly hat and stuff it in my pocket. Strictly speaking, anyone can travel this footpath and anyone can stop to look into the playground if they choose to. Maybe he's a parent. After all, I've been standing here too, and taking notes to boot. It must have looked very odd to him. On the other hand, such terrible things happen. What if – heaven forbid – something happened to a child here and I'd done nothing, said nothing?

Then again, maybe I'm overreacting again. It's rattled me badly, seeing with my own eyes what's happening with Adam. I have to decide when and how I'm going to approach the school with my findings. There's a lot to think about and my head is reeling. I'm going to have to take some deep breaths, go home, have a cup of tea and try to regain my equilibrium before the school run.

In the end, that is exactly what I do.

*

I am quite calm by 3.30, and ask Adam and Luke to wait while I see Miss Cluny. I've bought them a magazine each, and they wait in the car, which I've parked where I can see it from the classroom window.

Judith Cluny listens. She seems a little ill-at-ease, and suddenly interrupts me to say "Mrs Harper, there's something I have to tell you." I wait. She says, twiddling a strand of hair, "It's about the missing pen I mentioned. I have to apologise. It wasn't missing at all. I'd zipped it into a pocket of my bag."

I knew it! I knew Adam wouldn't have taken that pen. She ought to have known too. But I forgive her. We're all human.

Confession over, she straightens. "But there are still the other items. He did take those."

"Yes, he did," I admit. "He's been pilfering from home too. But now I know why. It's protection money, so to speak. I have a description of the boys who've been terrorizing him."

I can see she does not like the word *terrorizing*. I hand her my notes and tell her what I've seen. She nods; she recognises the boys.

"What will be done about it?"

She's uneasy again. "Well, the school does have a bullying policy. I'll have to talk to the Head when she's back tomorrow. Then we'll decide what action to take."

"And in the meantime?"

"We'll keep a close eye on the situation. Harry Dent does seem to have some problems –" She stops, maybe realising that she shouldn't be talking so freely.

29

"Harry Dent? Is that the sandy-haired boy?"

She nods, biting her lip. I'd hate to be in her situation. All the same, my maternal hackles are up and I want to see justice done. I've got the name of the ringleader, tracked down by my own efforts. Maybe I can make a few more enquiries on my own. Harry Dent. This is a small town where everyone knows each other, but I've never heard of a family called Dent. I intend to find out more.

Chapter Six

I've forgotten all about Caroline's planning meeting – oops! Fortunately, Jo rings early that morning, tactfully mentioning the meeting in case I haven't remembered. She knows me well. I haven't given it a thought! I'll have to move fast. I assure Jo that everything's under control, and get to my feet without finishing my coffee.

The faded pinks and greens of the sitting-room chintz look a little shabby, but it's wonderful what plumped-up cushions, polished furniture, a tasteful arrangement of evergreens and a little pot of early snowdrops can do. A pity about the hall though. A couple of long yellow streaks on the wall and a huge cupboard in the middle of the upstairs landing are somewhat embarrassing. I'll try to avoid directing the ladies to the upstairs bathroom, although the downstairs facilities are no great shakes, having the battered and grubby look of a place much used by heedless men and boys. I sigh as I whisk down the banisters with a duster. My house falls far short of *Beautiful Country Homes* perfection, but I hope that at least it's homely and welcoming. I'm quite looking forward to entertaining the ladies, and get out the best wedding-present bone china with delicate trailing roses. It's only when I go to get a packet of elegant finger-biscuits from the treats shelf that my bubble bursts. Anther pack of small chocolate bars has definitely gone missing.

*

Six of us are gathered in my sitting room. There are several apologies for absence. I decide to begin with tea and biscuits rather than serve refreshments afterwards. It gives everyone a chance to greet each other and settle themselves. Caroline feels that the proper time for tea is after a meeting and has tactfully mentioned this to me before. But I've chosen to forget her little word in my ear. Caroline, unlike some of us, doesn't have to rush to collect Primary school children.

Caroline is rather beautiful, her eyes large and cornflower-blue, skin smooth, honey-coloured hair swept back into a faultless French pleat, expression serene. Caroline doesn't get into flaps. She sings alto in the church choir; her voice is low and sweet. Her wool trousers are perfectly cut, her sweater looks like pure cashmere. How on earth she manages to dress like this on the pay of an Anglican priest I can't imagine. However she does it, she's reckoned to be a great asset to the parish.

I would be more irritated by Caroline if it were not for her daughter Rebecca, of whom I am rather fond. Becky is sixteen years old and refreshingly normal. Paul and Caroline have high hopes for her, even Oxford or Cambridge. I know Becky is bright as a button because I taught her in Sunday School. I'm pleased she's come along with her mother and greet her warmly. "How are you, Becky? No school?"

She gives me a faint smile. "It's a reading day for me. I was a bit bored, so I thought I'd come with Mum. Is Michael home?"

"No, afraid not. School as usual for him."

I see a flicker of disappointment in her brown eyes. She and Michael have known each other for ages, but she's a year ahead of him at school and they don't have much to do with each other these days. But then again, he's grown into an attractive lad...

Becky's attractive too, but today she seems a bit moody, down-at-the-mouth and scruffy in old jeans and a cardigan with the sleeves pulled down over her hands. Her hair's lovely but could do with a wash. She hasn't made much of an effort if she'd been thinking of impressing Michael.

Caroline seems to be reading my thoughts. She says ruefully "Teenagers today! I don't know how we mums cope!"

I think, meanly, that she can't complain, with only one child and a cleaner for the vicarage several times a week. I also catch Becky throwing her mother a look of pure venom. Jo meets my eyes and her lips twitch. I smile, and suggest we leave the teacups until later.

The meeting goes smoothly, mostly thanks to Caroline. Tasks for the Fayre are designated. Deirdre Burns, our librarian, volunteers for the bookstall as usual. Deirdre is forty-six, unmarried, and wonderfully well-read. Books are her life. She eats, breathes and sleeps them, and now that she's computer-literate, has the whole Internet at her fingertips, and can locate, order and purchase any book in existence. I'm a little envious. I did Deirdre's job once, and things were more laborious then.

Maisie and Myra Meadows will do the plant and flower stall as they always do. They are sisters, one unmarried, one widowed, who live together in a cottage with a picture–book garden. I love them both dearly.

"Janet has agreed to organise bring–and–buy," says Caroline, making notes on a pad. "Bert French has promised some of his poker–work art. How about your older two, Alison? Would they be interested in helping out?

I cannot see either Lauren or Michael jumping at this. But I say "Well, I'll ask."

"Good. Then there's the cake stall. Alison?"

Good heavens, is she serious? My cakes are a standing family joke. Is she suggesting I bake the cakes, or just mind the stall? Either way, it's not my scene. Fortunately Jo comes to my rescue and volunteers for cake stall duty. I breathe a sigh of relief. I owe her one. The minutes tick by, tasks are appointed, notes taken. I agree to run the bran–tub, which will mean wrapping up about two thousand little prizes. Caroline thinks that Miss Taylor and Ruth Prentice will organize the tea stall; they've done it before and are always so willing. Caroline's pen flies over the page. It's not until later that I realise she has no allocated task herself, and then I quickly have to chide myself for unchristian thoughts.

The meeting ends amicably, no–one has been seriously offended or taken the huff, and that's a victory in itself.

*

Jo hangs back as the others leave in a flurry of goodbyes and waves of gloved hands, followed by the sound of car engines purring into life.

"Ali, I need a favour – again."

She looks peaky, standing on the steps, winding her long purple scarf round her neck. Jo has the kind of olive–skinned colouring that looks marvellous with the slightest hint of sunshine but sometimes takes on a sallow tinge in winter. I pull her back into the porch, out of the cold. There's still fifteen minutes before the school run.

"Not your dad again? He's all right, isn't he?"

She nods. "Yes, he's fine. The heart scare was just a warning really. Maybe a blessing in disguise – he and Mum have gone into healthy living in a big way since it happened." She smiles wanly, hands thrust into the pockets of her big check jacket.

"It's me being silly, really. You know I have this thing about hospitals, a kind of stupid phobia. Seeing Dad hitched up to wires and tubes only reinforced it. I'm really scared of the places." She pauses. "Thing is, I

33

have a hospital appointment myself. Tomorrow."

She is scared, and suddenly I am scared too, with a horrible clutch to my insides like a kind of foreboding.

"What kind of appointment?"

"Well – a biopsy. A needle biopsy, they call it. They'll do it there and then. At the General. I've noticed this lump, probably nothing much –"

It's not nothing thought, I can see it in her eyes. I put my arms round her and she is tense under the big padded jacket.

"Darling, I'll come with you. It'll be okay."

I make my voice stay steady and feel her relax a little. I pull her back towards the sitting room. "Let's pray. We have a few minutes."

She smiles. "I hoped you'd say that. I wanted to ask the group for prayer, but, I don't know, I just couldn't face the thought of Caroline saying "Oh, Joanna, we'll put your name on the prayer chain. It works so well. Just give me the details". I don't want my details to go on a prayer chain, like some spiritual conveyer belt. I want to be with someone who cares."

She is near to tears and so am I. Jo is one of the sweetest people I know, a friend in a million. God won't let anything bad happen to her. He can't.

*

It's a half-hour drive to the city, but we allow three-quarters because sometimes the traffic is horrific. It's a gloomy day, with a thick blanket of fog clinging to the river all down the valley. The bare top branches of trees poke out from the fog, looking strange and sinister. Several times along the road I notice a buzzard sitting motionless in the hedge. Sometimes a couple of carrion crows are perched in the hedgerow too. Graham tells me they're waiting for roadkill, of which there's a lot on these winding country roads – unwary foxes, badgers, rabbits and smaller mammals. Those birds give me the creeps.

I give myself a mental shake and try to rise above this mood of doom and gloom. Jo is pale but composed, putting on a brave face. For some reason, we have both dressed to the nines, make-up and all, as if to prove we're a force to be reckoned with. We even crack a few jokes as we go.

Jo is tense and even paler though, when we've parked the car and entered the hospital. She grips my arm as we travel miles of corridor, take the lift, traipse miles more and finally arrive in the right department. Then a long wait, on blue plush seats facing a print of sunflowers. Brisk nurses and suited administrators with clipboards bustle in and out, efficiently going about their business. It's warm, too warm, even when we've shed our coats.

Jo looks beseechingly at each hospital worker, but they just smile brightly or ignore us altogether. I begin to feel cross, want to say – look, this is my friend and she's worried sick and scared of hospitals, and why are you in this so-called caring profession anyway if you don't really care…..

Jo reads my thoughts, and says "Probably they've all got problems with mortgage repayments, or the child-care has let them down, or their husbands have run off, or their mother-in-law is coming to stay….."

"Or they won the lottery but forgot to buy a ticket –"

Jo actually giggles. Then a blonde nurse consulting a list appears and calls her name, and she looks stricken again. I squeeze her hand and promise to wait.

It's a long wait. I could get myself a cup of tea, but I'm not sure where the cafeteria is. This is a new hospital, huge and many-floored, and I'm not really familiar with the layout. Besides, I promised I'd wait. Even though I'm gasping for some fresh air.

Eventually, Jo reappears, white but composed. I get up and reach out to take her arm. "How was it?"

She pulls a face, wincing a little. "It hurt a bit. Look, Ali, I'm sorry, but I've got to wait again. They'll have the results in half an hour."

Well, in for a penny in for a pound. If need be I can ring Sue and ask her to pick up Adam and Luke. We take the lift downstairs and have a coffee, trying to be positive, but inside I'm on pins and I can't imagine what Jo must be feeling. The half-hour drags, and of course it's much longer than that by the time they call her back in. I stare at the sunflowers and pray desperately.

Jo doesn't say anything when she comes out. She looks tired out, makes a further appointment with the receptionist. I'm shaking with apprehension.

"Well?"

"Inconclusive."

"What?"

"Inconclusive. That's what they said. I'll need more tests."

She looks really drained. What an anti-climax. I'm drained too, confused, relieved, or what, I'm not sure. It's a good sign, isn't it? Surely anything really bad would have shown up right away?

Wearily, we make our way downstairs again. I just want to get home now, get away from here. It all seems like a bad dream.

In reception, while Jo nips to the loo, I'm suddenly snapped back to reality by two things. One is the sight of Becky Rees, looking up at the department signboard. She hesitates, and then seems to make up her mind where she's going. The other is my mother, coming from the Cardiac unit.

Chapter Seven

Becky hasn't seen me, and she's disappeared round the corner. My mother has, though, and is approaching me across the reception area, immaculate in black trousers, a black suede jacket with a black and cream Gucci scarf knotted at the neck.

All these are designer items and look wickedly expensive, though I know she got them for comparative peanuts, on EBay. She has a little frown between her eyebrows.

"Alison, what a surprise! I didn't expect to see you here. Is everything all right?"

"Yes, Mum, I'm fine. I'm with Jo. She's just nipped to the ladies."

I think, more to the point, what are *you* doing here Mum, and is everything all right with *you*?

I say casually, "Are you visiting someone?"

She's evasive. "Not exactly" and immediately my suspicions are confirmed, and there's fear clutching at my guts. My voice sounds accusing, even to myself. "You had an appointment?"

She pauses then nods. The fear rises to my throat and I feel sick. "Who with? Why didn't you tell me? I could have driven you here."

"Your dad's perfectly capable. I didn't want to worry you." You always make such a fuss, is what she really means. She's not wrong. I want to grab her shoulders and shout – Of course I worry! You're my mum and you mean the world to me! But I say nothing, and she goes on "It's just a little heart thing. Palpitations, you know. Nothing much. I may need a pacemaker. It's a very simple operation."

She's playing it down for all she's worth, to stop me overreacting. As I am, with panic playing havoc with my insides. My own heart is thumping fast. First Jo, then my mum! What on earth is God playing at?

At the same moment, Jo appears from the ladies and my dad comes in through the revolving doors. There's a flurry of talk and greetings. Dad suggests we all have a coffee together, or maybe a late lunch, but Jo and I decline – we'll just be in time for the kids if we go now. Mum and Dad go off arm–in–arm without a care in the world, and Jo and I drive wearily home. Both of us want the comfort and reassurance of our own husbands and kids.

It's only much later that I remember that Becky was at the hospital too, heading for the gynae department.

*

Two days later, and I've finally plucked up courage to say something to Michael. I tap nervously at his door and go in. He's lying on the bed, tablet in hand, on Facebook. I can see the little thumbnail photos on the small screen, but he clicks onto something more impersonal when he sees me. He looks none too friendly.

"What's the matter?"

I weigh my words carefully. I've spent the last half–hour praying desperately for wisdom, for courage, for guidance. I must not blow this, whatever happens.

"Michael, I need to talk to you."

He looks guarded, suspicious. "What about?"

"Well – about Becky."

I could swear he's gone pale. He sits up abruptly and bends forward so I can't see his face. "What about her?"

I take a deep breath. "I saw her at the hospital the other day. Michael, is Becky pregnant?"

He jerks upright again and stares at me, and I can see the answer in his face.

"So you've been snooping!"

I make myself breathe slowly, in, out. "I haven't been snooping. I was at the hospital with Jo. I couldn't help seeing her."

"So I suppose you told Caroline and Paul?" His voice is nasty and aggressive – and frightened.

"I didn't tell them anything."

Relief brings the colour back into his face. "Well, don't! Not a word. You've got to promise."

I'm not promising anything, but I don't say so. I feel sick to my stomach, apprehensive, heartbroken. First Jo, then Mum, now this. They say trouble goes in threes.

"Michael, they'll have to know. Becky will need support, help, you both will."

He stares at me again, eyes suddenly wide and incredulous, and then gives a short, bitter laugh. "Oh, I get it. You think it's me! Well, thanks a lot, Mum!"

A fresh wave of relief floods me so that my knees suddenly feel like jelly. I sit down suddenly on the messy bed beside him, with his smelly socks and grubby T-shirts round my feet. He edges away from me. He's just a kid. I should have known.

He's angry now, with a look I've never seen on his face before. He swivels away from me again and says "That's the trouble with you, Mum. You always think you know everything. Well, you don't! You don't know anything about Becky. Or me."

I can't bear this. "Look, I'm sorry, Michael. I did jump to conclusions. But Becky does need help. Who – who is the – father?"

He shrugs dismissively. "Some jerk, friend of a friend or something. He lives abroad. They met at some party over Christmas, the creep."

"Does she love him?"

He shrugs again, scornfully. "No way."

"Then – why –?"

Never in a million years could I have imagined I'd be having this conversation with my fifteen-and-three-quarter year old son. Discussing the sex lives of his friends is not on his agenda, or mine. But both of us are in it up to our necks now. He turns his head half away and says "Why did she do it? Well, maybe she's fed up with being the good little girl, the Vicar's daughter, being an example to everyone. Maybe she wanted to make a decision for herself for once."

Maybe a few drinks were involved too. And look where it's landed her, I think. But Michael is letting it all hang out now. "You don't know what it's like for us, Mum. Having your opinions pushed down our throats all the time, having to live up to your rules."

What rules are these? I always thought we allowed our children a fair amount of freedom. Have we been kidding ourselves?

Michael is in full flow. "How can we ever learn if we're not allowed to make mistakes for ourselves? How can we know what we believe if we're not supposed to see what else is out there, what other people think and do? It's hard trying to live up to people like you. Even harder for Becky –"

I'm beginning to be a little hurt. "I didn't think your life was as awful as all that."

"I'm not *saying* it's *awful*, but that's the thing, you never do think about anyone else's point of view – "His voice sounds croaky suddenly and he leans forward and begins to fumble about on the floor for his trainers.

"Where are you going?"

"See? You always have to know everything!"

This is a ridiculous conversation.

"Please wait a minute. Becky needs help, she really does. By the way, I never realised that you two were such good friends."

He straightens up, holding a shoe with laces dangling.

"No, well, you wouldn't. Although you've shoved us together since we were little kids, all nice little church kids together." His mobile buzzes and he stops to read a text message. I don't know whether to laugh or cry. One moment he's saying we interfere too much in his life, the next that we don't know or understand him at all. He's confused, but no more than I am. And underneath it all I'm beginning to feel a real respect for my son. He's standing by Becky like a true friend, he's thinking outside the box. Despite the confusion, he's growing up, fast.

I dare to ask "What is Becky planning to do?"

He thrusts the mobile into his pocket and his foot into the shoe. "It's all sorted. Termination. And don't you dare say even one word to her parents. I promised."

*

Graham has remembered Valentine's Day, bless him. I haven't. My mind is buzzing, so overloaded with new revelations and their possible outcomes, that the ordinary things of life are almost pushed out.

Graham's sunny nature, however, overlooks and forgives my weaknesses. He has brought me flowers, a beautiful bouquet of lilies and carnations and maidenhair fern, done up in red–spotted cellophane and a big satin bow. And he's booked a table at the Three Knights, an ancient pub that's been tastefully refurbished. We sit at a small table in an upstairs room with original beams and uneven floorboards, in our own little candlelit oasis. Graham looks younger and relaxed, candlelight smooths out the strain lines and frown furrows that life has brought. I hope it airbrushes away my worry wrinkles too. At any rate, the food is lovely. Graham looks into my eyes and plays a little footsie under the table. He refrains from discussing corn prices, outstanding bills, tractor repairs, bank loans or anything else that might cast a shadow, and I don't mention Jo, Mum, Michael, Becky – or any other disquieting matter. We laugh and reminisce about other meals we've had, special times we've shared. It is a little time of peace.

Uh– oh, I'm soon down to earth again with a bump. By Monday morning, winter is back and trouble is brewing. It's been ominously cold over the weekend and then a chilly rain began to fall, with sleet mixed in, which is turning to proper snow. The valley and mountain view is blotted out in a cloud of grey, peppered with whirling dots. I wonder about school, but Graham assures me the bus will make it okay. "It'll be sleet and slush a little further down the hill. And it's all going to stop mid–morning, by the forecast."

I watch Lauren plod off alone to meet the bus, wearing, under duress, my big padded coat and bent double like Captain Oates walking out into the freezing Arctic. Michael hasn't appeared for school. I assume he has another free day. But as I'm bundling the two small boys out of the door he thumps downstairs, dressed for outdoors in a parka, beanie hat and boots.

"I need a lift."

Michael has been monosyllabic with me ever since our showdown. He won't meet my eyes and walks away if I try to talk. I feel he regrets saying so much. Or maybe wishes he'd said more. Either way, I'm not his favourite person. I've grown used to Lauren being like this, but Michael and I used to have a good relationship. Or so I thought. It breaks my heart.

"Take the Nissan," Graham advises. I'm glad of the 4 x 4 this morning. My little Ford Fiesta isn't up to these conditions. Even so, I drive carefully, peering ahead between whirring wipers and shifting the gears as blustery gusts throw handfuls of slush against the windscreen. We creep down the hill. Michael shifts impatiently beside me. "Can't you go any faster? I've a bus to catch."

This is news to me. "What bus?"

"The 9.10. Jeepers, I wish I was driving!"

I'm glad he's not. "Why are you going into town?"

"Meeting someone. Mum, it's pathetic, crawling along like this. The kids'll be late for school."

Adam and Luke are rather enjoying the distraction. They're in no hurry at all.

"Better a bit late than lying in a ditch. There, I told you!"

My concentration has lapsed. I've misjudged the distance, skidded a little and nicked the verge. We jolt to a stop and I get out into the slushy snow to take a look. No damage to the vehicle, thank goodness. Michael is livid. Getting back in, I hear him mutter something that sounds like "Bloody women drivers!" By the time we're back on track, we've lost more valuable minutes. We deliver the boys to school and by the icy silence I know that Michael knows he's missed the bus. What was the urgency about getting to town, anyway?

And then, suddenly, I realise. I turn to look at Michael's stony profile. "It's Becky, isn't it? At the hospital?"

He nods and looks near to tears. "I promised Becs. I said I'd be there. She went in on the early bus, wanted to walk round by herself for a bit–"

Oh, God, help me! There's nothing else for it.

"I'll drive you there, Michael."

He accepts with a very bad grace. It's Hobson's choice really, but he hates the idea of being obliged to me. And now he's going to have to listen to what I have to say.

It's sleet rather than snow here in the valley, as Graham had predicted. Even so, driving is hazardous and I need to keep my wits about me. But I can't pass up this opportunity. Too much is at stake. So I take a deep breath, and say "I can't believe this is right, Michael, what Becky's doing."

He scrunches down in the seat, sinking his neck into his coat collar, trying to blank me out. But he hasn't got even the protection of his ipod today, and isn't even bothering with his phone. I talk to him about the wonder of God's creation, the value of each human life, the miracle of birth. I even quote verses from Psalm 139, about the wonder of an unborn child in the womb.

He is not impressed, sinking lower and lower in his seat. And then, suddenly, he shoots bolt upright. His face is red and angry, fists clenched,

"You don't have to go on, Mum! Actually, I agree with you. I've been saying this kind of stuff to Becky. But she won't listen. She's scared."

"Her mum and dad would help–"

"Would they? Paul's always busy; he's got no time for anything other than his parish, that's what Becs thinks. And Caroline – well –"

I concede that Caroline might be difficult. But surely, surely, they both should know about this. They should be given the chance. Becky shouldn't be facing this alone.

The windscreen wipers whirr and the wintry countryside goes by. I'm gripping the steering wheel tightly, with icy fingers. I'm sure the heater isn't working properly.

"She won't be alone. I'll be there, if I can ever get there."

He is so vulnerable, so petulant and childish one moment, responsible, caring and loyal the next. A boy soon to be a man. My heart yearns over him.

"You needn't wait for me," he says dismissively as we approach the outskirts of town. "We'll come back on the bus, after–"

I don't argue, but there's no possibility that I will let either of them go home on the bus, as though this was nothing more than a dental appointment.

I know it's going to be a long, hard day.

Chapter Eight

Sometimes things happen so suddenly, and so fast, that you go into a kind of automatic pilot control. Or is it God taking over?

This happens today. One minute we're driving into the hospital car park, wipers whirring, looking for a parking place. I'm full of sick apprehension.

Michael can't wait to get out. Before I've hardly had time to park, before we've got a ticket from the machine (it's a scandal we have to pay in hospital car parks), he's out of the car and heading for the entrance. It's slushy underfoot and still sleeting, more drivers are coming in. I see events take place as though in slow motion. As he reaches the hospital entrance he slips, or trips, trying to dodge across in front of an approaching vehicle. He staggers and then he falls; even from a distance I hear a dull crack as his head connects with the low wall. He doesn't get up.

I have no recollection of leaving the car and crossing the car park but I must have done it at a run. Michael is white and still, eyes closed, as I kneel beside him. My heart stops. But others are there; someone is pressing a finger to his neck and calling for help. Boots and shoes swish past, voices murmur. Someone asks "Are you his mother?" and I nod dumbly. It seems an eternity, yet no time at all, before a trolley erupts from the doors and someone is giving instructions on how to lift Michael. It's like a scene from Casualty. Someone even jokes about it being the best place to choose for an accident.

A nurse holds my arm as we hurry through corridors to A & E. She speaks soothingly. "He'll be seen quite soon. We're not too busy this morning, for once."

My voice quavers. "He's – he's not – dead?"

"Oh my goodness, no! His vital signs are fine. He's concussed, and his arm may be injured. He'll be OK."

She's right. By the time we reach A&E, Michael's eyes have flicked open and he's moaning with pain. His head turns towards me. "Mum?"

"I'm here, darling." His silly beanie hat has fallen off and I smooth the damp hair back from his forehead. "You'll be okay. You had a fall."

His face twists. "My arm hurts. Mum – you'll have to go to Becky. Please."

I'd forgotten Becky. I want to stay with my boy. But his eyes are begging me. Then he's whisked away, disappearing through swing doors and I'm left standing. Someone is asking me for his details. I give them, automatically, and a nurse pats me kindly and shows me where I can wait. Michael will go to X–ray and then straight to the plaster room if necessary, but I should be able to see him soon.

I have no choice in this. I decline the offered seat and head off down the corridor to find the lift.

Becky is in another waiting room, huddled up in a big puffa jacket, looking small and lonely. She looks up and gives a huge start when she sees me, and seems to shrink further into the jacket. Her eyes are enormous and frightened. I sit down beside her and say gently "It's okay, Becky."

She's terrified, looking over my shoulder to see if anyone else is there. "Is Mum here? What's happened? Where's Michael?"

I reach out and take her hand. It's cold as ice and she's shaking. I repeat "It's okay. Michael's had a bit of an accident. He's in A&E. Your mum isn't here. I came instead."

My heart goes out to her. She's just a frightened, vulnerable kid, scared half out of her wits. Now is my chance to try and talk her out of this, get her to involve her parents, but I find I can't say a word. I squeeze her hand and she squeezes back, hanging on for dear life. Then a dark–haired nurse is calling her in, and she goes, with one last pitiful look at me. I say "I'll be right here, darling."

The nurse assumes I'm Becky's mum. She smiles reassuringly, and says "She'll be okay. It's always scary for them."

I don't bother setting her straight, but say "Could you tell me how long she'll be? My son has just gone into A&E."

She clicks her tongue, tsk tsk, it never rains but it pours, tells me I've time and once again I have the surreal feeling that this is something that's happening in a TV drama.

I'm getting to know my way round this hospital. Back in A&E, I'm told that Michael has a broken arm and is being plastered, a simple break, but they'll need to keep him in overnight because of the bang on the head and slight concussion. If I'd just wait....

I wait, but not in A&E. Upstairs, another girl and her mother are now in the waiting room, silent and pale, pretending to look at magazines. They glance at me and then away. The girl looks even younger than Becky. I sit down, my legs are like jelly, I have a headache and I'm suddenly oh, so tired. I must look strange, dishevelled and distraught, because the receptionist asks me if I'm all right. I find myself explaining again about a son in A&E, and she clucks sympathetically and then turns back to her buzzing intercom.

I don't know how long I sit there, staring at a print of Monet's water lilies. How long does this take? Will she spend time in the recovery room? Will they call me in there?

And then, the door opens, and Becky appears with the nurse, already wrapped in her big jacket as though she can't wait to get out of here. She's chalk white, her little face pinched, bowed over as though she's in serious pain. I feel I should speak to the nurse about pain relief and after care. And what about counselling? Do they provide details of that? But Becky is coming over to me and grabbing at my arm. "Alison, let's go!" She almost drags me through the doors into the corridor.

"Becky, we ought to speak to someone. I'm sure there must be some instructions about after-care, and won't you need a follow-up appointment?"

She's pulling me towards the lift. Waiting for it, she leans against the wall and I have the awful feeling she's going to pass out. My heart aches for her. I say "Was it terrible?"

She nods, and then suddenly lifts her head and looks at me. "I thought about what Michael said, about life and that, how a baby can move and is all perfectly formed in just a few weeks. I was all prepared and up on the table and everything, and then – and then– I wanted to scream, and I was saying "I can't. I can't." And I just kept on until they let me go. I couldn't do it, Alison. I couldn't."

*

Much of the rest of the day seems to pass in a blur. I dimly recall that I visit Michael again and find him sedated and sleepy, that I drive Becky home, that somehow I exact a promise that she will tell Caroline and Paul about her pregnancy. I remember volunteering to be with her when she does, to help in any way I can, but much of the conversation is lost in a kind of haze. For all I know, I might have offered to adopt the baby myself when it comes.

46

I do recall slipping and sliding on our road as I climb the hill; it's snowed on and off most of the day up here on the high ground and every tree, every mound and hummock is blanketed in white. It's almost dark and the yard lights are on, shining across the whiteness. Graham is there before I've stopped, scrunching through the snow and pulling open the door.

"Where the hell have you been all day?"

I never even thought of calling him on the mobile. I just disappeared after the school run this morning and didn't return.

"Why didn't you answer my calls?"

I get out stiffly. "I switched it off. At the hospital. Then I forgot to switch it on again."

I forgot everything, even the boys. The school rang Graham and he had to get hold of Sue, who took them home with her. Everyone's been worried sick, he tells me as he walks me to the house, holding my arm none too gently. And why was I at the hospital? And where's Michael?

"I'll tell you in a minute." I'm so weary I can hardly think straight. Only Lauren is in the kitchen, standing by the Aga and looking scared. Something is beginning to burn on the hotplate, a tin of beans or something they're heating in a saucepan. I automatically pull it to one side .A couple of potatoes are turning in the microwave. It's warm in here, warm and bright and familiar and safe. They've left the curtains open, I walk over and pull them against the night. Then I turn to their accusing faces, both of them waiting for an explanation. Ben has scrambled into the armchair, where he's not allowed. My headache is pounding. I'm a little faint and dizzy. The smell of burning is making me feel sick. I open my mouth to speak, but a strange little sound comes out. And then the tatty old blue hearthrug is rushing up to meet me.

*

"You fainted!" said Lauren. She sounds well impressed, but scared too, as though she doesn't know how to handle this new unpredictability of mine.

"Rubbish, I don't do fainting," I say groggily, trying to get a smile out of her. But her expression doesn't crack. I'm in the armchair, my feet on a footstool. Graham is hovering with a glass of water. Did he intend to hold it to my lips? Dash it in my face? A smile twitches my lips and I see relief in both their faces. I must explain. But I'm tired. So tired. I begin to tell them about Michael's accident, but somehow I can't finish properly. My head is lolling back, my eyes won't stay open.

"You'd better get to bed," says my husband. "When did you last eat?"

I really can't remember. Breakfast? I can't recall anything since, not even a cup of tea. But I'm not hungry at all. Just completely drained and tired.

"I'll just take the water." I gulp it down and he helps me up. I wonder if he intends to carry me upstairs, and am fleetingly thankful for the memory of him ringing that strong–man bell all those years ago. But he doesn't offer, although he does come up with me and attempts to tidy the unmade bed while I get undressed. He's not very good at it, but it's no matter, all I want to do is crawl under the duvet and sleep.

And sleep I do, right through the night and most of the next morning, while sleet showers slither and scratch at the windows and life goes on without me. Graham appears now and then with a cup of tea, which I can hardly rouse myself to drink. I get up only for the loo. Lauren comes every so often; didn't the school bus run today? The phone rings now and then and someone else deals with it. On one of my trips back from the loo I hear Graham and Lauren talking in low tones in the hallway below.

"Is Mum having a nervous breakdown? Paula's mum had a nervous breakdown."

"I don't think so. I think she's just tired." But he doesn't sound too sure.

Is this a nervous breakdown? No, I don't think so either. Emotional overload is the phrase that springs to mind.

Sometime in the afternoon I'm aware that Michael is in the room, arm in a pristine sling. Graham must have been to fetch him home.

"All right, Mum?"

I nod, all right, but haven't the energy to ask him how he is himself. I'm already more than half asleep again.

MARCH

Chapter Nine

The month has come in like a lion, with rain driving across the hillside, winds that rock the bare trees and shake our old house to its very foundations. Some tiles blew off the roof, and a leak appeared in the doorway of our downstairs loo, just where everyone has to walk to get in and out. It's because the room was part of a later extension to the rest of the house. Graham says there's a fault in the flashing where it joins. He goes up a ladder to investigate, and while he's at it, goes on up to replace the tiles. I hate it when people go up ladders, especially when it's someone near and dear to me, and get vertigo just watching. Anyway, the tiles are on and the leak stopped, so I mop up the muddy water around the doorway.

Lambing time is in full swing, and I'm so thankful we no longer keep livestock. I thought I'd miss the animals when Graham turned to arable farming but I adapted quickly. Everyone thought he was mad, growing crops on a hill farm where many of the fields are impossible to plant or cultivate, but he lets the unsuitable fields to our neighbours for grazing and rents extra land for crops along the valley bottom. It works well. I can enjoy the sight and sound of gambolling baby lambs in springtime, without having to do anything about them. I remember all too well those endless nights at lambing time, with midnight patrols in the cold and wet and nobody getting more than a couple of hours sleep at a stretch. I recall times when the kids were babies and teething or colicky at night, with lambs coming thick and fast, when Graham and I were never both in bed at the same time and walked around like zombies all day. That I don't miss.

Graham is temperamentally better suited to dealing with machines rather than livestock or people. You know where you are with a machine, he says. It doesn't fight back or answer back or make sudden unpredictable moves. It doesn't turn moody and reject its young, or skittishly leap hedges into the next field, or fall prey to some lethal and horrid disease. Sheep know a hundred and one ways to die before their time, he says, and will try out each one until they succeed. Give him a tractor any day.

He's not wrong about sheep. They must surely be the most foolish and ornery creatures God ever created. Driving the boys to school this morning, I encounter the perfect illustration. A ewe with twin lambs has somehow managed to squeeze herself through a small gap under the wire fence and into the lane. Now she's frantically running up and down the verge, trying to get back to her pathetically bleating babies. I stop and get out; she looks at me belligerently out of yellow eyes, but resists my attempts at guiding her back to her exit hole. I have to make the hole much bigger, pulling away more strands of wire, and then get Adam and Luke to stand in the lane while I try again to drive her in the right direction. It works this time, she gets the message and squeezes through and there's a great reunion with much bleating and wiggling of tails.

I mend the fence as best I can, twisting strands of wire together. I must remember to tell Sue and Mike about this weak spot in their fence. Of course we're late for school again. Adam is still taking goodies to school, but as long as his protection currency is forthcoming he's content. It can't go on though. I must do further follow-up investigation soon, without fail. But not today. This morning Paul Rees has asked me if I could call at the Vicarage to see him.

*

St John's vicarage is near the church, an imposing stone building with high sash windows looking across the water meadows to the river. Paul lets me in, apologising for taking up my time but saying that he is expecting several important phone calls this morning and can't leave the vicarage to come to the farm to see me. We go into his study. I hear Mary Miles, the cleaning lady, busy with the vacuum cleaner somewhere upstairs, but of Caroline there is no sign. I gather she and Becky were in church on Sunday morning. I stayed home, taking it easy after my spectacular collapse. The rest did me the world of good. I feel fully charged with energy again.

Paul offers me the comfy armchair in his study and takes the swivel one behind his desk. This is where the distressed and needy of the parish, the bereaved, depressed and perplexed, come to be comforted and counselled, as well as the hopefuls seeking marriage or confirmation or baptism for their infants. He and Caroline have been here for several years now. Paul runs his fingers through his hair. He's a nice–looking man in his mid–forties, though distracted and haggard just now; his face in repose is a little sad and careworn, but he has a smile of extraordinary sweetness.

He says "Alison, I want to thank you. For what you did for Becky."

So he knows. I let out my breath in a sigh of relief. "I didn't do a lot. I was, kind of, just there at the crucial moment. It all sort of – just happened." This sounds so silly, the kind of thing teenagers say when they're in a spot.

Paul runs his hands over his face, wearily. He doesn't look as though he's slept much lately. He says quietly "You were there for Becky. God's provision in time of need. Without you, I can't bear to think –"

He seems close to tears. I want to put out my hand and touch his, but I don't want him to misunderstand me. Instead I say "How is Becky?"

He sits up, more composed. "She seems fine. Relieved it's all out in the open."

"And Caroline?"

He pauses. "Caroline is dealing with it in her own way. It was all a dreadful shock, of course, to both of us. We never suspected – We've made mistakes, Alison. I've sometimes overlooked the needs of my own family in favour of my parishioners, and Caroline –well, it's very difficult for her. We decided it would be better for Becky not to be here for a while. Caroline took her across to West Wales to stay with my sister."

Of course. It wouldn't be good for Caroline's image of perfection to have a pregnant unmarried teenage daughter about the place. I try to suppress the mean thought, but Paul seems to see it in my face.

"Maybe, in the circumstances, I ought to tell you a little more about Caroline –"

Suddenly, I don't want to hear. Whatever it is, I'm sure she wouldn't want Paul to be sitting here in his study telling me. It's bad enough that I knew about their daughter's pregnancy before they did, and that I was the one Becky hung on to in the hospital like a drowning person.

"Paul, I'm sorry, but I really have to go. Things to do, you know."

He sighs, then nods. "Maybe you're right. But thank you again."

His phone is ringing as I get up, one of those important calls, and he picks it up with one hand while reaching out to shake mine with the

51

other, and on his face is that extraordinarily sweet smile.

*

I've decided that, after all, I may as well do a bit of reconnaissance work on Adam's behalf while I'm here in town. I leave the car where it is in the car park and set off on foot.

I love our town, nestled as it is right on the English/Welsh borders, with the river marking the boundary between two countries and the narrow little streets wending their way uphill to the castle walls. The castle is Norman, a huge grey hulk brooding over the town. It's surrounded by high walls and peacocks strut the grounds. It must have been an impressive place in mediaeval times, with the huts of shopkeepers and traders huddling against its walls. Now partly-ruined, it's a huge bookstore, like many other of the town's building, because this is the Book Town, the place with the biggest collection of second-hand bookshops in the world, which draws tourists in their thousands from all parts of the globe. Gone are the days my mother remembers, when this was a sleepy country town coming to life only on market days when farmers brought in their livestock and produce to sell. Now, while other towns along the borders are quiet and slow-paced still, ours is vibrant and bustling with life and culture. Some of the old families bemoan the change, but most of the tradespeople know which side their bread is buttered and cater to the visitors. Mother and I love it for the books, apart from anything else.

Over the years, new buildings have gone up – flourishing businesses, medical and dental centres, a large supermarket. New housing estates straggle out in all directions over the fields, creating a network of new streets and roads and car parks.

I am walking along one such road on the newest estate, searching among the raw new red-brick houses for number seventeen. Discreet enquiries among a couple of other mums have yielded the information that this is where the Dent family lives.

*

It's drizzling a little as I turn into Warren Road and I flip up the hood of my anorak. A man is hurrying in the opposite direction along the pavement, detouring a little to let me pass; his hood is up too but there's something vaguely familiar about him. He keeps his head down as we pass and doesn't meet my eyes. When he's passed I realise with a small shock that he's the same man I'd seen watching the schoolchildren. I shrug off a slightly uneasy feeling and scan the house numbers.

Number seventeen stands back from the road a little, a plain, red-brick house in a plain square of front garden with a patch of grass, a boy's bike lying on its side and not much else. The windows are tightly curtained, the door firmly closed. I hadn't intended to do this, but I find myself taking a deep breath and walking up the front path.

It seems a long time before the doorbell's answered. The young woman in the doorway is pale, fair-haired, unsmiling. She wears a blue hoodie and faded jeans and her nail-polish is slightly chipped. Her eyes are beautiful, long-lashed and a deep sapphire blue, she could be quite stunning if she made the effort, but her eyebrows are drawn together in a frown and she doesn't look friendly.

"Yes? Can I help you?"

I'm at rather a loss. "Er –Mrs Dent? My son is at school with your son, I believe. In the same class. Adam Harper?"

The name apparently means nothing to her. She waits for me to go on. Suddenly, I don't know how. Do I come right out with it and accuse her son of bullying, and demand something be done about it? Something in her face stops me. There's more here than meets the eye. I somehow know that this young woman has suffered, is still suffering. I say, feebly "I thought it would be good if the boys got to know each other a little better. Would Harry like to come to tea one day? We live on a farm two miles out."

Part of me is incredulous – why on earth am I taking this line? – Adam's going to freak out – while I hear myself babbling on about maybe when the weather's nicer, Harry could bring his bike –

She listens but seems to be only half paying attention, her eyes flicker as though her mind is partly on something else. She says, somehow on the defensive, "Well, maybe. We'll see. Thanks for asking."

At that moment, a young child cries from somewhere in the house behind her, a strange, high-pitched wail, like nothing I've ever heard. She says quickly "I've got to go," and closes the door in my face.

Chapter Ten

"I know what it is! It must be drugs," I say, kicking off my fluffy slippers (a Christmas present from Luke) and climbing into bed. The explanation came to me in the bath, the reason Harry's mum seemed so strange and spaced–out.

Graham is propped up in bed, with my pillows as well as his own, reading Jeremy Clarkson and laughing like a drain. He says "Mmm," and I know he hasn't heard. I tug back one of my pillows.

"Did you hear me?"

"Yes. It must be drugs."

"I mean, it would explain a lot. She looked so pale and weird. She didn't want me in the house. And it might account for Harry behaving the way he does. There's another child there too, younger. I heard it crying in a strange sort of way. Do you think Social Services ought to be involved?"

"Alison" – He's listening properly now, and his voice has a note of warning. "It's none of your business."

"But there are *children* involved. That's the trouble with society nowadays; nobody wants to be involved with other people's problems. Anything could be going on in that house."

"You have enough fingers in enough pies. Keep your nose out."

He leans over and gives my nose a tweak, to prove his point. He can be infuriating. I yank back my second pillow and lie down. He sighs and closes his book. We settle down to sleep.

We are drifting off, and Graham is beginning his snuffly snore, which I find wonderfully soothing, when there is a shuffling at the door and a small figure comes in, outlined against the dim landing light.

"Lukie? What's the matter?"

"I don't feel well."

He climbs into bed without more ado, scrambling over me and settling himself between us with much activity of knees and elbows. He's become very bony this last year, baby fat gone for ever. Graham wakes with a snort and then a groan. He needs his sleep, and I'm tempted to feel cross with Luke, but he does feel a bit warm to the touch.

"Where are you ill, sweetie?"

"My ears. They hurt. And my throat."

Doctor's surgery in the morning. Meanwhile, a dose of Calpol. I struggle out of bed and along to the bathroom, where I rummage in the medicine chest until I find a box of sachets. When I get back, Luke is asleep, sprawled across my side of the bed. Do I wake him to give the dose, or not? In the end, I decide against it, leave him undisturbed and spend the rest of the night in his bed under the lurid Spiderman duvet.

*

The doctor's waiting room is crowded. Mostly feverish children with their mums, or elderly patients with carers or attentive middle–aged daughters. There's a lot of coughing and spluttering, a GP's waiting room must be the ideal environment for the spread of bugs and viruses. The world and his wife seem to be in here today.

I sit beside a fellow mum whose small daughter is displaying the same symptoms as Luke, and we commiserate about the nasty bug that's going round the school. Then out of the inner door comes another mother with a child in her arms, a woman I recognise, Harry Dent's mum. For a second our eyes meet, but she instantly looks away. She isn't going to acknowledge me. She hands in a prescription note and stands by the desk waiting for it. The child, a girl, has her head buried in her mother's shoulder and her arms tightly round her neck. All I can see of her is a red hooded jacket and a pair of skinny legs in striped tights and boots.

My talkative neighbour sees me looking and says in a conspiratorial low voice "There's something wrong with that child, if you ask me. She's disabled or something. You never see the mother out with the child. She's hardly ever at the school to meet her boy. There's something odd about that family."

The surgery is a hotbed of gossip as well as viruses. I'm saved from having to reply by Luke's name coming up on the patient board.

It's as I thought, an ear infection, or a 'nasty red ear' as the doctor puts it. "Should settle in a few days, but I'll give you a script," the doctor says. She is female, pretty, and younger than me. A script? I thought that was what actors learned their lines from, but these days it's Newspeak for prescription, apparently. Clutching it, we head out into the waiting

55

room and to the desk. Luke suddenly breaks free and dives in among the waiting patients, having discovered his grandma in their ranks. By the time I join them, he is ensconced upon her knee, and outlining his symptoms to her sympathetic ear. She gives him a comforting squeeze. "Poor lamb! Never mind, here comes Mummy with some nice medicine! And here's some money to get a treat for afterwards."

"And how are you, Mother?"

"Fine, dear, just fine."

I don't believe her, entirely. Most people in a doctor's waiting room are not fine. I want to ask about the palpitations, the heart problem, find out just what is going on here. Maybe I should speak to Dad, though she's probably got him well briefed. Not for the first time, I wish that my younger brother Mark was not thousands of miles away in California. Maybe I'll call him this evening. We haven't spoken since the New Year.

"Oh, look!" says my mother brightly "Isn't that Jo just going out?"

It is. She hasn't seen me and is heading through the door and out to the car park. I grab Luke and run to catch up with her.

She's standing by her car door and the tears are streaming down her face.

"Jo!" I put my arms around her.

"Ali. I – just got the last test result."

My heart flips sickeningly. I can't bear this. "Jo – we'll stick this out together. We can beat it."

She sniffles and then sobs. "No – no, it's okay. The results were negative. I'm all right, Ali. I'm fine."

*

I call Mark at 6pm, while the rest of the family watch the Simpsons. For some reason, the Simpsons take priority even over the six o clock news, which I find slightly disquieting. Graham says it is teaching the children to appreciate satire and not take things at face value, which I'm still trying to work out. But at least it gives me a little private space.

It's morning in California, and I'm calling Mark at his work. He's area manager for a sports company that teaches English soccer to American kids. He loves the lifestyle, the beaches, mountains, snowboarding, cycling, the tanned blonde girls, the sunshine. Especially the sunshine. He was here at Christmas, sun bleached and tanned, spreading goodwill and expensive presents. The kids adore him and tag about after him, Michael and Lauren chat to him on Facebook, although I don't understand half the stuff they talk about. I speak to him less often, phone calls to California come expensive, and Skype is something we haven't got round to installing yet.

He says he didn't notice anything amiss with Mum at Christmas. "She seemed okay to me. Great. Has something come up?"

"I'm not sure. There's a heart problem, it seems."

"How's her blood pressure? Cholesterol levels? Has she had an ECG recently?"

I feel that I must be a very bad daughter, that I don't know about these things. Mum's policy is not to dwell on illness as so many older people do, but to live each day to the full. She doesn't seem like an older person to me. But I realise, with a pang, that she and Dad are both now older people.

They will not live for ever.

"Sis? Are you there?

I shake off the icy chill that has settled over me. "Yes. Sorry. Look, Mark, you know what a worrier I am. I'll go and see Mum, check out what's happening. She seems fine anyway. And how are you?"

We chat about his work, sport, the kids, and he says he's hoping to get home again for Easter. That's only a month away and it'll be good to see him.

"Have a nice day," he says, forgetting it's already evening here. Or is it something that Americans say anyway, whatever the time of day?

*

Caroline is back in church on Sunday, immaculate as ever in a chic cream jacket and long black skirt with a slit at the back displaying an expanse of shapely leg. She greets me as usual, cordial but cool, chatting about the trip to the coast, how winding the roads were on the way home, and the rough seas along the front during the recent gales. I'm not letting her off the hook though. "And how's Becky?"

"Very well, thank you. Enjoying the change of scenery." I wait for more, but that's all there is. Caroline is not discussing the situation with anyone, least of all me. Not a word of thanks or appreciation.

The theme this morning is humility, and I'm not sorry it's my morning for Little Tiddlers so I'll miss the sermon. I don't seem able to do humility this morning. Jessica has moved up a class, and away from the ministrations of his young aunt, Rhys is blossoming. His habitual hangdog demeanour has changed to one of lively confidence. In fact, he's keen to take part in every discussion, answer every question, give out pencils, and offer advice freely.

I write key words from the story in big letters on the blackboard. LOVE, JOY, PEACE , warning the children not to shout out the words until I ask. Rhys is on his feet immediately. "Miss, miss!"

"In a moment, Rhys. When I've finished."

"But miss –"

"Wait, Rhys."

He subsides. I write KINDNESS, GOODNESS, and turn to the class. "Now, Rhys, you can tell me the first word." I point to LOVE. Silence.

"Come along, Rhys, you wanted to answer."

He hangs his head, twiddles a pencil. "I can't read yet. Only – I've got a rubber stuck up my nose."

He has, too. He's put his pencil up his nose, twiddled it around and the rubber has dislodged itself up there. Try as I might, I can't get it out. I really don't need this, but unless I'm much mistaken, another trip to A&E is on the cards.

*

In the event. Rhys's mum takes him to the hospital and the rubber is removed without any damage and with minimal fuss. She is gracious about it, though Jessica at home time has an air about her which says, there, see what happens when I take my eye off him for a second?

We are able to go home to our dinners, rather later than usual, and to our teenagers who absented themselves from church this morning. Luke, in the manner of most small children, has made a speedy recovery and is in buoyant mood; he and Adam scrap in the back of the car all the way home.

I am cheesed off with Caroline; in fact I'm mad as hops. I want some news of Becky. Surprisingly, I get it from Michael later in the afternoon. He's still none too friendly with me, elusive and monosyllabic, but this afternoon he needs help changing his grubby sling for a clean one. It goes against the grain to ask, but I'm the only one who can do a decent job of it.

"Heard from Becky," I ask casually, adjusting the length before I knot the material at the back. The back of his neck reddens a little. He grunts something which I take to be a yes.

"Is she ok?"

Another grunt. Then he says, unexpectedly "She's really good. Likes it there a lot better than here. She likes walking on the beach with the waves crashing, and her aunt's really cool. Not like –" he doesn't finish. Does he mean Caroline? Me?

"Becs is going to some classes at college; she's even got a part–time job."

He stops again, remembering that we're not all that good friends any more, and says grumpily "That's too loose, Mum. Tighten it up."

I tighten and tie. I daren't push my luck by asking about the pregnancy, plans for the future – . For now, it's enough. I picture Becky exercising in good sea air, eating her cool aunt's nutritious meals, getting colour back in her cheeks. And I allow myself just a tiny thought of a baby, growing day by day, strong and well, and waiting for its appointed time to come into the world.

Chapter Eleven

It's 2.30 in the afternoon, and I'm sitting in the kitchen by the Aga, reading *A Day in the life of Ivan Denisovitch*. This is the kind of book that should be read tucked up in bed with a howling blizzard outside and several feet of snow. Today it's bright and breezy, with white clouds scudding across a blue sky and the ground drying fast. Graham is busy from dawn to dusk, planting spring barley. He appears only for meals, or if there is some mechanical breakdown requiring an SOS call or trip into town to pick up some vital part.

I should be doing something productive at this moment, before it's time for the school run, like baking a batch of fruit cakes to last several days, or restoring the boys' rooms to some kind of order. But I love this book and can't put it down. Solzhenitsyn has such an optimistic way of affirming life and holding on to it, considering it a good day when there's an extra bit of black bread to eat, or your turn comes round to dry your felt boots overnight on the inadequate stove before going out into the bitter Siberian winter. It brings things into perspective, big time. I'm a compulsive reader, like my mum, and sometimes the only chance I get is when the house is empty. I can sneak in an hour or two on a quiet day, and I do.

I used to be a librarian in the far off days before children appeared in our house, and I adored the job. Books wall to wall, floor to ceiling, people to deal with who loved books too, and on quiet days the perfect chance to read. I kept the job for a while after Michael was born, toting him to work with me in a carrier. But it had to end when he became mobile. Books and crawlers just don't mix. I always intended to go back when all kids were at school, but it never happened. So I indulge my habit, secretly, like a drinker or a chocoholic, stashing my books about the house with markers in place. I haven't yet graduated to e–books, I do so love the real thing.

Ben is at my feet, asleep, twitching and snoring. He's not been well these past few days. A chest infection, Jo's vet husband Stuart says, and gives me a canine script. "Don't forget he's an old, old man now," he adds.

Ben has been with us for ever, since before Luke and Adam were born. I can't even quite remember who came first, him or Michael. He's aged a lot this last year, growing slow and deaf and grizzled round the whiskers. But he's a tough old character. He's survived many an accident and mishap, and recovered from several serious illnesses. Just last winter he came through a bout of pneumonia against all the odds. Graham and I were discussing him yesterday, after dosing him with the prescribed antibiotics. We both felt he'd make it again, get through to the warmer days of spring and enjoy one more summer at least.

I lean down and touch his nose. It's dry and warm. Not good. He opens his eyes and looks at me mournfully. I put down the book and make a big fuss of him, rubbing his bony head and stroking his floppy ears. And I pray from the heart, as I've prayed many times before, for his return to health and strength.

And suddenly, a voice speaks. Now, I'm not one of those Christians who are in the habit of hearing voices. I do not stand up in gatherings and share some word that the Lord has spoken to me. I've asked many times for guidance, often in the grip of panic, and it comes, somehow and at some stage, usually in a way that I'd never even considered. But never in words, clearly articulated, not heard by ears but at some deep level inside me. "It's time to let the dog go."

I give myself a mental shake. My imagination is running away with me again. Ben doesn't look any worse. In fact, if anything, he seems a bit better, pulling himself up and thumping his tail in response to my petting. Anyway, I don't want to hear this. I want him to get better again and be able to go for sedate walks, sniff the fascinating scents of spring just around the corner and let the sunshine soak into his old bones.

I am pleading now. "Lord, don't let him die yet! He's got better so many times, let him get well again.!" I'm even beginning to think of bargains I could strike, though I know very well that God doesn't work like that. *All things work together for good to those that love God and are called according to his purpose,*; that's what the Scripture says. But what possible good can come from the death of an old dog?

"Let the dog go, it's time," says that inner voice again, and I know there can be no more argument.

I go into the downstairs loo and cry and cry, big gasping sobs of grief and loss and relinquishment. Then I scrub my face and return to the kitchen. It's time for the school run. Ben is lying head on paws. He rolls his eyes at me and sighs deeply and seems so normal that I'm tempted again to doubt what seems to be happening. But deep down, I know. I fetch him a drink, sit on the floor beside him stroking his ears and telling him what a good dog he is and how much we've loved him. Then I say "Go in peace, old timer," and smooth his domed head one last time. It's time to leave for school. He heaves a sigh and lifts his head again, watching me go through the door.

I feel I ought to prepare the boys in some way that will soften the shock, and ask Jo if Stuart might have a word with them. She thinks I'm being previous, but we go home with them and the boys play for a time while we have a coffee. Stuart has a few spare moments, so he takes Adam and Luke into the hospital area and chats casually to them, throwing in a brief mention of the shortness of the lifespan of animals as compared to our own.

"The main thing," he says cheerfully as we're preparing to leave, "is that we make sure our pets have happy lives while they're with us, and not be too sad when they're gone. "

I feel like giving Stuart a big hug, though Jo still thinks I'm a bit OTT in my assumptions. Maybe I am . I could be quite wrong.

As soon as I walk in the door I know I was not wrong. Michael and Lauren are home, and they and Graham are sitting silently round the kitchen table. They have mugs of tea which they're not drinking and Lauren has been crying, though she pretends she hasn't. Ben's place is vacant.

Graham clears his throat. Adam and Luke have clattered straight upstairs, noticing nothing amiss. "It's all right," I say quickly. "I know."

Michael looks near to tears. Lauren says dramatically "Ben died at twenty minutes past four, just after we got in. We went to fetch Dad." And then she bursts into tears again.

We have the funeral that evening at dusk, at the end of the orchard where many of our pets have been laid to rest. Ben's grave is under the Bramley apple tree. Snowdrops tumble down the bank from the hedge above. We say a prayer; lay a posy of forsythia buds and periwinkle, and Michael puts up a small wooden cross. There are some tears and a few reminiscences, and for a brief space of time we're united in loss, and grief, and our memories of someone we all loved.

There are a few more tears at bedtime.

"But he did have a happy life, didn't he?" says Luke with a final sniff.

"Yes, he did," I agree, and bless Stuart for his choice of words, and thank God for wise friends, and children, and dogs, and for all his goodness.

*

I go over to my parents' house next day to tell them what's happened. They were fond of old Ben and it's not a piece of news I want to break over the phone.

Dad is busy in his office, arranging for a container of woodworking equipment to be sent to Poland. All over Eastern Europe new enterprises have sprung up, new businesses growing, and he's busy. Mum is working at her computer but switches it off when I go in. She always makes people her top priority, whoever they are, and gives them her full attention. Other people have told me she makes them feel as though they're the most important person in the world, the very one she was longing to see. She makes coffee for me in her sunny kitchen, the kitchen I grew up in, but now somehow less cluttered and more spacious and sparkling these days, with new granite worktops and an oak floor with red rugs replacing the ageing vinyl flooring. *Tete-a-tete* daffodils and muscari in ceramic pots bloom on the windowsills; Mum has something in flower all year round. She is sympathetic about Ben, but not shocked or unduly sad.

"Think of it as a good life, a full life, now complete," she says, handing me a coffee mug with a yellow sunburst on it.

I look at her, smiling and serene in comfort-fit blue jeans and a loose fitting red polo-neck jumper. Am I imagining it, or has she lost a bit of weight lately?

I blurt out "Mum, tell me the truth. Do you have a health problem, I mean, something I ought to know about?"

She pauses for the briefest moment, then sits down opposite me at the oak table, pleasantly cluttered at one end with books, magazines, the morning's post.

"There is something, Ali. Maybe I should have told you earlier, you and Mark, but, well, you have so much to worry about already, and Mark is so far away –"

I'm holding my breath. She says, cradling her coffee mug "They've found a heart problem. It may have been there some while, apparently."

My own heart is thumping. "Mum. How serious is it? Can't something be done? Didn't you mention a pacemaker?"

She takes a sip of hot coffee. "A pacemaker wouldn't make a great deal of difference, it seems. I have some medication which may help. But really there's not a lot they can do." She pauses again, and says quietly "I may go on for years. On the other hand, it's just possible I might pop off, just like that, without much warning. I didn't want to tell you that, I know how much you worry. But maybe it's fairer that you know."

I put down my mug with shaking fingers, feeling panic rise. I can't get my head round this. I need my mum, need to know she's going to be there for a long time yet. This can't be happening, it just can't.

She reaches across and takes my hands. Hers feel cool and strong, capable hands, hands that can soothe a feverish child, fly over a keyboard creating wondrous tales, mix the lightest of shortcrust pastry, reach out to welcome a stranger, plant peas and beans...

The world can't manage without Mum. *I* can't manage.

I say, shakily, "Surely, if you're careful– if you get plenty of rest –"

"Listen, darling. I don't want to turn into a little old lady, forever worrying about my health, fretting in case I'm doing the wrong thing, running about looking for remedies. I intend to go on just as usual. Live every day to the full. That's all we have, anyway. Let's try to live in the moment, enjoy every day as it comes. Think about old Ben. Remember it's God who plans out our lifespan. Your dad and I are going to go on just as usual. And please don't say anything to those lovely children of yours. I don't want to cast any clouds across their skies."

I try to pull myself together. I must be strong, mustn't make things worse for Mum by going to pieces.

"You'll adjust," she says. "Give it a few days and you'll see. You're stronger than you think, Ali."

Maybe. I don't want to adjust. I want things to be as they were, without the heaviness and heartache of this knowledge. Then I remember the way God answered my prayers for Jo. He'll surely do the same for Mum. Because he has promised never to give us anything we're not able to bear, and I know for a fact that I couldn't live without my mum.

Chapter Twelve

I will not fuss, I keep telling myself, I will not worry, fret or be anxious, because those are all things the Scriptures tell us not to do. I will trust God and hand all my cares over to him. Which I do, sitting in my prayer spot beside the Aga, with Ben's vacant place beside it. The trouble is, though my cares have been cast upon the Lord, they often have a way of sneaking back, little by little.

Still, I have gone four whole days without calling my mum to ask how she is. This morning, though, I feel I must get into contact with her. I try to sound casual. "Hi Mum! How are you and Dad this morning?"

She sounds bright as a button on this dull March day.

"Fine, dear. We're just off."

Off? What is this? "Off where, Mum?"

"Oh dear, I've been meaning to ring you but I haven't had a moment, what with packing and so on. We're going to Prague."

"Prague?" For a moment I have difficulty remembering just where Prague is.

"Yes, dear. One of those special City Break things. Your dad arranged it as a surprise. Isn't it lovely? We're travelling down to Heathrow, staying overnight and flying tomorrow."

What can my dad be thinking, dragging a sick woman halfway across Europe? He's hit the right note with her though, she's positively bubbling. "It's such a beautiful city! I've always wanted to go! Of course, your dad's got a little ulterior motive as well. There's a prospective customer in the Czech Republic he wants to meet up with, so we've been invited to his home as well. It's all so exciting!"

My mouth opens and shuts. I want to warn her about over-exerting, taking proper care, etc, etc. But she's thrilled to bits. I can't cast a damper on her enjoyment. Secretly, I'm a little bit envious too. I'd love it if Graham whisked me off on weekend breaks, even with ulterior motives. I won't utter a word that would spoil it for her.

"Have a wonderful time, Mum," I say, with genuine warmth, and don't even add "And take care."

*

"Paula and I are going to Glastonbury," announces Lauren at tea time. I am in the act of dishing out shepherds' pie; my serving spoon falters for a split second and a blob of gravy falls between two plates. Over my dead body, you are, is my knee–jerk reaction, but I keep my silence for the moment. We have been discussing Mum and Dad's trip, and my daughter obviously considers this an opportune moment to mention her own travel plans.

"What's on there?" asks Graham absently, helping himself to broccoli. "School trip or something? How much this time?"

Lauren rolls up her eyes to the heavens. "The Festival, I mean. It won't cost much. It's not until June."

She eyes me across the table, daring me to object. "Does Paula's mum plan to take a tent?" I ask casually.

"Paula's mum is not going. We'll be camping on our own." Lauren is looking daggers at me, knowing very well that I knew that all along, and challenging me to make an issue of it. I put down the dish. If she wants a fight, she's got one.

"No, you won't, Lauren. Not this year. You and Paula are only thirteen, remember?"

"We'll be fourteen by then, or at least, she will, and I will almost." She puts down her fork. I wish we'd finished eating before all this blew up.

"Mum, *everyone* goes to Glastonbury! I've wanted to go for ages. Everyone else's mother lets them go without kicking up a fuss!"

I'd like to meet this much–quoted and permissive woman, everyone else's mother. She has a lot to answer for. Michael is keeping his head well down, shovelling his food in with one hand with the plastered arm resting on the table. Graham has one eye on the magazine crops supplement beside his plate. He will intervene if absolutely necessary but will stay out of it as long as he can. Adam and Luke are squabbling mildly over elbow room.

I say, trying to sound reasonable "Maybe in a year or two we could think again. Especially if a properly supervised group was going. It's really more suitable for older teenagers, anyway."

"Oh, and what would *you* know?" Lauren's cheeks are pink and her purple streak is falling over her face. She is mad at me, and suddenly I want her not to be. I want her to *like* me again, like she did when she was little and we rolled pastry together and made new clothes for her doll. But those days are long gone. Her blazing eyes hold something almost like hatred. She pushes back her chair, and says, bitterly and sarcastically "Thanks, Mum, for spoiling my life *again!*"

*

It's one of those evenings when I have to get out of the house. The days are lengthening fast; it'll be light now until seven or so. I don't stop to wash up, piling the dishes into the sink to soak. If I'm lucky Graham will do them, if not, well it's not the end of the world.

For once I don't go across our own fields or up the hill, instead I get in the car and drive into town, parking by the bridge and pausing to look down at the wide sweep of river, brown and full now after the rain we've had. Its ages since I went along the Bailey walk, a tree shaded footpath that runs along between the river and the disused railway line. I go through the kissing gate and set off under the trees, hands in coat pockets, pondering the complicated relationships of mothers and daughters. Why am I still so dependent on my own mother? Do all daughters provoke in their mothers the complex emotions I feel about Lauren, the hostility and the longing, the rivalry and the empathy, the anger and the sheer blind fear that I won't always be able to protect her? I love her so much, my beautiful, stroppy, moody, fearless daughter.

My eyes are suddenly full of tears. There's a seat beside the path and I sit on it for a moment, letting the tears come. It's quiet here, the river clucks and gurgles below the bank and the trees are just beginning to burst their buds. There are catkins on the hazels, dripping with dusty pollen, and pale yellow/green powder puffs on the willows. The path is beginning to be a little overgrown; people don't walk here as much as they used to. There's someone coming now, though. I hear a faint rhythmic squeaking; a swish of tyres, and then a figure pushing a baby buggy comes into view.

I straighten up and scrub the tears from my cheeks. I didn't even comb my hair before I came out, I must look a sight. I glance up and mutter "Good evening" as the buggy passes, and then look again, because the woman with the pushchair is Harry Dent's mother. She doesn't pause and her greeting is even briefer than mine, just a nod. I catch a glimpse of the child in the pushchair. It's muffled up in a blue blanket against the chill, with a woolly hat pulled down over its forehead.

Then a few yards further along, the woman stops and slowly, almost reluctantly, retraces her steps, pulling the pushchair behind her. She peers at me, standing a few feet away. Her fair hair is pulled back in a ponytail and her face looks cold and pinched.

"Are you okay?"

I must look worse than I thought. I smile and say" Yes, I'm fine."

She hesitates. "Only – well, most things can be sorted, can't they?"

And suddenly I realise that she thinks I'm sitting here sobbing in desperation, maybe planning to chuck myself in the river.

I'm so touched that I almost weep again. This woman obviously has no wish to be friends with me, she made that plain enough when I called round, yet she cared enough to make sure I was okay. I get up and smile. "I'm fine, really. Just a bit of family trouble. Can I walk along with you for a bit?"

She doesn't really want me, I can see that. I guess she's already wishing she hadn't stopped. But she nods ungraciously and sets off with the pushchair, pulling over to make room for me to walk beside her. She says "My boy is at Cubs but he'll be home soon."

I say "Mine never seemed to get into Cubs. How old is your little one?"

Again a slight pause. "Three. She's fast asleep. I often take her for a walk at bedtime to get her off."

"Is she better? Only I saw you in the surgery the other day. My little boy had that nasty bug that's been going round."

"Yes, so did Victoria. She's okay now." She frowns, easing the buggy over a protruding tree root.

I'm determined to keep this conversation going. Maybe I can get back to the problem of her son Harry and my Adam. I say "There's always something with them, isn't there? Kids! I'd just been having a spot of bother with my daughter before I came out. It really upset me."

She says "Oh yes?" not in an encouraging way, but I plough on regardless.

"Girls are more difficult than boys, I'm finding, especially when they get to their teens. You've got all that ahead of you, I'm afraid."

She stiffens suddenly and turns to look at me with the strangest look I've ever seen. Grief, despair, anguish, are all there in her face. She says, in a voice tight with pain "No. No, I won't."

Oh, God! There's something here, something that is pushing a mother to the limits of agony and beyond. Instinctively, I reach out and touch her arm. She says, shakily "I stopped and spoke to you because I've been where I thought you were. I've stood by the river and wondered if I had

68

the courage to go in, me and Victoria. But – there was still Harry –"

"Do you want to tell me?"

She looks at her watch. "I'd ask you for a coffee but Harry'll be home. I could do with someone to talk to. When you called round that day I thought you were some nosey do–gooder, but now I can see you're just an ordinary mum –"

"Tell you what," I say quickly "Why don't I come round another day, then maybe we can arrange for Harry to come to tea or something –"

She nods and gulps, bending to tuck the blanket more snugly round her sleeping daughter. We've come to the end of the path, where it takes a sharp turn away from the river to join St. John's Road near the church.

"My name's Alison Harper," I say as she begins to wheel the buggy in the direction of the new estate.

"Sonia Dent," she says, and is gone, walking fast along the darkening pavement.

*

I drive home in the dusk feeling awed afresh at the workings of a God whose ways are not our ways, whose thoughts are not our thoughts. The 'all things work together for good' verse is in my mind again. And the 'all things' include that sharp exchange with Lauren, and my going off on my own. There's a woman in some deep trouble here, and I'd never have had the chance to help....

I don't know what the trouble is, or how I could make a difference. But I can trust it to him who knows all things.

I left home in turmoil and am going home with that peace in my heart that passes all understanding, that I can't explain or really describe, but that can with gratitude experience, full and wide and deep as a river.

*

The kitchen lights are on as I drive into the yard, curtains undrawn. Lauren is in there alone, a slight figure in jeans and a purple top that matches the streak in her hair, with the sleeves pushed up. She is toiling over the sink, tackling the pile of dishes and cutlery left from the meal of six people. She is listening to music and hasn't heard the car. She brushes back the hair from her face with a forearm, and picks up another pile of plates from the draining board.

I let myself in quietly. Graham and the little boys are in the sitting room, watching the Simpsons movie yet again and laughing at it in the way Bart and Lisa laugh at Itchy and Scratchy.

Lauren gives a start as I enter the kitchen. She looks at me a little uncertainly. "I didn't know how long you'd be. You didn't take your phone." The statement sounds more forlorn than accusing. This could be my cue to say "Well, that's how I feel when you're out somewhere ...'

But instead I want to hug her, hold her, tell her how precious she is, and how much loved – I say "Sorry. I met someone and we got talking. Thank you so much for doing all this. You've done a fantastic job!"

She has, too, done all the extra bits that men forget – like cleaning down the worktops and shaking out the tablecloth. She shrugs, casually. "Well, Dad got to watching that film with the kids. They've already seen it about four hundred and twenty times!"

Another burst of laughter comes from the sitting room, Graham's loudest of all. She actually grins and we exchange a look that says "Men! They're all just big kids at heart. Thank goodness for a few sensible females like us!"

Chapter Thirteen

I'm awakened by Luke and Adam standing by the bed in their pyjamas, tugging at the duvet. "Mum! Mum!"

It must be early yet, but Graham has gone and his side of the bed is already cold.

"Mum! You've got to get up!"

"What's the hurry? What time is it?"

"Don't know, but you've got to get up!" Adam is pink with anticipation, jumping from one foot to the other, and Luke looks fit to burst with excitement. He says, in a strangled squeak "There's a snake in the kitchen!"

My blood runs cold. I have a total fear of snakes, large or small, slowworms, serpents, eels or any kind of long sinuous creature. Can an adder have got into the house somehow? There are sometimes adders in our area, and they're poisonous, but I thought they were only seen in the summer.

"Don't move!" I tell the boys, and scramble out of bed. I'm wondering where I left my mobile phone. It's not by the bed. Bathroom? If I can reach it, I'll phone for help, but I'm not venturing downstairs until it's dealt with.

I'm fumbling for my slippers – no way am I going barefoot with a snake in the house – when I become aware that the boys are behaving strangely, spluttering, gasping and struggling to hold in their mirth. They can contain themselves no longer. "April Fool!" they shout in unison, and when I collapse with relief on the bed they fling themselves on top of me.

*

Spring has sprung, and suddenly the patch of woodland up behind our farmhouse is teeming with life. Buds are swelling; the bare branches are being transformed by a haze of tender unfurling leaves. Lambs call in the meadows, and the birds are busy from dawn to dusk, claiming their territories and constructing new cradles. Everywhere I look, fresh green is pushing up from the grey detritus of winter, covering the monochrome drabness as warmth and light and colour return to the earth. Standing outside the back door, I hear the yaffle of a woodpecker and then the tattoo of his beak against wood. The air is melodious with birdsong and grey squirrels leap from branch to branch in the tall sycamores.

The squirrels are a sore point with Graham. Far from admiring their graceful leaps and athletic prowess in the branches, he considers them vermin, little more than rats with bushy tails, and mutters about getting the gun to them. The problem is they don't stick to nibbling the fresh shoots of sycamore buds, but also use the trees all winter long as a launching pad for reaching the grain store, where they soon find a way of getting into the corn bins and helping themselves. No wonder they're so fat and sleek!

"I thought squirrels hibernated over the winter, with a nice store of nuts," I ponder. I hate it when anything has to be killed, even pests like rats and crows.

"Not any more they don't! Maybe they used to when winters were longer and harder. But why should they bother collecting nuts when there's a nice stash of barley and wheat all handily harvested for them?"

"But their tails are so beautiful..."

"Tails, shmails!" But he leaves the gun locked up in its steel cabinet, for now.

Today I'm taking Michael to the hospital to have his plaster removed. What started out as a white and pristine cast is now a grubby grey, decorated with graffiti in the form of signatures, cartoons and rude remarks from his mates. It's been quite a handicap for him, he's missed out on a lot of sport, quad bike riding (though I've seen him round the fields illicitly once or twice, steering one handed), swimming and working out. I hope his studies haven't suffered; he'll be taking GCSE's this summer. It'll be a huge relief to him to get rid of the thing.

I can't help contrasting this mild, balmy spring day with the cold, ice and snow that dominated the scene the day Michael had his accident. He's much more relaxed too, especially when the plaster is off and the healed break pronounced a text-book perfect job. His arm looks pale, wasted and skinny, but we're assured it will build up again in no time with exercise. Michael is cheery as we leave the hospital, and I venture to strike while the iron is hot, by asking for news of Becky. I'd be very surprised if the two of them weren't in text and email contact daily, if not oftener.

"She's fine," he says, flexing his arm and examining it critically, as though he expects the muscles to develop there and then. "She'll be able to take her exams. Probably stay over there to do A-levels."

"And the baby?

I try to sound casual, but I'm longing to know.

"Adopted. Or will be. It's all arranged, no big deal."

Maybe not for other people, I think. But a very big deal for some, like Paul and Caroline, and the adoptive parents, and a huge deal for Becky and that little unborn baby. I want to talk again to Michael about the value of each individual, of how precious and unique is every new child born into the world. But he's a fifteen-year-old boy. He won't want to hear any of that stuff today.

I drop him at school and think that now might be a good time for popping in to see Sonia Dent. It's hardly worth going back home before lunchtime.

She answers the door to my knock, hair in a blue towel turban, obviously she's just been washing it. Bad start, I hate it when people come to the door when I've just washed my hair. But she smiles, in a strained kind of way, remembers my name, and says "Come on in, Alison."

The living room is ordinary enough; worn sofas livened up with tasselled red throws, a small pair of child's shoes under the coffee table, toys scattered about.

"Victoria's asleep," she says, moving a battered teddy and a couple of books from a sofa so I can sit down. "She usually has a nap before lunch. Coffee?"

I wait, listening to sounds from the kitchen of a kettle being filled and the clatter of spoons and mugs. Boys' comics and colouring books are jumbled together on the coffee table. There's a TV set on a stand near a wall-mounted gas fire, a red rug covering worn beige carpeting. Not much money for luxuries here.

When Sonia comes back with two mugs and a sugar bowl on a small tray, she's taken off the towel and pulled her damp hair back into a ponytail band. I think she'd be very pretty if she took a bit of trouble with herself and then I remember something Lauren said to me the other day. "If you had a decent haircut, lost ten pounds, toned up at the gym and found out what people wear these days; you'd be quite nice looking."

I smile at the memory, and Sonia's eyebrows raise enquiringly as she hands me a coffee mug. I say "I was just thinking about something my daughter said. Teenage girls can be quite cutting with their remarks."

The bleak look is back on her face again. I remember the way she reacted when I spoke about Lauren the other day. She sits opposite, cupping her hands around her mug, leans forward and takes a deep breath.

"I think I'd better tell you about Victoria."

I nod encouragingly, sipping my coffee. She takes another breath, and says "My daughter has Progeria. Do you know what that is?"

I feel I may have heard the name, maybe seen a TV documentary. A rare condition? I can't remember much. I shake my head.

"It's an extremely rare syndrome. Only one hundred or so recorded cases in the world, ever. Basically, it's premature ageing. Instead of living a normal lifespan, the child ages quickly. Ten times as fast. They don't grow properly, they lose their hair, develop the illnesses of age – arthritis, heart disease, stroke. A child with Progeria normally dies before thirteen, dies of old age, technically."

I feel winded, as though I've been punched hard. So this is the tragedy that lurks behind Sonia's eyes. "I'm so sorry," I say, and realise, how foolish, how inadequate, that sounds. I put my mug down carefully on a cork mat on the coffee table, my thoughts whirling. How on earth does a mother cope with a sorrow like this, the daily care of a child who will suffer terrible changes and then die?

Sonia is speaking again. "We noticed it first when Victoria was about eight months old. She didn't seem to be growing. Then her hair started falling out. Something wasn't right. She got ill a lot and wouldn't eat properly. Eventually she went into hospital for tests and was diagnosed. There's nothing that can be done for the condition. They said take her home and love her."

Her face twitches and she works hard to keep it under control.

"It must be so hard for you and your husband."

She gives a short, bitter laugh. "Oh, he's not around any more. He couldn't take it when we learned the score. Victoria was his little princess, you see. He absolutely adored her – we all did. Then when the changes started happening – hair loss, skin texture, when she

74

started looking a bit odd and different, it seemed to hit him what was happening. He just buggered off. Walked out to work one day and never came home. I got one text message saying he was sorry but that he couldn't hack it. And that was it. We haven't seen him since."

"Oh, how awful for you!" I wish I could think of something to say other than these silly, trite remarks. But my brain feels numb.

"We're better off without him, I reckon. We moved down here last year to be near my mum. And to be in the country, for the kids. Then Mum died, only a few months later. There's only the three of us now."

Sorrow upon sorrow. How on earth can she bear it, go on from day to day? But I can only say, stupidly "It must be hard."

"It's hard. I've been suffering from depression. Don't like going out much. People are starting to stare at Victoria. That's why I mostly take her out in the evenings. I don't want her to hear any snide remarks. We keep to ourselves. I get an allowance for Victoria. We get by. It's hard on Harry, though."

I'd forgotten Harry, and the reason I wanted to speak to Sonia in the first place. I say, tentatively "Is Harry happy at school?"
She shrugs and frowns. "I reckon so. I should go there more, I suppose, speak to the teachers. They did say he was having a bit of trouble relating to others, whatever that means. I thought he'd settle in time. He's a big boy, he knows how to take care of himself."

I don't quite know what to say to that. I begin to understand, though, why Harry demands attention, sweets, respect of a sort, friendship as he sees it. Poor lad, he's missing out in all kinds of ways. No dad around, a depressed, preoccupied mum, a sister who's not going to live many years.

Here at least is something I can offer to this heartbroken, overburdened woman.

"Adam is in Harry's class. Could Harry come out to tea one day after school? We're on a farm, he might enjoy it. I could always run him home afterwards."

She nods and sips her coffee. "Thanks. He'd like that, I expect."

My mind is racing. What Sonia needs is support, a group of caring people around her who she can trust, talk to in confidence, depend on for practical help when needed. A group such as I have, in my church and with my friends. She could be part of that group. But I also sense that I'll have to tread very warily here. She's not someone who easily trusts. I must not jump in feet first. At the same time, though,

I also sense that here is a woman who is desperate for friendship and understanding.

At that moment there is a sound from upstairs, a child calling in a thin, high-pitched voice, a rattle of cot bars.

"She's awake," says Sonia. "I'll bring her down."

I don't know what I expect to see when she comes downstairs again, carrying her daughter. What I do see is a tiny girl, more the size of an eighteen-month-old than a three year old child, in green cord dungarees, a stripy top and a green velvet mob cap. She turns and looks at me solemnly from her mother's arms; she has the most beautiful dark brown eyes, velvety as pansies and slightly prominent, but I notice that her eyebrows and lashes are almost non-existent. She stands shyly for a moment when her mother puts her down, sizing me up.

"She doesn't see many people," says Sonia. Sonia's face is transformed as she looks at her daughter, softer, lighter, loving. Having decided I'm harmless, Victoria trots to the toybox in the corner and rummages in it. She finds a sheet of characters from Frozen stickers, peels off one of Elsa and offers it to me solemnly. She has a small nose, a pointed little chin and round cheeks. I stick the sticker carefully onto my jacket and say "Thank you very much, Victoria."

She speaks for the first time, in a high, piping little voice. "Have you got any little girls?"

"Yes, one. But she's bigger now. Her name's Lauren."

She digests this information, then finds a piece of paper, gathers her crayons and begins to draw, kneeling by the coffee table, head on one side, tongue out in concentration. At some stage her hat tips forward over her eyes; she plucks it off and casts it away from her. I see her head, almost bald except for a covering of light-coloured hair, like a thin crew cut. She finishes the picture, signs it with a wobbly red V and presents it to me with a flourish. It shows a lurid orange sun, a square box I presume is a house, and a figure with arms and legs attached to its large round head.

"That's me," she explains.

I am captivated. "Thank you so much, Victoria. I'll take it home and stick it on my fridge."

She thinks about this. Victoria is obviously someone who carefully weighs up every piece of information. Then she says "Do you have Fruit Shoots in your fridge?"

Her mother laughs, and I'm amazed at the transformation it brings.

"Victoria! That's not very polite!"

"Actually, I do have some Fruit Shoots" I tell her. "My little boy likes them. His name is Luke. His favourite is blackcurrant." I pause for a moment. "Maybe you'd like to come to my house one day, Victoria, and meet my little boy, and perhaps have a Fruit Shoot?"

Her little face lights up. "Can us go now?"

Her mother intervenes quickly. "Not this minute, sweetie. We have to go to the clinic for a check later, after lunch. But perhaps another time."

"How about next Wednesday?" I suggest. "Maybe after school, then your brother could come too."

She jumps up and down, her cheeks growing pink. I get up to leave, holding her picture carefully. It will get pride of place among the other assorted postings in my kitchen.

Somehow I feel that there's a difference in the atmosphere between Sonia and me, a lightening and softening. Maybe the beginnings of trust. I don't know quite how it's happened, or why, but I know that God must be in it somewhere. And that Victoria, this sweet little girl in a body already beginning to age, has captured my heart.

Chapter Fourteen

Mark will be home next week. I am at my mother's, helping her get his room ready. It's full of his stuff, clothing, sports equipment, books, shoes, football memorabilia, years of accumulated possessions, so much that it's spilled over into other rooms.

"Mark's the only person I know who occupies three rooms, even when he's not here," says my mother with a smile.

She and Dad got back from Prague, not exhausted as I'd feared, but positively glowing with shared experiences and tales to tell of new people, places and happenings.

"Prague is so beautiful," she says, getting clean bed linen from the cupboard. "Walking round Old Town Square and seeing the Astronomical clock was magic! And we managed to get tickets for a concert at the Dvorak Hall – just imagine! That was thanks to Emil. His family were so lovely and welcoming."

I'm so glad they had a good time. And so relieved they were not overtaken by illness, accident or collapse, and that they didn't get lost, stranded, let down, mugged, disappointed or out of money, all of which had crossed my mind during the time they were away.

My mother is good at reading my thoughts. As I wrestle a mulberry-coloured cover onto Mark's duvet, she says thoughtfully "You know, Alison, you really mustn't worry so much. Jesus talked a lot about not worrying. We really ought not to."

"Yes, I know." I've read those Bible verses too. "The only thing is, Mum, it doesn't say how not to worry."

She plumps the pillows into place, thinks for a moment and then goes off into her own room. She comes back carrying a shoebox with a slot cut in the lid. She puts it down on the bed and motions me to sit down beside her. I raise my eyebrows questioningly.

"You know, dear, you're just like me. By nature I'm a terrible worrier too."

"You?" I don't believe it. Mum is so serene. I've long envied her ability to live in the moment and let tomorrow take care of itself.

She nods. "Oh yes. I've always struggled with thinking I know what's best for people or situations, and then trying to persuade God to bring it about. Trying to play God, in fact. Just what we mustn't do."

Well, that makes sense. "But what's with the shoebox?"

She pats it. "My solution. When I've got something really scary or upsetting going on, and there's nothing I can do and I don't know where to turn or how to go on, this is what I do."

She pulls the lid off the box. Inside are dozens and dozens of little folded bits of paper. "I write down my concerns and anxieties, add the date, fold the paper and pop it through the slot. And leave it there. Then, when I begin to worry again, I remind myself I've given it over to God."

"And it works?"

"Oh yes. Sometimes we're like kids; we need a little visual aid. And now and again I look at one or two of the papers to remind myself of what God has done."

She picks a piece of paper at random and smoothes it out, reading 'We need a Vicar at church so badly.' It's dated more than ten years ago, just before Paul was appointed. "You see? That seems to have been a fast answer! Others take longer. But that's God's responsibility, not mine."

She replaces the paper and lid and carries the box away. I shake out the duvet and smooth it over the bed. How fortunate that Adam needed yet another pair of new trainers just last week, and the box hasn't yet gone for recycling. I'm going to go straight home, dig it out, and cut a slot in the lid.

*

The phone rings as Graham is leaving the kitchen after his hasty lunch. The poor guy hardly has time to breathe these days, let alone eat. His crops have to be fertilized and treated for pests and disease this time of year and it's a long never-ending slog. He pauses only long enough to learn whether the call is for him, and then is gone.

It's Jo, with a proposition. Stuart has heard of a family of unwanted kittens needing hopes, a.s.a.p. They know we recently lost Ben and are wondering…...

Three of the five kittens have been promised homes already, but there are two left, nice friendly little things, both males, ginger. The local rescue lady would love me to get in touch.

All of us declared that we never, ever, wanted another dog after Ben went. Nobody ever mentioned cats, though. It's a year or so since our old black and white tom, Thomas, died, and cats are useful about the corn bins which attract rats and mice like a magnet.

I'm convinced. I make a couple of calls and arrange to meet the rescue lady, with kittens in tow, at the car park just before school time. She arrives in a beat-up old van with the back seat taken out and a large, gangling mongrel dog with an injured leg lying on a blanket on the floor. Her name is Delyth and she's a middle-aged, smallish lady who lives, sleeps and breathes the animals she recues. She would give her life-blood for them, one feels. The kittens are in a carry basket in front. She lets me take a quick peek at them, pretty little things looking up at me appealingly from pointed small faces. But first I have a grilling on my motives, background, family set-up and intentions.

"I shall be checking on you," she warns, wagging an admonishing finger. "Oh, and as they're both males they'll need to be neutered at eight to nine months. I insist on neutering for both sexes. Far too many strays running around. And don't let your husband take pity on them and talk you out of it. I know what these men are." She rummages in the dashboard cupboard and brings out an official-looking form.

"Sign there, please."

I sign, give the suggested small donation, transfer the carry-basket to my car, and get ready to introduce the two new members of the family to the present ones.

*

I can't believe it. Graham and I are having a day off, driving to Heathrow to meet Mark's transatlantic flight from San Francisco. Graham is up to date with his work, the sun is shining, it's a beautiful spring day.

We start early and stop for lunch at a pub in the Cotswolds, with an open fire, exposed beams and excellent food. I begin to think longingly of little breaks, a weekend away maybe, or even a holiday in the not too far distant future. Graham is looking out the window, murmuring with a hint of envy about the beautiful, flat, fertile farming land of the Cotswolds, but that doesn't spoil my enjoyment. I feel free as a bird, looking forward to seeing my little brother.

Heathrow is busy, packed, noisy and confusing. I used to love the hurly-burly of airports, train stations, even motorway services with everyone on the move and going somewhere. Now that security checks are so much longer and more complicated and there's so much waiting about, a lot of the shine has gone from travel situations. There's a long wait between the time Mark's plane come in and when the passengers start appearing down the exit way. But they're trickling out now, scanning the waiting faces at the gates for their friends and families. And suddenly, there's Mark, tall and tanned amongst a group of winter-pale complexions, a jacket slung over his shoulder and a big grin on his face as he spots us. Even after a long and exhausting journey, he's able to attract admiring glances from several females.

My brother greets us both with big bear hugs and kisses. Mark is the only man I know who Graham would allow this kind of familiarity. He doesn't go much for public physical shows of affection.

"Nice tan!" Graham says as we head for the car. "Snowboarding?"

"A bit," says my brother. "When I can wangle time off. I've got a new part-time thing going though. Voluntary sheriff's department Search and Rescue."

I listen to him and Graham discussing the duties, how Mark's training will at some stage involve him staying out in the woods for three days entirely dependent on his own survival skills. There are bears in the North California forests, snakes and I daren't think what else. What Mum's going to think about this new venture I don't know, but I have the feeling she'll regard it as one more new and interesting development in her son's life. She'd probably do it herself, given half a chance.

"How is Mum?" Mark asks, when we're in the car and negotiating our way out onto the motorway. Suddenly he's looking serious. I've explained on the phone about the heart condition. I tell him about the recent trip to Prague. He's thoughtful for a bit. Then he says "Sis, do you think I ought to come home?"

I can see he means it, and would do it. There have been times when I wished he was not half way across the world, but I know that Mum rejoices in the fact that he's living the life he loves, that she wouldn't clip his wings or tie him down for anything.

So I say, and mean it from the heart "No, I don't. Mum and Dad look after each other. And what would she do if she couldn't boast about her son in sunny California! And him a part-time sheriff, at that?"

*

Sunday lunch at our house is hilarious with Mark there. He tells funny stories about the children in the teams he coaches, their pushy moms, and the training he's doing for Search and Rescue. I'm not quite sure where fact ends and fiction begins. Luke and Adam sit on either side of him, vying for his attention, begging him for a game of football later. Lauren preens and is looking for opportunities of showing off her cool uncle to her mates. Michael laughs at Mark's jokes in a way I haven't heard for ages. Graham is relaxed, and the pressured look he wears at busy times has smoothed out. Even the new kittens love Mark, twining themselves about his ankles and trying to sharpen their little claws on his jeans.

Mum and Dad are quietly happy, pleased to have their family together, giving each other that special look now and again. Mark is so laid-back that some of it rubs off even on me. He is one of those sunny, charming people who take a feelgood factor with them wherever they go.

*

It's Palm Sunday, and Paul has decided that an enactment of Jesus' triumphant last journey into Jerusalem would be a meaningful way of celebrating it, complete with real donkey. In a moment of rash confidence, I mentioned that our neighbour Dai had a donkey he might be persuaded to lend for the occasion. When approached, Dai was willing but a little dubious about Jacob's ability, or willingness, to perform.

"He's a stubborn creature, Jacob," he said, pushing back his old tweed cap and rubbing his head. "Awk 'ard and stubborn. He might decide to go at a gallop, or then again, he might not go at all."

It was decided we'd take our chances with Jacob, and trust that he'd be in an obliging and co-operative mood. This afternoon, he's transported by horsebox to the field by the river, from whence he'll make the journey to the church, led by a few young 'disciples' and greeted by a crowd of children with palm branches.

Dai is dubious too about the palm branches. "He'll most likely panic and take off like a rocket when they start waving things at him."

Paul directs that the waving and cheering be kept very low key. He and some others of us seem to be having a few doubts about the wisdom of the whole idea. I begin to have visions of a panic-stricken donkey breaking loose and running amok among the tombstones.

But Jacob rises magnificently to the occasion. Gripped firmly in Dai's strong hands, he even permits 11-year old Stephen Parry, who is taking the part of our Lord, to sit upon his back. Then he plods sturdily along the lane to the church, where the 'crowd' waits. His ears flicker a little but he never falters when the palm branches wave dangerously near his face and there's an enthusiastic outburst of loud Hosannas.

I feel a lump rise in my throat. The boy dismounts at the church and I see clearly the imprint of the cross on Jacob's back, lighter grey against the dark, a reminder, they say, of that first Palm Sunday, when the untamed young colt was gentled by the tender hands of the Saviour on his last fateful ride into Jerusalem.

Chapter Fifteen

I wonder how Adam will take to the idea of Harry Dent and his family coming to tea next Wednesday and am pleasantly surprised when the idea doesn't appear to cause any consternation. In fact, he rather seems to be looking forward to it.

"He'll be on his own territory, you see," says my mother when I mention the matter to her. "It's bound to give him that extra bit of confidence."

I pick up Sonia and Victoria along with the schoolchildren and we all travel home together. Victoria is wearing a smart pink hat and her brown eyes sparkle as I strap her into Luke's old car seat. Sonia doesn't have a car and I guess that outings are not all that frequent in Victoria's little life.

"Us are going to a *farm*," she tells her brother joyfully as the boys scramble into the car. Harry mumbles a reply, half embarrassed and a little out of his depth. But I notice he is kind to his little sister, he picks up her fluffy rabbit when she drops it, and points out the river to her as we cross the bridge. He and Adam seem a little wary of each other but not unfriendly. Luke is chattering non-stop which covers up any awkwardness.

I see in the driving mirror that Victoria's eyes are like saucers as we leave town and begin the climb up our mountainside. Every sheep or cow or pony in the fields as we pass brings forth a delighted squeal. Her feet, dangling in the car seat, drum into the back of my seat as she flails them in excitement, a not altogether welcome experience I'd forgotten since Luke passed that stage. But it's well worth it to see her pleasure.

Harry seems a little disappointed when we pull into the yard and begin to pile out. "I thought it would be a *real* farm." Evidently he had expected it to be an Old MacDonald's kind of place, with ducks quacking, pigs grunting and cows mooing. Our sprawling stone farmhouse with its supporting structures of corrugated-roofed barns and tall corn bins, softened just now by the new green of spreading sycamores and oaks, does not quite fit the bill.

"It's an *arable* farm," Adam is quick to point out. Harry does not understand what that means, but looks suitably impressed.

I usher them all into the kitchen, where at once Victoria spots the kittens, Spit and Spot, curled up in their basket, and has to be restrained from killing them with kindness. Victoria's hat falls off and her balding head and pointy elf's ears are on show for all to see. I have grilled the boys on not making remarks, explaining that she looks a little different from other children but is an ordinary little girl inside. It is Harry who snatches up her hat and replaces it, skew-whiff, but gently, and says "Look, Victoria, there's a Barbie car in the toybox."

I'm glad I thought to hunt up some of Lauren's old toys. I'm beginning to warm to Harry. He's had a lot to adjust to, and maybe it's no wonder that he sometimes relates to others in an inappropriate way. I make tea and sandwiches and the boys wolf them down, then I steer them in the direction of bikes and footballs and the outdoors. Michael and Lauren have arrived home, exchanged polite greetings with the visitors and drifted off to texting and social media and, I hope, some homework.

"Some exercise will be good for Harry," says Sonia ruefully, wiping a milkshake moustache from Victoria's mouth. "He's got overweight – too much TV and play station and not enough exercise. And I'm afraid all too often we have easy quick meals instead of proper freshly cooked ones."

I can sympathise. I cut corners myself quite often. She doesn't need to beat herself up all the time. She and I take Victoria for a gentle walk down the lane to see the lambs in Sue and Mike's field. It's a perfect spring evening; a blackbird is warbling his heart out from the high branch of the big ash tree and the lambs are running races up and down the meadow. Victoria is enchanted, wanting to run up and down too, but we persuade her to stand on the gate and watch from there instead.

"She's such a sweetie," I say as we walk back to the house with Victoria running ahead.

Sonia smiles, but there's pain behind her eyes. "Yes, she's very special. It's so hard – soon her joints will stiffen and she won't be able to run like that anymore –" Her voice trembles. I touch her hand. I just can't imagine how hard it must be.

We are beginning to round up the boys when a vehicle can be heard coming up the hill. It's Mark, driving my dad's car. He jumps out and apologises, flashing his sweet smile. "Oh, sorry, sis. Didn't know you had company."

I introduce him to Sonia and Victoria, and we go indoors to make more tea. The boys don't need rounding up now; they come running as soon as they know Mark's here, mobbing him like football fans. Harry hangs back a little.

"Uncle Mark! Come and play football with us!"

He agrees he will have a game later, which will keep them nicely occupied while I run Sonia and the children home. Mark perches on a kitchen stool with a mug of tea and chats to Sonia and Victoria. Victoria takes to him right away, edging nearer until she's at his knee.

"Can I play football too?"

He laughs and tickles her chin. "Not with this bunch of ruffians, honey. Tell you what, fetch that woolly ball and I'll show you how to shoot goal." And he does, laughing and jumping around like a big kid, right there in the kitchen, and cheering when Victoria gets the ball between the makeshift goalposts. Sonia laughs too, looking quite animated and suddenly very pretty, with pink in her cheeks. I'm constantly amazed at the effect my little brother has on people.

Victoria is asleep almost the moment we strap her into the car seat. Harry looks cheerful and relaxed. He and Adam part company with amicable thumps. The visit has been a success.

"I suppose your brother will be going back before long," Sonia asks casually as we approach town, and when I reply that yes, he'll be off next week after the Easter holiday is over, I catch a wistful look flitting across her face.

*

We have a new tradition for Good Friday, which Paul started the year he and Caroline moved here. There's a service in church in the morning, and afterwards a group of us carry a wooden cross around the town. I don't manage to make the service this year, but I join the rest at the lych gate as they prepare to carry the cross.

We're a motley crew. Most of the church ladies are there, a few of the men who are retired or have the day off, a sprinkling of children. Luke is the only one of mine I could persuade to come with me; for Graham, it's field work as usual while the weather stays dry.

We gather round the cross, held by Paul, who says a brief prayer before we set out. Then Paul shoulders the cross and leads us out into the town. Graham made the cross out of two pieces of oak held together by a strong iron bolt. It's nothing fancy at all, not shaped or polished, but rough, hard and heavy, and it takes a strong man to carry it. We follow, straggling out over the pavement, young and vigorous up front, slower and more infirm bringing up the rear. Deirdre Burns has her elderly mum in a wheelchair, Fay Jones her toddler in a buggy. Half way up Warren Bank we meet Janet French riding a bicycle; she dismounts, turns around and wheels the bike beside us. One or two more join us as we make our way to the castle and car park.

Paul sighs with relief as we reach the castle forecourt with its patch of grass, and rests the cross, rubbing his aching shoulders. The town is humming with Easter visitors, here mostly for the books. People are crossing and re-crossing from the car park to the alleyway running beside the castle walls and into town. We get some curious glances, one or two people smirk or make some snide remark, but the vast majority are indifferent, intent on their own business and pleasure. I wonder if this is how it was on the day that Jesus carried the cross.

Paul reads, slowly and distinctly, the story of that day, more than two thousand years ago, while people come and go and mill around. I pray that some word will stick, that some seeking heart might discover a gleam of hope in the retelling of the suffering and death of the one who gave his life for the redemption of mankind.

We don't stay long, standing in silence for a few minutes. One or two people come up and ask for the literature we carry. Someone laughs and makes a rude remark about us. I feel overwhelmed by the privilege of being identified with the Christ who was mocked and spat upon.

Then Paul shoulders the cross again, we assemble and follow it on a route through the busy streets and back towards the church, where it is set up on the grassy mound that was the site of the original castle. It will stand there over Easter, a silent witness to an event that still changes lives.

*

Lauren has an Easter concert performance at school which Graham and I and Mum and Dad are going to while Mark babysits the boys. Lauren would like Mark to have been there, and sulks and grumbles because there are only four available places. Showing off her cool uncle from California would have done wonders for her street cred. She's not pleased either with the crisp white cotton shirt I've carefully laundered to go with her black trousers.

"Nobody wears *those* any more."

"I thought you needed a white shirt."

"I need a white *top*. That doesn't mean some school blouse from the last century."

Uh-oh, I got it wrong again. She rummages about in her wardrobe and pulls out a skinny, clingy tiny garment. When she's pulled it on it leaves an inch or two of bare skin around her slender midriff. I open my mouth but close it again. Pointless to argue.

A lot of the others are wearing skimpy T-shirts, or strappy things or little tops that wouldn't look out of place at a night-club. Not a crisp white shirt to be seen. I've been proved wrong again.

"Doesn't Lauren look beautiful?" whispers my mother, as the instruments begin to tune up. She does, blonde and lovely and colt-like with those long, slim legs, studiously avoiding any eye-contact with her family.

"I think she wishes I'd stayed at home and let Mark come instead," I whisper back, only half joking.

Mother pats my knee and says "No, dear, you're the one she wants to impress most of all."

You could have fooled me. But I am impressed, overwhelmingly, as the music begins and the pure, piercing notes of Lauren's flute rise in a haunting descant to the rafters of the school hall. They're playing Schubert, the beauty of it brings tears to my eyes. I am proud of my daughter, so proud it makes my heart leap and my toes curl in my pointy-toed shoes.

Chapter Sixteen

I don't send out Easter cards, personally. Not any more. The Christmas card list is bad enough, especially when it seems obligatory to exchange cards not only with loved ones at a distance, but also with someone just down the road, or someone you see every day. I used to buy a few Easter cards and send them hastily to anyone who sent them to me, but I gave that up as being pointless and hypocritical.

A handful of people still persist in sending them to me. Graham's mum is one. She and Graham's dad, Bob, lived here, in our farmhouse, and farmed for many years until Bob decided to hand over to Graham. They moved to a modern bungalow in town but in the event were not there long, because Bob became ill and died within two years. We realised afterwards that he and Molly had known of the illness when they decided to move. Molly stayed for a while to be near her only son and his family, but when her sister Jane was also widowed, the two of them bought a house together on the Pembroke coast, somewhere, apparently, that both had always fancied living.

Molly periodically descends on us and stays for a visit. I'd half–expected her this Easter, and am slightly relieved she stayed put. I'm fond of my mother–in–law, but cautiously so. I feel I never *quite* measure up to what the wife for her perfect only son should be. When she's here, she pointedly bakes fruit cakes for him, and substantial puddings, brushing aside my weak attempts at advocating healthy eating. A working man needs fuel, she says. She frowns disapprovingly at any rip in a shirt sleeve or toe poking accusingly from a hole in a sock. She always did her mending and darning routinely, like washing and ironing. When I tell her that modern socks aren't designed for darning, she tut–tuts, and goes out to buy Graham a dozen pairs of wickedly expensive pure wool socks, the kind Bob always wore. She recoils in horror at the thought of Graham ever getting together a scratch meal for himself, or washing the odd plate or dish, or doing anything that's officially women's work. She was brought up in an era when men, or at least farming men, were lords of the household and women their willing slaves, and does not approve of modern trends and the flighty ways of modern young women.

If ever I moan to Graham about his mum, he agrees to a point but modifies my complaints. "She thinks the world of you, you know."

"She does?"

"Yes. I've heard her boasting about her wonderful daughter-in-law, how clever and creative she is, just like her dear mother, how her children are a credit to her, and how kind-hearted she is."

"I wish she'd say a bit of this to my face."

"Well, her generation didn't. Heaven forbid anyone would become big headed from too much praise and get above themselves!"

"Some chance, with the kind of people I have to live with."

I recognise the precise handwriting on the envelope that arrives in our mail. It gives me a sense of relief, that, (a) Molly is alive and well, and (b) she doesn't plan to visit just now. Also a stirring of guilt. Graham and I haven't seen her for a while and must make the effort to visit her and Jane, soon.

The card is a pretty one of primroses on a sunny bank. Molly has green fingers, and the pleasant side of her visits is that she takes my neglected flowerbeds in hand and even tackles the vegetable plot. There's something else inside the card, a folder with 'Happy Anniversary' on it. Oh my goodness! I'd forgotten it will be our wedding anniversary the week after Easter. Molly never forgets; she has a calendar in her kitchen with everyone's particulars and dates on it. It would appeal to her thrifty nature to enclose the two cards in the same envelope.

The smaller card reads 'With love to you both on your anniversary' and contains £400 worth of travel vouchers, to be used whenever and however we wish.

I have to eat humble pie and take back all the niggling criticisms I have of my mother-in-law. Sometimes she really hits the right note and comes up trumps, so to speak.

*

Graham and I spend a pleasant hour or two this evening reviewing the possibilities. Timing is the first consideration. Any time from July to October is out, harvest prevails. So it's before or after. Next month would be cutting it fine, I feel. Autumn is often wet and blustery, unless our money would stretch to taking off for sunnier climes. Flying is not such an attractive prospect these days though, all that waiting about

90

does not appeal. June? I remind him that Michael's exams are coming up. Maybe the first couple of weeks of the month?

Children and animals will need to be catered for. Mum will probably have the two eldest, and maybe I could farm out Luke and Adam to a couple of friends. Dai might pop in to feed the cats and keep an eye on things generally. The hamster can go with Luke.

Next, destination. We soar in fantasy to Caribbean islands, Italian culture spots, the Dordogne or the Swiss Alps. We could take a trip on the Orient Express, explore romantic Venice, take a Mediterranean cruise. Graham loves the sound of the motor-cycle trip across the Mexican Baja desert that Mark did last year, but it happens in September and motor-cycles aren't quite my thing. I also think it would cost rather more than £400.

There are so many possibilities. There's no hurry to decide, but we've had a good time talking about it, and go to bed in a relaxed and carefree mood, which is a gift in itself.

*

Our church stands with its back to the river, facing towards the town. It is Norman built, with a square tower and the green hill beside it which was the site of the original Norman castle. This Easter Sunday morning, the wooden cross on the hill stands dark against a pale, rain-washed sky, empty, and I feel, with an assurance that suddenly floods my being "He is risen!"

We are all here this morning, two car loads of us. The church is full for Easter Sunday. Lauren scuttles off to join the music group. Michael skulks into a seat near the back. The children will stay with us this morning, no Sunday School, it's a family service. I had half-hoped Becky might be home for Easter, but she isn't, or at least, not in church. Caroline looks as calm and serene as ever, in a chic new linen jacket and slim skirt. I wonder how she can bear to have her daughter away; doesn't it hurt her beyond belief to be apart from her at a time of celebration like Easter? But I put aside judgemental thoughts of Caroline and join in with the rousing opening hymn.

The church is pale stone with a gallery and massive pillars marking the nave. The pews are polished mahogany, cushioned with red velour but still not the most comfortable of seats. Graham and I disagree over church seating. I maintain one should not be too comfortable in church; we need to stay wide awake and pay attention. Maybe that's why pews are built as they are. Graham says it's very difficult to pay proper attention when one has to be constantly shifting position to ease the crippling pain in one's back. Over the archway to the sanctuary there's gold lettering urging us to 'Enter into his gates with thanksgiving and into his courts with praise.'

That's easy today, the rafters fairly ring with voices raised in Easter praise. My parents are sitting a few rows ahead; my mother turns and smiles at us with a face radiant with joy. She sings with all her being, feet tapping, her hands raised as though they can't help themselves, as though this moment is the most wonderful she's ever known. Maybe it is. I feel a lump rise in my throat.

There are stained–glass windows each side of the nave, scenes of Jesus and his disciples, fishing, blessing, breaking bread, healing. After the morning rain, the sun has reappeared and its rays cast a rosy glow across Paul's face as he gets up to speak. He has had a sad, wistful, withdrawn look about him these last weeks since Becky left, as though something had died within him. But this morning, with the light on his face, suddenly there is new hope there too, a promise of light after darkness, joy after sadness, hope after despair.

He begins his message with a quote from St.Augustine, spoken out in a strong, clear voice: – 'We are an Easter people, and Alleluia is our song!'

And in the church, this morning, that is what we are – an Easter people, with death defeated and the promise of beauty for ashes, the oil of joy for mourning, and instead of a spirit of heaviness we are clothed with a garment of praise.

MAY

Chapter Seventeen

As soon as May begins, or even before, a kind of madness comes over our town. Shops and businesses smarten up their premises, buildings are painted and decorated, the garden centres hum with activity and hanging baskets and window boxes appear in a riot of colour on walls and steps and patios.

In the big flat seven–acre field on the outskirts of town, a jungle of scaffolding, steel girders and canvas appears as the Festival Village takes shape, for later in the month the annual Literature Festival, sponsored by one of the leading National newspapers, will begin.

For ten days, our tiny town, with its population of fourteen hundred souls, will be literally swamped by hundreds of visitors who descend on our little piece of paradise.

Last year, 150,000 came. Wall to wall people block the tiny streets, stopping the traffic, giving us simple country folk a taste of the urbane and exotic and sophisticated. The locals grouse, but not too loudly; they know which side their bread is buttered. The Festival is a wonderful opportunity for the entrepreneur; in fine weather ladies throw open their gardens for refreshments and the pavements blossom with parasols and bistro furniture. When it rains (as it often does), the local sports shops will have laid in a good stock of wellies, and farmers put their tractors to good use by pulling cars out of the muddy parking field. Suddenly every other house is a B & B.

*

On the brink of the Festival, Caroline has called a planning meeting to finalise details for the Summer Fayre, also an annual event, timed to coincide with the literary shenanigans. This time she's hosting the meeting herself at the Vicarage. Caroline is the perfect hostess, charming and gracious, serving tea and finger biscuits in her drawing room, beautifully furnished with antiques.

"I bet Mary Miles was in this morning," Jo mutters as we settle into the cream damask sofa. My bitchy side is inclined to agree. I bet those delicate biscuits aren't home-baked either, in a temperamental Aga that never knows whether to blow hot or cold. I try to bring my compassionate side to the fore, and don't altogether succeed. Caroline seems in no need of my compassion, seating herself opposite and crossing her elegant legs. The Meadows sisters are watching her admiringly. Becky's situation is all round town now and the general opinion is that Caroline is just so wonderful the way she's taken it, bravely carrying on with her duties about the parish. There's sometimes an undercurrent of criticism regarding Becky too (how could she do this to the poor vicar and his dear wife) that makes my hackles rise, but so far I've kept my lip tightly buttoned.

Caroline is checking off details in a businesslike notebook. The Fayre will take place in the Vicarage garden, which is huge, and will be on the Saturday of the Festival, when the maximum number of visitors might be attracted. In the event of inclement weather, the Parish hall will be available as an alternative venue; despite its being sought after for Festival events, Caroline has managed to ensure that it will be kept free.

"We'll lose money by not letting it out, but the Parish Council felt our own Fayre should have priority," explains Caroline, with the air that somehow suggests she's personally sacrificed a substantial sum of revenue on our behalf.

"And hopefully the Fayre will bring in as much, or more," points out Jo.

"Quite," says Caroline, flicking through the pages on her lap. "Now, are we all clear about our respective responsibilities?"

We run through them, just to make sure. A few minor hitches are mentioned and quickly disposed of. Caroline uncrosses her shapely legs. There's a photo of Becky on the small gate-legged table in the window, a childhood snapshot of her aged about five, standing on a beach and squinting into the sun. I wonder if Becky is walking on another beach today, listening to the waves crash and maybe feeling the first fluttering movements of her child.

"Perhaps your Michael and Lauren would like to help in some way?" Caroline is suggesting. "Take charge of a stall, maybe? Or design some banners for us? I'm sure we could harness their talents in some way."

I say I'll make enquiries, but I'm not holding my breath on this one. The church fete will definitely not be high on their lists of Saturday afternoon priorities. Michael will be off playing in a football match, or watching one. Lauren might agree to playing her flute and collecting money, but I feel that Caroline might not consider busking to be a suitable side event. I can't see either of them standing behind a stall, and banner–making would be considered on a par with making paper chains.

But I've judged wrongly again. Or have I inadvertently used reverse psychology? When I say, casually, at tea–time "The Fayre committee wondered if you'd be interested in helping out. I said I didn't think so, really," Lauren immediately replies "Why on earth did you think that? I don't mind helping." Furthermore, she adds that she'll get Paula to come along and help too. They could run a little crèche for the toddlers. Maybe do face–painting, or balloon sculptures, or plasticene modelling. She just *loves* working with kids, and so does Paula. Why on earth didn't I ask before, to give them time to organise properly?

Why, indeed? My daughter constantly surprises me, and I try to remember, not for the first time, if it was particularly busy on maternity the night she was born, and whether there's a remote possibility that babies could have been switched.

*

It's a lovely day for the Fayre, anyway, blue skies, soft breezes and balmy spring sunshine. Graham and I both go early to the Vicarage, to help set up stalls and fetch and carry. Paul is there, in jeans and shirtsleeves, wrestling with trestles and lugging heavy loads of assorted stuff from the Vicarage basement where it's all been stored. He's glad of our help, relieved it's a fine day, and hopes optimistically for a good turn–out. His hopes should be realised, already the town is buzzing with visitors heading purposefully towards the Festival village and their early morning events. Festival visitors come in many guises; there are the ordinary, everyday people in casual gear, often with kids in tow, the terribly posh ones (male and female), the hippie artistic types, the show–bizzy luvvies, the exotic and the downright weird. It's an entertainment in itself sitting and having a coffee in the village and watching the people go by. Not that I do much of that, even a plain coffee in the village is priced at a sum that brings tears to the eyes.

On our very doorsteps, we have the chance to hear the rhetoric of politicians and statesmen, media people, entertainers, eccentric one-offs, as well as the book people. The place reverberates with music, from jazz to opera. Artists exhibit and paint on the pavement. I've seen an elderly aborigine sitting playing a didgeridoo at the entrance to the main car park. Celebrity spotting becomes an obsession, although the really big cheeses sweep in and out in darkened limos. When a former US president came to speak, a helicopter circled overhead and the town's sewers were checked for possible bombs. But you never know who you might see mixing with the hoi polloi.

I would love to linger about the streets and gawk, but duties call, I have a family at home who will expect to be fed. As we make the return trip over the bridge, I see, just behind a knot of strangers heading into town, a face I recognise. It's that man again, the one I've seen a couple of times before, always alone, always watchful. He gives me the creeps somehow. I shake off the feeling and tell myself that my imagination will get me into trouble one day.

By 1.30 lunch is over and Lauren, Adam, Luke and I are heading back into town, freshly washed and dressed and ready for action. The groups of visitors have turned into a heaving mass of humanity; strange people fill the pavements and straggle out over the road, glaring at any motorist who has the temerity to try to drive through. We locals are supposed to fade into the background while the Festival is on, apart from providing essential services like B&B accommodation, lunches, teas, gardens to visit, horses to ride, amenities to use and other entertainments. A friend of ours, going home from work past one of the designated car–parks, was determinedly flagged down by a zealous attendant in a luminous yellow coat, who tried to direct him into the car park.

"I'm not going there. I'm going up the lane," insisted our friend.

"No no, there's nothing up there, no parking. All vehicles into the car park."

"I don't want to park. I want to go home."

"Home?"

"Yes. I live up this lane."

Parking attendant, amazed, "People actually live up there?"

Yes, they do, believe it or not. The Festival brings a buzz and a lot of business to the town. I love the opportunity to hear well–known speakers, but often I'm in complete sympathy with those who mutter about ignorant townies.

We negotiate the crowded streets with some difficulty and reach the sanctuary of St. John's vicarage. It's busy there already; people are drifting in even before the official opening time. By the time it's properly up and running, the place is buzzing. I'm kept busy at my Bran Tub, all those small prizes I laboriously wrapped are fast disappearing into eager little hands which rip off the paper in two seconds flat. I'm glad there's a litter bin nearby. Deirdre Burns over the way is doing a brisk trade in used paperbacks too. Lauren and Paula have their pitch under an apple tree, an orange tent which proudly proclaims KIDZONE in large letters on a black ground. I have a feeling we may be on shaky ground as regards Health and Safety, or age of the proprietors (Paula is fourteen, Lauren not quite) or the whole legality of this venture, but it's only for a couple of hours, it's non-profit making and I hope we'll get away with it. At any rate, KIDZONE is proving popular, there are toddlers and pre-schoolers going in and coming out clutching balloons or with their faces gaudily painted. I'm relieved that several mums have stuck around to keep an eye on things, that I'm only a few yards away and there are plenty of others within screaming distance in case of emergency. Luke and Adam drift about with a gang of other small boys. They have strict orders to stay within the confines of the Vicarage garden.

Caroline drifts around too, never a hair out of place, in beige linen trousers and a cream top, making me feel like a bumpkin in my T-shirt and denim skirt. She makes a few alterations to the cake stall, rearranges Deirdre's books which have become a little disturbed, tweaks Bert's artwork display into a more pleasing pattern. There's not much she can do to my bran tub, though she tidies away the odd bit of paper that I've missed. She is definitely the star of this show, us others her supporting cast.

"She's so *wonderful*, after all that's happened." says Janet French admiringly. I exchange a look with Jo at the cake stall, where Jo is surreptitiously repositioning the things Caroline had moved around. Jo's eyebrows shoot up and she mouths "Sooo wonderful!"

Caroline soothes a shrieking toddler who has been poked in the eye by another outside KIDZONE, and passes on. Lauren is beginning to have a frazzled air which I recognise all too well as the one worn by most mums of toddlers. We needn't have worried about numbers. I've never seen so many people at a church do, many of them Festival goers and strangers. I notice that several have ignored the signs and trespassed into the private part of the garden, pointing out this plant or that bloom that has taken their interest and trampling down others in the process. Oh dear! But surely we'll make such a profit this year that any minor inconveniences will be worth it.

Suddenly, I'm aware that something is happening over by the refreshments stall, which has been busily employed all afternoon. People are clustering round someone, others are rushing about and there's an ominous feeling that something bad is happening, or has already happened. Maisie Meadows comes over to me, frowning.

"A little girl has gone missing. Rose Westlake's child, Lily. Rose is hysterical. She was just queuing up for tea and orange squash, turned round, no Lily."

Lily is three years old, a cute blonde moppet. Panic rises in my airways and threatens to suffocate me. I run over to Lauren's tent to check that the child is not there – no, she was in earlier but was getting tired so left with her mum to get drinks. I see my own two youngest approaching in the midst of a group of other boys and feel a guilty relief that they are accounted for. They are faintly mystified when I pluck them out of the group and order them to stay by Lauren's tent.

"But why? It's a babies' place," protests Luke in tones of outrage.

"Because I say so!" I snap, and then add, "Look, a little girl's gone missing, I'm going to help search and I need to know where you are."

"We could help search," Adam offers hopefully.

"No! You just stay here."

They promise grudgingly, with the bribe of being in charge of the bran tub in my absence and having a free dip themselves. People are leaving their posts and running round, peering into tea chests and behind stalls, and among the bushes, calling Lily's name. My heart is racing, but suddenly it almost stops with sheer horror. I've remembered that man, the one who hangs around looking at the kids in the school yard and who behaves shiftily. I saw him this morning; he's here in town again. What if he's abducted Lily? Oh God, no please! And then comes the dreadful realisation that I could have reported him, could have said something, and didn't do a thing. And now it may be too late.

Panic is spreading through the vicarage gardens like wildfire. Mums are clutching their children, people are running hither and thither, calls are made on mobile phones, there's a new scent of fear in the spring air. I'm sickeningly aware that I must voice my suspicions to someone; time could be of the essence here. Lily's mother is having hysterics by the tea stall, several women are trying to calm her, without much success. I look round for Paul, but see only Caroline, standing transfixed, her face ashen.

Then, suddenly, it is over. Someone calls "She's here!" The call is relayed from group to group. Lily's been found, safe and sound, fast asleep on a big floor cushion towards the back of Pam's Textiles, out of sight behind an embroidered screen. Pam explains breathlessly that someone bought the cushion and asked her to put it away to save carrying it around. We rush over to view Lily, flushed and sound asleep with her thumb in her mouth. Her mother falls upon her, still sobbing but this time with relief. Lily wakes, rubs her eyes and demands a drink, querulous at having her nap disturbed.

My knees are like jelly and I'm shaking. I go back to my own children, my head in a whirl. As I reach them, two things happen simultaneously. A police car pulls in to the vicarage drive, summoned by a quick-thinker with a mobile. And at the same moment, I see the man again, standing half-hidden by the vicarage lilac bushes, silently watching.

Chapter Eighteen

"One of these days you will land yourself in serious trouble," says Graham, giving me one of his looks, which I interpret as 'How on earth did I end up with such a dumb cluck when I had the pick of all those worthy and sensible farmers' daughters?'

I have no answer. I only hope his mother will never get to hear of this.

I'm in no mood for a lecture; all I want is a nice cup of tea and a chance to hide my head in a dark place, preferably for several days.

"Lauren, be a love and put the kettle on," I ask weakly, and sink down in the chair by the Aga.

She does so, but is suddenly overtaken by a fit of helpless giggling.

"It did look funny, though! Well embarrassing, but funny! The police come marching in, Mum rushes up to them and points to some man standing there and says 'There he is, officer! He may try to get away!' And the poor man hasn't a clue what on earth's happening–" She doubles over with mirth, clutching her stomach.

I suppose I may see the funny side one day. At the moment I'm so mortified I feel I may never recover. I've spent what seems like hours at the police station, being questioned about the allegations I'm making. The constable is patient with me. I suppose bearing with foolish women is part of his training.

"What exactly are your concerns, Mrs Harper?"

"Well, I've noticed him – er – lurking. Hanging about."

"Doing anything suspicious?"

"Well – er – no. But I did see him watching the children in the school playground once."

"Was he speaking to them, interfering with them in any way?"

"Er – no. But he looked – um – shifty."

"Shifty." He's making notes of all this. My remarks will probably be forever recorded on some police computer. They've brought the man to the station too; presumably he's being questioned elsewhere. He went with them willingly enough, though looking very confused. I begin to think I've made a terrible mistake.

"And was this why we were called to the vicarage today?"

"No. A child was missing. I thought –" I am digging myself into a deeper and deeper hole, and I know it. I say weakly "It was a mistake. The little girl had just fallen asleep nearby. I'm sorry."

"So there are no allegations?"

"No."

The constable sighs. He says "I think you should go home, Mrs Harper. Your husband is here, in reception."

Graham is none too pleased at being called from his work to retrieve his wife from the police station. We drive home in our separate vehicles, the children having been taken under Jo's wing when I was hauled off. I'm feeling like a criminal myself now. But I have to make a stab at defending myself as we walk across to the house.

"I couldn't just stand by , not when a child was involved."

"There wasn't a child involved. The little girl was having a quiet kip, quite safe."

"Yes, but, I've noticed that man before, just kind of hanging about watching people, watching children – he's a stranger here."

"Along with about 100,000 other people around here at the moment. You're lucky you didn't get charged with wasting police time."

He seems unable to drop the subject, even now we're safe home and I'm getting some kind of meal for everyone. And the others are quick to jump on the bandwagon too.

"That poor guy will be out to get you now, Mum," says Lauren gleefully.

"You'll have to watch your back," says Michael, grinning.

"As I said, you'll get yourself in serious trouble one of these days," says Graham, cutting a hunk of cheese. "And don't think I'll bail you out, either."

As I see it, a nice, cool, bare police cell would seem at this moment to be quite an attractive haven, for an hour or two at least. This Summer Fayre will certainly go down in memory. I'd like to draw a veil over it all for now, though, although there's no chance of that with the kind of family I have.

*

Gardening fever has set in with a vengeance. Every autumn, I vow that we must make a plan – get a really good gardening manual to study over the winter, and then do the appropriate digging planting and cultivating month by month, so that we have fresh produce is season all the year round. It never works out. Graham, like most farmers, is no gardener, holding the opinion that an arable farmer like himself, used to cultivating rolling acres and sweeping stretches of rich soil, cannot demean himself by scrabbling about in small enclosed plots. I have convinced him that it's lovely to have our own fresh home–grown produce, and he can't argue with that – he audibly smacks his lips when I serve up new green peas or tender runner beans or the first new potatoes, not to mention juicy strawberries and blackcurrants. So some years ago he agreed that we will work on the vegetable garden together.

I'm not the most knowledgeable gardener, but I believe that different veg should be planted at different times. For example, purple sprouting broccoli should sprout and be ready to eat early Spring, and therefore need to be planted in the Autumn.

Graham can't be doing with any of that messing about. Come April, he sets aside a few days for the garden, cultivates our plot and plants everything from runner beans to radish and lettuce, in one go. From then on, it's all expected to sink or swim, apart from the weeding, watering and de–bugging, which is my designated part.

This year, our vegetables were in around the middle of April and a month later they are a sight to behold. Hopeful young cabbage plants are getting a grip, tender green pea–haulm poking up from the soil, carrots showing feathery topknots, rows of tiny radish and lettuce sprinkling themselves against the dark earth. The runner beans are sending out inquisitive tendrils and already need sticks to support them.

Slugs are our worst enemy, plump, black and sinister, they are out on the prowl at night seeking tender new greenstuffs to devour. I try all kinds of 'natural' deterrents, coffee, soapy water, aromatic plants adjacent – to no avail, and have to resort to a chemical product from the garden centre. While I'm there, I can't resist the bedding plants, yard after yard of lovely colourful trays, busy–lizzie, petunias, marigolds – just what we need to brighten us up after a gloomy winter. I come out with several boxes.

An elderly acquaintance eyes them as I head for the car. "Hope you're not thinking of planting those out, love. Frost about."

If it's not one thing it's another. I stash the plants away in the old garden shed for a day or two, and go to look for some black plastic to cover up the vegetables tonight. Graham isn't wrong when he says that gardening means a lot of fiddling about.

*

I've been reading a book by a new young writer who's local to this area, or, at least, local–ish. It's a first novel, set in this border country, a rather depressing and downbeat tale of a farming family in the 50's. Brilliantly written though, this young man will go far, I have no doubt. Half–way through the book I get a bit annoyed – the country people seem to be portrayed as unfeeling, avaricious and rather thick, while the incoming townies are the perceptive, caring 'goodies' in the story.

He's speaking at the Festival and I'd like to hear what he has to say. I ring the booking office and get a couple of tickets, and also look up his website. There's a picture of him, looking soulful and Byronesqe, with big dark eyes and long curls.

I'm looking forward to his event. In the meantime, Michael will go with me to hear another speaker, a TV personality who I've heard of but who apparently is a wow with the younger element. The venue is crowded. Michael grins and snickers along with most of the rest of the audience as the speaker rattles on. I'm rather bored, I don't understand some of the 'in' jokes. I resort to surreptitiously looking round at everyone else in the marquee – and suddenly I see the young novelist, sitting in the audience and apparently as impressed as everyone else.

I nudge Michael. He glares at me and mouths "We're supposed to be quiet", and edges as far away from me as he can go, which isn't far – the seats are tightly packed with very little leg room. He's obviously wishing he'd chosen a more congenial companion.

This is too good a chance to pass up, though. When the event ends I make a beeline for the young man, dodging the departing crowds. He looks rather startled to be addressed by name, but concedes that yes, he is the author of 'The Darkened Dawn.' He is even more Byronesqe close up, and very young, but I harden my heart and present my complaint about his portrayal of my fellow country people. He seems quite upset. I have the feeling he's had a lot of praise for his book and not much criticism. "I'm sorry you got that impression," he says, in a soft, hesitant voice with a posh accent (obviously he was not educated round here). "It wasn't at all intentional. I wouldn't upset anyone for the world." His big brown eyes almost brim with tears – or is that my imagination again? Anyway, I'm sorry for him and I hasten to add that his writing is brilliant and I enjoyed the book. He smiles tremulously, reassured, and

103

thanks me for my comments, and says he'll bear them in mind for the future. I feel quite kindly towards him now and say I'll look forward to his next novel.

A steward approaches and speaks. "Excuse me, but the tent is cleared now ready for the next event."

It is, too. The seats have emptied while we've been standing there in the aisle. We exit hastily, side by side, he's telling me about his next novel as we emerge, walking out between the queues of people waiting to hear the next speaker, and shake hands warmly as we part.

Michael is waiting to one side, scarlet with embarrassment.

"Everyone was staring," he hisses. "What did you think you were doing?"

"Just making my views heard. He thanked me for it."

He doesn't believe me, and neither do the rest of my family when he recounts the tale at home late.

"Thank goodness I wasn't there," says Lauren with a shudder, and I get the feeling that neither she nor Michael will ever willingly accompany me anywhere again.

Chapter Nineteen

The Festival is over, and suddenly our town belongs to the residents again, we can shop without having to fight our ground and pass the time of day in a leisurely way with our friends without being pushed off the pavement. The Festival organisers, pubs and B&B's can gleefully tot up their takings. Crossing the bridge, I look down at the smoothly-flowing water and am reminded of the closing paragraph of the book by Norman McClean; *'In the end, all things become one and a river runs through it.'* It's true. Big events, big names, come and go, but the natural world turns and the seasons change regardless.

Still in philosophical mode, I almost bump into Paul Rees coming out of the haberdashers, where I've been detailed to pick up wire cutters for Graham. Paul stops. "Alison, I've been wanting a chat with you. Could you call by for a coffee?"

"Er – yes, thanks, Paul." I can't think of any excuse not to, though I haven't seen Paul or Caroline, except at church services, since the debacle at the Summer Fayre. I'm sure Paul must be dreadfully embarrassed about that, and as for Caroline…

Caroline, however, is not at home, having gone to visit Mrs Parry in the local cottage hospital. "She's a real tonic when she comes," another elderly lady told me recently. "So charming and so beautiful to look at. She lights up the whole ward."

Paul makes coffee in the sunny kitchen. He says not a word about the Fayre, and I don't mention it either. Mrs Miles is there again, I hear the hoover upstairs and a radio playing classical music.

"She's a Bach fan, Mrs M," says Paul with a grin. "I must say I find it very soothing. She could be someone keen on reggae or hip–hop!"

There is something rather hypnotic about the beautiful music and the soft hum of the cleaner. I begin to relax a little. There's another picture of Becky in here, as a seven–year–old with a kitten and a gappy–toothed grin. Paul puts down his mug. "Alison, does Michael hear from Becky?"

He sounds wistful, as though they don't hear much themselves.

"I think so. They're in touch all the time, aren't they, these youngsters. Texts and tweets. Not that he tells me anything, and it doesn't do to ask." Paul sighs. "I miss her, Alison. It's hard, like a bereavement, almost. She'd have left before long, anyway, for college or university, but this was too soon, too sudden…"

He sits down and turns his face away a little, but not before I've seen the real pain there. This man is suffering. I wonder if he and Caroline go to see their daughter.

"She doesn't want to see us," he says heavily, reading my thoughts. "My sister says she's fine, but it's just as though – as though Becky blames us for what's happened. As though she's rejecting us. Punishing us."

I feel I've got to stop this negative train of thought somehow.

"Look, Becky's young, she's confused, her whole life has been turned upside down from one silly mistake. She doesn't know what she wants, or thinks. But she needs you both. You've got to keep trying, building bridges. The longer you're apart, the harder it'll be."

"It's very hard for Caroline…"

"Caroline! Surely this is about Becky!" I put my mug down harder than I intended and it makes a sharp sound. Paul turns to me, startled. He's silent for a moment, and then says "Alison, normally I wouldn't speak about Caroline but there are things I think you should know."

We've been here before. I didn't want to hear then and I don't now. But somehow I sense that I'm going to have to know, and that it matters that I do.

He rubs his hand over his face and through his floppy hair, and says, "I know Caroline can be difficult. I know she's not liked by everyone –" he looks at me and I feel my cheeks grow warm. Guilt? Shame? I have a mental image of all the snide, sneaky things I've thought (or even said) about Caroline flashing by on a continuous feed like an autocue.

He goes on slowly "The thing is, Caroline had a raw deal herself in many ways. Her upbringing was strict; she was the only child of an older authoritarian father and a mother who deferred to him in every way. Caroline had to be perfect, to excel in everything."

I nod. That follows. That's exactly how Caroline is herself.

"Well, she rebelled. Becky's age, or younger. She ran away from home. They disowned her."

I stare at him, aghast. "They did what?"

"It's true. They completely cut her off. Never spoke to her again. She had word they'd died some years ago; making it plain that she had no part in their inheritance. As though they'd never had a daughter."

"Total control freaks. How terrible."

He nods, rumpling his hair again. "Poor kid, she'd probably have gone back home after a week or two. But there she was, under sixteen, running round London, money ran out." He pauses, a long, painful pause, and when he speaks again his voice is taut and agonised. "She was raped. I don't know the details, but she was put into the care of Social Services and then a foster home. She was found to be pregnant."

I catch my breath. I'm beginning to understand, just a little. What dark, complicated, tangled threads can lurk on the underside of a life.

He's talking now in short, sharp phrases, bare facts.

"The child was adopted, of course. Caroline came through it so well. Studied hard, got to a good university. That's where we met. She came to my Christian Union. I can see her now, the day she made her decision to follow Christ. She said 'Paul, I can start again. Everything new!' And it was, bless her. She's been such a wonderful wife and helper. She's so beautiful. I love her so much."

He lifts his head and it's there, blazing in his blue eyes, the love he has for his beautiful , flawed, brave, damaged, courageous wife, who cannot be anything less than perfect, who cannot allow herself any human weakness lest the edifice she has carefully built should fall to pieces about her ears.

I think, oh, Caroline, we've failed you. How we've failed you, how we've judged and mocked and resolutely refused to look below the surface. How we've fallen so far short of the love and compassion of Jesus.

I want to weep with remorse. I say shakily "Paul, I'm so sorry. Is there anything we can do to help?"

He thinks for a moment, and then says, hesitantly "I don't suppose you could go over to visit Becky, could you? I think she'd welcome a visit from someone from home. Maybe Michael would go too."

I'm sure he would, even with his mother in tow. In fact, the more I think about it, the more I feel this is the best idea I've heard in ages.

Chapter Twenty

Michael not only agrees to go, he seems positively keen; moreover, he suggests that we go on his birthday, which comes up a week Saturday. I'd been wondering about his birthday. How does a sixteen-year old celebrate? Too often, I suspect, with drink and other substances, convincing themselves they're having a good time. Not that Michael's into drinking – well, I don't think he is, though you can never take anything for granted. Anyway, a run to the West Coast seems to be an acceptable way of spending the day.

So we set off early, my other responsibilities discharged three ways into safe hands, those of Dad, Grandma and Jo. It's a beautiful day, breezy, white clouds scudding across a blue sky, hedgerows clad in the luxuriant white and tender green of early summer, froth of may blossom, lacy cow-parsley fringing the verges. Michael seems in good spirits, though irked that he has to be the passenger while I drive. He is critical of my driving skills and apt to fiddle with things inside, adjusting the passenger seat to accommodate his long legs (he's now passed six feet), altering the angle of the wing mirror, tuning the radio. He reckons I clash the gears and am hopeless at reversing.(This last is true!) I realise with a slight shock that in just one year he'll be legally able to drive himself. The thought gives me the heebie jeebies. But, hey, that's a year away. Let's take the day and live in the moment, I say.

"I just love this time of year, I think it's my very favourite," I enthuse, as we travel the tree-lined river road on the first lap of our journey. Bluebells stretch away beneath roadside trees and the river has little white-caps rippling its surface. Michael concedes with a grunt that it is pretty, but adds tersely "You need to keep your eyes on the road, Mum. You never know what idiot might be coming round the next bend."

I hope he bears this in mind when he begins to drive.

We leave the river and begin to climb up through forestry and out into hill country where sheep far outnumber people. I brake hard to avoid one wandering into the road, and Michael mutters under his breath. He sounds uncommonly like his dad.

We are up into red kite country, and suddenly, I see one and then another, massive wings and forked tails swooping and twisting against the blue.

My exclamations of delight make Michael nervous. He reminds me again that I'm at the wheel and that gazing heavenwards as I drive is not recommended. We're reached the little roadside café out in the wilds, and both agree it's time to stop for a coffee.

Neither of us has mentioned Becky since we set out. Facing each other across a check tablecloth, I wonder if I should say something. I sip my coffee and decide not. We are rubbing along fairly well together so far, Michael and I, and I don't want anything to spoil that. Looking at him, so hunky, tall and handsome, I can't believe that this is my baby, my first-born. The teenage girl behind the counter can't take her eyes off him. I reach over and pat his hand.

"Happy birthday, darling. I'm so proud of you."

Oh dear, I've overstepped the mark. He says "Mum!" in an agonised voice and pulls his hand away. His mug slops a little coffee on the tablecloth. He drains what's left and gets up to leave, muttering goodbye to the girl, who simpers and smiles. He'd like to pretend I'm nothing at all to do with him.

Aberystwyth is always a bracing kind of place and today it seems more blowy than usual, the sea slate-coloured and choppy along the front. Becky's aunt and uncle live in a comfortable, solid house at the edge of town; her uncle is a tutor at the university and her aunt is a supply teacher. Today, Uncle is off on a project with some of his students, but Aunt Eunice greets us warmly at the door. I've met her once or twice when she's visited the vicarage. She's fiftyish, plumpish, smiley and pretty; I can see the resemblance to her younger brother in her eyes and the shape of her mouth.

"Come in, come in," she urges. "Lunch is ready. I'll call Becky and tell her you're here."

We're ushered into a chintzy sitting room. Michael seems tense, awkwardly arranging his long limbs on an overstuffed chair, cracking his knuckles. Then there are steps on the stairs and Becky is at the door. Michael is on his feet again, towering over her, although they greet each other casually, as though they'd spoken quite recently, which they probably have, as Michael has fiddled with text messaging most of the way here. He says "All right?" and she nods, and then says "Hello, Mrs Harper," and gives me an uncertain little smile. I get up too and give her a hug. She doesn't exactly hug back, but doesn't resist either.

The awkward moment is broken by Eunice ushering us into the kitchen for lunch. Becky is looking well, I have to admit, a different person from the unkempt, scared, confused girl I saw back in the winter. She's in her second trimester, a time when pregnant women usually blossom, and it's true in her case. Her hair is glossy and shining, cut a little shorter to chin-length, her skin faintly tanned and with a peach skin bloom to it. She has a little bump just showing, which she makes no attempt to conceal beneath the snug white T-shirt and low-slung khaki combats. She is lovely. Michael can't take his eyes off her and I don't blame him.

We eat smoked salmon, potato salad and a tossed green salad with fresh crusty bread. No amount of awkwardness can detract from Michael's appetite, he shovels in the food with gusto and accepts second helpings. Becky eats a good lunch too and drinks a glass of milk. She is taking good care of herself. I note all this to relay to her parents.

Nobody mentions Paul and Caroline. Eunice keeps up a cheerful chatter, passing plates, bringing in strawberries and cream, pouring coffee. It all seems a bit unreal somehow, as though we're actors on a stage, each with our part to play.

When lunch is over, Eunice shoos the two young ones out of the house, instructing her niece to take Michael for a nice walk along the beach, saying we'll maybe join them later. I sense they're glad to escape. They have some catching up to do.

"He's a nice lad, your Michael," says Eunice, as we wash and dry lunch dishes together. I agree, and then wonder if Eunice might have the idea that Michael is the father of Becky's baby. She quickly dispels any such concerns, however. She knows the situation, and more impressively still, accepts it.

"Becky talks to me," she says quietly, hands deep in soapsuds. "Poor lamb, it's not easy for her."

"Will she come home, do you think?"

Eunice gives a little shrug. "Paul would like her to. Caroline – I'm not sure." She hesitates briefly. "Caroline has her own demons to face."

I tell her that Paul has told me some of Caroline's history. She looks relieved. "Then you'll understand a little. I feel that Becky should be told at some stage, though maybe now is not the time. Becky doesn't want to go home. She's happy here with Fred and me, is doing well with school work, even has a Saturday job. And we're happy to have her. I always wanted a daughter."

"And when the baby comes?"

She pauses for a moment and a cloud crosses her face. "She's adamant it's to be adopted. It'll be painful. But we'll see her through it somehow. She comes to church with us, you know, we've lots of young people here and she's got a good circle of friends. And there'll be A-levels on the horizon, and uni to aim for."

I think Eunice is one of the nicest people I've ever met, and her realistic but positive attitude is so comforting. I can see why Becky loves her. There's still a shadow, though, when Paul and Caroline come to mind. To all intents and purposes they seem to have lost their daughter. The thought of it breaks my heart. How could I ever bear it if I lost Lauren?

I shrug off gloomy thoughts and say that I'll take a walk too, along the front and maybe the beach. She says she'll have the kettle on when we all get back.

The beach here is not a smooth, sandy one; it's pebbly, stony and shingly. Today is on the cool side, but there are families with toddlers and kids playing at the water's edge. People are walking dogs, and far across the beach I see a couple of figures, one tall and broad and one smaller, who might be Michael and Becky. I shade my eyes and yes, I can see it's them, walking close but not touching, his head bent to hers, deep in conversation.

I sit on the breakwater and wait for them. They're both windblown and have colour in their cheeks. It's hard to tell what their expressions are, but they actually look quite pleased to see me.

"Want an ice-cream, Mum?" asks Michael, and suddenly he's a little boy at the seaside again, squinting against the sunlight and pulling his peaked cap lower over his eyes.

There's a queue for ice-cream. While he waits, Becky and I sit on one of the seats on the prom. She seems nervous suddenly, fidgeting with her hair and nibbling her nails.

"Do you walk on the beach a lot?" I ask, saying the first thing that comes into my head.

She nods. "Every day, if I can. Even if it's raining or really rough. I really like it then, actually. I always liked staying here with Auntie Eunice and Uncle Fred."

This might be my cue to enquire about her plans, but all of a sudden I'm reluctant. A seagull screams low overhead and lands close beside us, strutting about in search of titbits.

"Uncle Fred hates them," says Becky with a grin. "He says they're filthy, greedy, and a pest."

He might have a point there, but I love the sight and sound of them. I guess living inland as we do; they seem part of the very essence of the coast. This one waddles near to us, picks up a piece of biscuit and flaps into the air with a shriek. Becky speaks again, hurriedly and shyly, not quite meeting my eyes. "I want to say thank you for that day, you know, at the hospital. I'm glad you were there. I'm glad I didn't go through with it."

Suddenly, her confidence fails and she's a lost, confused little girl again, the girl who clung to me in terror at the hospital. She says, the words coming in a rush "The baby's going to be adopted. It's all arranged, but –" she pauses, wistfully, and says, "I sometimes wish that Aunt Eunice could keep it, and then I'd get to see it sometimes, when I was home from uni in the holidays –"

My heart goes out to her. I say, as gently, as I can "I don't think that would be possible. Your aunt's in her fifties, she couldn't really start again with a little baby. I don't think it would be allowed, and it wouldn't be fair on someone her age –"

She sighs, and her hair swings forward to cover her face. "I suppose not. It might work, though, mightn't it? I could get a place at uni here. Or I might just get a job –" I feel that the tears are not far away. I search for the right words, something that will encourage her without giving false hope. But before I can speak, Michael is there, holding two ice-cream cones precariously in one hand and one in the other. He sees at once that Becky is upset and looks accusingly at me. "All right, Becs?"

"Yes." And, amazingly, she is all right again, flicking her hair back and taking one of the cones from him with a smile. They sit devouring their ice-cream and cracking jokes about the people they can see on the beach as though they haven't a care in the world. I lick mine thoughtfully, wondering once again at the resilience of youth.

JUNE

Chapter Twenty-One

June is busting out all over, with a profusion of fresh greenery lavished and heaped on the hedgerows and along the verges with a profligate hand as though Mother Nature got carried away and didn't know when to stop. Red campion, yellow rattle and the white stars of stitchwort glow from the ditches, and in the 'jungle' behind our house a sea of bluebells ripples away under the hazels and oaks. Now the trees are in full leaf, I can leave my back door, walk twenty yards into the woodland and be completely cut off from sight of civilization in a green world of my own, with the only sounds the rustling of leaves and a cacophony of birdsong. I love it when the sun is out dappling the ground with moving patterns of light and shade, and I love it when it's been raining and the woodland is heavy with wet greenery and the scent of damp soil. When I'm here I truly feel I'm walking in Eden, and even the reminder of human activity, like Graham's tractor roaring into life across the fields or a faint shriek from the farmhouse, can't take away the peace I experience. I'm truly blest, and I know it, and I'm thankful.

A less welcome harbinger of early summer is the outbreak of allergies that afflict us at this season. Lauren gets spasmodic outbreaks of eczema, Adam is asthmatic, the three eldest all suffer from varying degrees of hay-fever, and I come out in a fine case of hives every year about this time, a reaction to I know not what. Various theories abound as to the causes of these ills; tree pollens, blossom pollens, insecticides, sprays, diet allergies, food additives, etc etc. We've had our share of tests and charts and graphs, but not come up with much, likewise tried most regular and homeopathic remedies, with varying degrees of success. Mostly I rely on the old faithfuls; anti-histamines, calamine lotion, inhalers. It seems hardest on Michael and others his age this year, sitting exams with runny noses, bouts of sneezing and itchy eyes. They do make allowances for hay fever sufferers, I hear, but how that works in practice I haven't a clue. Anyway, it's usually a short-lived thing, in a week or two the allergies will settle and we'll be back to normal, or what passes for normal round here.

*

We've finally decided on our holiday destination. Not Greece, not Italy, or the Canaries or Seychelles or a trip on the Orient Express! Not even Provence, for which I've had a longing since reading *Chocolat* and other books by Joanne Harris. The places I long to visit are always ones that fire my imagination in books, ever since reading *The Oregon Trail* as a child and longing to cross the prairies of the Mid West in a Conestoga covered wagon.

No, we've decided on a tour of Scotland, inspired by the books of George Macdonald and Rosamunde Pilcher. Graham reckons we can squeeze in a week before the winter barley is ready to cut.

First, though, we have a week-long visit from his mother, a kind of penance-in-advance for the holiday she's provided. I remark on this to Graham, as I iron the creases out of the best Irish linen pillowslips.

"Now now," he remonstrates mildly, barely looking up from his beloved Top Gear. "You know you love her really."

The thing is, I do, but she does conjure up ambivalent feelings in me, particularly the idea that I'm not quite up to scratch, which makes me at first try harder and then lapse into contrariness.

Molly arrives by train, carrying a great many bundles and packages that I have to be careful with. There's Graham's favourite date and walnut cake, ('I'm sure you don't manage to find the time to do much cake making, dear'), a pair of Art Deco jugs she saw in a sale and thought I would like (I really dislike Art Deco) and some bedding plants in little trays – bizzy lizzies, petunias and lobelia. Now, these I'm delighted to see. You can never have too many bedding plants. Molly wears a simple but top quality cashmere cardigan over a neat blouse and skirt, and flat leather pumps, her greying hair is short and feathery. She gives me a peck on the cheek and hands me most of the packages. "You're looking a bit tired, dear. You do too much running around."

Tell me about it. I say "We'll just pop these in the car and then I've got a few things to pick up from the supermarket. You could have a coffee in the restaurant."

"Well, no dear, that seems a bit unnecessary. I'll have a nice cup of tea when we get home. Don't worry about me. I'll just sit in the car."

And sit she does, with the window wound right up against traffic fumes, fanning herself with the train timetable while I dash around snatching up grocery items. I can already feel my teeth beginning to grit, and we're not even home yet.

There's more teeth-gritting later that evening, when supper is over and I'm clearing up while Molly unpacks upstairs. She has Adam's bedroom, while Adam squeezes in with Luke for the duration, not without protests from both. Lauren wanders in and casually gathers up the last of the cake crumbs and pops them into her mouth. "That cake was yummy."

I agree. The cake disappeared in a trice, to Molly's gratification. "There! I knew they'd enjoy something home-made!"

Well, fair comment. I did cheat a little this evening by resorting to a bag of frozen crispy roast potatoes, to save time. The children prefer them anyway, to home-peeled and prepared ones. The salad and the local gammon were fresh though. I let it pass.

"You used to make cakes," Lauren mentions accusingly.

"I still do, sometimes. Anyway, I thought cakes and stuff were frowned on, these days."

She gives me a withering look. "They're all right in moderation. You have to have *something*, *occasionally*, that you enjoy."

She drifts out again with the air of one who personally finds very little to enjoy in life. A few minute later the plaintive notes of her flute come floating downstairs.

Molly appears in the kitchen, knitting bag over her arm.

"Oh, you've finished already. I was going to help."

"It's okay." I'm being quite truthful here. I have my own system in the kitchen, and I quite like the feeling of putting things in order, in my own way. I say "You must be tired after travelling. Would you like another cup of tea?"

"If you have one in the pot, dear."

"It might be a bit stewed. I'll make some fresh."

"No no, don't go to the trouble just for me."

"It's no trouble."

"Well, if you're sure, dear. Not too strong, if you don't mind."

She sits down at the table and hangs her knitting bag over the back of her chair. Molly knits a lot – hats, gloves, jumpers – for the children, poor dears; they seem to have nothing but those dreadful hoodies.

"Maybe we could go raspberry picking," she suggests, as I pass her a fresh mug of tea. "Raspberry jam is so quick and easy to make. Adam and Luke could come too. Graham used to love raspberry picking when he was little. He used to put a raspberry on every finger, like a row of cute little hats."

I'm afraid Adam and Luke are way beyond such charming games. Not sure how keen they'd be on this idea, period. But I'm not going to argue the point. Instead, I pour myself more tea, pull up a chair, and ask Molly's advice on getting rid of carrot fly. Gardening is a safe area, and one we mostly agree on.

*

Molly and my mother get on well, in fact they get on famously, which rather mystifies me. Molly is highly competent and practical, her well–shod feet firmly on the ground, whereas my mother, dare I say it, sometimes has her head in the clouds. In the nicest possible way, of course. It's her artistic temperament, I suppose. Mother has no sympathy with me at all if I ever venture the teensiest moan about Molly to her.

"She's a very wonderful woman," she insists firmly.

"But she always makes me feel kind of – inadequate, like I don't quite measure up," I complain, feeling like Adam when he's having a confidence dip.

"Maybe that's your problem, not hers." says Mother, and gives my shoulder a little squeeze to take the sting out of her words. We're standing in front of her open wardrobe, seeing if there are things I can borrow for my holiday. I'm skinnier than her, but she has some lovely sweaters and shirts that would go well with my jeans. I pull out a deep pink T–shirt and hold it up against myself.

"Not your colour, dear," says Mum. She hands me a jade green one and nods approvingly. "Much better."

"I feel I fall far short of what she thinks her son's wife ought to be," I say, returning to the subject like a dog worrying an old bone. That jade green does look good against my dark hair; I add it to my 'to take' pile on the bed.

"Look at it this way," says my mother. "Be grateful to her for producing and raising such a wonderful young man to be your husband. And admit that you probably have a few expectations of your own of how your sons' wives should be."

I haven't given this matter a lot of thought, as yet. But she does have a point.

"Are you all right for nightwear?" enquires Mother, pulling open a drawer. "Only I have a really pretty set, champagne satin, that I bought in a hurry for Prague and never wore. Slippers to match. You'll need some nice stuff for the hotels."

Hotels! My heart gives a little skip and jump. I'm going to be staying in hotels! Where someone else cleans, makes the beds, provides fresh linen, cooks – and I'm the guest! And it's all thanks to Molly. An ungrateful cow, that's what I am. I'll stop at the florist on the way home and buy her a big bunch of flowers. Or will she think that's wickedly extravagant, given that flowers are coming into bloom in the garden? Who cares! I'll do it anyway!

Chapter Twenty-Two

We're on our way! Free as a bird, everyday life left far behind, the wind in our hair, the miles being swallowed up under our wheels as we head north. Or something.

Not that it was plain sailing, reaching this point. For a start, my carefully planned child-and-animal care plans met with a big hitch. Jo had the misfortune to tread on a discarded Lego on the stairs in bare feet (ouch!), fall and end up with a wrist in plaster. So our contingency plans had to be rearranged, as she was the chosen surrogate mum for our two youngest during holiday week.

I cast about for alternatives. I was hesitant about asking Mum; two small boys plus one teenager would be too much for someone in her state of health. Bev's kids have chicken pox, the boys have had it but it wouldn't be fair to add another pair of kids to her burden of fractious invalids. Luke tearfully pleads to go with us, and for a while I'm on the point of scrapping the whole expedition and trying to see if we could get our money back.

In the end, it's Molly and Mum to the rescue, and between them they really come up trumps again. Molly will extend her visit; instead of leaving the week before we go away, she will stay on, and Mum and Dad will move into our house too for the duration. Moreover, Molly's sister, Jane, will hop on the train and come too. All the kids can then stay home if they wish; the animals likewise, the house will be occupied, and if we're lucky the garden may even be weeded! Bingo! I do wonder whether running our household may be too much for four older people, but they all assure me that they will just love it, the kids are so good and they'll enjoy spending time together. It will be a tight squeeze but they'll manage; it'll be like those house parties they used to go on. The kids are charmed by the idea; to a man they all decide they'd rather stay home after all.

So I put aside any misgivings, pack our bags, get bedrooms ready, make sure there are plenty of supplies in, write extensive lists and numbers of emergency services in large letters, which I leave in prominent positions, likewise our phone numbers, hotel details and anything else that comes to mind, and finally wave goodbye to our assembled family with a huge lump in my throat.

"I wonder if we've done the right thing," I mutter for the nth time as we bowl along country roads between rich farmland, with hedgerows laden with deep cream hawthorn blossom and verges starred with cow parsley. Graham has given up replying to my fretful ponderings, he's enjoying looking over the hedges to see how other farmers' crops are doing. "Lovely land here," he comments, in the wry tones of one who knows only too well the hardship of scratching a living on the sparse soil of a hill farm. I make a conscious decision; I will stop fretting, trust God and live in the moment. "It is lovely," I agree. "And it's such a beautiful day. This is going to be a wonderful holiday."

And now we've left the country roads and pretty black–and–white villages behind and have joined the wide stream of speeding vehicles that is the M6, heading North. I must say I like travelling, I always have. Airports, railway stations, motorway services, have a kind of magic for me. Everyone here is transient, on the move, going places. I travelled a fair bit as a student and a single girl, though travel has been drastically curtailed since marriage to a farmer and the appearance of several kids. Graham and I did take a couple of trips to the continent in the first year or two, toting Michael in a backpack, but more offspring and increasing responsibility with the farm put a stop to all that. I realise with a shock that this will be the first holiday on our own that Graham and I have had in almost fifteen years.

We stop at a motorway station and have soup and sandwiches, which Graham considers criminally overpriced. Our first overnight stop is in Cumbria, at a small hotel in the hills which looked beautiful on the Internet site. We planned all our stops carefully, booking in advance and choosing hotels or B & B's in strategically scenic locations with reasonable travelling distance in between. They will take us up though Edinburgh, on to Fife and over the Tay estuary to Dundee and across the beautiful countryside to the West Coast and the Islands. My heart gives a little leap of anticipatory joy.

On the road again, I rummage in my bag to look at the hotel details, to check its name and location. I made a list of all the stopping places, with post codes and relevant info. The list isn't there. More rummaging, getting more frantic by the minute, brings the sickening realisation that the reservation details, travel directions, phone numbers – have all been left behind.

*

"How on earth did you manage to do that?" demands Graham, as though I'd plotted, connived and worked to effect such an oversight.

I have no answer, no excuse, and no idea where I might have left the darned list.

"I'll have to phone home and see if they've found it," I say. "Could you pull in while I make the call? I can't hear properly with all the traffic noise."

"Of course I can't pull in, this is the M6, not some country lane with a handy gateway," says Graham irritably. I recognise the first signs of fuming, which I try to avoid at all costs. A fuming driver, especially when it's my husband, is not a comfortable travelling companion. He says tetchily that he'll stop when he can, and I pray silently as several more miles speed by.

When at last we come to a halt on the hard shoulder, I am shaky and sweaty. It's warm today, there's a smell of heating tarmac mixed with the traffic fumes. I pull off my cardigan and dial our home number.

"Hello, this is Oak Tree Farm," a voice announces importantly. It's Luke. I don't allow him to answer the phone; obviously the rules have already been relaxed.

"Lukie, this is Mum. Sweetie, is Grandma or Grandpa there? Or Nanny Molly or Auntie Jane? Can I speak to one of them please?"

Now Luke has control of the phone, he's making the most of his opportunity. "Mummy, is that you? Guess what, we went to MacDonald's! I had a Happy Meal, Adam had a double cheeseburger with fries –"

He obviously plans to run through the lunch choices of the entire family, in some detail. I interrupt, and say "Luke, I need to speak to a grown–up. See if you can find one, please."

"All right, but I wanted to talk. I miss you –" The phone goes down, there's some shuffling, a door opening, a cat mewing, shouts and a burst of laughter outside. They seem to be enjoying themselves, anyway. We wait, Graham tapping his fingers on the steering wheel. Now we're stationary, I realise just how fast motorway traffic travels. It flies past in a blur, and every time there's a truck or heavy vehicle there's a huge whoosh and the car shudders.

At last the phone is picked up and there's Molly's voice on the end. "Hello?"

I explain in a rush, rather relieved it's Molly. If anyone can locate that list, it'll be her. My mum can be vague about finding misplaced things, and my dad, being a man, can never find anything. Molly promises to look, but doesn't sound all that hopeful.

"I cleaned right through this morning," she assures me. "All the children helped. (Goodness, however did she manage that?) None of us noticed any lists. Where would it have been?"

That's the thing, I have no idea. My heart is sinking as we talk.

"Can you remember any of the addresses of the places?" she asks, sounding as though she's clutching at straws. I can remember a few details, but very sketchily.

"We'll just have to keep looking and ring you immediately there's news," she says. "Try and remember the areas you booked, or hotel names. Or anything that might help." As an afterthought, she adds, "Don't worry too much, dear."

She's surprisingly calm and reassuring, seeing as it's her money that might be going down the drain. I try to remember what deposits we paid, whether they were refundable, what the conditions were.

"It pays to keep a back–up copy," Graham says infuriatingly as I say goodbye to Molly. "I'm always telling you."

I bite back a swift retort to the effect that maybe he could have helped a little with the planning. Playing the blame game isn't going to help here. Neither is panicking. I take deep breaths.

"We'll just have to play it by ear," decides my husband, starting the engine. "One step at a time. First, get to the area we'd planned to be tonight. Keep a lookout for any hotel that might be the one. If all else fails, we'll go to a Travel Lodge. There's sure to be one not far away."

"Sure to be," I echo faintly, trying to convince myself as we pull out again to join the speeding traffic.

As the afternoon wears on, so does the air of despondency inside our fast–travelling metal box on wheels. We don't know where we're heading for, we have no guarantee of comfy beds and hot water awaiting us; we're both getting tired and tetchy. And it's all my fault. The bubble has well and truly burst.

No longer can I relax and watch the world flash by, even if it amounts to no more than long stretches of motorway, speeding traffic, bridges and fields. At least we were getting somewhere. Now we're heading we know not where. My eyes are aching from scanning every likely-looking hotel sign that might be our destination. Graham's hands are tense on the wheel and he has that pursed-lips look. At intervals he asks me tersely if I've remembered anything yet. I haven't. And now we're up in the hills, with a wonderful sense of space, and towering mountains on every hand.

There's a motorway stop up ahead, miles from anywhere, and, yes, it has a motel attached. Graham and I glance at each other and we're both ready to call it a day. He asks "Shall we?" and I nod. We pull into the station.

Actually, this is a very beautiful place. The grounds have been tastefully landscaped to blend in with the scenery, there's a huge grassy area with trees and a pond. The sun is dipping low as we climb out, weary, travel stained and disillusioned, and with great relief find that yes, they have a room, a ground-floor twin, no smoking. Meals in the restaurant adjacent. The price makes Graham's eyes stand out on stalks, he moans about it to the receptionist, which embarrasses me horribly and renews my feeling of guilt. But we take the room and lug our overnight bags down the long corridor to find it. There we collapse on the blue covered beds and review our situation. It looks a bit iffy. I find myself thinking longingly of my bed at home (this mattress is on the firm side) and of my kitchen and the little faces of my children. Time to get up and plug in the plastic kettle for a nice cup of tea.

Chapter Twenty-Three

What a difference a day makes, or even eight good hours of uninterrupted sleep! We both wake with a different view of the world, shower in the pristine bathroom, dress and prepare for a brand new day. I don't even have to hang up the towels or make the beds; we just take our bags to the car and then sashay along to the restaurant for breakfast.

The breakfast proves to be excellent. We have worked our way leisurely through grapefruit, muesli, scrambled egg and bacon and have just ordered more toast and coffee when my mobile rings. It's Mum. "Good morning, darling. Did you sleep well? Yes, yes, everyone's fine. Boiled eggs all round for breakfast. Yes, Lauren too. Yes, we remembered Luke's eczema cream. No, Adam hasn't needed his inhaler. Do you have a pen and paper handy? We've found your details."

"You have?" I almost choke on my toast and marmalade. "Where had I left the list?"

"I haven't a clue, dear. But Michael wondered if it was still on the hard drive. It was. So can you jot down the details if I dictate?"

I certainly can. I fumble in my bad for notebook and pen, while Graham rolls his eyes across the table and mouths 'Why didn't you think of that before?'

Why, indeed! But nothing can spoil our relief and anticipation this morning, even the discovery that we pay extra for breakfast. The day is new, bright and sparkling, our equilibrium restored, and the world is our oyster.

We set off through magnificent mountain scenery. The mad rush of traffic is calmer here. The hills are dotted with sheep and crisscrossed by dry stone walls. Graham gives me a brief history on the craft of dry stone walling. We cross the border mid–morning, more hills and valleys and now there's a covering of purple heather on the slopes. Skirting Glasgow it's busier again for a while, but already I sense the slowing pace, a relaxation of tension, and when we're amongst hills and valleys again I find myself taking deep breaths, filling myself with the sense of freedom, of clean air and sanity and peace.

*

What can I say about the holiday except that it is magical, wonderful, an exhilarating shared adventure, a glorious interlude? Somewhere between Glasgow and Oban, Graham and I manage to put aside responsibilities, burdens and niggling anxieties and for six glorious days become again the carefree youngsters we were when we met at a Young Farmers' function all those years ago. Together we explore remote glens in the mountains, walk hand–in–hand on heather-covered slopes, watch a golden eagle soar majestically against the sky and catch a glimpse of a russet–coated pine–marten leaping among tussocks of tall grass. We island–hop; across to Skye and back, over to Arran with its deep blue waters and high peak of Goat's Fell, we cross to Mull and, magic! from there take a little ferry as foot passengers and land on Iona.

Iona is a place I've read about and longed to visit. It's a bit touristy, with a gift shop and restaurant and an enterprising lady with a horse and trap who takes visitors on tours round the island. But it's a place of striking beauty, the sea here is sparkling turquoise when the sun shines, bottle green in the shade, the sand is gleaming white and the cliffs pink granite. We visit the abbey, grey and solid and busy with pilgrims from all over the world who stroll its cloisters, soaking up the atmosphere. Iona is said to be a 'thin' place, meaning that there's little between this world and the world of the spirit. I try hard to capture this feeling – thereby maybe defeating my own purposes – and am disappointed until, walking on the cliffs, I realise that God's spirit is not confined to any particular place, but is here, closer than a heartbeat, within me, and within every person who has trusted in the sacrifice of his son.

In the afternoon we walk to the other side of the island, to St. Columba's bay, where the saint landed in his coracle bringing the gospel from Ireland in the sixth century. It's so peaceful, there are no cars on Iona and people travel by bike or on foot. The bay is deserted, tall grasses blowing gently in the dunes, sand fine and warm as we take off our shoes and walk down to the water. Graham points to two faint dark smudges on the horizon. "Coll and Tiree," he says. "I looked at the map."

Even the names have a magical sound. Time seems to stand still here. I don't want to leave, but tomorrow we must be on our way south.

"Glad we didn't choose the Canaries, or Benidorm?" asks Graham, and puts his arms round me. We haven't felt this close in ages.

"Very glad," I say from the heart. This holiday has been a brief one, with a dodgy start, but it's exceeded my wildest expectations. I've had my own little taste of paradise.

*

In this relaxed, refreshed, optimistic and happy frame of mind, we leave behind our highlands and islands, our lochs and heather-covered slopes and head south to join the M6, plunge into the crazy rat-race of the Midlands, and pass on through to the more peaceful environments of rural border country. I feel as though I've been away months, or even years. Every familiar landmark I greet with nostalgic delight, as though I'm surprised it has remained the same in my absence. It is still daylight as we approach our own patch; I wave enthusiastically to anyone I see whose face seems vaguely familiar. Some wave back, others seem slightly mystified.

"Don't overdo it," says Graham. "They'll think you've finally flipped your lid."

The sun is going down as we climb our own hill. Hedgerows are resplendent in full leaf, birds are warbling in the branches. Graham slows to a crawl, eager to inspect the progress of his growing crops. For the last fifty miles or so he has resumed arable farmer mode, worrying lest his barley should have been stricken with a plague of fungal stem rot or the neighbours' sheep broken into his winter wheat, which will now be at the flag-leaf stage. I am anxious now to see my own lambs.

It's a perfect summers' evening, long shadows are stretching across the yard and the Montana clematis is a riot of bloom over the end of the house. One of the cats is curled up on the garden wall, but there's no other sign of life. We pull onto the yard and toot the horn.

Lauren is the first to emerge, with Paula in tow, both of them dressed to the nines in cropped jeans and brief tops.

"Oh, it's you," she greets us with a hint of disappointment.

"Who did you expect?" I enquire wryly as she leans in through the open window and favours me with a peck on the cheek.

"Paula's dad. He's picking us up to go to a barbecue at theirs .Then Grandad's fetching me later. It's all arranged."

She tosses her carefully styled hair and gazes past us down the lane, eager to see an approaching vehicle that will whisk her away from the dull parents she hasn't seen for a week. She looks pretty and suntanned.

Paula remembers her manners and asks if we had a good holiday, and I reply that, yes, we had a lovely time, as we begin to unload our luggage from the boot.

"Where's everyone else?" enquires Graham, lugging out the biggest case.

"Oh, they're all playing poker. ," says Lauren. "Grandad taught us. We play it every night. For money. Good fun."

Obviously. So good they can't tear themselves away to greet returning parents. But I judge too hastily, because just then Luke appears at the window, sees it's us, and disappears with a shriek, reappearing at the door in a flurry of Spiderman pyjamas and bare feet. He's seen joined by Adam and Michael, with the elders bringing up the rear.

There's an excited babble of voices.

"We had a sleepover!"

"Michael crashed the quad."

"Shut up, you dope!"

"Luke had to go to the hospital!"

"We might be getting a dog!"

"What did you bring me?"

We are escorted indoors in the midst of an eager crush of bodies and hands grabbing at various bits of our luggage. The four elders greet us with smiles and kisses; we're relieved to see that all of them are looking reasonably fit and compos mentis, though Jane's hair looks as though she's recently been running her fingers through it. Someone helps bring the last bags in; someone else goes to put the kettle on.

"Your bed is all made up and ready, dear," says my mother, and the words are like music to my ears. "Dad and I will be off home later – we'll drop Lauren back here first."

The house seems fairly tidy, it's cool and inviting. Spit is curled up on the rocker; Spot has uncurled from the wall and sauntered in to join us. Everything seems to be normal, but a few questions need to be asked.

"What's this about hospital and crashing the quad?"

"The crash wasn't anything," Michael assures us quickly. "Just a few bruises." He pulls up his T–shirt to reveal spectacular black and blue patches around the ribs. "It's almost better now."

"Luke did go into hospital," admits my mother, exchanging a look with Molly. "We suspected a broken wrist, but it was just a sprain."

Luke wriggles his left wrist about, pulling up his pyjama sleeve to reveal bandaging. "I fell off the woodshed roof."

I have the feeling he was not meant to impart that information, but the moment passes.

"Spot was sick on the clean washing," Adam volunteers, filling a vacuum.

"Dai has got a dog we can have," says Luke. "Can we have it? Ple – eese?"

Both of them are dancing about in front of us, waving their arms, demanding attention as we sip our mugs of tea, taking furtive peeks into the bags to see what we might have brought.

"Let Mum and Dad have a bit of peace to drink their tea," says my mum, but she might as well speak to thin air.

"They've been so good all the time you were away," says Molly, with the vague intimation that our homecoming is greatly to the detriment of the boys' behaviour. Graham and Dad have been attempting a little discussion about the performance of the car on the journey, the weather, the state of the crops en route, but they are overwhelmed by the competition. I sigh, put down my mug and reach for my holdall. There'll be no peace until presents are distributed.

"We stayed up late every night," shrieks Luke as I rummage about.

"Granny told us not to say that, you dope!" yells Adam and gives him a shove, which causes Luke to theatrically clutch his bad arm and aim a kick. In their hyped-up state, they'll soon be punching the living daylights out of each other, bad arm or no bad arm. The two grandmas are hastily gathering up the mugs and beating a retreat to the kitchen.

We're home, all right.

Chapter Twenty-Four

It's good to be home, though by Monday I'm feeling a twinge of regret that the closeness my spouse and I have enjoyed for the last week has already dissipated somewhat. This morning, he is up at the crack of dawn, inspecting the crops. At lunch time I get a full report. Thank goodness the wheat appears to show no sign of fungus and the barley no mildew. No stray sheep or cattle have encroached on the fields. He wolfs a sandwich and is off to catch up with the fertilizing and spraying.

Molly and Jane departed this morning, no doubt glad to see the back of us all and return to their neat, peaceful coastal cottage and garden. All the children are at school. I've done five loads of washing and am taking a moment to catch my breath.

The phone rings. It's Dai, down the road. "Oh, you're back then, from gallivanting round the world."

"Yes, we're back. It was only Scotland."

"All foreign parts. Me, I never been to London and only once to Cardiff."

"Well, you're probably wise, Dai. How are you keeping?"

"Very fair, thanks. This nice weather do suit me." Pause. "What I'm wondering is, when do you want to pick your pup?"

"Pardon?"

"Pick the pup. Your pup."

"Er – I'm not sure I'm quite with you, Dai. Has Jess had pups?"

I'm well acquainted with Jess, who is one of those over-defensive sheepdogs with the habit of hurling themselves barking and slavering at the wheels of any passing vehicle. She is perfectly docile when you meet her face to face, but everything on wheels is considered a threat to her patch and must be seen off aggressively. One of these days she'll misjudge the enemy and come to grief.

"Ar – her has. Four. Three weeks old now. Your nippers came over to have a look, with your Dad and the three ladies. They said one of them would be just what you could do with, seeing as your dog is gone. It's all arranged. But they said better wait till you get back before picking one."

Did they, indeed! All arranged, is it? What on earth was Dad thinking to go along with all this? Sheepdogs are working dogs, they need to be on a farm with sheep, if they're at a loose end there's a danger they'll be tempted to investigate other people's sheep, unsupervised. Anyway, we said we didn't want another dog, not for ages, at least.

Dai is patiently explaining. "They won't be any good for sheepdogs, see, so I got to find other homes. Not easy, because of the pedigree."

"The pedigree?"

"Ar. Her got out when her shouldn't have. Looks like there's hound in them." Pause. "Like that hound of yours."

"Ben's dead."

"Ar. But he wasn't dead a few months back, was he? I'll say there's a definite possibility he's something to do with them pups."

I'm at a loss for words. Ben was old and he was infirm and I'd have said he'd long been past any such capers. But you never can tell...

I say weakly "I see. Well, I'll have to talk it over with Graham, and then maybe we'll come and have a look."

I try to think of excuses for not having this pup as I hang up. But already I'm feeling a kind of strange responsibility towards this new litter, who may be almost related, so to speak. I feel it won't be long before we have yet another family member.

*

I'm at Sonia's, having called by on my way to stock up at the supermarket. This past week, since coming back from Scotland, we've seemed to get through twice as much food, for some reason. I also have to pick up selective weed killer from the farmers' Co Op, and make haircut appointments for Luke and Adam for next week. Today they're both on a trip to a theme park from school, so at least I don't have to collect them, and that has left me a little time to pop in on Sonia and Victoria.

They're in the garden at the back, and Victoria is playing in a paddling pool, in a pink swimsuit and a big floppy sunhat. Her skinny little body has a faint tan.

"She's talked of nothing else since that day we came to the farm," says Sonia, smiling and replacing the sun hat, which has been tossed aside. She adds "A hat is an absolute must. And lashings of sun cream. Her scalp would get sunburnt in no time."

We go inside, where Victoria is dried off and dressed in shorts and T–

shirt while the kettle boils. I've brought her a present, a long–outgrown party dress of Lauren's, shiny green and pink taffeta with a petal–shaped skirt and spangles on the bodice. It's a little too big for Victoria but she puts it on at once over her clothes, her little face wreathed in smiles. She dances around excitedly, holding out the skirt and shrieking "Look, look, I'm a princess! I'm a princess!"

"So you are," says her mother, smiling. Sonia looks better, less pale and strained. The summer has put a little colour into her cheeks. I mention an idea that has occurred to me, choosing my words carefully. "Sonia, I've been thinking. I teach a Sunday School class at St John's, tiny ones. Little Fish, they're called. Would Victoria like to try coming?"

Sonia's face clouds and she puts down her mug. "Well – I don't know. Would – would things be said? Children can be so cruel. I don't want Victoria to get hurt, to be made to feel different –"

I look at her, wanting so desperately to protect her daughter, to keep her from the harsh realities of the world, and I look at Victoria, denied many of the normal experiences of childhood and all too soon to be denied life itself. My heart aches for them both. I say, carefully, "I can't guarantee that all of the other kids would behave with perfect tact. As you, say, kids usually come out with whatever's on their mind. But I don't think they'd be deliberately unkind. And I think Victoria's resilient enough to cope in a group and to benefit from it. I'd keep a close eye on her, of course."

Sonia is silent, biting her lip. "Well, she coped okay at your house. I was surprised. She does like to be with other kids. It's just –"

"I know. You don't want her to be hurt. But think about it."

She promises she will. I finish my tea and get up to go. I wish I could do more to help them both, but I'll have to be patient.

It's a lovely afternoon again. I've left my car in the main car park, so I decide to walk back into town along the river walk. The water is calm and brownish, dappled with sunlight. A few canoes are drifting downstream. I pause for a few moments to watch them.

"Good afternoon." Someone has approached from the other direction, footsteps so muffled on the dry leaf mould that I haven't heard a thing. I look round with a start, and my heart gives a lurch and then seems to stop. It's that man, the one who lurks mysteriously, the one, I remember with terror, that I caused to be hauled off for questioning at the police station. I look frantically to left and right; the path is quite deserted in both directions, shaded by overhanging boughs of hazel and beech. On one side is the bank with the old disused railway track, overgrown now with briars and nettles and a profusion of red campion and stitchwort. On the other side is the river.

He's half–smiling, or maybe it's a sneer, I'm too terrified to tell. He's wearing a blue check short–sleeved shirt, jeans and trainers, sunglasses and a peaked cap. But I can tell it's him. And he recognises me too.

"We've met before, haven't we?" he asks, in an accent that's not local. Midlands? Black Country? His voice is soft, a little uncertain.

"Have we?" My own voice comes out breathless and shaky. I try to pass him to go on my way, but he's blocking the path and I can't get by. The river chuckles and murmurs peacefully below. He could push me in there in a moment and no one would ever know. Nobody would hear my screams.

And then, suddenly, the terror leaves me. I realise he's as nervous as I am. He takes off his shades and rubs a hand over his face in a weary gesture. There are tired lines around his eyes. He says, almost diffidently "You were the one that set the police on me."

"Yes, I – I did. It was a mistake. I'm sorry."

"Why did you do it? That's what I want to know. Two hours I was in there, answering questions. What have you got against me?"

"Nothing. Nothing. Only –"

"Only what?"

I'll have to explain. I really have no choice. I've got myself into another predicament, as Graham would say. But somehow, I'm not scared any more, just mightily embarrassed.

"Look, I've got kids to meet and I'll have to get going, but if you'd like to walk along with me I'll try and explain –"

And so there I am, walking along the path chatting with a perfect stranger and one who might be a dodgy proposition to boot, and I'm telling him just what my suspicions of him are.

"You seem to keep popping up all over the place and yet you're not local, and often it's when children are about, and you seem to be watching but not wanting to be seen. You hear such things –"

He nods slowly and sighs, hands in pockets, eyes on the ground. Then he says "I've been a bit of a plonker, haven't I? Should have thought of all that."

He sighs again, looks at me, and says "You've got kids, you say?"

I nod.

He's silent for a moment, then says "Maybe you'd understand then."

Suddenly I have the strong conviction that this man desperately needs to unburden himself, to talk to someone, to get help. I feel he's lonely, needy – but not dangerous. All the same, I shouldn't be doing this, and certainly not alone, in a place where there are no other people.

We've reached the gate now, and I can see the main road, with traffic and people passing on the pavement. Even as I speak I know I'll regret it, but I hear myself say, not quite believing I'm saying it, "Look, I've got to go. But if you'd like to talk I can meet you somewhere. There's a little café down Lion Street, tables outside on the pavement. Two thirty tomorrow?"

*

This evening it's decided that we will stroll over to Dai's and inspect the litter.

"Just to look, mind you," I warn, lest anyone thinks we'll be coming home with a cute little bundle. At least it'll be something to do, to take my mind off the weird appointment I have tomorrow. I haven't said a word to Graham about it, which gives me pangs of guilt as well as apprehension. He would definitely not approve, or understand. I'm not even sure I understand myself why I'm doing it.

The pups are in Dai's woodshed, ensconced on old hessian sacks on straw. Jess looks inordinately proud of them, and pleased with herself. Smug is the word that comes to mind. The pups are round, soft, warm and velvety smooth. They're a mixture of hues, brown, black, tan, white, they totter about on wobbly legs and play–fight with each other, and, yes, they have the beginnings of long droopy ears and short stumpy legs.

"See what I was saying?" says Dai meaningfully. "Not much sheepdog there."

We do. And, strangely, the feeling uplifts my spirits. Ben was a good old friend, we miss him, and maybe one of his progeny is just what we need to fill the gap. Graham and I look at each other.

"We can have one, can't we? Please, please, please!" implores Adam. "We'll tidy our rooms and put all our socks and pants in the laundry basket, for ever!"

Well, strike while the iron is hot, that's what I say. Nothing like killing two birds with one stone, so to speak.

"I think maybe we can," says Graham, and before his sons can fall in a body on the pups and smother them with love, he adds "They're too young to leave their mother yet. But we can choose the one we'd like. That little one with the brown ears is nice, don't you think?"

JULY

Chapter Twenty-Five

So here I am, first day of a new month, when I'd intended putting in a good day's work on the vegetable patch. The lettuce and onions need weeding, cabbage whites have been fluttering ominously and I should check for caterpillars. There should be enough tender green peas ready to pick and have with today's supper.

Instead, I'm heading to a café in town to meet a man.

The thought gives me a little *frisson* of amazement, excitement, curiosity and terror. Mostly terror. I don't know this man from Adam, really, and there's something strange and mysterious about him. I have to admit I'd like to get to the bottom of it.

It should be safe enough, in the little tea garden at the back of Avril's Café, bright with pink geraniums and striped parasols over the small round wrought-iron tables and chairs, with Avril and her teenage helpers well within screaming distance.

He's there already, sitting rather uncomfortably on one of the small chairs and studying the afternoon tea menu. Maybe I should have suggested we met in the privacy of a pub, but I think I subconsciously wanted this meeting to be in the open. He's wearing his peaked cap and shades again, which surely must mean he wants to avoid recognition. There again, though, I went to some lengths to disguise my own appearance, with my own rather outdated blue-rimmed sunglasses and my hair pulled back and tied with a scarf. The tea-garden is not very busy, an older couple at one of the small tables, and a larger group of animatedly chatting ladies who seem to be having some kind of reunion.

He looks up with a start as I sit down opposite.

"You came."

"Yes. Didn't you think I would?"

He shrugs, putting down the menu. "Wasn't sure. Hoped so."

He looks tired behind the shades, sad, defeated somehow. One of the teenage waitresses appears and we order tea. I know her by sight and she gives us a curious glance. This all seems so surreal, as though I'm having a clandestine meeting with a lover or something. We exchange banal remarks about the weather until the tea arrives, with flowered china and a twee little milk jug. I pour and hand him a cup, he sips it awkwardly. His hands are square and capable, not as rough and calloused as Graham's, but strong –looking, too awkward for the fiddly little cups. I wait, sipping my own tea.

He puts down the cup and looks at me, clearing his throat. "I'm not proud of this." The Midlands accent is more pronounced now, as if he's being his real self, putting off all pretence. I wait again. He says, slowly "My wife and family live here, in this town. My name's John Dent."

Dent! I recognise the name immediately. It's Sonia's name, and Harry's, and Victoria's! This man is Sonia's husband, the children's father.

I put down my own cup and say shakily "I know them."

He nods. "Yes. Thought so. I've seen you go there, to the house. That's why I spoke to you."

"But – but – why the secrecy? Why not go there yourself?"

He sighs, passing his hand over his face in that weary gesture. "I – can't. Not after what happened. You see, I ran out on them, just upped and left. I couldn't take it, when I saw what was happening with my little girl – with that illness – it was cruel."

He looks away, shifts in his seat, cracks his knuckles. I don't know what to say. I sit and look at him and think, yes, it was cruel. Cruel to walk away from someone you love, to cut and run, just 'bugger off' as Sonia had put it so bitterly, leaving her to face the heartache and struggle and pain all on her own, to see her son unhappy and disturbed, her daughter dying by inches, alone –

I'm silent, fighting down my feelings of anger and contempt, but it must show in my face because he goes on, not meeting my eyes "I'm not proud of myself. Pretty soon realised what a shit I'd been. Thought about coming back. Then got offered a job, a good one, on the oil rigs. Took it. Was there two years, almost." He's talking in short staccato sentences, as though he wants to get it all out in as short a time as possible. "Then had an accident, had to leave. Had a bit of a breakdown. Then got work nearer here, factory work, shifts." He pauses. "I – wanted to see Sonia, but couldn't. Hadn't got the guts. Found where she lives, used to go by the school now and again to get a glimpse of my boy. Saw Sonia and Victoria once or twice, in the distance". He spreads out his fingers, looking at them miserably. "Gutless as ever, I guess. Can't seem to stay away, but can't seem to get up the courage to speak to her either. Maybe they're better off without me."

I'm still silent, torn between anger and sadness and pity and a kind of rage, against a world where children sicken and die young, families are fragmented, hearts broken, where there's loss and pain and suffering and despair. Why am I sitting here with this man? Is there any order, any purpose to life? I'm an ordinary woman – what in the world can I do or say that will make a difference?

He lifts his head and looks at me and I see a world of emotion in his face; shame and regret, loneliness and longing, despair and maybe the faintest flickering of hope. And I know that whatever else I do I must not extinguish that hope.

I choose my words carefully, or maybe something or someone infinitely greater and more loving chooses them for me.

"I've got to know your family. One of my boys is Harry's age. And little Victoria is such a sweet child –"

He's hanging on to my every word. When I pause, he says quickly "And Sonia? Does she talk about me? Is there any chance she might have me back, do you think? I know that her mother died. I've got a fair bit of money saved from working on the rigs – is there any hope?"

That money would have made all the difference in the world to her, I think silently, and remember how bitterly Sonia spoke of her desertion by this man, and the times she'd walked by the river contemplating suicide, and the cowardly way he's sneaked around, no better than a stalker, and my mind says, no way, mate, if she's got any sense she'll stay a million miles away from you, and you sure don't deserve a second chance –

But that other presence is there, overriding my judgmental reasoning, my blinkered view and smallness of mind, and I hear a voice from my heart saying "I think there is a chance. I don't know how and it may not be easy, but if I can help I will, and, yes, I think there's always hope."

*

News travels fast in our town. Adam and Luke have dental checks after school, and by the time we're back the others are home and the smell of chicken casserole is filling the kitchen. I put some jacket potatoes in the microwave and think regretfully of the new green peas – no time to pick and pod them now, but never mind, they'll have another day to grow and fatten in their pods. I've bought Danish pastries all round for dessert and ask Lauren to put them onto plates.

She gives me a funny look as she does so. "Have a nice afternoon, Mum?"

I automatically begin to answer, yes thanks, when I realise she's getting at something. "Why do you ask?"

She grins infuriatingly, lining up the plates on the sideboard. "Oh, I just heard you met a friend. Don't worry, I won't tell Dad."

She sniggers. I sigh. That's the trouble of living in a small town. One of those teenage waitresses probably texted a friend, or her sister, or someone who knows Lauren, and it's got back to my daughter. I'll have to come clean, though I'd hoped to keep this quiet while I work out what to do next, if, how and when to approach Sonia.

"I can explain. That man wasn't a friend. I hardly know him – or didn't until today. He's actually the husband of, er – a woman that I know –"

I'm digging myself in deeper and deeper. I'm loath to mention names, but I can't have my daughter jumping to the wrong conclusions. She's now looking rather shocked, eyebrows raised and a prim expression. We both hear Graham's boots in the back porch.

"As I said, I won't mention a word to Dad," she says primly. Goodness, the girl really believes I was up to no good! But Graham and the boys are all piling into the kitchen, pleading desperate hunger, except for Adam, who is complaining that the dentist wiggled a tooth and made it loose.

"It was loose anyway, you idiot," Michael tells him, and Adam aims a nudge with his elbow, though he ought to know better because Michael pins both his arms tight against his sides until he pleads to be let go.

It's all normal. Graham is eagerly relating that the winter barley should be ready any day now, and Luke is asking for the hundredth time when can we have our new puppy. All through the meal though, I'm conscious of Lauren's eyes on me, cool, reproachful and accusing, until by the time we reach dessert I'm actually feeling guilty myself. I'll have to get Lauren alone and explain it all in detail.

I grab the chance when the menfolk have left to view the news and the Simpsons, in that order. Lauren is still throwing odd looks at me. I begin hesitantly "Look, about this afternoon –"

She purses her lips, and I'm afraid she's going to say she doesn't want to hear. But instead, she suddenly bends over double, clutching her stomach and bursting with laughter. "Oh Mum, your face! All red and guilty! As if you'd really been meeting someone on the quiet!"

I feel limp with relief. She's been winding me up, the little madam! But I'm so glad she doesn't think badly of me. I laugh too, and begin to stack the plates. Lauren flips back her hair and picks up her rucksack. "I'll help you with those in a minute. Just got a few texts to do." She shoulders the bag and heads upstairs, laughing again and saying casually in departing "I'm not that stupid, Mum! I guessed all along it was one of those sad people who're always wanting to talk to you. I mean, someone your age wouldn't be up to anything, would they? As if!" I hear her chortling to herself as she climbs the stairs.

*

Barley harvest is under way, and suddenly our days, and much of our nights, are taken up with the roar of machinery and with streams of golden grain pouring from combine to trailer, from trailer to store, and, if moisture content is high, to the corn drier that looms like a giant factory chimney over the other buildings. Graham is busy from dawn to dusk, driving the combine while one of Sue and Mike's boys follows with the trailer, fuming over mechanical breakdowns, depending on me to be on hand to supply sandwiches and drinks on request whatever the hour, or to run emergency errands. He comes in bone weary each night, streaked with dust and sweat, eats, showers, falls into bed and is asleep in seconds, to repeat the process next day and the next. The only respite comes if there's a shower of rain, which brings with it much fretting, worrying, scanning of weather charts, speculating, and general stress to the farmer and to everyone around him. He reminds me, if I venture a hint of protest, or suggest he slows down a little, that this is the culmination of a year's hard slog, the end product he's worked and slaved towards, the means of providing for us all in the manner we're accustomed to. Farming is a gamble at the best of times, he tells me, the weather and wheat prices, fluctuating markets and the trumpery machine parts you get these days are all stacked against us and it's a wonder we scrape by at all. He sometimes wonders why he bothers, and there are times when I do too.

At other times, though, I know exactly why, like this evening. I'd half planned on seeing Sonia Dent, but abandoned the idea when Graham decided it might rain before morning, he must press on and finish Nine

Acres before it comes, couldn't stop for supper and would I bring him something down? I make thick sandwiches with the gammon I cooked earlier, big slabs of cake, cheese and fruit. He eats on the move, shoving in the food with one hand, taking swigs of tea, all the while controlling the roaring red monster he drives. Then he crawls away down the field, followed by tractor and trailer, into which the grain is flowing in a dusty golden stream.

I stand and watch for a moment, seeing the shadows lengthen over acres of golden stubble, watching the oak spinney darken as the sun dips down behind it. Across the valley the hills are blue and misty, there's a streak of red in the sky and, contrary to Graham's fears, I think that tomorrow will be another lovely day.

And I wouldn't change this life for the world.

Chapter Twenty-Six

Only another few days and then school breaks up for six and a half weeks! I can't wait! Most of my friends consider I'm nuts and think I'm joking when I say I just love the long summer holidays and find them restful. Well, I do.

A school morning begins the night before, with hunting up everyone's clean socks, shirts, underwear, PE kit, swimming togs, football strip, drama costume, or whatever else is appropriate to next day's activities. Needless to say, I am the one who is expected to remember when, which and where said activities will happen, my family's capacity for recollecting these details being faulty at best. Also, homework has to be chased up, located and checked for completion, or at least some attempt at completion. Not that my evening efforts always succeed, all too often these preparations are carried over to the morning.

Come the dawn, the scholars must be fed, checked over for cleanliness and correct dress code, equipped with packed lunch/dinner money, and packed off to meet the bus at 7.15 (two eldest) or ferried to school at 8.45 (two youngest.) By the time I've returned, surveyed the breakfast debris, fed the animals who've been overlooked in the rush, picked up belongings scattered en route, I'm badly in need of a reviving cup of tea before I begin my morning's work. And often by then, the farmer, having been out on the tractor since first light, is either at the door for mid-morning refreshment, or, most likely at this time of year, requiring me to pop down to the field with a little something. Then, before I know it, it's lunch time, and then 3.15, when I have to take off again to pick up the two youngest and begin the evening routine.

So, yes, I love the summer holidays and find them very relaxing. There are more hours in the day. There's less pressure. I'm looking forward to breaking up even more than they are.

First, though, I've agreed to attend Adam and Luke's Sports Day, having been reproachfully informed that I'm the only mother who never goes. I admit I wriggle out of it if I can. Although I do remember coming second (or was it third) in the mum's egg–and–spoon race one year.

I still haven't spoken to Sonia since seeing John, but today had an idea of how I might kill two birds with one stone. So I set off early and call by Sonia's to see if she'd come to Sports day with me. She looks dubious. "Well, I don't usually go to the school much. I find it – difficult."

I stand my ground. "You'll be fine with me. It's a nice day, be good for you to get out. You'd enjoy it. And Harry would be so pleased to see you."

Victoria is there, peering at me from behind her mother's legs with that big smile on her little old/young face. She hasn't a clue what we're talking about, except that an outing is in the offing, but tugs at her mum's skirt and says pleadingly "Can us go, Mummy? Can us go, please?"

Sonia relents. "Well, all right. For a little while."

She covers Victoria up in her usual floppy face–shading sunhat and adds a pair of pink Hello Kitty shades. We load up the buggy into the car. The school sports ground is packed with eager parents, grandparents and smaller siblings in summer clothes. Nobody takes particular notice of us, they're all intent on their own particular young sporting hopefuls, but I make a point of introducing Sonia to a few of my friends. Jo makes a big effort, chatting about kids and the event, and talking to Victoria about her smart shades, but Sonia is ill–at–ease, deflecting attention away from her daughter. I feel I want to take her by the shoulders and give her a big shake, but Victoria is enjoying the experience, kicking her heels against the buggy footrest and watching everything with keen interest.

The little ones go first, running their races with earnest concentration, there are a few tears from losers but a fast recovery rate. Mums and grannies cheer in unashamed partisanship, small siblings run onto the track and are retrieved and restrained. The older children's events are more dignified affairs; they've been in serious training. Luke wins the sack race and collapses in triumph, Adam does not excel but manages a fair result in his events, without a sign of a wheeze, which is a victory in itself. Harry Dent, still on the overweight side, has the slightly embarrassed air of one who does not shine at any kind of sport.

I get the chance to speak to Sonia about her ex–husband during a quiet spell, when lemonade is going round and we're all waiting for prize giving. We've subsided onto the grassy bank at the right of the school grounds, with Victoria facing us. She has fallen asleep in her buggy, with her hat covering half her face. One or two people I know drift by, peer at her, and comment on the 'sweet baby.' She does look more like a twelve to eighteen month old than a child of three-and-a-half, with her skinny little legs and arms covered in a cotton smock and trousers. Sonia is a little more relaxed now. I feel she's glad she came, especially as Harry waved to her and said "Hi. Mum!" My own two have studiously ignored my presence all afternoon, though I've noticed a sideways glance or two in our direction, just to make sure I'm watching.

I seize my courage in both hands and turn to Sonia. At the same moment she turns to me and says "I've been thinking –"

I close my mouth and raise my eyebrows enquiringly. She goes on, slowly "About what you said, the other day, about Victoria coming to Sunday School."

"You're going to bring her?"

But she shakes her head. "No – well, not yet. Maybe later. But I did think I'd bring her to the church service, and stay myself. I've never had much to do with a church. I'd like to know what it's about before I involve the kids. Would that be all right?"

I nod warmly. "Of course. We'd love to have you. I wonder fleetingly what she'll make of Caroline. Sonia is so defensive; she's running so scared, that it wouldn't take much to put her off. It's a huge thing for her to think of coming at all.

I send up a little silent prayer of thanksgiving. This is a big step she's taking. I realise that now is not the time to make any mention of her errant husband.

*

We have a lull. Barley harvest is complete, wheat not quite ready. Arable farming is a fine art. The crops need to be examined, watched, judged and harvested when they're at the peak of ripeness; in theory, all that wholegrain goodness started on its journey which ends in the nourishing staff of life that we butter for our sandwiches and thrust into our toaster. I sometimes wonder how many of the children today have an inkling of how their bread is produced. Do my own children fully appreciate the significance of the hours of work put in by their long-suffering father? Lauren went through a phase a couple of years ago when she was deeply ashamed of being the daughter of farming folk. When she first started at High School she used to plead with me never,

ever, under any circumstances to turn up at school in the old utility vehicle, even if it was an emergency.

"But what if you had an accident in games, for example, and I had to get there quickly, and the ute was the only vehicle available," I argued.

"Then please just send for the ambulance," she implored. "Don't show me up by coming to school in the ute. There's *mud* all up the sides and *straw* hanging out the doors – everyone would laugh –"

The picture of her classmates hanging out of the windows convulsed with mirth while she was taken off to hospital in such a vehicle almost had her in tears of mortification. I began to think she must either be abnormally sensitive, or that Graham and I had managed to raise a little snob. Fortunately, the situation to date has not arisen, and she's got over that phase anyway. She's more than happy to bring her friends to the farm, and has even been known on occasion to exaggerate a little the extent of our acres. It's cool, too, to bounce around in the back of a utility vehicle, mud, straw and all, and would be cooler still if we'd let her drive it.

Anyway, there's a hiatus while we wait for the wheat to ripen. It'll be at least three days, declares the expert. So we have three days in hand. School is out, Michael's exams behind him; Lauren is staying with Paula for a few days. They are toying with the idea of holidaying together in August, the Glastonbury idea having been shelved.

So, what shall we do?

*

There's a pleasant little spell of relaxation. Nothing complicated or expensive. One day, we go pond–dipping, take a short drive to an isolated pool on the hill, set among whinberries and heather. It's teeming with life when you really look, and I'm glad I brought my old pond–life book for the identification of the various wriggling and squiggling creatures enthusiastically dipped up, examined and returned. There are several frogs and even a couple of common newts, which I have to say give me the creeps.

Another day we take a picnic and go swimming in a safe stretch of the river, which used to be polluted but is now wonderfully clear again and even has fish. The next day we have an impromptu barbecue, which is great fun and only slightly marred by Luke having a painful encounter with a colony of ants. I congratulate myself on a very enjoyable few days with hardly any outlay and plenty of fresh air.

Luke is still complaining next day. "My hair is full of ants," he says, scratching. "They won't go away."

Oh my goodness! Warning bells are ringing. I do a spot check, and it's as I feared. Luke has an infestation, and not of ants. I wonder where on earth he picked them up, now the holidays have started. But then, the little monsters take time to hatch, don't they. Fortunately I have an unopened bottle of the necessary medication. But I can't find the required grooming tool. I'll have to go to the pharmacy.

I'm always mortified by this kind of thing. Useless to tell me that there's an epidemic of the things in almost every school, that they actually prefer clean heads. This episode reinforces the nagging feeling that as a mother, I often fall short. At the pharmacy, I look round furtively to make sure nobody I know is nearby, then approach an assistant who I don't recognise, and whisper my request.

"I'd like –er – a fine–tooth comb, please."

She looks but can't find any, so hollers across to her colleague at the other desk "KATH! ARE THE NIT COMBS OVER THERE?"

The eyes of several interested customers swivel in my direction and fix on my scarlet face. No use to feign nonchalance, I'm the picture of shame. Oh well, maybe it's good for me. As my mother sometimes says, pride goes before a fall.

Chapter Twenty-Seven

Oh dear. More trials are looming.

I'm out early next morning, heading for my veggie patch with watering can in hand – the weather is so dry now that I water twice a day. A scene of devastation meets my eyes. Something – a very large something – has walked through the vegetable garden wreaking havoc as it went. Cabbages and lettuces have been trampled, scarlet runner beans and their supporting sticks knocked askew, deep holes gouged in the soil among the potato plants, and my hopeful rows of carrots and onions trampled and trodden. A large hole in the hedge between the garden and our small meadow bears witness to the intruder's entrance, and, yes, there is the culprit herself, standing knee deep in meadowsweet and lady's smock, with a long wisp of timothy-grass dangling from her mouth. If I'm not mistaken, it's a heifer belonging to our neighbours Mike and Sue along the road. Our little meadow is a conservation area; we are paid a certain sum annually to keep it unmown and so preserve the wildflowers and grasses that flourish there. Dai remarked to me only last week that it must be a great temptation to neighbouring livestock, looking over the hedge, especially when grass grows scarce, and he's right. The temptation was obviously just too great for this one. She could have been satisfied with the meadow though, and not passed on to dessert in my vegetable patch! I sit down on a pile of wooden pallets I use for potting and don't know whether to laugh or cry. All those hours I put in, planting, weeding, watering!

Sitting sobbing isn't really an option though. It doesn't solve anything and it doesn't put my garden back together. I get to my feet and drag one of the pallets across the hole in the hedge, lest the culprit should think of returning sometime soon, and go in to tell the others.

Graham is less sympathetic than I could wish. "That's what comes of gallivanting around day after day. Something's sure to happen."

"Well, I want that creature out of our meadow. You'll have to take her back to Mike's, sharpish."

But this morning he's not to be browbeaten. The magic moisture point has been reached, the wheat is ripe and ready to harvest. Within seconds he's out of the kitchen, and the combine is roaring into life and heading for its next assignment.

"You and the boys'll manage to get her back okay," he flings over his shoulder as he departs.

I wish I had his confidence. There's nothing so skittish as a skittish heifer, from my experience. Mike and his sons will already be hard at work, evidently too busy just now even to notice a hole in the hedge and a missing heifer. I could ask Sue to come and help, but that will only prove what I suspect she thinks already, that I'm a bit of a wimp when it comes to livestock.

Well, she could be right. I was brought up on a mixed farm, but we've been arable people for so long that I'm a little rusty and lacking in confidence when it comes to animal husbandry. Nevertheless, the boys and I arm ourselves with stout sticks and set forth to do our best.

The small Hereford heifer sees us coming, seems to guess our intentions, and she isn't having it. Oh no, not when she's found a beautiful grassy meadow like this, with juicy vegetables handily adjacent. She tosses her head and trots to the far hedge, tail held jauntily high, passing the gap to her home field and ignoring it.

The boys and I go into a huddle to discuss strategy. We must redirect her, press her towards the gap, cut off other escape routes until she is obliged to go through. She has other ideas, breaks free of our cordon and gallops off again. Adam and Luke are not a great help, whooping and waving their sticks in a not altogether helpful way that further excites the heifer. At one point she lowers her head and I fear for the safety of my youngest, but instead of charging him she suddenly sees sense and turns to the gap, bursting through with a great splintering and crashing. We get our breaths, flushed with exertion and triumph, and do what we can to 'glat' the hedge, using branches and sticks to make a temporary barrier until it can be permanently repaired.

The errant heifer rejoins her friends and surveys us reproachfully from a distance.

Next, we must trudge across the fields and report on events to Mike and Sue. As I expected, Mike and his sons are at work, but Sue is at home, treating a pen of sheep for parasites in the yard, single handed except for her youngest son and two collie dogs, who set up a cacophony of barking as we enter the yard.

Sue is what Graham calls a 'proper farmer's wife.' She's maybe in her late forties or early fifties, large, fair and raw–boned, as strong as a man and well able to do a man's work. She and Mike have five sons, all large, strapping and blond; the youngest, Jack, is eleven and towers over Adam, making him look particularly frail and delicate. They stop work and listen to my tale with expressions of concern and apology. Sue puts aside the worming gun, releases the lamb she was treating and wipes her hands on the tail of her work shirt.

"Jack, you go and see if you can find a bit of corrugated zinc and patch up the hedge, just for now," she instructs. "I'll go down myself and do a bit of hedging later. You boys go with him."

The boys depart, and Sue leads me towards the house, for a cup of tea, and, as she puts it "to take the weight off our feet."

Now, my kitchen is no great shakes, being usually cluttered and far from the Ideal Home version of a classic Aga–saga kitchen, but Sue's is something else again. Large boots of all descriptions vie for floor space with buckets, dog beds and machine parts, while on the work surfaces pots and pans rub shoulders with animal medicines, sheep drench, fly spray and sundry other remedies. A big pot simmers on the Rayburn; Sue gives it a casual stir and drops in some chopped potatoes and root vegetables while the kettle boils. She mentions that she's heard of some new product that might be just the thing for Adam's asthma. I murmur a vague reply. Graham swears that Sue uses the same medication on her family that the vet prescribes for their livestock. True or not, her family never seems to have a day's illness.

I move a large tabby cat slightly to sit down on a sagging armchair.

"Expecting again, she is," remarks Sue, pouring water into a teapot. The cat does not look unduly plump to me, but then, another tale about Sue is that she has a kind of sixth sense and can spot any pregnancy, human or animal, almost from the moment of conception. I accept a mug of tea, suddenly feeling rather warm and uncomfortable and a little light–headed. I remember I've had no breakfast this morning.

Sue sits opposite, in a dilapidated old rocking chair that looks as though it's seen sterling service, and looks at me consideringly over the rim of her own mug. She pauses a moment, and then puts into words what I've been thinking these last couple of weeks.

"Speaking of which," she says slowly, almost diffidently, "although it's none of my business and you can tell me to keep my nose out if you like, but – you are too, aren't you?"

I put down my mug, unsteadily, beside a pile of farming catalogues on the sturdy coffee table. It's no good pretending I don't know what she means. Sue's clear grey eyes are holding mine steadily.

I nod my head, in assent.

I can't deny it.

I am.

*

"How on earth do you reckon that happened then?" says Graham incredulously.

We are in bed, at the end of another long hard day, and maybe it's not the best time to break such shattering news. But I can't put it off any longer. Today I went to the pharmacy again, this time to buy a pregnancy-testing kit, and watched with a conflicting mix of feelings as the line turned blue. He had to be told.

"The usual way, I imagine," I answer, with something like a sniff. I am tired too, with that familiar numbing weariness that has little to do with energy expended and everything to do with hormone activity. I'm still struggling to come to terms with this turn of events, and I'd hoped for some kind of helpful response from my spouse. After all, it's been a shock for me too.

He fidgets with the duvet, and says tetchily "But you're nearly forty!"

I'm getting irritated now. "I'm aware of that! So what? Many women these days don't even start a family until their forties."

He grunts, whether in disapproval or just general grumpiness I can only guess. But if I'd expected a reaction of joy and delight, or expressions of loving concern, I'm sadly disappointed. I'm not even going to ask him how he feels about it. He hasn't asked me.

He's quiet for a bit and I think he's fallen asleep. Then the duvet twitches again and a sleepy voice mutters "It was that holiday, wasn't it?"

I nod and gulp in the darkness. "I rather think it was."

Another silence. Then he says "If it's a girl, we'd better call her Iona. Or Arran for a boy."

And then he really is asleep, snoring gently into his pillow. I reach out and touch his hair, soft and floppy from the shower and with a few grey streaks in it now, and think of his eyes, clear and grey-green like sea water in the shadows of island rocks, and suddenly I feel I am a privileged woman.

*

I wait until all the children are home again before sharing the news with them. Their reactions vary, once they've worked through the initial blankness, disbelief, and astonishment that such a thing could happen.

Luke is pragmatic. "Does that mean we can't have a puppy now?"

"No, of course not," I say, and he sighs with relief. "Because if I had to choose, I might choose the puppy."

"Plonker," says Michael, I suspect for want of something better to say. He looks rather nonplussed, confused and yes, even a little put out. It's one thing being supportive to a pregnant teenage friend, quite another when it's your pregnant almost-forty mother.

Lauren puts this view into words. "It's going to make life difficult, isn't it? I mean, I hope I'm not going to be asked to push it out in a pram or anything. People might think it's mine!"

Michael sniggers and she gives him a dig with her elbow.

Adam has been thoughtfully considering the situation. "I would quite like a new brother or sister younger than me. It might be better than the one I have now, if we trained it properly."

All in all, I am happy with their responses.

*

Now the family are in on it, I can't wait to tell the world, or at least, those who matter most to me. Jo is thrilled to bits, bless her, rushes off to buy a ridiculous pair of white lace-trimmed baby shoes that I'm sure no infant of mine will keep on its feet for more than two seconds.

At church there's a quiet buzz of interest and congratulation. Caroline doesn't avoid me exactly but she isn't going out of her way to spend much time with me either. I do understand; baby talk between us might be difficult in the circumstances.

My mother is quietly pleased, but cautious, and concerned for me. "You'll have to remember that you're no spring chicken, dear. It's harder for older mothers. You must take proper care, don't rush about more than you have to."

Easier said than done. But I appreciate her concern. I certainly won't get any cotton-wool wrapping at home. I do feel a little more tired than usual, but I get a huge adrenaline rush when I realise, with a kind of awestruck wonder, that a new, unique, complete little human being is already living and growing and beginning his or her journey into the world.

Chapter Twenty-Eight

The thing most dreaded among harvesting farmers has happened – the weather has turned. After our pleasant June and warm sunny July, the month is ending with lowering clouds and an intermittent drizzle. The hopeful moisture content result has taken a dip, and some days it is pointless to try harvesting at all.

Graham is near to tearing his hair out, boiling with frustration. He searches daily for fatal signs of *growing* – shoots of new growth from the heads of wheat which will render the grain soft and useless. On good days he works like a madman, far into the night, with combine lights moving across the fields like some roaring fairground monster. On bad days he frets, unable to rest, constantly checking weather reports, moisture contents, scanning the skies and doing repairs. He is on a very short fuse. The kids have learned to stay out of his way, keep the noise down, avoid confrontation. I do what I can, which isn't much, and usually wrong.

It's difficult all round, but there have been times like this before, and they pass. Nothing can get me down, even the tiresome little bouts of morning sickness that bother me some days. I cherish my pregnancy like a hidden jewel, swallow my vitamins, rest without a twinge of guilt, even early afternoons with the kitchen piled high with unwashed lunch dishes and a layer of dust gathering on the dresser. Life flows around me, while I sit cocooned and untouched by the events of the outside world. I am a bearer of new life, and I feel invincible.

*

I am quite relaxed these days, even to the point of only getting half-dressed in the mornings. Well, there's no school run, I still feel a bit yucky first thing, and it's so easy just to pull on a T-shirt and a pair of jog-pants, and thrust my feet into comfy old deck shoes with holes in the toes. Is this what's called letting oneself go? I tell myself I'm only letting go of the superficialities of life.

It's mid-morning and I haven't even run a brush through my hair when the telephone shrills. I do hope it's not for Graham, he's supervising the corn-drying in the yard. It's Jane. Her voice sounds odd, tight and strangled, as though she can't quite get her breath. "Alison? Is Graham there, dear?"

I tell her that he's tending the roaring inferno of a machine, and that I must only interrupt him for situations of life or death ... As I speak, I hear my own voice tail away uncertainly, and a coldness seems to creep up from my feet in their tatty deck shoes. There is a silence. "Jane?" I say, suddenly full of foreboding "Jane –?"

"Oh, Ali!" She crumbles suddenly, her control breaking. "Ali, it's Molly – she – she passed away last night. In her sleep. A massive heart attack, the doctor thinks–" She is weeping uncontrollably now. "Ali, I'm so sorry, what with the new baby coming and everything – and Graham so busy – she had been so well, you see, a little tired, but then we're neither of us getting any younger – and then she said she'd get an early night. This morning I took her a cup of tea – she looked so peaceful, I felt so glad she was having a good long sleep –" Jane is sobbing heartbreakingly. I picture her in her flowered housecoat, hair in curlers, sweet, quiet Jane, always a little in the shadow of her sister –

I am clutching the phone so hard my hand is hurting. I take a deep breath. "Jane, Jane darling, hold on. We'll come. Is there someone – a neighbour, who could come in to be with you?"

I hear a gulp. "Mrs Bailey next door is here now. She's so good –"

I hear myself say comforting things, give reassurances, and hang up. My heart is pounding, head whirling. This can't be happening. Not Molly. It's my mum who has the heart condition, who I've schooled myself to leave in God's hands. Not Molly. Not practical, bustling, bossy, organizing Molly. It can't be true. No. There must be some mistake.

*

There is no mistake. At mid-morning the unthinkable happens – the busy corn-drier is silenced, the golden stream stopped in mid-flow. The two of us cling together, one sweat-streaked and grimy with corn dust, the other dishevelled and tearstained, while we try to take in this world-shattering turn of events.

And our world is shaken to its foundations. Graham says little, but there is pain behind his eyes as the realization comes that now both his parents are gone; he is a forty-two year old orphan. I have this strange feeling of somehow being smaller and less important, diminished is the word that comes to mind. Someone who mattered to me and to whom I mattered, whatever our differences, has gone from the world. I feel I am of lesser account, less me.

Little time for philosophising though. For now, we must collect ourselves, make phone calls and then take the hundred mile round trip to fetch Jane.

Jane is tremulous but composed. She has not gone to pieces as I had feared. She has already seen to some of the arrangements. Molly's paperwork is efficiently up-to-date, including detailed arrangements for the funeral, which will naturally be back at our church, where her husband has his resting place. I read through the neatly-typed instructions, the words dancing in front of my bleary eyes. I'm ashamed to say I cried all the way to Jane's in the car, snuffling and sobbing my way through a box of tissues and deeply ashamed of not being the strong, supportive wife Graham needs just now. He doesn't seem to hold it against me. In fact, when we take a short toilet stop (my bladder takes no heed of events), he gives me a squeeze as I get back in the car, and says "I'm really glad you and Mum got on so well together."

I don't know whether to laugh or sob afresh. Getting on was hardly how I'd describe Molly's and my relationship. But under the odd niggles ran something strong and deep. Over the years, we had grown to understand each other, Molly and me, to respect, and yes, to love one another.

*

In a rural community like ours, a funeral is a thing of wonder. Even in the midst of seedtime and harvest, drought or disaster, everything will stop for those few hours. From every farm, large and small, up and down the valley, from cottages and shops and businesses and pubs, they will come to pay their respects, to remember the absent one, to offer what they can to the bereaved family, flowers, hugs, handshakes, a fruit cake, a few words, a casserole, some poignant memory. If for reason of accident or infirmity or some other crisis, someone cannot attend, a representative will be sent, and the fact duly noted in the newspaper report.

It's surprising how much it helps, this volume of familiar faces, this gathering of sober-hued figures, the hands, the flowers, the messages, the support and solidarity. At times like these I am so glad to be part of a farming community. I am saddened by those town burials that consist of a handful of huddled figures in a huge bare cemetery. Here the church is full to overflowing, the gallery packed tight, men in Sunday suits and women in dark dresses and jackets standing in the aisles and spilling out into a crowd standing outside, where a relay sound system has been fitted so that all can hear the service. There'll be much speculation about numbers present, folk noticing who is there, hushed talk about Molly, her age, Bob, their farming and family histories.

It's strange to be the ones in the forefront, Graham and me following Molly's simple oak coffin, with family flowers, through the lych gate and along the gravel path. It's a brighter day, the sun slants through the old yews and there are dust motes dancing in its rays. The church porch is dim and cool. Behind us comes Jane, escorted by Michael, Lauren with my dad, my mum with a small boy clutching each of her hands. A few cousins and their offspring fall in behind.

We pause in the porch, and I have a moment of confusion when I cannot think why we are here, what we're all doing. And then I see the flowers on the coffin, Molly's favourite lilies, and am overtaken by a sense of grief and loss. Molly! Green–fingered Molly, who brought me trays of petunia and begonia and marigold, which are now in full bloom in my pots and tubs. She cannot be dead!

Paul is there, in surplice and cassock, to greet us with a few reassuring words. And then we are walking into the church, Paul ahead of the coffin, and his wonderful, rich and resonant voice is proclaiming words that seem to soar to the skies. *'I am the Resurrection and the Life, he that believes in me, though he were dead, yet shall he live, and he that believes in me shall never die!'*

There is hope, and triumph, and glory in his voice, and the grief slips from me like a garment, and suddenly I am clothed with joy. I turn to Graham, and see an echo of that same joy in his face, and I squeeze his fingers tight. Molly is alive, more alive now than she has ever been!

Paul speaks about Heaven, our home. Molly had even dictated the title of his address, would you believe, and Paul, bless him, has risen to the occasion. He speaks meaningfully of that place where time will be no more, there'll be no partings, and every tear will be wiped away by God's own hand. It's not a long homily. I smile, thinking of Molly's neatly–typed instructions; 'Don't make the service too long. People get fidgety, and it's hard on those who have to stand.'

Michael gives a tribute, standing straight and tall in his new suit, his hair burnished, making me think somehow of a knight in armour. I'd offered to help with the writing of it, but he'd waved me away. He'd do it himself. And he does, just a few childhood memories of his Nan that I'd long forgotten, but that nevertheless bring a lump to my throat. A few jokes, which raise smiles. And then Lauren plays her flute, a hauntingly beautiful melody that has the congregation reaching for their hankies again. Tears, and smiles, memories and laughter. A life remembered.

The little boys are taking it all in ,wide–eyed and inquisitive. I feel a pang that they had Molly for such a short time, that our unborn baby will not know her at all.

But later, at the graveside, as we sing Molly's favourite hymn *'When the Roll is called up yonder'*, I stop singing suddenly, because some other words have come into my mind, very faintly but with that clarity that belies any human origin.

'I have done all things well.'

And I know that Molly's life and times on earth are complete, that she is safe home and that all things with her are indeed well.

*

We are totally exhausted by the time we've negotiated the crush of people at the tea in the Church Hall afterwards, spoken to everyone and conveyed our thanks, wished goodbyes and safe journeys and promised to stay in touch. Graham and I would like to crawl into bed straight away but there are still a few stragglers and the family to be fed. Jane proves a tower of strength, making tea, cutting sandwiches, clearing up.

The two small boys seem energised by this unusual day.

"Nanny Molly won't be able to make me a birthday cake this year," observes Adam, stuffing his face with iced sponge that someone has donated.

"Unless she makes one in Heaven," says Luke. "Mum, do people make cakes in Heaven?"

I am too weary to think of an answer to this one, but Lauren gives me a quick glance and says "Come on, I'll play a game on the play station with you before bed."

Bless her; she's trying to spare my feelings. She bundles them both out of the room, and I hear Luke say "Anyway, it would get squashed, wouldn't it, dropping down" and both of them collapsing in giggles. My own mouth twitches. I catch Graham's eye and he is positively grinning. It's good they don't feel the need to tiptoe around, that they can laugh and remember their grandmother with joy and tales and terrible jokes. They're good kids, all of them.

Jane puts a cup of tea down beside me and I kick off my black patent pumps and wriggle my toes in relief. Tomorrow I have my first scan appointment. Today we said goodbye to a loved mother and grandmother, very soon we'll have the chance to say hello to the next family member.

Chapter Twenty-Nine

Sonia comes to visit, bringing Harry, Victoria, and a lovely bunch of pink roses for me. She has acquired a second-hand car, and is getting about a little more these days. The weather has picked up, and it's dry and pleasant with the slightly dusty feel of summer moving on.

The boys soon migrate to the stream, slowed to a trickle now but still with the power to draw kids like a magnet. In the far wheat fields, harvest is going on apace. The boys begin to build a dam, a hopeful construction of stones and mud. Victoria toddles after them, in denim pedal pushers, a cap with a sun flap at the back, and pink crocs that make her feet look enormous on the ends of her spindly legs. Sonia flutters nervously, anxious that she doesn't get wet, but Victoria seems content to stand on the shingle, scooping up handfuls of pebbles and flinging them into the water.

Sonia and I, with a big jug of fruit juice between us and a stack of plastic beakers, seat ourselves on the battered café chairs at the round table I constructed last summer with an old metal stand and a heavy circular marble top. I placed it under the shade of the old willow by the stream, with romantic notions of breakfasting to the sound of gently murmuring water. Well, it was a nice thought. And it is very pleasant sitting here, listening to children's voices and doing absolutely nothing.

"It leaves such a massive hole, when a parent dies," muses Sonia, gazing up into the gently moving willow fronds. "I mean, they've always been there. If not nearby, somewhere in the background. Your backup, so to speak. Then there's nobody to fall back on. You're on your own."

I remember that Sonia's mother died not very long ago. And she is truly on her own. It makes me feel a little ashamed. I'm feeling keenly the loss of Molly, but I still have my own mum and dad, a husband, kids, Jane. I have friends and neighbours in abundance.

This is surely as good a time as any to talk about her husband. It would make such a difference if he was back in their lives. She leans forward, smiling suddenly as she remembers something. "By the way, how did the appointment go?"

My own face splits into a big grin. "Oh, fine! Everything's great!"

I fumble in the breast pocket of my denim shirt. Since the scan a few days ago, I've carried the photo around with me, pulling it out every so often to look again and make sure it's all real. It's beginning to look dog-eared already. I push it across the table to Sonia. She bends her head over it, studying the large drooping head, the round tummy with thick umbilical cord attached, the skinny little budding limbs.

"Oh, how beautiful! It's wonderful to see, isn't it? A real baby, living and growing!"

My own family's reactions had been less gratifying. Graham professed not to be able to understand the picture at all. Jane seemed faintly embarrassed, Michel loftily disinterested, though that could have been an act. Lauren thought it grotesque and asked if the baby was deformed. Adam and Luke giggled in a mystified kind of way.

Well, it takes another mother to see beauty in an eight-week foetus, I guess. I feel a warm fellow-feeling towards Sonia. Then quick empathy as her eyes go from the grainy picture to her daughter, squealing and jumping up and down at the water's edge, and cloud over with sadness. I tuck the photo away into the pocket over my heart and take a deep breath.

"Sonia?"

She looks at me enquiringly. The slight tan she's gained over the summer has made her look younger and more relaxed. Harry's looking fitter too, less pale and podgy. He's hardly recognisable as the bully who terrorised Adam and made his life such a misery. They're working together as a team, painstakingly constructing their dam stone upon stone, while Luke fetches mud in a plastic seaside bucket. All of them are getting wet and very filthy, but, hey, it's high summer and they're having a whale of a time.

Sonia's eyebrows are raised, looking at me. I take another breath. I'm not finding this easy. "The thing is – well, I hardly know how to say this, but – I've met your husband, Sonia. Recently."

She goes white suddenly, then the colour rushes back in two red spots on her cheeks. "What? You've seen John? What do you mean – where –?"

It's been a real shock. I pour a glass of juice and push it across to her. All those times John has lurked about the area and she's had no idea. None at all.

She stares at me in disbelief and amazement as I tell her as completely as I can about my dealings with her husband. I do gloss over the affair at the Vicarage Fayre, and the police station, although I'm surprised she hasn't heard that story from someone else. But then, Sonia doesn't mix much.

She looks more and more incredulous. And when I come to John's request that maybe he could see her and the kids, her expression becomes tinged with anger.

"Oh, so he thinks he can just waltz back in where he left off," she says bitterly, putting down her beaker so hard it slops over. "Typical John! And then push off again if he finds he doesn't like it!"

"I think he may have changed" – I say tentatively, noticing that Victoria has looked round at the altered tone of her mother's voice. "He seemed genuinely sorry and wanting to make amends" –

"Amends my foot! And fancy sneaking about, trying to get round me through some other woman! No chance! He blew it once, left us in bits. He'll not get the chance to do it again!"

Oh dear, it's all gone pear-shaped. She stands up and calls "Victoria! Harry! Come along now, time to go."

"Oh – but they're having such a great time. And I thought you'd all stay for tea" –

She gives me a steely look. I am obviously deemed guilty of conniving with her husband in the most underhand of ways.

"Sorry," she says shortly "Things to do. Come on, Harry! There, look, now you've soaked your shoe." She actually gives him a slap, and yanks Victoria by the arm. The little girl's eyes well up with tears and her mouth wobbles. She's not used to this.

If I'd expected this kind of reaction I'd have kept my mouth firmly shut. I don't know quite what I did expect. Some ray of hope, at least. But my name is definitely mud to Sonia at the moment, almost on a par with her errant husband. I watch her stump off across the yard, a reluctant kid in each hand, to her car parked under the sycamore.

"She looks mad as hops," observes Adam, coming up from the stream with mud up to his elbows and squelching trainers.

I have nothing to add to that.

*

157

I am in West Wales, at the house overlooking the bay, with its beautifully kept garden tucked down behind the house that was Jane's and Molly's. We have driven here, Jane and I, to sort out and pack away some of Molly's things. It will be hard for Jane, I think, going back to a lonely house, and maybe my being here that first day will soften it a little.

I stand for a moment on the little deck area, with French doors opening from the dining room, looking towards the sea. I've stood here many times, watching the water in all kinds of moods and at every season, usually waiting for the moment when my children, having headed for the beach the moment they got here, would suddenly burst out from among the gentle dunes and tall marram– grass, and appear as small figures on the sand, sometimes turning to wave to us watching from above as they headed for the water. They considered that one of the coolest things about Nanny Molly was her house at the seaside, and a trip here has always been a real treat.

Today, the children are busy with their own activities back home and Molly is no longer here. The sea is calm, ultramarine, with fluffy waves ruffling the surface like frills on a party dress. Maybe there'll be time for a quick walk to the beach before I leave. I breathe in lungfuls of the salty air and turn back to the house, with its neat flower beds planted with geraniums and lobelia, bright and blooming. It's often too windy here for hanging baskets, but Molly has planted up wooden tubs, stone troughs, sturdy window boxes with ivies and trailing plants spilling out of them.

Jane is in the kitchen at the back, standing at the table with her hand pressed to her heart. Unusually for her, she hasn't put the kettle on yet. The house is still and empty, silent except for the ticking of the flowered china clock on the wall.

I say gently "Are you okay?" and she looks up and nods, and says "It seems so – strange. One of us was usually here if the other went out. If I'd been to the shops, or the library, or to some appointment, she'd be here when I got back, kettle on, something baking, and her in here chopping things for chutney, or stirring jam, or pricking out little plants – I can't believe" – She sits down suddenly on one of the ladder–back chairs, her face working. "Ali, what am I going to do now she's gone?"

I pat her shoulder and fill the kettle at the tap. This is going to be harder than I thought.

Later, we go through the house, trying to decide what should be done about Molly's things. Everything is in apple-pie order, of course. Molly's clothes hang neatly in her wardrobe, plastic bagged and scented with the little pot-pourri sachets she made herself from her beloved rose petals. I look at the bed with its pretty sprigged duvet, where Molly quietly breathed her last. Someone has tidied it and pulled up the covers. Jane and I pick out a few things for Oxfam, but it's a harder job than I'd thought, my back begins to ache and we fill only one black bin bag.

Somehow, we find ourselves sitting on the bed with a shoebox of old photos between us. Some of these I've never seen before. Molly has meticulously kept albums of family photos, her and John in their young days, Graham as a baby, a small child, growing up, our wedding, the grandchildren. Others date back much further. There's a black and white one of two young girls in print dresses, squinting and shading their eyes against the sun, laughing.

"That's Molly and me," says Jane, picking it up. She smiles, the first I've seen today. "Our mum made those dresses. We hated them. Wanted proper ones from a shop, or a real dressmaker, with puff sleeves and lace collars. Mum couldn't do puffs, just plain sewing. It was wartime, you see. Everything rationed and scarce, we had to make do and mend. I think those dresses may have started out as curtains."

She pauses, the photo still between finger and thumb, her eyes going far away, remembering. "We were evacuees, you know, Molly and me." I hadn't known, and am surprised. "You were city kids then?"

"Oh yes. Londoners. We were evacuated down to the Welsh borders. Most kids were sent somewhere. You heard terrible things about the way some were treated."

"Were you badly treated?"

"Oh no, not at all! We were with a lovely couple, older, he was a retired farm-worker, they were wonderful to us, treated us just like we were their own. They kept chickens and ducks, and we each had our own little garden plot. Mostly vegetables. Digging for victory, they called it. But they gave us flower seeds to plant too, mignonette, larkspur, night-scented stock. I think that's where Molly got her passion for growing things, and her green fingers."

I smile, imagining those two little girls in their shapeless print dresses, earnestly cultivating their garden plots.

Jane says "We went home, after the war, of course. But we couldn't wait to get back, we missed the country so. When we'd both finished school we got back as soon as we could. I worked in a market garden for many years. Molly got a job in an auctioneers' office. That is where she met Bob. He came in with his father one day to settle up for some heifers he'd bought, and as they say, the rest is history."

History indeed. Part of Graham's history, and our children's. I hadn't known any of this. I wish I'd spoken more to Molly, about her life, to my own mum and dad for that matter. Time slips by so quickly and is gone. I sigh, and change position to ease my aching back. It's afternoon already. We've made a scratch lunch from supplies in the cupboards here. I must be on my way soon. I replace the photos in the box.

"Should we do a quick shop before I leave? Milk, fresh bread, that kind of thing?"

Jane says "Oh no, there's no need. There's a little 24–hour shop just down the road." She hesitates. "You've been so kind, Alison. I've loved being with your family. So full of life. Bert and I were always sorry we didn't have our own family."

She bends her head, gets up and smooths the bedspread, but I have seen the tear slipping down her cheek. I look round the quiet bedroom, so neat, so full of Molly's presence and yet so lifeless. Her things are here, photos, clothes, bed, but she is gone.

Jane is closing the cupboards, shoulders bowed. Realization hits me suddenly. Jane will not be happy here, without her sister. The coast, the sweet little house, the lovely garden, will be meaningless with none to share it.

Hardly thinking, I hear myself say "Jane, if you'd rather stay on with us, we'd love to have you. We've room. The kids would love it. You could sell this place, or rent it out – perfect for holidays. You could come here yourself if you wanted a change. What do you think?"

She turns, and her face says it all. "Oh, Alison! I would like that! It needn't be permanent, just for a while – I would pay my way, of course. And I could help when the baby comes –"

So it is, that, when I leave a little while later, it is with Jane beside me and her cases still packed, in the boot. We will decide about the cottage when Graham can be consulted.

I didn't get my walk on the beach after all. I am very tired all of a sudden, and the ache in my back has not eased. We are within a few miles of home when it becomes something else; a sharp, persistent pain that shoots around to the front and for a moment takes my breath away.

Chapter Thirty

Strange, that in the space of a mere twenty-four hours, everything can change, the roof of my world cave in, and still the larger world keeps turning, the sun rising and setting, life going on.

I have little recollection of those last couple of miles home, gripping the steering wheel with Jane white-faced beside me, wishing she'd learned to drive, while pain strikes again and again with deadly persistence at my insides, and I know with a mind-numbing certainty that it's not going to be all right. I do remember Jane fumbling with my mobile phone, trying to read the little numbers, to get hold of Graham, or ring 999, or both. She must have succeeded, because the ambulance arrives at almost the same time as we do, and I remember the paramedic opening the car door and trying to prise my hands from the steering wheel.

It was a long night, alone in a side ward, punctuated by nurses questioning and checking me, and a doctor, ridiculously young, peering over his spectacles. I remember the sound of their shoes, squeaking quietly on the hard shiny floor. There's a lot of pain, blood and sweat; the tears come later, when it's all over. I bleed heavily and the young doctor decrees a D&C, 'just to clear everything up', and another night in hospital. In between, I doze, waking with a start every time and feeling the tears spring afresh. Graham is there sometimes, and my mum and dad, but I'm woozy from the anaesthetic and they seem hazy and unreal.

Foolishly, I refuse the offer of a sleeping pill when night comes. I've dozed all day and now, when I'd give anything to escape into deep sleep, it eludes me. All night long tears seep out from under my eyelids, open or closed, seemingly of their own accord. The pillow is soaked; nobody has thought to bring me more tissues. A nurse looks in sometime in the wee small hours, looks at my red swollen face and says "Oh dear, we can't have this, you know." She brings a cool wet flannel and bathes my face, fetches a box of man–size tissues and a fresh pillow, then she actually sits by the bed and strokes my hand. It's kind of her, she must have plenty else to do.

"You are an angel," I say weakly, and she smiles at my foolishness and gives my fingers a squeeze. "No angel, just someone who's been through this myself. It will get better."

I can't see how, but I drift off with her holding my hand and sleep for an hour or two.

In the morning, the same young doctor discharges me, frowning over his spectacles. He says I should be back to normal in a week or so. Has he been on duty all the time I've been here? No wonder he looks so tired and has a dark stubble round his chin.

Graham picks me up and drives me home, not saying much. What is there to say, after all? 'Never mind, it might be for the best?' 'You never know, there might have been something wrong with it?' 'You'll be as good as new in no time.' I've heard all those things said regarding other miscarriages, and if he said any of them I would scream. He has the wisdom not to.

Mum is at my house; she and Jane faff about putting me to bed and bringing cups of tea. They tell me my friends have stepped in once again and taken the boys off for the day. Everything is under control. Nothing to bother my head about. Just get some rest, dear. That's what you need most.

Wrong. What I need, with a desperate hunger that consumes me and scares me, is my baby, who is gone.

*

The summer is wearing on, school holidays going by at lightning speed as they always do. The winter wheat is gathered in, and the spring crops being harvested. We have a dry spell; the leaves have lost their fresh green and have that tired, dusty look. Lauren is off on holiday with Paula's family for two weeks, to Tenerife, no less. Michael's O–level results came, three A's, four B's, one B+. He celebrates with his friends and comes home late, and I suspect a celebratory drink or two has been consumed. Now he's off on a camping trip in Snowdonia with an Outward Bound group.

I am up and about, back to normal. Except I'm not. I smile, and laugh, and get on with things. But inside I'm aching, screaming, asking questions and finding no answers. Shouting, raging, demanding. Why? Was it my fault? A punishment? I know better than that. Then what?

A lesson? Am I such a slow learner, so hard of hearing that my heart needs to be broken before I will take heed? I shout at God to tell me, but no answer comes.

I wonder at myself amidst all this inner confusion. The baby was not even planned. I've only known about it for a few weeks. A few weeks of knowing and planning, of dreaming and anticipating, and a black and white scan picture. That's all I have to show. I'll never know if it was a son or daughter, whether it was dark or fair, intelligent or plodding, a doer or a thinker, an athlete or a scholar. It came and it passed, a non-event.

Paul and Caroline visit, with a bouquet of greeny-cream lilies, my favourite flower. I'm left tactfully alone with them in the sitting room, after Jane has served tea, with cups and saucers, and little shortbread biscuits. Caroline seems ill at ease. She's usually good in this kind of situation, gracefully bringing in order and calm, the right words and a touch of beauty, that all adds up to comfort and reassurance. I've often heard her described as a wonderful visitor by those about the parish who have received her ministrations. This, though, seems to be a little too near the knuckle, too close to home. After a peck on the cheek and a few well-chosen words, she drifts elegantly across to the sideboard and begins to arrange the lilies in a vase Jane has brought. I remember with a pang that Becky's baby must be due in just a few weeks.

Paul puts down his cup and saucer and leans towards me from the opposite sofa. Half of my mind registers the fact that the chintz is looking a little grubby again. Maybe the person who warned me that flowered cream, green and pink chintz was not the best choice for family upholstery, was right.

"And how are you, Alison?"

I open my mouth and begin to form the words that say "Oh, fine thanks, just about back to normal," but, looking into his steady brown eyes, I hear instead a tight, unsteady voice declaring "Actually, I feel like *shit*!"

I see out of the corner of my eye that Caroline stiffens, and although she doesn't turn her head she stands frozen for a moment, a long-stemmed lily in her hands. Then she resumes her tasteful arrangement.

Paul nods encouragingly. "Go on."

I haven't meant to say all this, but I do, feeling that a dam has burst and cannot be held back now.

"I'm angry, Paul. I don't understand. Why? Why? What's the point of something starting, then stopping, just like that? What is God thinking? It's as if he offers you something, lets you see how wonderful it's going to be, and then snatches it away. And it's not just me. Every time I look at the news, there's some child that's been abused, or is starving to death with flies crawling over its mouth and nose, or sold into prostitution, and there are all those refugees, and children disappearing – and..." I can't stop now, everything is flooding out, all the sorrows an injustice and suffering that God does nothing to stop, and maybe does not care about at all –

Paul reaches over and touches my hand very gently. "Maybe it's not the best idea to watch the News programmes just now, Ali."

What kind of answer is that? I feel some of my anger turn towards Paul. He's supposed to be God's representative, isn't he?

"But it's still happening, whether I watch it or not. And what about kids like Victoria Dent"– I am sobbing now and my words are not making much sense.

"Paul, I want to know. Why does God let – why doesn't he stop the dreadful things" – and then I lose all control, and my voice is a wail, "Where is my baby, Paul? Where is my baby?"

Suddenly, Caroline is beside me on the sofa, in a whirl of white cotton and flowery perfume, and she is holding me tight, and I am clinging to her for dear life, and the tears that are falling onto my green scatter cushions are not all mine.

Paul sits quietly across from us and doesn't say anything but I think perhaps he's praying. Caroline doesn't say much either, just sits close and weeps with me, and I think of that first baby that she gave up, maybe never even held, and I am glad she's holding me, and I begin to see why she is reckoned to be such a treasure as a visitor, and a vicar's wife, and why Paul adores her so much.

At last the storm is over and we draw apart a little. She produces a pack of scented tissues from her bag and we both mop. I must look a sight, but she has the kind of face that doesn't go red and blotchy when she cries, or eyes that puff up into slits. She doesn't say anything at all, but after a moment gets up, smooths her white cotton skirt and goes to finish the flower arrangement.

Paul clears his throat and says "I'd like to give you some answers, I really would. But I'm afraid I don't have many to give. I only know that we're part of a fallen, sick world and that in such a world the innocent are often the ones who suffer most. But I do know that God knows and cares about every one of these little ones, that his heart breaks over them, that he knows each name and commends each one who will reach out to help them. That he will gather them in his arms at the last and wipe every tear from their eyes." He pauses and then goes on, very gently "And he knows every detail of your precious baby, Ali, and in his wisdom has taken that little one back to himself. What his purposes are we don't know, maybe one day we'll see what greater blessings may have been possible because of this. But rest assured – all those little ones, lost by miscarriage, or abortion, or stillbirth, are with him, safe and happy, and that one day you'll meet your little boy or girl."

I am silent, drained and empty but with something that might be the beginnings of peace. He glances across at Caroline, and adds, very softly "And he knows about every child separated from parents, or adopted at birth, or kidnapped, or forced to flee their homes, or ill–treated – and there will be a time when healing and restoration comes."

I see, just for a moment, the lily stems tremble in Caroline's hands. She bends her head for a moment, and then raises it, and looks at Paul, a long steady look that carries gratitude and love and the kind of courage that makes me feel that maybe, I, too, will manage to get through.

Paul has just one more word of advice for me, before they leave.

"Don't forget to tell Graham how you're feeling, Ali. Remember he's lost a child too."

Chapter Thirty-One

The summer is wearing on; all too soon it will be the end of the holidays and the start of a new school year. Michael will be a sixth-former, studying A-levels, one step nearer to his chosen career and his future as an adult.

"Strange, to think of being the parents of men and women," muses Jo, who has invited me round for coffee. "I mean, when do we get to the stage of feeling grown-up ourselves?"

I shake my head. I don't know, I haven't got there yet. Do any of us ever feel we have become the person we were created to be? I comfort myself with the thought that surely Molly did, and my mum and dad do – or do they? It's too big a thing to get my head round.

"I suppose we'll have to think about school uniforms," says Jo with a sigh. "Kids seem to sprout like weeds in the summer; nothing ever fits from the last term."

I sigh too. "I know. At least Michael won't need uniform in the sixth form. But Lauren's stuff is not the 'in' thing any more, and both Luke and Adam say their shoes have shrunk. Another trip into town, I suppose." I sigh again and take a sip of coffee.

Jo puts down her own mug and gives me a keen look. "We can go together, if you like." She pauses for a moment, and then says "Ali, if you don't mind me saying so, you're not looking all that wonderful. Think you should see the doctor?"

"No, he says I don't need to see him again. I'm just a bit run down, that's all, with everything that's happened, and it being the busy time of year."

"All the same, you should get checked out. You may be anaemic."

"Maybe you could sneak me a bottle of Stuart's iron pills," I say lightly. "Or I'll get Sue to fix me up one of her potions. Perhaps not, though. I tried one of her tonics once and it nearly blew my head off."

We both grin, and I hope she will drop the subject.

*

To be truthful, though, I don't feel too clever at all. Although the deep anger and grief have eased since my visit from Paul and Caroline, I'm not feeling myself. I'm tired all the time, short tempered, and I'm horribly anxious about every little thing. The boys think I've turned into a real spoilsport and Lauren eyes me warily and avoids me whenever she can. She is off on holiday with Paula and her family, to sunny Tenerife, which necessitates a trip to shop for tiny bikinis and miniscule tops and flip-flops. I'm full of forebodings about randy foreign men, or drunken Brit boys on holiday, or kidnappers, though Paula's mum assures me they'll be well supervised. Lauren herself is utterly confident, beautiful and sanguine about the whole thing. Even my mother thinks it will be a good experience for her. But then, Mum and Lauren are very much alike, poised, talented, confident and not given to too much self-doubt and introspection. It's me who's the odd one out, who fails so often, ties herself into knots, and who, when push comes to shove, cannot cope with life.

Once or twice I've caught my mum and Jane having low-voiced little conflabs in the kitchen, which fade into silence when I appear. Graham, I am ashamed to say, gets the brunt of my fretfulness. Poor chap, as my mum observed one day, he can't do right for doing wrong. If Molly was here, I'm sure she would tell me to pull myself together and snap out of it.

I'm exhausted by night-time, in spite of the fact that Jane has taken on a lot of the household chores, yet I can't sleep for more than an hour or two. Hour after hour I lie awake in a tangle of warm sticky sheets, while Graham slumbers beside me. My mind will not relax, busy with problems real and imagined. I've tried to talk to Graham, and, to give him his due, he tries hard to understand and sympathise, but I know he's well out of his depth. More than once, I have waited for an answer to my confused ranting and received only a gentle snore. He is so tired himself, so hard-pressed with getting the harvest finished, his mind already running ahead to ploughing and sowing for next year. To him my concerns must seem mere trivialities, my tendency to drama-queen status gone over the top.

Frustrated and frazzled, desperate and sad, I often get up again and walk around the silent house, envying the sleepers behind their closed doors. One night, I do not go back to my own bed, but turn into Lauren's room. Her bed has been neatly made up with fresh linen by Jane and my mum. I crawl in between the clean fresh sheets and press myself against the far wall. Somehow, the feel of my forehead and hands and body against the cold hard plaster surface brings a measure of relief. I go there again the next night and the next. And then I don't go to our own bed at all, but look forward all day to that narrow firm mattress, that quiet space and the feel of cold plaster against my skin.

*

My mother has finally made me promise to see the doctor, after I dropped a perfectly ordinary white pottery cereal bowl on the tiled floor at her house one day and burst into tears so unstoppable that you would have thought I'd destroyed a prized piece of Crown Derby.

I promise, and she stands over me while I make the call from her house. The lines are busy, so I say I'll phone when I get home. She gives me a look that says "You'd better!"

My memory is suffering too. I forget to make the call, and it's only when I'm passing the surgery on my way home from the Co–Op next morning that I remember. Maybe they can fit me in at the end of morning surgery, which won't be long. Should be a quick in and out job.

Wrong. There's quite a queue at the reception desk, and they seem a little short staffed. The girl on duty is dealing with a white–haired man who seems quite sprightly but hard of hearing. She's handing him an appointment card and speaking loudly and clearly. "That's your appointment for Hearing Aid clinic next week, Mr Baines. And below it, I've put a reminder that you'll need to come in again a couple of weeks later for your flu injection."

"Eh? What's that? Why do I need to come in a new direction? I usually come straight from home along the footpath."

"No, no, not a new direction. Your FLU INJECTION!"

"All right, no need to shout. Why couldn't you have just written it down for me?"

The queue is slow–moving. I'm almost tempted to slip out, convince myself it's almost lunchtime and I'll come another day. But suddenly there's movement and I'm at the desk, and the receptionist is looking at her computer screen and saying that I'm fortunate, there's just been a cancellation and I can go right on in now.

The doctor asks a few pertinent questions and I disgrace myself by bursting into tears again. She hands me tissues, scribbles a few notes, clicks her mouse and checks the screen. Then she turns back to me.

"You're suffering from clinical depression, Mrs Harper. Not

surprising, considering what you've told me. Two severe emotional shocks, one hard on the heels of another, plus all the hormone activity that's going on just at the moment. But we'll have you right as rain again. I'm prescribing a course of anti–depressants, and maybe you'd like to see a counsellor? I do warn you though it may take a few weeks to set that up – they're very busy."

I murmur that I'll have to think about that, and that I'm not over keen on pills either, and don't want to become dependent. She smiles. "You won't. A course of anti–depressants is just that, a course, like you'd take a course of antibiotics. It will probably take three to four months. They're not tranquillisers, although as you take them at night you may find they help you sleep. It will take two or three weeks for you to feel a marked improvement though, so don't give up after a day or two. And go easy on yourself. You've been through a lot."

I thank her and leave, clutching my prescription. I think I'll have to hide them from Graham, he's a bit funny about pills and has to be in a great deal of pain before he'll consent to take anything. Even then, when the prescribed dose is one or two tablets, he'll probably take half. He gets it from his mother, who had a real aversion to pill–taking. I can remember trying to get her to take a couple of paracetamol when she had a miserable streaming cold, and her firmly refusing to give in to such weakness.

"Oh no dear, I don't take *pills*! A nice dose of hot lemon does just as much good!"

So she takes a glass of Lemsip, which does the trick, as she smugly informs me an hour or so later. I refrain from telling her Lemsip has the maximum dose of paracetamol allowed, plus other assorted chemical additives.

*

I dutifully take my pills, though they don't seem to be helping much. Michael is back from camping, looking tanned and fit, with holes in every single sock he took with him and his clothes practically in rags. They did a lot of rock–climbing, it seems, and some abseiling and mountain walking and a bit of pot–holing thrown in. It was all great. He leaves a pile of ripped, torn and stinking washing on the utility floor and heads off for a hot shower. They've been doing their ablutions in cold mountain streams, he tells me cheerfully, and one time a passing sheep nibbled holes in someone's thermal underwear. All good stuff, but he seems glad to be home. He's thumbing his mobile as he goes, apparently they could not always get signals up in the mountains and he has loads of texting to catch up on.

I go shopping for kids clothes with Jo and am exhausted at the end of the day, but it's more of a normal kind of tiredness. Jane, bless her, has made shepherds' pie and plum crumble in my absence, and I find I'm really hungry for the first time in ages. And I even find myself laughing at one of Luke's terrible jokes. I'm beginning to feel a little more human again. Maybe the medication is beginning to work after all.

A night or two later I pause at the door to Lauren's room. She's due home soon and will want her bed back. Suddenly, the narrow bed and hard cold wall seem far less attractive than my own fleece-topped king-size and the warm familiar shape of my husband. I close Lauren's door and tiptoe along the passage to mine and Graham's room. He is asleep already, snoring gently, sprawled half across my side of the bed as well as his own. He's got used to me not being there. I slip under the duvet and he mumbles a little and turns over to give me room, not really waking up.

In the morning, I wake to find his arm flung across me and his breath gently ruffling my hair. I feel wonderfully rested and, for the first time in ages, without that deep crushing feeling of loss and despair. I turn my head to look at the clock – uh-oh, it's later than I thought. Graham is waking up, sees the time too and begins to disentangle himself. It's so good just to watch his little morning routines, the yawn, the way he rasps the stubble on his chin and runs a hand through his hair, the kicking off of the duvet and swinging his legs over the side. He sees me watching and leans across again, nuzzling my neck. "I'm glad you're back. I missed you."

Yes, I'm back, and I'm glad too.

Chapter Thirty-Two

Now that I'm better, as Graham remarks some days later, maybe we'll have some sense around here. I'm aware of the sighs of relief that have gone up following my marked improvement, but I wasn't aware that things had particularly gone to pieces in the last few weeks. In fact, I'd imagined that we'd managed rather well, thanks mainly to the sterling efforts of Jane and Mum in the kitchen, Dad ferrying people around and my friends entertaining the boys. Maybe I'm not as indispensable as I'd thought. The children, without exception, reckon that it's been the best summer holiday they've ever had. So I am grateful to my husband for crediting me with some contribution, however small, to the smooth running of the household.

Lauren arrives home, sleek, tanned, and rather smug. She shows us pictures of her and Paula by the pool, her and Paula in a boat, her and Paula dressed up for dinner, her and Paula – what's this? – in a group hug picture with a couple of dark-haired, white-toothed teenage boys.

She whisks that photo away quickly, a tinge of pink in her cheeks.

"They're Carlos and Juan, two – er – boys we met."

"Yes, so we can see. Are they waiters or something?"

"Oh, Mum! Course not! They were helping at the Kids' Club. Coaching, sport, and that. Paula and I helped too, as they were short-staffed and we'd had experience."

I hardly think a one-off event at a vicarage fete counts as valid qualification.

"Did the people in charge know you were only fourteen?"

"Don't know, they didn't ask. It wasn't an issue. Not everyone is so uptight about things like that. Much more relaxed."

Hmm, I wonder to what extent this relaxation applied? Thank goodness Paula's parents were there, and they're sensible people whose judgement I trust. But that little comfort is dispelled when Lauren seems to read my thoughts (she knows me well) and remarks that

Paula's mum and dad are so cool. "We had a system worked out so we wouldn't get in each other's hair. Mornings we went to Kids Club and then to the pool while they were on the beach. Afternoons we went to the beach while they stayed by the pool."

Not much supervision, there, then. Whatever could they have been thinking, with those two Romeos hanging around. Lauren goes on "They didn't want to go out in the evenings, being older, so they usually stayed in the bar while we went out clubbing – most nights we got in before dawn, though."

The little madam, she's winding me up again and I fall for it every time! She collapses in giggles on the sofa, kicking up her feet in their rope–soled sandals. "Don't worry, Mum, we hardly escaped from them for five minutes at a time. Who do you think took all the pics? And Paula and me think Carlos and Juan are both gay – anyway, they did nothing but pose and look in the mirror and make sure their hair was just so"– She gives her own hair an exaggerated pat, and then begins to rummage in the rucksack for the gifts she's brought.

I've missed Lauren, and I'm so happy to have her home.

*

Tragedy isn't quite done with us; Luke's hamster has finally shuffled off her mortal coil and been discovered in a lifeless heap beneath her running wheel. Luke is inconsolable, despite our assurances of the long and happy life his pet had enjoyed. This one had lived for almost three years and become a part of the family. We called her Charles Atlas, despite her gender, because of her large size and superhuman(or should that be superhamster?) strength. Our hamster residence has a door in the top, and Charley very soon got the knack of standing on the top of the intricate system of tunnels and tubes and reaching up with her little paws to push open the door from below. Even when we resorted to weighing down the door with a collection of phone directories and hefty catalogues, she still managed somehow to push them aside and squeeze through. Having an exploring bent, she was retrieved at various times from Lauren's old Barbie hairdressing salon, where she'd made a cute little nest of Barbie hairpieces, from the sitting room coal scuttle, from holes in the walls and gaps behind the skirting boards. Only when we installed a strong wire fastener was she obliged to stay home and content herself with hours and hours of spinning in the wheel.

And now she's gone, and that squeaking wheel will be heard no longer. We hold the obligatory funeral service, with a Ferraro Rocher box coffin and a posy of daisies and periwinkle, and lay her to rest near the graves of Ben and numerous cats, rabbits and guinea pigs who have shared our home and hearts over the years. I say a short prayer and Luke wails with an intensity that would put a professional mourner to shame.

To provide a distraction, we decide that now might be a good time to install our new puppy. He's been ready to leave his mum for some while now, and looking at Luke's woebegone face, I feel this might be the right psychological moment. I'd intended waiting until the school term started, but, hey, what's a few days?

We always seem to travel en masse when it's anything to do with some animal, so a whole gang of us traipse over the fields to bring home the new family member. Even Jane comes, which rather surprises me. I'd somehow felt that Dai's eccentricities and questionable bachelor habits might put her off, but not a bit of it. They've met once or twice about the place, and seem to have taken quite a shine to each other. She says he reminds her of her foster dad from her evacuee years. And Dai remarked to Graham one day that his aunt seemed to be 'a tidy little 'ooman.'

Anyway, it's a lovely evening, and there might not be too many more nice summer evenings. Already the days are beginning to draw in a little.

Our puppy is the only one left now, and his sheepdog mother is well fed up with him. He craves company and tries to trail after her, but is discouraged by Jess, who has given him many a sharp nip for his pains, and by Dai, who has to shut him away every time Jess is needed for working sheep.

"No idea at all," says Dai disparagingly. "I did try him running with Jess once or twice, but he's got no notion what to do, runs in among the sheep, wants to play with them, the fool. And eating his head off. Sooner the better you takes him away and lets Jess and me get on with our job."

We have caught Dai in a grumpy mood, but he brightens when we tell him we have indeed come to take the pup away. I notice Jane peering round his cluttered kitchen, taking in the piles of Farmers Weekly cheek by jowl with unwashed dishes and what looks like mildewed porridge in a saucepan on the stove.

"I haven't had time to clear away yet," he says by way of apology. "But you're welcome to a cup of tea if you can wait for the kettle."

The pup has appeared, his mournful eyes brightening with a ray of hope as he sees the influx of new people – Jane and myself, Lauren and the two boys. He already has the long velvety ears of a Bassett, the domed head and drooping jowls and sad demeanour. But the other side of his pedigree shows in the shorter body, the longer legs with feathery trimmings, and the smaller, neater paws. He's rather odd–looking but I think he might turn out quite an attractive dog.

The two boys fall on him with whoops of glee. The pup looks first nervous, uncertainly wagging his collie's tail, then hopeful, and finally a spark of joy lights his sad eyes. The boys offer him an old raggedy rabbit toy they've brought, and he tussles with them, snarling baby snarls and gripping the rabbit and shaking it, while Jane and I drink tea from thick mugs and Lauren looks at Dai's family photos on the cluttered sideboard. I see that the pup has the powerful shoulders of a Bassett Hound too, the strong jaws and firm grip. And he seems very much at home with children, another Bassett trait.

The shadows are lengthening as we walk home across the fields, the pup being passed from one to the other of the three children and carried home in style.

"I know it's not my place to say it," remarks Jane thoughtfully, "but have you ever thought of asking Dai to Sunday dinner?"

I have to admit I never have, though he does call by for a cup of tea and slice of cake now and again. "Do you think I should?"

"Well, it might be a kind thought. He looks as though he doesn't feed himself properly or cook a decent meal. Must be a lonely life."

It must. I don't know why I've never thought of asking him before. I wonder how many other lonely farmers there might be scattered around the hills and valleys and rural places of our land. You hear of a very high suicide rate among farmers, mostly due to the loneliness of their occupation and lack of communication. Not that Dai is the suicidal type, he's far too cantankerous for that. Just like his donkey. Which reminds me; Caroline has further plans for that donkey, and it might be helpful if I tested the waters, so to speak.

"I'll ask him for next Sunday," I promise.

*

The pup settles in surprisingly quickly, barring a few minor hiccups in the early days. He is friendly and anxious to please, so anxious that he is constantly pressing up against the nearest person, all wagging tail and eyes beseeching us to love him. We have learned not to turn too quickly and to watch where we step, as there's a good chance the pup will be in close attendance. The cats do not like him at all at their first meeting, they both stare with undisguised horror, arch their backs and fluff their tails. The pup, ever hopeful, pads over to make their acquaintance and is rewarded with venomous spitting and a double sharp–clawed attack to his nose. Whimpering and bewildered, he takes cover in a far corner while both cats, quivering with offended outrage, retire to the back of the blue armchair. After a time of regarding each other from these vantage points they seem, by some animal telepathy, to come to a truce, and all cautiously emerge to get to know each other. In a short time, all three are the best of friends, with the stipulation that a strict pecking order is observed – cats are boss and pup the underdog. All seem happy with this arrangement.

There's a lot of discussion about names for the new family member, and so heated does it get that it's obvious we're never going to have unanimous agreement. Luke, as the youngest, is nominated to choose. He gives it a lot of consideration and finally comes up with Benson. "Well, you said Ben was his dad, so he ought to be called Benson, didn't he? You know, Ben's son?"

It's sound logic, and it's as good a name as any. Benson it is.

Chapter Thirty-Three

We're having another of Caroline's planning meetings, and once again it's at my house. Actually I'm rather well prepared for once; Jane has removed all the chintz covers, washed and replaced them, and polished the furniture to a burnished shine it hasn't seen for many a day. She's joined the meeting, but is poised to make tea, hand round dainty home-made cakes and generally act as my parlourmaid, secretary and anything else I might require. This all rather embarrasses me, but she says she loves it; it really gives a purpose to her days and makes her feel part of the scheme of things. What scheme that might be I have no idea, but she's happy, I'm happy, Graham's happy and the kids adore her, so who's complaining? She may decide to be on her own again one day, so let's enjoy it while it lasts.

We've been planning the Harvest services next month, but beyond that, Caroline has her sights set on a new kind of Christmas celebration. "I read about this village in Gloucestershire," she says, flicking through the sheaf of notes on her lap. "They have a Nativity play that involves the whole community. Streets are closed to traffic, lights dimmed, the clip-clopping of hooves is heard in the cobbled streets, and Mary and Joseph appear on a real donkey, weary and footsore. They knock at an inn door – no room. Several different venues, same reply. Then, they make their way to the church where a stable scene awaits, with choirs and congregation ready to take part, and the Nativity story begins."

She pauses and looks round at the circle of faces. Is she suggesting we enact a similar performance in our own community? Surely not.

She is. "It would work well, I think. St John's Road could be closed off, people could gather and watch from that wide pavement. The Blue Boar could be the first pub called at, then the Barley Sheaf, then Ron Powell's B & B. The proprietors could be in costume. We could get others involved as angels and crowds and to sing in the choirs. The whole community could be drawn in, as I said. What are your thoughts?"

My first thought is of plump Ron Powell, in a dressing gown and tea-towel, shaking his head solemnly and saying "No room!" The second is of the necessary donkey.

"Er – would it be Dai's donkey you're thinking of?"

"Why, yes, it did so well at Easter, it would be perfect for the Christmas donkey. Don't you agree?"

I'm not sure. I feel it might be pushing it a bit. A gentle jaunt on a Spring evening was one thing, but if it's dark and cold, with lights going on and off, slippery surfaces underfoot, and angel visitations –

I venture a question. "Er – the donkey wouldn't actually go into the church, would it?"

Caroline obviously thinks I'm being obtuse. "Well, of course not. Just up to the little side door, and then while the lights are dimmed, the congregation would file in, Mary and Joseph take their places, and the whole thing would begin."

"It would take a lot of work and organization," ventures Jo, rather nervously, and Caroline nods. "Yes, it will. That's why we need to plan carefully. Contact the right people in plenty of time. Get as many as possible involved. I thought some of the teenagers could be angels. Tall young lads in white robes –"

Oh my goodness! Jo is trying to catch my eye, and I am avoiding meeting it. What is Caroline letting us in for this time? I look at her, calm and serene in pressed jeans and a white shirt, blonde hair tumbling gently over her shoulders. She is beginning to delegate, checking out who will do what. I realise that in less than a month Becky will be giving birth to Caroline's grandchild. Surely this will shake Caroline's equilibrium, ruffle her calm? Or will it leave her completely unmoved?

The familiar feelings, part resentment, part admiration, part bafflement, begin to rise in me. And then I remember, here on this very chintz sofa, Caroline's arms holding me and her tears mingling with mine, and the relief of it, and the sorrow and then the healing.

I look her right in the eye, and hear myself saying, with real warmth "I think it's a fantastic idea, Caroline. What would you like me to do?"

*

This time of year I am often overtaken by the urge to harvest and squirrel away supplies for the winter to come. There must be some deep instinct in our genes, the hunter–gatherer syndrome. I eye the produce in my vegetable garden – prolific runner beans still flourishing and asking to be picked, sliced, blanched and stored away in the freezer. They're nothing like the fresh green beans when they come out, but they're better than supermarket ones that may have been sprayed, treated and contaminated with goodness knows what. Or so I tell myself. Graham begs to differ. He says sometimes I spout a load of piffle and don't know what I'm talking about anyway, and that if I knew just how some of the healthy 'organic' veg are produced and fertilized I might have a big surprise.

Anyway, I pick and slice my beans, smug in the knowledge that I'm providing for my family against the winter cold and hardship. I pull my onions and plait them into ropes, dig my potatoes, carrots and parsnips and plant winter brassicas in their places. I pick apples, the big luscious Bramleys that cook like a dream, the smaller eaters that always seem to go a bit wizened in store. I carefully lay them on newspapers in our attic, although the mice and maybe rats will surely have a nibble at some over the winter. Windfalls I pick up, peel and stew into puree for the freezer.

I'm not finished yet. There are the hedgerows to scour for blackberries, which I freeze or turn into jelly. Blackberry jelly is delicious, with a real taste of the hedgerow. Crab apples likewise, and I even sometimes make jelly of rose–hips. And after an overnight shower there's often a crop of mushrooms in a corner of a field, creamy–white buttons with salmon–pink gills. They freeze well too, and are delicious in soups or cooked with a little oil.

Trouble is, things don't always go according to plan. Today, a Saturday, I have a big basket of luscious blackberries to turn into jelly. We had an early lunch, and the two youngest have taken Jane on a long hike across to our far fields, where there's an amazing view of the valley she's never seen. They took Benson too, to my relief. He does get underfoot and, furthermore, has turned out to be a chewer. He soon got bored with the ancient slippers we offered, and much prefers Lauren's silver flip–flops, or the boys' new school shoes, or, best of all, wellie boots. Once he got shut into the back porch for a whole evening, and reduced Luke's wellies to ankle–height galoshes. The upside is that it's made us all ultra–careful about putting our footwear away.

Anyway, the coast is clear, I have battalions of clean jars lined up, and the kitchen is filled with wonderful sweet brambly smells. I love the look of full jars on my larder shelves – deep purple for blackberry, delicate rose-pink for crab apple, deeper pink for rosehip, yellow-green for quince. My household jewels. Today, though, there's a problem, simply, that the jelly won't jell. Time after time I test a little on a cold saucer on the windowsill – it's supposed to form a skin that wrinkles when it reaches setting point. For some reason, the samples are remaining resolutely liquid. I'm beginning to feel hot and bothered, sticky and frustrated. I'm very tempted to give up and fling the whole panful onto the compost heap.

I'm placing yet another saucer of dark juice on the windowsill when there's the sound of a vehicle powering up the hill. It's Sonia Dent's little Citroen, missing the gatepost by a whisker and raising a dust cloud as she turns into our yard. She fails to miss the bit of stone wall that used to be steps to the granary and I hear a horrid scrape as she comes to a halt. She's in a state. Something must be badly wrong. I turn off the heat under my jelly pan and hurry out to meet her.

Sonia has got out of the car and is surveying a long scratch to her paintwork. I see with relief that Victoria is strapped in her seat in the back, quite unperturbed by the bump and grinning with delight at the sight of my red perspiring face. She's fine, anyway.

"Sonia! Are you all right?"

She pulls a rueful face. "I've pranged the car. I was in a bit of a hurry. What an idiot!"

"What was the rush about? I thought one of the kids must be ill –"

"No, no. We saw your boys and your aunt in the field by Dai's and they said it was all right for Harry to go with them."

"Well, come on in."

Inside the kitchen, Sonia stands awkwardly by the table. "Ali, when I was here last I was so rude, storming off like that. I've come to apologise, for one thing."

Victoria has headed for the huge box of Lego in the corner and is prising off the lid. She dips in both hands and begins to pull out handfuls of pieces. I put the kettle on to boil. "Sonia, it's okay. Please sit down. It was just reaction – maybe I could have been more tactful. Let's forget it."

She sits, but I know there's more to come, she's full of tension like a coiled spring. I'm putting teabags into mugs when she suddenly bursts out "Ali, I've seen John!"

I stop what I'm doing, feeling my eyebrows lift. "You have?"

"Yes. He – came to the house. Last week. Quite out of the blue. Just turned up on the step."

I'm holding my breath. "And?"

"Well – we talked. He's changed, Ali. Much older somehow, more grounded. He told me about seeing you, and how it gave him the courage to make contact again. I was tempted to shut the door in his face at first, tell him to bugger off. But – well, I ended up asking him in."

I put a mug in front of her, not saying anything. She wraps her hands around it and looks up at me quickly. "Oh, he didn't stay the night or anything. We're not back together, don't go thinking that. But – we talked. And he came again the next week to see the children."

"How did they take it?"

"Harry was very iffy at first. He remembers his dad leaving. Kept his distance, didn't really want to know. John had the sense not to push it. But when he'd left, Harry started asking questions, like what team his dad supports, what kind of car does he drive, that kind of thing. It'll take time, but I think he'll come round."

"And Victoria?"

"Oh!" Sonia's face lit up. "Victoria just accepted him as though she'd always known him, toddled over and climbed up on his knee. He was gobsmacked – in a good way. When Harry took Victoria out in the garden for a bit, John cried. I'd never seen him cry before. It was weird." She ponders for a moment, sipping her tea. "Those tears did more than any amount of talk. Maybe men should cry more."

Maybe. Graham certainly isn't given to shedding tears, and I sometimes wonder whether he should. Jo and I were discussing that very thing the other day, and were both in agreement until she suddenly said "Mind you, it would be a bit unsettling if they went around bursting into tears and sobbing on each other's shoulders, wouldn't it?" She had a point.

Sonia and I both look across at Victoria, who is dividing the Lego into two piles, one red, one yellow. Once again she has worked her magic. I am slightly gobsmacked myself. Despite my well-intentioned meddlings and near disasters, God seems to have worked for good, big time. I remember the biggest mistake, and say "Sonia, did John mention I'd almost had him locked up in the cells?"

She smiles. "He did. He doesn't hold it against you though. Thinks you are a woman with guts." She takes a sip of tea and puts down the mug. "You're a good friend, Ali. I want to say how sorry I am too – about your baby. That must be so hard."

I can't help it. The tears still come, whenever I'm reminded of that little one that I won't see this side of eternity. Sonia reaches out and takes my hand in both of hers. Victoria looks up and gets to her feet, leaving the Lego and toddling over to us, putting her arms around my upper leg and laying her cheek against my knee. I look down through my tears at her little balding head with its tufts of hair, and am glad that she'll have a daddy in her life, and something is moving in my messy kitchen, something that is pure and peaceable and transcends human tragedy, something that I know is the Spirit of God, the spirit of pure love.

When Sonia and Victoria have left to find Harry and go home, I return to my cooling pot of blackberry juice, my jars and sticky saucers. There is a skin forming on the jelly, and the liquid is thickening. My jelly has jelled after all, and by God's mercy, in time the Dent family may jell again too.

Chapter Thirty-Four

Dai has been to Sunday dinner. He accepted my invitation with great alacrity, arrived promptly at 12.45, scrubbed, shaved and sporting a collar and tie and polished brown boots. He's even had a haircut for the occasion, so closely trimmed that it gives him a scalped look. He confides in me that he always has a good short cut for economical reasons – that way, he can go for six months before needing another one, or even longer if he trims it up a bit himself in between.

Once at the table, Dai munches slowly and methodically, jaws working in a kind of circular rhythm reminiscent of cud-chewing. He has put in his teeth for the occasion, he tells me – usually doesn't bother wearing them, just keeps them in a mug on the sideboard for mealtimes. That way, they last longer. Now economy is an admirable thing in this day and age, but I feel this is a little too much information. Dai works his way through roast chicken, bread sauce, roast potatoes, veg, and anything else that's offered him, accepts seconds and would no doubt take thirds too if anything was left. And still has room for apple pie and custard. Mum and Dad have come for dinner too, so altogether there are ten of us around the kitchen table. I'd have difficulty catering for so many if Jane was not there to peel potatoes and apples, mix batter and stir the gravy. Mum brought a big tub of luxury ice-cream too, which is a great hit with the younger members, though it's the one thing Dai refuses. "Never took to that cold cream, so I'll say not for me, thanks, if it's all the same to you. I always wonders what effects it has on one's insides."

All in all, it's been a pleasant lunchtime. Afterwards, Dad and Dai go into the sitting room to have a yarn about harvest and the price of store lambs, and I tell Mum and Jane to put their feet up too. Graham gallantly offers to help with the washing up, which I quite enjoy, we make a good team at the sink.

"You realise we'll have Dai round all the time now, now that he's got his feet under the table," Graham remarks, swishing up bubbles in the bowl. (Why do men always seem to use too much washing–up liquid?)

"Well, he's an old man on his own, it doesn't hurt us to show him a bit of kindness, does it?"

"Rather pleased with ourselves, aren't we?" says Graham, and dabs a dollop of foam on my nose. I give him a sly dig in the ribs, just where I know he feels it most. I'm so glad the strained distance between Graham and me has vanished. He's looking rather nice, freshly shaved and deeply tanned after the summer, and I consider giving him a quick snog while we're alone for a moment. No chance of that though. There's a thunder of feet upon the stairs and I draw quickly away. Any sign of parental messing about deeply embarrasses Lauren and may throw her into a bad mood.

It's not Lauren though, it's Michael, with a mobile phone in one hand while he's struggling into his jacket with the other. He has an intense, pale look about him.

"I'm going to Aberystwyth."

Both of us gape a little, Graham up to his elbows in soapsuds.

"What?"

"I'm going to Aberystwyth. With Paul. Becky's had her baby."

I close my mouth and then open it again. What's this? Paul preached a perfectly calm and normal sermon this morning, neither he nor Caroline made any mention of a baby. It's not due for another couple of weeks at least.

"Are you sure?"

"Mum, for crying out loud! She just texted me!" He waves the phone and thrusts the other arm into the jacket sleeve.

"She texted you? After just having a baby?"

"Yes! This is the twenty–first century, for Heaven's sake! I'm off, meeting Paul at the top of the lane. I'll be late, I expect"–

"But"– He's already gone, with a slam of the back door and a thudding of footsteps.

Graham and I are left staring at each other. Then Graham says "Well, he's in a hurry."

For some reason this remark stirs up some deep disquieting thing in me that I can hardly identify. "What do you mean by that?"

"Nothing. Just that he's in a hurry. Don't look so wild. He'll be okay with Paul."

But my relaxed mood has evaporated and I am filled with a confusion of unanswered questions and fretful imaginings. He didn't even say if the baby was a boy or girl, if they were both okay, if there's some emergency, if – I have a picture of Michael's face, white and strained, and I'm just going to have to wait to ask any more questions. I don't like to ring his mobile and speak while Paul and Caroline are in the car with him. Nor do I want to make nosey enquiries among other people in the parish.

I dump a load of dinner plates in the suds and resign myself to a long wait.

*

The rest of the day does seem to drag. Dai, having got his feet well and truly under the table, does not seem inclined to leave until after tea, cake and sandwiches have been consumed and it's time for feeding his dogs, checking the sheep and doing evening chores. He thanks me and stumps off homeward, and Mum and Dad make their farewells soon afterwards. I haven't mentioned Michael's hasty exit, nobody's remarked on his absence, and I decide to keep my counsel until after he's home.

It's a long wait. I assemble school clothing for next day, check on homework, put together ingredients for packed lunches. Jane and I watch Songs of Praise together, then Graham comes in and enquires if I know where his clean boiler suit might be, and could I find it, because he's got an early start in the morning. I do so with a bad grace. Jane asks if I'm feeling all right, and I say I'm a bit tired, and she says no wonder with having so many to feed – but she'd thought it was so nice of me to ask Dai, and that he confided to her that I'm not a bad cook at all, considering I'm a bookish kind of person.

I calculate the length of the journey – two hours to Aberystwyth, two hours back, plus however long they're at the hospital. If only I knew more. Was there some problem with the birth, or afterwards? What are visiting hours? Will Michael be allowed in anyway? My mind seethes.

*

It's past eleven and the rest of the family are tucked up when I hear a car come up the lane, stop at our gateway, door slam, and then Michael is letting himself in. He seems surprised that I am still up, curled in the old blue armchair.

"Are you waiting up for me?"

"I was, yes." I uncurl myself and get up to push the kettle onto the hotplate. Michael looks pale still, but a little more relaxed now.

"How were things – with Becky?"

"Oh, fine." He takes off his jacket and drapes it over the back of a chair. "Mum, is there any of that chicken left? I'm starving!"

"None at all, I'm afraid, the bones were picked clean as a whistle. But I've got some nice gammon. Would you like a sandwich?"

"Yes please. Plenty of pickle."

The gammon was for tomorrow's packed lunches, but I can stop on the way to school and get those ready–made sandwiches in plastic boxes for Adam and Luke, for once. I get out the ingredients, bread, gammon, spread, pickle. Michael stands at the Aga, leaning on the rail.

"So Becky and the baby are okay?" I ask, keeping my eyes on what I'm doing, hoping I sound casual. Michael hates being third –degreed, but I'm bursting with questions.

"Yes, fine. It was a bit early, so it's in an incubator thing for a day or two. But it's healthy."

"And?"

"And what?"

"Well – what is it, boy or girl? What weight? Was it an emergency delivery?"

He frowns a bit as though he can't quite remember. Is he being deliberately awkward? Or is it simply that these details haven't really registered with him, or at any rate not seemed important enough to retain.

"I don't think it was an emergency. Becky never said really. Paul talked to the nurse, she might have told him all that labour stuff – I don't really understand it. Anyway, it was quite small – about five pounds I think, not quite sure – and it's a girl."

A little girl! Paul and Caroline have a granddaughter. I let out my breath and dump the sandwiches onto a plate. Michael sits down at once and begins to wolf them down. The kettle is boiling and I make a mug of hot chocolate and put it down beside him.

"And Becky's okay?"

"I said, Mum, she's fine. She walked us to the lift."

My, they do get them up on their feet early these days, and often pushed out of hospital within hours too. My mother tut–tuts like crazy at modern post–childbirth practices . When Mark and I were born, she tells me, mums stayed in hospital for at least a week and had a good rest. But Becky is young and resilient. I feel a sudden pang, realising that maybe Becky will not be taking the baby home at all. How do things work with adoptions?

I dare not question Michael any further tonight. He has devoured the sandwiches, gulped the chocolate and is heading for the door.

"Wake me tomorrow, Mum. I've got Physics first thing and I don't want to miss the bus."

He's off upstairs and he's going to wake everyone in the house at this rate with the noise he's making.

I sit for a while longer, letting it all sink in. Michael is relieved, he's been able to help see a mate through a hard time. But I know that the hardest times are maybe yet to come. How will they all cope, Becky, Paul, Caroline? I think of that tiny newborn girl, who one day, however lovingly raised, will know the sting of rejection. The tears begin to fall, and I'm mopping them with the check teacloth on the Aga rail, and after a while I'm not quite sure whether the tears are for Becky and her baby, or for my own lost little one who is never far from my mind.

Chapter Thirty-Five

I'm tired but I don't sleep too well, my mind seeming to run in circles of endless questionings, confused gropings, vague misgivings, and coming to no real conclusions. I'm torn with conflicting emotions and half-formed ideas – relief, grief, doubt, gratitude, apprehension – all these battle in my mind and deny me rest and peace. There are things I'm still not sure about, and I'm not even completely clear what those things are. I wonder if I'm breaking down again, but no, it's not that. Maybe I'm looking for answers when I can't expect any. Have any of us the right to demand answers from God? Have we any rights at all? Is there any sense or order in this state we find ourselves in, willy-nilly, where we seem to have little or no control, this thing called life?

In the end I fall asleep, dream of Dai, reaching out to grab a ewe with his crook so that he can pull her in and treat her for liver fluke, and wake feeling strangely comforted. It's a new day, and one thing I can do is phone Paul and Caroline and speak to them. I can let them know I'm there for them.

I have no need to make the call, because Paul is on the phone the minute I'm back from the school run. He sounds uptight and anxious, unlike him.

"Alison? Michael will have told you the news. I'm sorry about dragging him away like that, with never a word of explanation. Everything's happened in rather a rush–"

I smile, relaxing, and go to sit down. Now maybe I'll get filled in on some details.

I do. Paul explains that Becky went into labour early yesterday morning and Eunice took her to the hospital. Paul's voice sounds choked as he says ""You know, bless her, she wouldn't let Eunice call us – said it was Sunday morning and I'd have the service all prepared. She made Eunice wait until lunch time – but by then the baby had already put in her appearance. Becky rang me herself, asked if we'd come, and bring Michael too. It was all go–"

"But everything went okay? Michael hasn't said much."

"Oh yes, seems to have been a textbook first labour. The baby's healthy, but it's policy to keep them in intensive care for a day if they're premature. Tiny little thing, only five pounds three ounces, but perfect, absolutely beautiful–" There's a catch in his voice, and pride too. My heart aches for him. "And what does Caroline think?"

There's a long pause at the other end. Then Paul says, slowly "Ali, that's one reason I'm calling you. Caroline hasn't seen Becky and the baby yet. Yesterday she said she just couldn't do it."

I say quickly "Oh, but doesn't Becky want to see her? Surely –"

"Yes, yes, she does. She asked specially, pleaded almost. I guess every girl needs her mother most of all at a time like this. But Caroline –it's so hard for her, you see. With what's gone before – Ali, I know this is asking an awful lot of you, after all you've been through yourself. But – in a way this baby owes its life to you. We all realise that. And – and – well, I'm going to Aberystwyth again today, on my own. But – Caroline did say that she felt she could face it if you went with her. So I'm wondering – would you, could you, possibly consider going there with Caroline tomorrow?"

I'm silent for a moment. I hadn't expected this. I'd assumed that Caroline had gone with Paul and Michael yesterday. I want to ask – why me? What exactly is my role in all of this?

But I think of the two of them, Paul and Caroline, that day in my sitting room. Something loving and healing was there with us that day, in a way I hadn't expected.

I hear Paul clear his throat, and then he says "Alison, if I'm asking too much, please say so. Truly, it's all right."

I say, slowly "No, it's okay Paul. I'll go with her. Would a ten o clock start suit her?"

*

Caroline picks me up on the dot of ten. As ever, she is immaculate, wearing a black linen skirt and a black T–shirt with silver embroidery, discreet silver earrings, hair swept back and caught at the neck. But she is pale under her careful make–up and under her eyes there's a bruised look that tells of many sleepless hours. And she is quiet; after the initial greetings and exchanges she says hardly a word, gripping the wheel with manicured hands and staring straight ahead. I don't push conversation; Graham tells me there's nothing worse than a chattering woman in the car when you're trying to drive with things on your mind. And he should know.

We take the beautiful winding road beside the river, with its fringes of tall trees and bracken-covered hills beyond, just beginning to show a tinge of yellow that will soon turn to warm brown. The leaves show that first hint of turning too, a dry tired look that shows the sap is beginning to draw back deep into the trunk and roots, safe from winter frosts until the time when it's ready to rise again for another Spring. I love this route, climbing steadily as we leave the valley, neatly hedged fields giving way to wilder mountainside intersected with deep ravines and overhung in places with towering rock faces and granite outcrops. Sheep are everywhere, dotted across the hillside, grazing close to the roadside, so used to passing traffic that they sometimes decide to wander across right in the pathway of a vehicle. It's not unusual to see some unfortunate lying lifeless after being hit by a car.

"You'd think they had a death wish," remarks Caroline, and I have to agree. Caroline's hands are white-knuckled on the wheel, and it's not just from the possibility of hitting a sheep. I ask tentatively about Becky, whether she's still in the hospital, and she replies briefly; yes, they phoned this morning, the baby is still being observed for today and Becky opted to stay in too, though she could have gone home to Eunice yesterday. Fortunately they seem not to be short of beds, unlike most hospitals these days. For a moment we talk about hospitals, and soon find ourselves beginning to criticize the NHS, so that I wish I hadn't mentioned hospitals. Then we fall silent again.

We've made good time, so pull in for a coffee at the little café in red kite country where Michael and I stopped back in the spring. The same young waitress is behind the counter; she doesn't remember me but gives Caroline the once-over, taking in everything from her coiffed blonde head to her black leather sandals and gleaming polished toenails. We order coffee and sit in a booth by the window. The only other occupants are a youngish couple in fleeces and walking boots. The café is full of Welsh mountain memorabilia, woolly toy sheep, red kite posters, maps of the area, wooden love spoons. We sip our coffee from sturdy mugs with a red spot pattern.

Suddenly, Caroline puts down her mug and says "Ali, Becky wants to keep her baby."

I put mine down too, carefully, because my hand is shaking a little. Caroline is biting her lip, eyes down. I say, slowly "I'm not really

189

surprised, Caroline. She said as much that time I went to see her, months ago."

Caroline taps nervously on the handle of her mug with a long slim finger. "Apparently she had a long talk with Paul yesterday. We had the adoption all set up, everything in place. There's a couple waiting – a professional couple who can't have children – they'd be able to give a child a wonderful start in life."

Is she trying to convince herself, or me? I see that her fingers are trembling.

"What does Paul think?"

She's quiet for a moment. "I know, deep down, that Paul doesn't want her to give up the baby. He won't insist on anything I can't handle. But I can tell what he's feeling. He and Eunice have talked –Becky had some idea that Eunice might help her bring up the baby, but it's not on, really. Eunice and Peter are well on in their fifties, and now Peter has this health problem –rheumatoid arthritis, I think – and Paul reckons it would be asking far too much – it's years of hard work and commitment"–

She's agitated, talking fast, the words tumbling out one on the heels of another, as though now she's started she can't stop herself. She looks up at me with an expression that's almost piteous.

"Ali, they – Becky and I think Paul too – want to bring the baby home to the Vicarage. I can see it in Paul's eyes. I'd do anything for him – for Becky too, but I can't do this. I can't–"

I reach across the table and take one of her trembling hands. She goes on before I can say a word, "I'm not like you, Ali. I'm not good at coping. I'm not good with people, not at any deep level. I don't even like babies. The mess, the noise, all the clutter and disruption. After Becky, I couldn't face another. I was a lousy mother."

She's almost sobbing. This is the real Caroline, hurt, desperately insecure, frightened, vulnerable. I clasp her hand in both mine and say "Not lousy at all. Becky is lovely, an amazing girl, a credit to you and Paul. She's not perfect, but neither are any of us. We don't have to be. What we all need most is to know how deeply we are loved. And she is, and so are you, Caroline. Greatly loved."

She gives a kind of half–gasp, half–sob, and her fingers cling to mine. The waitress is regarding us with interest, polishing a glass over at the counter. I'm glad Caroline's back is towards her. I lean forward and say "Look, Caroline, if it came to it, it could be done. The Vicarage is huge; nobody need be on top of anyone else. You've got Mary Miles coming in. Everyone would support you. It could work."

She looks at me again, china blue eyes terrified and swimming with tears. "I don't think so. It – it might not even like me, the baby, I mean. A lot of people don't. Becky doesn't, for one – I sometimes feel she hates me"–

I think of Lauren, and say "Join the club! But that's just teenage girls. She doesn't hate you, Caroline. She loves you very much. She's asking for you, isn't she? Eunice has been brilliant, but as a substitute, not the real thing. It's you she needs."

"I don't know. I don't think I could do it. I'm not even sure I can face Becky today. I don't know what to say to her."

Caroline is terrified, afraid of doing the wrong thing, of failing, of not living up to her own ideals, of venturing into the unknown, of what people might think of her, of losing control. And most of all, of rejection.

I catch a glimpse of us both in the window reflection, her, even in deep distress, so beautiful, me in my jeans and sweatshirt, my hair in a ponytail, our hands clasped across the table. Two women, with different histories, both inadequate in our various ways, both needy, both incomplete, both weak in ourselves. But at this moment, we have one another and we have God , with whom all things are possible.

"We'll do it together," I say.

Chapter Thirty-Six

Aberystwyth is as breezy as usual, a stiff wind blowing and ruffling the hair of the people along the front. Caroline and I have plenty of time before visiting; we have a sandwich at a small café, though Caroline hardly touches hers, and walk a little along the prom. Caroline says she's too nervous to visit Eunice until after she's been to the hospital. Constitution Hill looms over to the right of us, the little funicular railway running steeply up its side. I've always told myself I'll take the boys on that one day, or maybe tackle the beautiful cliff path over the mountain to Clarach Bay, where you can get a bus back.

But today we're here for a purpose. As visiting time approaches, Caroline is increasingly nervous. By the time we're at the hospital, she's trembling and twisting a lacy handkerchief in her hands. I steer her into the reception area and get her yet another coffee from the machine. She must be awash, with all she's drunk. I try to get a few private moments so we can pray together, but it's difficult, with people coming and going around us. If only I'd thought of prayer before we left the car.

"Ali," says Caroline, with a kind of gasp in her voice. "Could you do one more thing for me? Could you – go ahead to the maternity ward and – and kind of see Becky first? Test the waters. Find out if she really does want to see me? I can't quite believe she does, after all that's gone before."

She's in a right old state, no trace at all of that cool, confident Caroline I know so well. Those deep hidden fears have all sprung to the surface, big time. I hesitate – we've come such a long way, visiting time is over all too quickly, and we shouldn't waste any of it. She sees my hesitation and tries to raise a smile. "Don't worry, I won't run out on you. I'll wait here until you come. Only – please go in first."

It's that shaky smile, trying to be brave, that does it. I pat her knee gently and say "Okay, Caroline. Take it easy. I'll go on ahead. Ten minutes, okay?"

Becky doesn't appear to be in the main maternity ward. A nurse directs me to a side room. "We put the mums in there, when baby's been in the special unit. Specially the young mums. Gives them privacy to get to know their baby, to learn how to feed and change, to bond."

My heart flips. Is bonding a wise thing, in these circumstances?

And there's another thought that's been buried deep inside me, and has slowly surfaced, a doubt that I haven't fully acknowledged but which is now pushing its way upward demanding to be addressed. I remember Michael's white strained face, the way he rushed here the day the baby was born. He and Becky have some special relationship, something I wouldn't expect between two kids their ages. He told me the baby's father was a visitor from abroad, a friend of Becky's friend, someone who was no more than a casual, defiant, one-night stand. I don't want to doubt my son's integrity. But deep down, I realise that I've always had the tiniest of niggling doubts, the small uncertainty that never quite goes away –

I look through the glass panel in the door of her room. She is sitting cross-legged on the bed, in a black tracksuit with a white stripe down the side, and big fluffy pink socks on her feet. She looks so young, more like twelve than seventeen, her hair is falling forward, half hiding her face. In her arms she's holding a tiny bundle, a little doll wrapped in a pink blanket, all that's showing is a small round head in a white crochet hat. Becky is bending over the baby, crooning to it, rocking it and gazing down at it, her whole being absorbed in the miracle of her daughter's being.

There are tears in my eyes. I blink them back and push open the swing door. Becky lifts her head and her face lights up. "Ali! I'm glad you came! Is Mum here too?"

She's already looking beyond me, hoping for a glimpse of her mother.

"She is," I tell her quickly. "Just catching her breath. I'll go and tell her you're ready for visitors, shall I?"

"Please." She bends to plant a soft kiss on her baby's face, and looks up at me. Her face is radiant. "Ali, isn't she the most beautiful thing? Come and look!"

I walk the few steps to the bed, drawn as though by a magnet, and catch my breath as I look down at the sleeping infant. She is lovely. Thick dark eyelashes fan out over her cheeks, there's a tuft of dark hair peeping from under the hat, tiny starfish hands, each with a perfect fingernail, spread against the pink blanket. And her skin is olive-tinted, with a hint of warm pink, her mouth and nose are perfectly chiselled, there is Mediterranean blood in her veins.

She is not Michael's child. But she is the most beautiful baby I've ever seen.

I touch a tiny hand, and a tear falls upon it before I can brush it away. Becky looks up quickly. "Oh, Ali, I'm so sorry! I heard that you lost your baby"–

Her own eyes are brimming with tears, with the passionate awareness brought by two days of motherhood that she can't imagine anything so terrible as the loss of a child. I hug her, cradling her and the baby together and say "Oh, darling, it's all right. I'm fine. And you're fine, and so is she"–

The baby stirs and moves a little, making small sucking sounds in her sleep. Her eyes open for a moment and close again –deep, dark pools, mysterious with the wisdom of one fresh–minted from the presence of her maker. I realise afresh that we women are privileged beings, chosen to share in the wonderful work of the Lord, the crowning glory of his creation. The three of us gently rock together for a moment or two.

Then Becky says, suddenly and fiercely "I won't give her up, Ali. I won't. They can't make me. They won't try to make me, will they?"

Her voice tails off piteously. I say, and I don't know where the certainty comes from, but it is there "No, they won't. You won't have to give her up, I promise."

There's a sound at the door. I'd almost forgotten Caroline, but there she is, standing as white and still as a statue inside the door. How long she's been there I don't know. I draw back a little and Becky says joyfully "Mum! Mummy – come and look!"

And Caroline comes, and she looks at her daughter and her granddaughter, and that something is moving again, this beautiful child is working her magic, and something melts and shifts in Caroline, and the love floods in, that perfect love that drives out all fear, and the healing presence of Christ fills that little hospital room, and I know it will be all right.

I get to my feet and tiptoe out, and they do not even notice me going.

*

We are even quieter on the way home, if anything. Caroline seems exhausted, the blue shadows under her eyes deepened into violet, and no amount of foundation applied in the hospital cloakroom can disguise her pallor. I offer to drive for her, but she says she's not sure about the insurance cover, and that she's fine anyway. And there is a kind of peace about her now, a quietness and new confidence.

I'm tired too, wrung-out and emotionally drained. I feel I could nod off to sleep if I closed my eyes, but I must stay awake for Caroline's sake. It's been a day of miracles and we don't want it to end with someone having to tell our husbands that we've careered off the road and rolled down some mountainside.

Near our coffee stop a pair of red kites are flying, wheeling and circling with cat-like mewing cries, plainly showing their forked tails and the yellow bars on their undersides.

"Such big birds," muses Caroline, glancing upward.

"More than six feet across their wing span," I say. "Or so I understand. Raptors. But they don't actually kill anything bigger than a mouse or a small rabbit. They'll wait for something else to do the killing and then join in."

"Amazing."

Yes, red kites are amazing, and so is the world and its wonders, and so is life itself. The sun is beginning to set, sinking in the sky behind us and sending long shadows across the hills, its last rays brightening the heather and gorse and gilding the grey stone. We move eastward as twilight begins to descend, and bats flitter from their homes in the rocks and the fir trees. Lights are coming on in the villages and birds are finding their roosts.

It's almost dark when Caroline drops me at the farm gate. The boys are in bed already, Jane has fed everyone and the kitchen is neat and tidy. Graham and Jane are watching TV in the sitting room, Lauren and Michael probably digitally socialising. Jane calls through to say that there is a lamb chop with veg ready to heat up, if I haven't eaten. I realise that Caroline and I haven't eaten a thing since that sandwich at lunchtime, though we've downed gallons of coffee, and I am famished. I get the plate from the fridge and pop it in the microwave, and rummage about in the bread bin for a cracker, a crispbread, anything to keep me going.

Michael comes quietly downstairs and into the kitchen, as I'm cramming in a dry cracker with more haste than decency. "All right, Mum?" He sounds casual, but I know he really wants to know. I swallow some dry crumbs, splutter a little and say "Yes. Fine. Everything's all right."

He gives me a long look and seems to relax, then peers into the microwave. "That's getting overdone, Mum. It's frizzling up." He opens the door with a ping and pulls out the plate.

Watching him, I'm overcome with a wave of love and gratitude and delight in this ever–hungry young giant, this steadfast friend, this man of integrity that he promises to be. He has burned his fingers a little on the hot plate and is waving them about and huffing. I go over and reach up to him, taking his face between my hands and planting a kiss on his cheek. He's taken by surprise. "What was that for?"

"Just for being you."

He grins, half pleased, half embarrassed, then says "Is that chop for you, Mum? 'Cos if not, I don't mind eating it."

"Well, that's big of you! But yes, it is for me, so keep your mitts off!"

"Okay, only asking." He turns away, heading for the stairs again, already fingering his mobile. "You know, Mum, sometimes I think you're seriously weird!"

Chapter Thirty-Seven

Harvest Festival time is here again, and thankfully, despite the vagaries of an uncertain summer and a rather better September, all of ours is safely gathered in. The barley, wheat and oats are harvested, dried and projected into the huge bins in the grain store, from whence they'll be taken in truckloads to the mills and the first stage of their transformation into daily bread.

I wonder again how many children today understand the origins of the loaf that goes into the making of their packed lunches. With this in mind, I have a flash of inspiration for a topical study for my Little Tiddlers. I make toast in the church kitchen, and then take them through the history of a loaf of bread, beginning with the seed going into the ground, through the dormant period, the action of winter, wind and sunshine to grow and ripen the corn, the harvesting and bread making process. I let them do actions to represent the various processes – very popular until someone gets poked in the eye by an over-enthusiastic combine harvester. When they have settled again, I run through the process, emphasizing the necessity of God's part in the scheme of things, and the need for our co-operation with him.

Rhys is looking thoughtful ,and I sense a question coming on. Since Jessica's departure to Little Fish, he has found his voice, and it is often an argumentative one. "Miss," he says now, wrinkling his brow. "Why does God make bread like that?"

"Well, he decided that was how it should be done. God likes us to work together, you see. We do our part, planting and weeding and harvesting and baking. He sends the rain to make it grow, and the sun and wind to ripen it."

Rhys's brow becomes more furrowed. "Miss, can you talk to God?"

"Why, yes, Rhys, you know we can. We talk to God when we say prayers."

"Well, next time you talk to him, could you tell him we don't need to do all that? Tell him he can get proper bread, all sliced, at the Co Op, like my mum does."

*

Our harvest services are the traditional kind, as befits a rural community. There are graduated rows of vegetables rising from a table beneath the pulpit. The gardeners among the congregation give their best for Harvest Thanksgiving – the reddest, juiciest tomatoes, the plumpest marrows, greenest and longest runner beans, shiniest and sleekest cucumbers, largest and pointiest carrots and parsnips. There are homely touches like a loaf of bread in the shape of a sheaf of wheat, and a hessian sack of potatoes, open, with some spilling out onto the floor. Jars of home made jams, chutneys and jellies gleam among the produce – I glimpse some of my own among them. There are taller jars of pickled onions and beets and a flagon of elderberry cordial. Sheaves of wheat and oats with grain in the ears flank the pulpit and the lectern – Graham saves some of the best each year from the jaws of the combine. And there are flowers – Michaelmas daisies, dahlias, asters, flaming colours mixed with autumn foliage and twined artistically with scarlet bryony and rosehips, the harvest of the hedgerows. It makes me catch my breath every time, this bountiful provision from the hand of a generous creator.

But we are mindful too of those less fortunate, and every year the collection will go to an African village in need of a well, or an orphanage in a war–torn country. This year it will be the hordes of displaced and homeless refugee children. Paul will speak about our duty to our fellow humans, and he'll get a ready response. The farmers will turn out in force to the Harvest services, even those who would normally never darken the door of a church. They'll congregate in the back seats, unfamiliar in their best suits, and their deep voices will add volume to the singing of the old familiar harvest hymns.

I suppose we're a little old–fashioned when it comes to Harvest Thanksgiving, but none the worse for that. For an hour or two we forget the hard toil and sweat, the struggle with wind and weather, the setbacks and disappointments, the falling prices and uncertain markets and recessions, and are united in thanksgiving and praise. And that can't be bad.

*

It's half term next week and I am laying in extra groceries against a week of kids home to lunch every day, not to mention the twenty–four hour dipping into the fridge and cupboards in search of snacks, or the possibility of friends around the place.

I'm putting the stuff away when the phone rings. It is Sonia, and she's incoherent. Something's badly wrong. In between gasps and sobs, I gather that Victoria has been taken ill and is going into hospital. They're waiting for the ambulance, and could I please pick up Harry from school and bring him home with me?

"Yes, of course. I'll keep him overnight if that'll help. Try not to worry too much. They'll get her sorted out in hospital."

Who am I kidding? Even to myself, my words seem trite and hollow. It seems that Victoria is listless and running a high temperature. Possibilities chase each other through my mind. Meningitis? That's the big terror that haunts every mother with a sick small child. Thank God the ambulance is coming.

"Try not to worry," I say again, lamely, but even as I speak there's the faint, wailing cry of a very sick child, and Sonia draws in a sharp breath and says she'll have to go.

That cry sounded so ominous. And I never even promised to pray. I hardly know how to pray. I replace the receiver and my hands are shaking. How do you pray in these kinds of emergencies? "Help, Lord!" seems all I can manage, and it seems inadequate.

Suddenly I think of my mother, and feel an urgent need for her calm, her quiet trust and her wisdom. I shove the rest of the groceries any old how into the cupboards and look at my watch. Two hours until school pick up. I'll go over and see her now. I dropped Jane off to visit a friend in town earlier, so I write a hasty note explaining my absence in case Graham happens to come in.

It's a beautiful autumn day. We've had a touch of frost and the trees are magnificent, with leaves in shades of yellow, orange, russet and every hue of green. Some are twisting and spiralling earthwards and beginning to gather along the verges. Normally I love to look at the flaming colours as the trees change, but today I'm too worried to be appreciative. I do notice Mum's Virginia Creeper as I draw up outside my old home, fiery red against the white walls. Dad's car is out and the place seems quiet. I let myself in by the back door, calling "Hello!" to let them know it's me. The kitchen is empty and peaceful, breakfast dishes draining in the rack, a bowl of hyacinths in bud standing on the window sill. The budgie chirps a greeting from his cage. Mum must be hard at work on her latest book. I feel a twinge of guilt – I don't know much about this latest one she's writing. I really should ask, Mum says writing is a lonely business and people often don't understand and take an interest as they would when one is a farmer or a teacher or a businessman.

The study leads off the kitchen and is a cosy room which Mum and Dad share. They each have a desk, one under each of the two windows, a filing cabinet and a computer. There's an easy chair, sagging and comfortable, where Mum sits to read and often to write too, in longhand in a hard backed A4 manuscript book. There are rows of such books lined up on a bottom shelf, all colours and patterns, journals and drafts, ideas and plots and long–published stories. But mostly the room is full of books, shelves and bookcases and books lined up between bookends and often spilling over onto the floor. It looks complete chaos, but Mum reckons she can put her hand on any title, any time she wants.

The study sharing is not always harmonious , it must be said. Dad's business paperwork and Mum's manuscript pages sometimes mingle and cause fuming and contention. Graham cannot understand why they don't have separate studies, after all, there are four bedrooms in the house and one could easily be spared. He's even offered to move furniture and put up shelves. But I know Mum and Dad will never change their arrangements. They like being together, even the disagreements are meaningful to them and they'd miss one another desperately if they were apart.

The door is slightly ajar, and I can see that Mum has been working on her manuscript. She is somewhat old–fashioned in some ways, despite her modern reputation with my children, and likes to keep a hard copy. The printer has been throwing out pages, the receiving tray is full and some have drifted off onto the carpet. Mum's chair is pushed back at an angle from the desk, as though she's gone out and will be returning soon. I wonder where she can be. There's not a sound in the house, no–one padding about upstairs or sound of running water from the cloakroom.

And then I see a foot in a dark sock and leather loafer, just showing from behind the comfy armchair. My heart stops and then jumps into my throat. I grab onto the back of the chair. She's lying flat on her back, in the middle of the very pretty rug that Mark gave her two Christmases ago, tomato red with blue and black patterned edging. She's wearing her comfy blue track suit. Her arms are flung out to the sides, her eyes are closed and she's not moving at all. An eternity passes and there's just one thought in my mind; this is it then.

I must have made some sound because suddenly her eyelids flutter open and she sees me there. She yawns a little, stretches her arms and grins ruefully. "Ali! I didn't hear your car. I must have dropped off for a few minutes."

She rolls herself over and begins to climb to her feet. I'm shaking so hard my legs won't hold me. I slump down into the armchair. Mum yawns again, sits down in Dad's desk chair and peers at me. "Ali? Oh dear – did I give you a scare? You're white as a ghost."

I nod, and find my voice. "Just a bit. Are you sure you're all right?"

"Just fine." She flexes her arms and rolls her shoulders. "Yes, much better. I get very stiff and cramped, sitting at the computer. So I do this thing Mark told me about. It's called the Alexander method."

"The which?"

"The Alexander method. Or is it the Alexander technique? Anyway, you lie flat on your back, your head is meant to be supported by the depth of two paperback books, but I find a cushion comfier. You stay flat for at least twenty minutes. Your spine is straightened and the muscles realign themselves properly. It works a treat."

My heart is returning to something approaching normal. Mum frowns a little and gets up. "I'll put the kettle on. You look really shaken up. You really mustn't worry so much, dear."

"But Mum" – I stop, choked up. I want to say, Mum, you have a heart condition. This could happen for real –

She pats my arm, reading my thoughts. "Look, sweetie. I'm here and I'm fine. When it's my time to go, I'll be ready. Let's not spoil today by worrying about tomorrow."

She's right, of course. Mum has a great capacity for seizing the day. Spooning sugar into my mug (I don't take sugar but she reckons she's given me a shock), she says "By the way, we're off to Dublin next week for a couple of days, Dad and I. A little business trip to see a customer. I've always wanted to see the Book of Kells."

There's no holding the woman back. But I feel myself relax, sipping the strong sweet tea and watching her potter about, putting the shepherds pie she prepared earlier into the oven for Dad's tea.

I look at my watch and suddenly remember why I'm here. I put down my mug and hurriedly explain. Mum perches on the stool opposite.

"Well, let's pray then, dear."

"Yes, but – Mum, I just don't know how to pray for Victoria. That's why I came. Any other child, you'd pray for their healing and recovery. But with her – well, what is her life going to be? Gradual ageing, stiffness, disability – do we ask for her life to be prolonged for that, or –?"

"Or would it be better to let her slip away now," Mum finishes quietly. The thought of losing Victoria makes my heart twist. I've grown to love her so much, that balding head, pointy little chin, sweet personality, brave spirit. We are quiet for a moment, while the big wall clock ticks softly. Mum has a wry expression, and suddenly I see something I haven't seen before. That every moment with a loved one is precious, and that we must live in those moments. Life is fleeting, even for the longest-lived among us. We can take nothing for granted, but we can remember that our times are in the hands of someone infinitely more wise and loving than ourselves.

"Let's not make the mistake of trying to tell God what to do," says my mother "Let's put Victoria into his hands and let him make the decisions. He's the one who knows what's best."

Chapter Thirty-Eight

Harry has an anxious look about him when I pick up the kids. Sonia has called the school, so he's been told what's happening. He asks almost before he's properly climbed into the car "Mrs Harper, is Victoria going to die?"

I say reassuringly "No, Harry, they'll find out what's wrong at the hospital and be able to sort it out, I'm sure," but I'm thinking – oh dear, is this what I should be saying? What if she dies? Will Harry lose all trust in adults? He's struggling a bit in this area as it is. Should I be strictly honest and say I don't know, or is that too much for a child to take on board?

Harry doesn't seem convinced anyway. I see his worried face in the driving mirror, sandy eyebrows drawn together in a frown, staring out of the window and taking no part in Adam and Luke's routine wranglings and jostlings for space.

When we're home, he declines their invitation to go and play upstairs and attaches himself firmly to me.

"Mrs Harper, what will they do to Victoria in hospital?"

I shrink from telling him about the possible blood tests, the pokings and proddings and – horrors! – the possibility of the pain and terror of a lumbar puncture.

"Well – they'll give her a good checking over –"

"But how will they do it, Mrs Harper?"

I am saved by the bell. The phone rings and it's Sonia, breathless and hurried. "Just a quick call – I have to get back. But they've found the problem – a touch of pneumonia. Got her on antibiotics – they actually started them in the ambulance. Thought I'd let you know. Harry okay?"

I tell her yes, and she's gone, saying she'll call back later, leaving me breathing a sigh of relief. Harry is at my elbow, frowning?" "Mrs Harper, was that my mum?"

"Yes." I tell him the diagnosis, and that it's good news. Harry just looks at me in silence for a moment, but I see the weight of the world lifting from his shoulders.

Then he says "Mrs Harper, could I go upstairs to play with Adam and Luke?" "You could, Harry," I tell him. "Would you like a Jaffa cake to take with you?" I produce a full new packet from the cupboard, but he says "No thanks, Mrs Harper. I'm not allowed biscuits."

Ah! I forgot – Sonia is on a healthy eating thing. It's working, too. As Harry heads for the stairs I notice that he's perceptibly less chubby than he was, and beginning to grow long in the arms and legs.

There's peace for a while, the muffled thumps, shrieks and giggles from upstairs far enough away to ignore. I'm deep in the fridge, rummaging for sweetcorn in the depths of the vegetable drawer when I hear footsteps descending again and a presence behind me. I half expect to hear Harry's voice with a new petition. "Mrs Harper"–

But it's Adam who has a request. "Mum, can Harry sleep over?"

I emerge, sweetcorn in hand. "Well, we'll have to ask his mum. She's phoning again later."

"Well, will you ask her? Plee– ese?"

"He's welcome if she says it's okay."

"Thanks mum." He's turning to go, and I'm reflecting how it's only months since he was lying, pilfering and conniving to avoid being bullied by Harry. And now they're bosom pals. How things can change.

"Mum?"

"Yes?"

"Could we have some Jaffa cakes? Harry says you have a whole packet in the cupboard."

I hand them over. So much for the healthy eating, but never mind.

*

Between tea and bedtime there is a hiatus, a space that must be filled, and the increasing volume of shrieks, thumps, loud footsteps up and down the stairs, and bickering over computer games, is beginning to grate on me. I have a brainwave, I'll enlist the boys' help in a recycling evening, thus neatly killing two birds with one stone.

Some while ago I became enthused about the role of the Christian in the environment, after reading an inspiring book on that theme. I began to recycle in earnest – no more half–hearted forays to the bottle–bank whenever I happened to remember. I commandeered a couple of tea chests and added some big cardboard boxes – the ones that hold toilet rolls in bulk are ideal – and installed them in the old garage. No council collections here, or colour–coded bins, it's all a do–it–yourself effort.

With our number of family members the boxes soon began to fill – plastics, glass, cardboard, paper, textiles, even shoes, all in their appointed place. In fact they filled very quickly indeed, and I have difficulty remembering to take a box or two to the bins in the Co Op car park when I'm dashing in that direction.

Yesterday I noticed that almost all my boxes were full to overflowing, with stuff piling up around them on the floor. Graham is beginning to mutter about rats. The boys and I will do a clean sweep, load everything into the back of the ute and take it to the car park. This idea gets a mixed reception. They are not keen on the drudgery of posting cereal boxes and plastic milk containers into the slots of the dumpsters. But they brighten when I remind them of the glass – the sounds of it smashing into the dumpster and shattering to pieces appeals to something in their destructive little psyches. We load up and set off.

As I'd thought, they're not keen on the dull stuff. That's mostly left to me, while they deal with the bottles and jars. They're having a fine old time, until there's a sudden shriek.

"Mum! Harry's cut himself!"

I drop a bundle of newspapers and rush across. He has, too, there's an impressive amount of blood already dripping into his shirt cuff. Darn it! I'd be in trouble if the Health and Safety police were around.

"It's only a bit," he says modestly, but I can see that he's rather impressed himself. Adam and Luke are full of admiration.

"There must have been a broken bit," says Adam helpfully.

I examine the cut – it's a small one on his thumb, despite the amount of blood. I hope he's up to date with his tetanus jabs. Maybe this wasn't such a good idea after all. I find a clean tissue and tell him to apply pressure.

The phone rings. It's Sonia. "I'm just getting Victoria settled, then I'm staying the night. Will it be okay for Harry to stay with you?"

"Oh – yes, they've been wanting to ask you that." I look across at Harry, who is pulling away the tissue to see what's happening beneath. "Still bleeding," he says with satisfaction. I wonder whether he should speak to his mum, whether she'll be mad at me, but, coward that I am, decide maybe not.

"I'm sure they're having a lovely time, thanks so much," she says warmly, and adds she'll see us tomorrow, and rings off. The boys are giggling and shoving each other, Harry is pretending to smear blood on the other two. Or maybe it's not pretending.

"Right," I say briskly. "The Co Op's still open, so we'll go across and get a plaster to fix that. And then it's home, and bedtime. It'll be dark soon, you're all getting tired now and you'll go straight to sleep."

Who am I kidding?

*

I go to the hospital at visiting time the next afternoon, taking a few things with me in case Sonia hasn't been able to get to the shops, a pair of flowery pyjamas for Victoria and some toiletries in a pretty pink bag. Victoria is sitting in a cot with high sides, twiddling the knobs on a yellow plastic game that is tinnily singing nursery rhymes. Sonia is in a blue plastic armchair, half dozing. Victoria is pale and frail-looking, but her face breaks into a delighted smile when I push open the door to the little side room they're in. There's a narrow bed against one wall for Sonia, a wall-mounted TV set and a wash basin in the corner.

Sonia is pleased to see me too. "Ali! It's good of you to come."

"How are you both?"

I show the pyjamas to Victoria, and hand her the pink bag so she can investigate what's inside. "This is my bed," she tells me, patting the cellular cover "and that's Mummy's."

Her words are cut off in an attack of coughing that shakes her little body. Sonia jumps up and holds her until it's over, and suggests she take a little rest, plumping her pillow invitingly and finding Victoria's favourite rabbit. Victoria seems glad to concur, the coughing has worn her out.

"But she's loads better than yesterday, a different child," Sonia hastens to assure me. "She even ate some breakfast and lunch."

"Children are so quickly up and down," I murmur reassuringly. But my heart aches for little Victoria. How much illness will she have to suffer in the short life ahead of her? But there, I must remember to take one day at a time.

I don't stay too long. It's early days for Victoria yet and Sonia looks as though she didn't sleep too well last night. Besides, I must get back for the boys.

"Harry's very welcome to stay for as long as you're here," I tell her.

"I was just going to mention that," she says, and lowers her head a little. "It's so good of you, but, well, the thing is, John's been here – he came in last night to see Victoria" –

I'd forgotten John, but I'm very glad he's been in.

"He's coming again this evening, and we thought it would be good if he brought Harry too."

I nod. "I think Harry'd like to see Victoria. He was very anxious."

"Yes, he adores her. And, well – we thought maybe Harry could stay with John overnight. John has time off work. Maybe they could – get to know each other again. If that's all right with you."

"It's fine with me. I'm just wondering about Harry –"

"Actually, I spoke to Harry at school lunch time today. He wasn't too sure at first. He does so enjoy being with your boys. But I think he's coming round to the idea."

I think for a moment and say "Tell you what, I'll catch John and have a word, Harry too, and we'll go from there."

"Thanks Ali. You're a friend in a million."

I get to school by the skin of my teeth, my boys are dancing with impatience and I see John Dent and Harry there discussing the situation with solemn faces. I hope there won't be any difficulty. Harry spies me and waves.

"Mrs Harper, I'm going to see Victoria."

"That's great. She's feeling much better. Hello, John."

"Hello. I understand Harry's been staying with you"

"Yes. " I hesitate. "Er – will he be coming home with us today?"

John looks at Harry enquiringly. "What do you think Harry? I could always pick you up from there to go to the hospital."

Harry seems undecided. Adam is at my elbow, jumping from foot to foot. He really wants Harry to stay over again. "We could play that Wii game again," he says.

Harry looks from Adam's face to his father's. Then he says "We could play it another day. I'm going with my dad now."

Adam's face falls, but he'll get over it, and the expression on John's face, relief , joy and hope, is something that warms the cockles of my heart.

Chapter Thirty-Nine

Becky and the baby are home, arriving one sunny October day with a mountain of infant necessities, and are now installed at the Vicarage. From what I understand, things are working out well. Becky is at Sixth Form College a day or two a week, and studies at home for the rest of the time. I had half-imagined Mrs Miles would be in charge of the baby while Becky is away, but no, Caroline is a hands-on grandmother and an extremely doting one as far as I can see.

When our next women's group meeting comes round, the baby is there beside Caroline in a wicker basket in the sitting room. I can't help noticing that the room is a little less pristine than it used to be; there's a pile of folded small garments on a side-table, a box of baby-wipes beside the bowl of pot-pourri on the coffee table, and the table itself has what looks like a faint layer of dust.

There's a chorus of oohs and aahs as each of the group peers into the bassinet. The perfect little sleeping face brings a lump to my own throat. I've not been quite able to bring myself to hold the baby yet – I'm still capable of bursting into tears at some inappropriate moment, but half a dozen pairs of hands are itching to get hold of her at the least murmur.

"She is absolutely beautiful," breathes Jo.

"Angelic," adds Myra Meadows, clasping her hands.

Caroline pulls a wry face. "Not at three in the morning!" she says, but her tone belies the words. Besotted is the description that comes to mind.

For some reason, the baby doesn't seem to have a proper name yet, what they put on the Birth Certificate I don't know, but it seems that discussion is still under way at the Vicarage. At present, she seems to be known as Bibs. Caroline rather affectedly calls her Bebe, which seems to fit well with the little smocked dresses and exquisite French outfits she produces from some unknown source to dress her granddaughter. Caroline herself, though, is a little less perfectly turned out than usual.

Her outfit seems less carefully co–ordinated and more thrown together, her hair is pulled back into a scrunchie band and there's a small damp patch on the shoulder of her jumper that just might be baby vomit. Already this baby is working miracles before our very eyes, enabling her grandmother to join the rest of us in allowing herself to be a little less than perfect.

*

This autumn has been particularly beautiful, as though to make amends for the unpredictable summer. The colours of the trees have been magnificent, from scarlets and oranges through all shades of green to butter yellow. There's a little touch of frost at night now, enough to crisp the fallen leaves underfoot, and still hours of sunshine as long as daylight lasts.

The days are getting shorter now. "Only a week until the clocks go back," observes Dai, who is here most Sundays these days. Meanwhile, potato harvest is going on at the big farms down in the valley. From my front porch I can see the big fields turning brown as the harvesters work their way along them, and smell the rich earthy scent of turned soil.

And the migrant workers are back. Every year they come in gangs from Eastern Europe- Ukraine, Poland, Romania, Latvia, Estonia, Bulgaria – and set up camp in the caravan site that's been prepared for the purpose, out on the fringes of town. We see the foreign workers in the Co Op, hear the sounds of East European languages. Mostly the migrants keep to themselves. I wonder about them, especially the women I see among them, who work as hard as the men. Do they have families at home, depending on the money they send back? Do their children miss them? Some of them have children with them, how do they fare? I wish there was some way of making contact, but my own life seems so full and busy and involved that I can't see how,

Not so my mother. She's back from the little jaunt to Ireland, and one morning I meet her in the Co Op pushing a trolley piled high with groceries. We arrive at the check–out together, and I help her pack her stuff into bags and transport it to the car. She has that slightly furtive look about her that means she's up to something.

"This is an awful lot of stuff for you and Dad, Mum. Have you taken in lodgers or something?"

She pretends she hasn't heard, wedging a bulging bag firmly so that it won't tip. My suspicions begin to rise.

"Mum? If you're stocking up you should have asked me to give you a hand. This is heavy stuff."

"Yes, well, I didn't think you'd approve."

"Approve of what? I think it's a good idea to keep your cupboards stocked up, but you needn't have done it all by yourself."

"Yes, well, it's not exactly stocking up. I'd have told you, but you tend to make such a fuss."

I slam down the boot and put my hands on my hips. "Mother! I think you'd better explain."

So she does. Apparently, she's been buying 'a few little extra things' and taking them to the families at the work camp. A few of them have children with them. And it must be so hard for the women, doing a day's work and then having to turn round and cook and clean up after their menfolk. They're very nice, she says, and very grateful for the few little extras she takes.

"I bet they are!" I'm torn between a mixture of admiration, exasperation and concern. "It's all very well, but you've worked hard to earn your money, Mum, and they get paid good wages, you know."

"Yes, but they save almost everything to send home, and live very frugally. A few little luxuries make a lot of difference."

There's no arguing with the woman. It's no good saying these women might be taking advantage, big time, maybe laughing behind her back. And I suppose she could be doing worse things.

She gets into the driving seat and winds down the window. "I expect you're busy, dear. See you at the weekend. And don't look so ruffled. I'm not breaking the law or anything."

"Well, I suppose not. But take care. I suppose it's not as though you're having them to live with you or something."

She looks at me rather strangely, key half in the ignition.

"Well, actually, I might be."

"What?"

"Having them to live with us – well, two, at any rate. I'll explain when I see you next. Have to be off now."

And she's gone with a crunch of gears, leaving me standing in the car park and staring after her like an idiot.

*

I'm not prepared to wait until the weekend. I want to find out what my mother is up to, now. So the next evening, when the boys are settled for the night, I head over to my parents' place.

The evenings are pulling in fast now, this time next week it'll be dark by five. It's windy tonight; leaves are skittering across the road in the headlights and beginning to gather along the verges in coloured drifts. The Virginia creeper is losing its leaves too, leaving a bare twiggy framework over the front of my parents' house. The place is in darkness, just a gleam of light showing from behind the sitting-room curtains. They're dug in for the evening.

Mum and Dad seem surprised to see me. I don't usually go visiting on the dark evenings. They are sitting together watching a documentary about whales with the wood-burner lit and just a small reading lamp giving light. My parents are creatures of habit these days. You'd never guess that my dad runs a successful business that takes him all over the place, or that my mum is a well-respected children's author. They like their evening routines. Supper at 5.30., then they watch the news before clearing up. Then they might spend an hour or two reading or doing Sudoku. Mum reckons Sudoku keeps the brain active, I find that if I do it I get frustrated and bad-tempered when I make a mistake that throws every line out of sync. If it's daylight they might take a walk down the lane or potter in the garden with the watering can. When it's cold and dark they settle down to watch TV for an hour or two. Nine o clock, hot chocolate. By ten they're usually tucked up in bed.

Mum says she'll make a cup of tea, and scuttles off to the kitchen. Good, this'll give me a chance to talk to Dad.

"What's all this about the migrant workers, then?"

"Oh – she's told you."

"Well, she didn't exactly. It's just I began to wonder when I saw her buying enough groceries for an army."

"Yes, well. You know what your mum's like. When she gets an idea in her head, that is."

"But don't you mind? Some of those workers look pretty rough and I bet there's plenty of vodka going round too. Is it safe for her going out to the camp?"

"Look, Ali, I had my misgivings when she first mentioned it, and I went to the camp with her the first couple of times. When I saw the women and kids, and the way their faces lit up when they saw her, well, I hadn't the heart to gripe about it."

"Yes, well" – I'm not letting him off the hook, and I've not forgotten what else Mum said. "What's this about some of them coming to live here. That can't be true, surely?"

Mum is suddenly at the door with a tray of mugs, and she's heard the last part of the conversation. "I told you, dear. It's only two. Two girls, Dorina and Sanda." She puts down the tray and hands me a mug. "They're sisters, Romanian, still only in their teens, not much older than your Lauren. They came with their brother. But they don't like it much at the camp. The work is all right, they're pleased to be earning money –it's for their education, bless them – but some of the young men are proving to be a problem. They say they don't always feel safe, especially if there's been some drinking at weekends."

Dad and I look at each other. "So, I thought the obvious thing would be to let them stay here. They can cycle to and from work. We've got plenty of rooms to spare, it's only for the season. Where's the problem in that?" She sighs and sits down with her own mug. "I'll even get some rent. And I really like young people about. I can't see any problem at all. Why must people make such a fuss?"

People being her daughter, of course. She is getting quite steamed up. "Do you really want me to be a little old lady sitting knitting?"

"No, Mum, heaven forbid. But I do want you to be safe, and not overdoing it, and staying well. And happy," I add, feeling that my litany sounds a tad dull.

"Yes, well, this makes me happy. And that's my last word on the subject."

*

By next weekend, the two girls have moved in, bringing with them a couple of bulging knapsacks and two pairs of muddy wellies. They are pretty girls; Dorina, the eldest, is seventeen, dark–haired and shapely, with melting amber eyes and an air of confidence. Sanda is sixteen, smaller and shyer, rather in her sister's shadow and inclined to follow her lead, but with an appealing way about her. Neither speaks much English. They work sometimes seven days a week, depending on weather conditions, so are out of the house from dawn to dusk. I pop over with the boys to meet them the second evening they're there. They greet us shyly, looking at Mum for guidance. She is in her element as Mother Hen, piling their plates with food and tending to their every need. They are freshly showered after work, and their hair is damp, with a faint aroma of the brand of toiletries I saw in Mum's trolley at the Co Op. I suppress a mean thought that they're on to a good thing here, and greet them warmly.

"Welcome to the United Kingdom," says Adam solemnly.

"And a Happy New Year," adds Luke, who has his dates a little mixed.

"Thank you, thank you," says Dorina

"Thank you," repeats Sanda.

"Can we show them our Crusaders Quest game?" asks Adam. I let them bring the tablet with them, thinking it might be a good way of breaking the ice. It is. Some things can be communicated without the need for language.

The four of them commandeer the sitting room, Dad is closeted in the study, Mum and I clear up in the kitchen. Gone is their evening routine, but they don't seem to be missing it.

"They did the dishes for me yesterday," says Mum in their defence. "And I'm really enjoying having them around. Dad and I were getting very set in our ways. The girls must meet Lauren and Michael too, soon."

A lot of whooping and laughter is coming from the sitting room, and a few thumps too. I hear a loud cry of what sounds like "Da!" They are getting on famously. I have trouble dragging the boys away when it's time to go.

"They're fun," says Luke on the way home.

Adam agrees. "They're teaching me Romanian", he says importantly. "I know one word already. Da. It means yes."

Chapter Forty

Stormy weather is on its way. Dai says that there are often high winds about the time of the Autumn equinox, and this year he's right. The wind is just pleasantly brisk on Monday, making my washing snap and dance on the line and getting it beautifully dry and fresh-smelling when I take it in. By the next day the wind is stronger and there's rain coming with it, the kind of rain and wind that drives in horizontally and seeks out loose tiles and roofing slates to worry at and dislodge if it can. The leaves are whipping off the trees now, no longer crisp and crunching underfoot but piling wetly wherever they come to rest, where they'll rot and become black, slimy and slippery. Our pleasant autumn weather is coming to an end.

Graham has been busy all day clearing buildings and making the grain store secure against the wind and weather. It's safely gathered in, but will face hazards before the winter's through and the bins empty. Marauding squirrels will try to gain entry and feast on the grain, the bins must be covered with squirrel-proof netting. When there's heavy rain the water sometimes pours off the steep fields and the drains become overloaded. There've been times when streaming rivulets have diverted themselves across our yard and crept into the grain store and under the bins, where the water will ruin the stored wheat and barley. Graham watches for the first signs of flooding, but it can happen so suddenly that we're sometimes taken totally unawares.

He thinks it'll be okay tonight; there's more wind than rain. Not long after Michael and Lauren arrive from the school bus, the gale begins in earnest, whipping small twigs as well as leaves from the trees. I'm glad to have my brood safe home in the warm kitchen with a casserole in the oven and the darkness and weather shut outside.

We've eaten, and the Simpson-viewing is under way when suddenly the lights flicker off, then on, then off again. Jane and I are in the kitchen in total darkness. I put down a pile of plates carefully and feel my way to

214

the cupboard where we keep emergency candles and matches.

There's a wail from the sitting room. "Mum, the telly's gone off!"

I'm obviously expected to be able to wave my magic wand and restore essential cartoon power. When darkness comes here it's dark indeed, especially on a moonless night. It's strangely silent, the fridge has stopped humming and there are no squawks from the TV next door, only a murmur of complaining voices. I'm just fumbling with the candlestick when the lights go on again. Jane is blinking at me, looking relieved. It's short-lived relief though. The lights flicker and then go off again. I hear Graham's voice issuing instructions that the TV controls must not be fiddled with, and Luke wailing in protest. Michael comes barging downstairs, torch in hand, complaining loudly. "Mum, what's going on? I was in the middle of something on my laptop and it just went."

"Yes Michael, it's called a power cut. Probably the gales."

"Well what are we going to do?"

"*I* am lighting candles. *You* had better make sure your computer is switched off. You don't want to lose important stuff."

Muttering, he goes back upstairs. For people raised in the age of technology, my children are remarkably dependent and lacking in initiative and resourcefulness when the said technology fails. Adam comes wandering in, looking ghostly in the flickering candlelight.

"I can't watch TV."

"No, that's true, you can't."

"Well, what am I going to do then?"

"You could tell stories, or sit in the firelight and play games, like guessing games, or we could do a quiz. That's what I sometimes did when I was little."

He looks at me as though I've totally lost it.

"Thank goodness we got the meal cooked," says Jane.

"Yes, and that we've got a conventional kettle that boils on the Aga."

"But Mum, it's Doctor Who. I always see that."

"Sorry, Adam, it seems likely that tonight you won't."

"Well, it's not fair."

"As I may have mentioned not a few times before, Adam, life is not fair."

"But there's nothing to do. I can't charge up the tablet. I'll be bored."

"As I have also mentioned on occasion, bored children are usually boring children."

He gives me a baleful stare and retreats disgruntled into the firelight of the sitting room, where I hear some scuffling. I call after him "And if your dad's taking a nap, don't wake him."

Lauren appears on the stairs. "Mum, how long is this power cut going to last?"

"If I knew that, my sweet, I would be a wiser woman and probably a much wealthier one."

She is not amused. "I can see you're in a mood. Is it all right if I have a bath?"

"Yes, there's plenty of hot water. You'll need candles though."

She brightens. "Oh yes. I could use those scented ones I got last Christmas. And tea–lights, loads and loads all round the bathroom."

The possible fire hazards of this plan spring to mind, but the risk is worth taking for the sake of peace and harmony. She departs with a box of matches, and I place candlesticks on the worktop while Jane and I finish the dishes. The candles flicker a little; this draughty old house has windows that fit less than perfectly. Outside, the wind is battering the east side of the house and the stems of the climbing honeysuckle rattle against the walls whenever there's a fierce gust. It looks like being a stormy night.

*

All night long the old house seems to shake rattle and roll under the buffetings that come its way. We all retire early, the electricity still being off, and are tucked up by nine thirty or so. I would normally rather enjoy this, snug and cosy inside while the weather does its worst outside our thick stone walls. But Graham feels obliged to get up two or three times, with waterproofs over his pyjamas and torch in hand, to go out into the storm and check on the drains and the rainfall situation. I lie awake each time until he returns, chilly and inclined to warm his cold extremities on his ensconced wife. The third time, he reports that he thinks it's stopped raining now, but that some of the apple trees may have lost their branches, and it's blowing harder than ever. I'm used to the howling wind by now, and before he's settled again I fall into a deep sleep.

In the morning we oversleep a little. The rain and wind have quietened, but the power is still off. I boil the kettle and make porridge on the Aga, and begin to worry about the freezer and its contents. Dealing with a freezer full of thawing meat and veg and melting ice–cream rates among one of my worst nightmares. But it's okay, because

216

by school time there's a sudden surge, the lights come on, the fridge hums into life, and the magic of harnessed electricity is with us again.

Outside, it's plain that the storm has wreaked some havoc. There are twigs and bigger branches across the road when I take the boys to school, and I notice that our old apple tree has lost two of its limbs. Anything not fastened down seems to have moved and shifted, there are buckets rolled on their sides around the buildings and black plastic sheeting has blown about and wrapped itself around whatever it encountered, or got itself stuck in hedges. The place looks like a tip. The dustbin has blown over and bits of sodden cardboard, plastic and assorted rubbish is scattered around the back door area. Uh– oh, it's going to be a clearing up morning.

"It's bonfire night next week," remarks Luke, as we steer our way between debris and out into the lane. "We could have a bonfire, couldn't we? Plee–eese!"

"We never have a bonfire," says Adam accusingly, and I know what's coming next. "Everyone else's mum lets them have a bonfire. Why can't we?"

I put the car into second gear to go down the hill and promise I'll think about it.

*

The bonfire idea has taken off, big time. When the branches and bits of wood from the storm are collected up, they make quite a sizable pile in our front meadow. Graham becomes fired with enthusiasm and adds all the bits of broken equipment, things past repair, damaged pallets and other assorted combustibles, including a couple of defunct tyres. These last I have my doubts about; smoke from burning tyres is incredibly thick, black, acrid and oily–smelling, likely to choke anyone unlucky enough to breathe in its fumes, and they sometimes explode like gunfire. At my request he puts these aside; if there are extra kids about we do not want accidents. Catching the general bonfire–fever, I pull out bits and pieces from the house, chairs awaiting reseating that's never going to happen, a rickety cane table that was a terrible dust trap, and old sagging armchair with the stuffing out, a cheap chest of drawers whose drawers fell to pieces in no time. I'm tempted to add all the plastic flower pots, fertilizer bags and packaging that accumulates so quickly, but remember that I'm committed to recycling these days. The bonfire has reached a towering height, and the sight of the old armchair has reminded the children of a guy.

"Could we have some old clothes?"

"And something for a head?"

A surprisingly lifelike guy is produced from an old holey boiler suit stuffed with straw. Someone has the idea of adding a hooded coat, with the hood stuffed and tied around the neck with a woolly scarf, and old boots tied onto the legs. With a pair of defunct glasses and a makeshift pipe he looks surprisingly lifelike, and Luke suppresses a shudder when the guy is seated in the chair, hoisted on high atop the bonfire and tied in place with baling string. It is strangely disconcerting to think that the poor chap will have to sit there until next week awaiting his fate.

The whole thing has somehow snowballed and is now looking like being the major event of the autumn season in these parts. Adam and Luke want to invite most of their classmates, Lauren is considering asking a few friends but wonders whether my cooking will be up to scratch or whether it might be best to have caterers.

"Caterers? I thought we'd just have sausages and potatoes baked in the Aga, maybe a few nibbles. Hot soup maybe – just the thing for a cold night. Maybe the two Romanian girls would like to come over with Mum and Dad. And Sue and Mike and the boys"

I toy with the idea of asking my friends in town, but decide maybe not. A cold, muddy field in November would be maybe a rural treat too far. Funnily enough, I'm quite looking forward to it.

Chapter Forty-One

In the event, the bonfire party turns out to be quite a select affair. Harry comes, minus Sonia and Victoria, as Victoria is not long out of hospital, and, as Harry solemnly informs me, she doesn't like loud bangs and scary things. I agree, a burning effigy of a life-size man in an armchair must be one of the scariest scenes imaginable. Lauren invites just Paula, who is her bestie and can be counted on to make allowances if proceedings turn out to be less than cool. I tentatively suggest that Michael could invite Becky, but he says she always gives Bibs her bath and puts her to bed about that time, and then she has an essay to write. Mum and Dad come and bring Dorina and Sanda, who seem mystified as to the origin and meaning of this strange tradition. (I'm a little mystified myself.)

I introduce the Romanian girls to Lauren and Paula, and they smile uncertainly at one another and say "Hey!" which seems to be the internationally understood form of greeting these days. I notice Dorina and Sanda looking covertly at the clothes that the other two are wearing. To the casual glance they would all seem to be dressed much the same – jeans, jackets, long scarves and the wellies obligatory for a fun evening in a cold muddy field. But there's a subtle difference in their clothes, and they know it. Dorina and Sanda are older, but Lauren and Paula are streets ahead in style, the confident way they wear their gear, the myriad little details that add up to a sense of knowing what is in at the moment and what is not.

There's a little frisson among the girls when Michael comes out to grace us with his presence. By now the fire has been lit and is taking hold, flames licking up through the newspapers and dry wood at the bottom of the pile. The boys are agog, little monsters, waiting for the moment when it reaches the hapless guy seated aloft. I fervently wish we hadn't built the bonfire quite so high, and urge the boys to stay well back from the flames. They think I'm a spoilsport because I won't let them pick up burning brands and wave them around.

We have a modest firework display, only a few, because, at risk of being a meanie, I can see no sense at all, in these economically difficult times, of spending good money for a few short moments of bangs, flashes and coloured stars.

The boys run around, churning up mud, the teenagers cautiously mingle. The two Romanian girls are very taken with Michael, giggling hopefully at his remarks even when they don't fully understand. He is showing off a little, playing to an audience. Lauren and Paula are exchanging knowing looks, with a great rolling of eyes and meaningful facial expressions. Mum, Dad and Jane stand together in a little group, hands in pockets and woolly hats pulled well down; it's quite a chilly night, though the heat from the fire is beginning to be felt. Graham, pitchfork in hand, tends the fire like a character from Dante's inferno.

Sparks from the fire begin to fly, thankfully the wind is blowing away from the house and buildings or I might begin to fret. The flames are leaping high now, crackling and leaping up round the old armchair and round the legs of the guy.

"It's really rather a horrible custom, isn't it, burning a human effigy, whatever old Guy Fawkes tried to do," remarks my mother. I have to agree. The kids love it though, cheering and hooting as the guy's straw innards catch light and when he collapses and pitches forward into the flames. A fresh shower of sparks flies up, the old chair is blazing merrily and I wonder uneasily whether we all have a little of the pagan fire-worship instinct still working in our subconscious. At any rate, when the fireworks are over, the bonfire past its blazing peak and beginning to die down and the show is over, people begin to lose interest and drift off towards the house in search of sustenance.

Everyone agrees it's been a good evening though, teenagers and all. It didn't rain, and nobody caught alight or even burned their fingers. When the hot potatoes and bangers have been consumed, the soup slurped and the crisps nibbled, the guests have departed and Jane and I are left with a kitchen full of debris, and bits of crisp and cake crumbs trodden into the mud on the floor, we agree that we're glad that Guy Fawkes night, like Christmas, only comes round once a year.

*

November is my least favourite month of the year, though every month has its own magic and I love the changing seasons, all of them, with passion. If it would stay fine, dry overhead and mud free underfoot,

220

the days getting shorter and the leaves gently falling, nature winding down to its winter sleep, it would be quite enjoyable. But there's always too much rain, or too much wind, and definitely too much mud. It's dark by five and will darken even more over the next few weeks in the rundown to Christmas. If the sun appears at all, it's pallid and half-hearted and soon gives up the ghost at the first hint of approaching darkness. Dead leaves pile up, lying in drifts over my precious piece of lawn and threatening to kill the grass beneath, and settling on paths and steps in slimy lethal black patches for the unwary to slip on. Wood has to be split and hauled in for the wood burner; there's always a trail of sawdust around the log basket and muddy wellies in the porch. But hey ho, it's all part of life's rich pattern, Christmas is coming and I really wouldn't have it any other way.

*

I bump into Sonia on one of my frequent forays to the Co Op. I'm a bit self-delusional when it comes to grocery shopping. In my head, I have a weekly budget that seems ample, even for a family of seven as we are these days. Supplemented as it is by my own garden produce, preserves, frozen veg and so on, I should easily manage from one Friday shop to the next.

I don't though. I'm always sure there'll be enough, even allowing for a hungry man, a fast-growing young teenage giant, two also fast-growing small boys, a picky daughter and two women who cheerfully eat anything that the others despise so there's no wastage. But my family don't play by the rules. When the fancy takes them they think nothing of using up a whole packet of bacon at a sitting, or consuming huge bowls of cereal at odd times of day, or eating half a tub of ice-cream while watching a late movie. I'm always running short, and running to the Co Op.

For once, Sonia doesn't have Victoria in tow. She's choosing steak from the butcher's counter when I spy her. "Is Victoria okay?"

She closes the cabinet door and stows the steak in her trolley, which also holds asparagus tips, new potatoes and a bottle of red wine. Graham says I have a strangely nosey streak in me. Maybe it's my Welsh blood; Welsh women are notorious for knowing other peoples' business. Whatever its origin, I love to listen in on other people's conversations and look into their shopping trolleys. You can tell an awful lot about them by the food they buy.

"Oh, yes. She's back to her old self, just about – hardly coughing at all

221

now. Thank you so much, for your help – and – your prayers."

She seems a little embarrassed, maybe it's the mention of prayer. But then the penny drops – best steak, out of season veg, red wine, Victoria presumably being minded by someone else …….. "Sonia! Is John back?"

She blushes a little, averts her eyes. She's looking rather pretty, a smart pink jacket I haven't seen before, a hint of make–up.

"Well, kind of. He stayed with Victoria while I came out – they're getting to know each other and she's happy to stay with him. I can't believe how much easier shopping is without a small child in tow."

"Tell me about it! So things are working out?"

She goes even pinker. "Well – yes. They are actually. Between you and me, he's staying over tonight." Suddenly she can contain herself no longer, joy is bubbling up and can't be held back.

"Ali, I can't believe it! It's like – well, when we first met. In spite of what's happened, we seem to be falling in love all over again! And it's really thanks to you."

She gives me a big hug, right there in the supermarket aisle, with shoppers giving us curious glances. I hug her back. This is amazing; surely it must be a miracle. It's what I'd dreamed and scarcely dared hope for. And what a difference it will make to little Victoria, and to Harry!

I've almost forgotten what I came in for in the excitement. I leave Sonia choosing between a raspberry Pavlova and a rather exotic cheesecake and go on my way, walking on air. Was it pasta or basmati rice Lauren said she wanted? Never mind, I'll get both, just in case. I'm not sure how much credit I can take for the mending of this marriage, but there's nothing like a bit of good news to bring brightness to a gloomy November afternoon.

Chapter Forty-Two

You just never know what dramas are waiting to unfold. On Sunday, I notice that Mum and Dad are alone in their pew. They've been bringing Dorina and Sanda along lately, but not today. Mum has a rather strange expression on her face too, kind of half mysterious, half wary – nobody else would notice a thing, but I can read my mum like a book. They're doing their own thing for lunch today, but she collars me after the service. "Alison? Can you spare a minute?"

Oh goodness, what now? I scan her face anxiously, but she appears to be fit and well, and Dad seems hale and hearty too. I have to admit that having those two girls around seems to have given them a new lease of life.

The rest of my family are socialising with their peer groups. Mum and I stroll slowly towards the church car park. She's very chic in a cream jacket over a deep red blouse and black skirt.

"Where are Dorina and Sanda this morning?"

"At the camp. The work's finished, they're packing up today and will be on their way home tomorrow."

Of course. Graham mentioned to me that the potato harvest appears to be all in, pointing out the bare brown fields. I'd forgotten.

"So they've left?"

"Yes." A pause. "Actually, that is what I wanted to talk to you about."

I wait. She goes on "There's been – a slight problem." A little frown has appeared between her eyes.

"But I thought you'd enjoyed having them."

Her face lights up again. "Oh, I have! We both have. They're such dear girls, so cheery, and so nice to have around. They've been helpful, appreciative of what I do, although my cooking was a little on the bland side for their taste. I've learned to spice it up a bit."

I laugh. When the girls first came to Mum's, they brought gifts from home, from the supplies they'd brought along. Two huge jars of honey

223

and a large jar of pickled fish. Mum passed one of the honey jars on to me, along with the fish. "The honey's delicious, dear. But – er – we didn't quite fancy the fish. I thought some of your gang might like them."

The fish resembled gigantic sardines, floating pale and lifeless in a glutinous green liquid, like some exhibit in an old–fashioned freak show. One look at them turned Lauren pale and faint, and had Luke and Adam clutching their stomachs and making exaggerated gagging, retching sounds. Michael cautiously unscrewed the lid and sniffed at the contents. "Phew! What do they pickle them in?"

A strong fishy and garlicky smell wafted out. Even Graham's strong stomach decided it was a tad too highly seasoned for its liking. In the end, we gave it to the cats and dog. The cats loved it, licking meticulously the last drop of oil from their whiskers. Benson passed on eating the fish, preferring to deposit his share on the utility floor and roll luxuriously in it, making him stink to high heaven until someone could bring themselves to give him a bath.

Mum and I laugh, remembering.

Then the little frown returns. "But as I said, there's a problem."

I wait. We've reached the car and I ask Mum if she'd like to sit inside. It gets chilly standing about. We both climb in, sitting side by side in the front seats. I prompt her: "What kind of problem?"

She's really having trouble with this. She fiddles with her rings for a moment, and then says "It's like this. The girls packed their things this morning – there wasn't much – and then Dorina cycled to the Co Op and bought me a lovely bunch of flowers. The two of them made me a little thank you speech and then they left. The thing is – I think they took my ruby necklace. It's gone, at any rate."

That necklace, with matching earrings, was Dad's ruby wedding present to Mum two years ago. I'm not sure if the stones are genuine, but it's very pretty, with silver dangly bits and the stones a beautiful deep red. Mum loves that set.

I'm silent for a moment, feeling a rush of indignation. How dare they, after Mum had been so kind to them! But I mustn't jump in with both feet. I say, carefully "Are you sure, Mum? Could it have just got moved, or misplaced?"

She shakes her head, looking down at her hands. "No, I don't think so. I wore it at the Watson's last Thursday night. Then got undressed in the bathroom, and I remember taking the necklace off and putting it on the shelf, in that little pink china dish, to be safe. I forgot to take it back to the bedroom. I remembered it this morning, when I was dressing for church. It goes nicely with this burgundy blouse. It was there when I showered first thing. It had gone sometime between then, and the girls leaving."

"And you looked for it?"

"Oh yes. I pulled everything off the shelves. Searched behind and underneath things. Searched the bedroom too, just in case. I haven't told your dad though – he bought it for me and I don't want him to get angry with the girls."

People are beginning to drift across the car park, homeward bound. I see Graham coming, having rounded up the two boys.

"Mum, what are we going to do about this? You can't just let it go, surely?"

She shakes her head. "No. I've decided I'm going out to the camp this afternoon. I wondered if you'd come with me."

Oh, glory! My first thought is that I'll ask Graham to go too; if there are going to be accusations I'm not sure I can handle it. What if there's an angry scene?

Mum says quickly "I'm not afraid of facing them, if that's what you're thinking. I've been there often enough, they know me and trust me. I wondered how I'd approach this, but it came to me this morning in church, and I think I know how to do it."

It's more than I do. The boys are at the car windows, clamouring to be let in. I unlock their doors.

"Is Gran coming home with us?"

Mum is climbing out. "Not today, boys. Grandpa and I have a nice casserole in the oven at home. I may see you later though. Mum and I may be going out for a while. Okay, Mum?"

She looks at me meaningfully and I nod. I can see I really have no choice.

*

There's a definite whiff of November in the air as Mum and I, clad in our Barbours and wellies, pull into the camp site and park the car near the gateway. The air is dank, damp and earthy, full of the smells of rotting leaves, turned soil and wood smoke. Beyond the site, the bare potato fields stretch away into the distance, by next week the ploughs will be out turning furrows for next year's crop.

The campsite is busy; people are packing their things into the vans and trucks that they travel in. A small fire burns at the far end of the field for burning up stuff they don't want or can't take home. I'm apprehensive, wondering what on earth we're letting ourselves in for. Wouldn't it have been better to let the police deal with it, or at least our menfolk? But Mum will have none of it. She's serene as ever, striding towards the caravans with a carrier bag clutched in one hand. One or two of the workers see her and call out friendly greetings; soon a few of the women come over, smiling and taking her hand. She squeezes hands and wishes them a safe journey home, exchanges hugs with one or two of them.

The caravan the girls share with their brother is a large grey one with a white van parked beside it. A young man in a baseball cap is doing something to the engine of the van. He is dark and rather good–looking, with a marked resemblance to the two girls.

"Their brother, Andrei," says Mum, going over and holding out her hand. The young man's face breaks into a grin. He shakes her hand warmly and indicates that we go into the caravan.

My heart is thumping. Everyone seems so open and friendly here, maybe – surely – Mum has been mistaken about the whole thing? The girls are sitting at the fold–down table, sorting a pile of clothing, folding jeans and sweaters neatly, matching pairs of socks, placing it all tidily into a wicker basket for transporting. They look up in surprise at the sound of our voices, and I know immediately that Mum was not mistaken. Dorina's face breaks into a look of surprise and delight. Sanda smiles too, but I see her give a quick, darting glance at my mum and then turn away. She carries on with the sock sorting.

I'm feeling sick. We sit opposite the girls, across the table, while Andrei puts a kettle on the gas. His English is better than his sisters'. It's not the first time he's worked here. He says "Is nice that you have come to wish goodbye. You are good lady. Kind to my sisters."

This is going to be even harder than I'd expected. How on earth are we going to tackle it? How will he react? I look at Sanda, head down, trapped on the inside seat, and try to be angry with her for creating this situation, but can see only a young girl not much older than my Lauren, awkwardly shifting in her seat with guilt written all over her face.

Mum clears her throat, rummaging in the carrier bag. She puts a big tin of Celebrations on the table top. "For your younger brothers and sisters. And," adding a folded tablecloth with printed pictures of our area "For your mother. I thought she'd like to see some views of where you've been. "She pauses, fishes in the bag again and brings out small boxes, giving one to each girl. Dorina opens hers and exclaims in surprise and delight at the dainty link bracelet inside. Sanda does not touch hers.

"Open it, Sanda," says Mum gently. The girl gives her a sly glance which turns into a defiant one, opens her mouth, closes it again and then obeys. She gives a little gasp and her hand flies to her mouth. Nestling in the box are the ruby and silver earrings that go with the necklace.

"They're yours, if you want them," says my mother.

Suddenly, Sanda's defiance crumbles, her mouth turns down and trembles a little, she seems tongue-tied. Her brother and sister realise something is up, and maybe they have some idea what it might be about. Dorina puts her arm round her sister, and Sanda babbles a whole lot of words, unintelligible to us, and begins to cry. She reaches into the rucksack on the seat beside her, fumbles in it and pulls out a wodge of tissue paper, from which she pulls the necklace and drops it on the table. Dorina and Andrei look from the necklace to the earrings, to us and to their sister, and I can see they know what's happened. Whether they knew before our arrival I have no idea.

Sanda is crying properly now, her flushed and tearstained face buried in her sister's neck, although whether the tears are genuine or not I don't know either. Dorina looks from us to her brother in shame and embarrassment, but I see pity for her sister too, in the way she holds her and doesn't let go. Andrei's face is unreadable. He says, in his halting English "My sister says she is so sorry. She steal this necklace, she want to give it to our mother, our mother has worked hard always and never had pretty things. She is so sorry, you have been very kind, like a mother yourself –"

It's a pretty speech, and he does seem genuinely sorry, but whether it's for the theft or because it's been found out, I can only conjecture. I look at Mum. She's got a tear in her eye herself. I wonder if she's really taken in by this show of penitence, because I'm not altogether convinced. She fishes in her bag again and brings out a box of tissues, pushes some across to Sanda, tries to take the girl's hands. She says gently "Sanda, I understand. It's all right. You can take the necklace to your mother. The earrings too, if you want." She pushes them across the table, but Sanda pushes them back, exclaiming "No, no!"

"My sister, she has never before been a thief," declares Andrei.

"And she's not a thief now," says my mother firmly. "She just made a mistake, gave in to a little moment of weakness. We all do it."

227

The kettle whistles on the gas. "I would love a cup of coffee," says my mother, and I know she's saying it to give Andrei something to do, because she seldom drinks coffee. It comes in tin mugs, black, strong and sweet, and we sip it while Sanda slowly grows calmer and the tension eases.

"I hope you'll come and stay with us again," says Mum, and I know she really means it. She would really let Sanda have the ruby set, too, but Sanda won't touch it now. Mum gathers up the necklace and earrings and presses another little box into her hand, which contains a locket on a chain, and amazement crosses Sanda's face as she mumbles words of thanks. We part with hugs and kisses.

Walking back to the car, I feel suddenly weak at the knees. I wonder about Mum's heart condition, but she seems sprightlier than I'm feeling.

"Mum, was that a wise thing to do?" I say weakly. "I wouldn't be surprised if the other two knew something about it. And did you see that sly, shifty look that Sanda had? I think they might have been taking you for a bit of a mug."

She stops and looks at me. "Maybe. But I try and think the best of people. You and me, we have a totally different way of life. They have nothing back home; everything's done by bribery and corruption....

"Maybe. But should we let them get away with it? Would you really have let them have the jewellery? Dad's anniversary gift?"

She thinks about that for a moment before answering. "Yes, I think I would. I love that set, and what it stands for. But, I have your dad, and we've had all those years together, and so much to be thankful for. And if I have to give account some day – as we all will– how can I say that I loved a set of jewellery more than I loved a fellow human being? Anyway, it all worked out. I still have the set, and we parted friends."

I have no answer to that. I shake my head and we walk on.

"How on earth did you decide what to do?" I ask.

"Oh, I just followed instructions."

"Instructions?"

"Yes. They came very clearly in the Scripture reading we had this morning. Luke seven, verses twenty–nine and thirty."

I think back and recall that these verses have something to do with giving someone your cloak when they've taken your coat. Well, it seems to work. There's nothing I can add to that.

Chapter Forty-Three

The flu season is here, and it's struck early, not even December yet. Maybe that's for the best; hopefully the worst will be over by Christmas. Adam comes home one afternoon feeling shivery and saying he has a headache. I'm on the alert immediately and swing into action, checking for fever (he has a slight temperature) administering Calpol and persuading him that early bed is a good idea. He agrees, after Jane promises him the loan of the portable TV she has in her bedroom, and sinks languidly between the sheets, where he makes plaintive demands for hot drinks, ice-cream, grapes, and maybe the lend of someone's tablet when he's a little stronger.

Graham disapproves of all this pampering and pandering to every little ache and pain. His mother brought him up on the premise that if you have a good healthy diet and plenty of fresh air you don't get ill, and if you should pick up the odd cold or sniffle the best thing for it is more of the same; good plain food, fresh air and maybe a dose of hot lemon and honey, but the minimum of fussing. There may have been something in it, he hardly ever gets ill.

I remember with nostalgia my own childhood ailments, when I'd be tucked up with extra pillows, a hot water bottle maybe, hot blackcurrant, a vapour rub for my chest, chicken soup, strawberry jelly, and a big soft muslin square, left over from baby days, which was the most comforting thing in the world for a red, sore, runny nose. Paper tissues just don't hit the spot in the same way.

Within a day or two, Luke is down with the bug, followed in quick succession by Lauren and then Michael, who, one by one, take to their beds. Four kids by necessity don't get quite the same TLC as one would, and there's a lot of wrangling about the TV sets, music systems and tablets, which they can't live without, sick or not. Jane and I are kept busy for several days, running up and downstairs to a background of coughing, complaining, and querulous voices. Thank goodness Jane has had her flu jab, and so have Mum and Dad.

By the time most of them have graduated to the sitting-room, where they complain just as much and argue more, I am quite worn out and feel I'd rather like a day or two in bed myself. But I can't go down with flu, of course. There isn't time. Mums don't, and that's an end of it.

When they're finally on their feet and have straggled back to school, more or less well again, I'm badly in need of some distraction. So when Mum phones and asks if I'll go to a book-signing event with her, Dad being a bit tied up with business that day, I jump at the chance. Anything to escape for an hour or two.

*

The signing is at a new little bookshop that's opened in the city. It's run by a couple around my parents' age, retired missionaries, who still have energy enough, and a friend with resources, to begin this new project. The shop is tucked away in one of the little side streets that fan out from the cathedral, it actually has cobble stones.

The little window has a tastefully arranged selection of books and a large notice which says "Local Author Emilia Banks signing here today." We had a bit of difficulty parking though, the shop is miles away from the main car parks and we had to find a spot in another side street and walk from there. I'm wearing a skirt and heels, as befits the occasion, and my feet are aching already.

I'd half expected a large event in one of the big chain bookstores, with books piled on a table and Mum seated behind, glasses on and pen at the ready, the way it happens at our Literary Festival. This seems very low key. A pleasant, white-haired lady bustles to meet us as we enter. It's small inside, every wall crammed with bookshelves, bookstands, spinners, with just room for a counter and a couple of chairs. The lady seizes my hand and wrings it warmly. "Mrs Banks? How lovely to meet you!"

I hasten to explain. "No, no – I'm her daughter. This is Emilia Banks."

Mum's books are arranged neatly on the counter, two piles of blue and lilac covers with titles in black '*Hacking It*'. This latest title for teenagers is set firmly in the technological age. I skimmed through it again last night to refresh my memory in case I'm asked any questions.

"I've sent flyers out everywhere I could think of," says the shop lady, who has introduced herself as Dorothy. "I'm sure people will come. Please take a seat. My husband will be back soon."

Mum seats herself on one of the chairs behind the counter. I wonder how long it will be before the rush, and browse the books on the shelves for a few minutes. There are some lovely ones, but oh! they're expensive! I know that bookshops are rapidly going under because it's so much cheaper to buy online, and I admit guiltily that I take advantage of this as much as anyone. And so many people read on e-readers these days. I make a mental resolve that I must support the shops, even if it means less reading material. Now I understand why Mum waived the fee they offered for this signing.

Standing in my heels is not a good idea, and there does not seem to be another chair, let alone space to put it. After a while, during which time Dorothy and my mother chat, I say "Er – would it be all right if I went and looked around the shops for a while?"

They both seem to think that's a good idea. I hate to think I'm withdrawing moral support from Mum, but she's not exactly overwhelmed at the moment, and she and Dorothy are getting along famously. I leave with some relief and head for the centre, where I'm delighted to find a pair of loafers just my size in a sale, which feel so blissful on my feet that I wear them to leave the shop. I hadn't intended buying shoes today, but, hey, I won't buy anything else, just window shop. I spend a pleasant hour or so doing just that, winding up with an espresso coffee and watching people go by, until I suddenly realise guiltily that I've left Mum unsupported for far too long. Maybe her books have all sold and she's waiting to go home.

When I return to the bookshop, Mum is deep in conversation with a middle-aged lady who is clutching a copy of *Hacking It*. The lady has seated herself on the other chair, while Dorothy is busy rearranging shelves. There's still quite a pile of books.

The lady jumps up when she sees me. "Oh, you have another customer. I'll be getting along. But thank you so much!"

She and Mum exchange warm hugs and kisses and scribbled phone numbers.

"Someone you know, Mum?"

"No, dear. Well, I know her now. She was telling me about her son and his children – what a time she's had, poor soul."

I scan the pile of *Hacking It*. "Sell many books?"

Mum glances towards Dorothy and they exchange rueful smiles. Mum says "Well –er –just the one, actually."

Dorothy is apologetic. "I'm so sorry, this does sometimes happen, I'm afraid. It's the recession, of course. But I thought that, with Christmas coming up" –

She spreads her hands helplessly. "I'm afraid you've had a wasted morning, Emilia."

"Not at all," says my mother, with her warmest smile. "I've had a lovely time, really. I'll come again whenever you like."

My mother and I agree to have lunch at the Garden Centre just on the edge of town. Mum seems not at all cast down by the non-event of the morning, and is glad I had a walk round the shops and got a comfy pair of shoes.

"You're taking it very well, Mum," I tell her over our soup and rolls.

"Not at all, dear. I really did enjoy it. That poor woman had just been longing to find someone who'd sit and listen. We're going to keep in touch. And then Dorothy and I had a lovely chat about her missionary work – do you know, she actually knows the Whittaker family who we were such friends with"

She breaks off a piece of roll and says reflectively "You know, dear, life's not all about success and money and status. That's not where the real treasure is. It's about people, isn't it?"

*

I'm up earlier than the rest this morning. Despite the hour, the light is bright from behind the curtains. When I get out of bed and peep out at the morning, I see there's been a frost overnight, the first of the winter. Everything is sparkling and glittering with myriad points of light as the sun comes up.

This kind of morning in the dark days of November is too good to miss. I leave my slumbering husband, pull on a track suit over my pyjamas and tiptoe downstairs. The cats yawn and stretch but are too idle to move yet; even Benson is reluctant to leave his basket as I pull on my wellies. He's his father's son, and likes his creature comforts.

Even wrapped as I am in coat, hat and gloves, the air strikes with a sharp chill that stings the inside of my nose. My breath is a white vapour as I cross the yard, climb the stile and walk up the gently sloping meadow beyond. My boots crunch in the frost-stiffened grass, every branch and twig has a delicate covering of white rime. Even a spiders' web is transformed into a tracery of sparkling silvery thread. When I reach the highest point of the meadow, and stand under the frosted bare branches of the hazels, I can see the valley stretched before me, mile upon mile of glittering white fields intersected by grey shaded hedgerows and stands of fairytale fir trees with icing-sugar frosting, and the silver ribbon of the river winding through it all.

The birds are quiet, still tucked up somewhere with their heads beneath their wings. But a sudden movement in the hedgerow catches my eye. A fox emerges, lifting his feet delicately against the stinging cold. He's preparing to take his usual route across the meadow after his night's hunting, to where he probably has his den in the clump of beeches and oaks on the higher ground.

He pauses, one paw uplifted, sniffing the air. I hold my breath. He's scented me, and slowly he turns his head and looks at me. I don't move, try not to blink.

I have ambivalent feelings about foxes and fox-hunting. I acknowledge the inherent cruelty of the species, have seen at first hand the terrible wanton destruction a marauding fox can do, killing not for food but for the sheer bloodlust, or so it seems. A fox will get into a henhouse and slaughter every last bird, leaving them torn and bloody, before making off with just one. They'll stalk a ewe giving birth and snatch a new-born lamb, if it or its mother seem weak and ailing. Foxes have no finer feelings, and invoke little sympathy among farmers. If Dai came across this one when he was carrying his gun, he'd have no hesitation in despatching it.

Yet I hate too the idea of hounding a creature to its death and revelling in the kill and smearing blood on a child. I would have said I was a hunt protester, but seeing the way the actual anti-hunt demonstrators behave, with not an ounce of real knowledge of how the countryside works, I've come down on the side of the hunt. Our local hunt still rides to hounds, regularly, ban or no ban, and I would support them if asked. Benson, like his father before him, adores the hunt, has to be shut in securely when the hounds are about. The hound blood in him is desperate to join in, and he howls and bays for hours after the hunt has passed by.

This fox is an old one, and he must be a wily one too; not many foxes make old bones. He has grey hairs around his muzzle and grey among the russet of his brush. He stares at me for a long moment. I can see the colour of his eyes, a dark amber. I wonder if his night's hunting has been successful. He seems to have no fear of me a long as I'm still, and after a moment turns and lopes off across the field along his accustomed track, leaving a faint trail in the frost.

I let out my breath, and realise my feet are getting cold despite the pair of Graham's thick socks I pulled on. I say softly "Go safely, old timer" and head homewards myself, marvelling at the wonder of God's creation, and the balance of nature, and that a time will come when all things will come into the harmony of his perfect reign.

Chapter Forty-Four

I'm not quite sure whose idea it was that we should add another member to our already well-populated household. Or more than one, to be exact. Maybe it was the introduction of a new hamster for Luke, a fat little caramel-coloured butterball by the name of Fudge. Once again the nights are punctuated by the sound of a creaking wheel.

Or it might have been the fact that Adam's class is doing a project on wolves and dogs this term. He is throwing himself into it with all his might. My mother rather likes wolves and is encouraging him with suitable reading matter. All good stuff. So how did it lead to us even considering getting another dog?

"Wolves are pack animals," declares Adam, with the confidence born of recent research. "They don't like to be on their own. They usually have a pack leader, who's, like, the boss wolf. Then there's the next one down. Some packs are big and some are small. But they don't like being on their own." He pauses, eyeing Benson speculatively. "Dogs are the same."

Aha, I begin to see where this is leading. I try to steer the conversation into safe territory. "You've really worked hard on this, Adam. Well done you."

He's eyeing me speculatively. "I think Benson is very lonely."

"Oh no, he can't be. He has all of us, and the cats. We're his pack."

"But we're not dogs." I'm not sure where Adam gets his stubborn streak, but it certainly is quite pronounced. "You know how he howls when he hears the hunt. He wants to be in the pack. He's lonely." We both look at Benson, prone in front of the Aga on this dull, gloomy November day. He rolls an eye at us, and sighs heavily.

"See!" says Adam triumphantly. "He's not happy. We should get another dog!"

Now the challenge is out in the open and is picked up very quickly. Everyone, it seems, thinks that another dog is a Very Good Idea. Even

Graham does not object as loudly as I'd hoped. He observes that we have plenty of space here, unlike some of the idiots who try to keep dogs in tiny little housing estate gardens and then wonder why they get into trouble. We've only just got over Benson's clingy– chewy puppy stage, but it seems to be soon forgotten. I find myself thinking that maybe another dog would be rather nice.

There's a lot of discussion about possible breeds. Anything with sheepdog in it is out of the question, with woolly bodies in the fields all around waiting to be chased. I've always fancied a black lab. Michael mentions Irish wolfhounds, which I reckon would cost even more to feed than he does. Luke and Adam just want another dog, any dog.

We consult Stuart, who is ever practical, and says any dog we get should be even–tempered and good with children, first and foremost. "And if you're getting a pup, make sure it's from a reputable breeder," he says in conclusion. "There are a lot of very dodgy dog people about, you know."

"Of course", I assure him. I've heard all about those puppy farms and the people who run them. Wouldn't think of buying from them. As if, as my daughter would say.

*

We have scanned local adverts and perused details of puppies for sale, and have finally decided on going to see one of them. It's at a place about ten miles away and sounds hopeful. "Whiteside Farm, Graveney," I read out. I know Graveney a little, a picturesque village up amongst the forestry on the English side of the border. The dogs are golden cocker spaniels, which we think would be an excellent choice of breed. We ring the number and make an appointment for Saturday afternoon, when the boys can come with us.

It's a pretty drive up among the trees, through the tiny stone–walled village which is not much more than a church, a pub and a handful of houses, and up a farm track just beyond. The track is pitted and bumpy and even steeper than our own. The farm is unremarkable, grey stone buildings clustered around a low farmhouse. But the moment we're through the gate and getting out of the car my heart sinks. I know we've made a big mistake.

It's a dull, lowering kind of afternoon with a hint of drizzle in the air. There's a smell of damp straw and rotting leaves and dogs. The farmyard is muddy; thank goodness we're all wearing wellies. The farmer greets us, a stocky, taciturn man in overalls, tweed cap and an ancient waxed jacket. He walks with a slight limp, leaning on a stick.

"Looking for a pup, then?"

We explain our mission and prior viewing appointment. "Come this way," he says shortly, and stumps ahead towards the buildings.

Graham and I exchange a look behind his back. This place doesn't have a good feel. Approaching the outbuildings, we can hear a growing chorus of yips, yaps and howls. There are a lot of dogs here. Looking round, we can't see any other signs of livestock or arable activity. I'm beginning to have a dreadful suspicion that this is one of those awful puppy farms we were warned about.

I'm right. We are led past several stalls that once housed cattle, and each one contains golden cocker spaniel mothers with offspring at all stages, from tiny wriggling newborns to gangling half–grown youngsters. The mothers look sadly at our faces peering in at them; the ones with small pups have that smug look peculiar to most new mothers, those with older pups wag their tails hopefully, they're at the stage when their children are becoming a trial to them. Do they get exercise away from the pups, I wonder? I want to question the farmer about the dogs, but he's stumping on ahead, not encouraging any lingering or chat. He stops at the furthest stall and says "This is the litter I'm advertising."

This mother seems to have the saddest face of all. Her eyes are droopy and a little bloodshot, long golden ears dangling on either side of her face, tail waving tentatively as though she doesn't expect much. She is being hassled by a squirming mass of youngsters, pushing and shoving and rolling over to get at her. I count at least six, there could easily be more.

"Bitches, all of 'em," grunts the farmer, "except that 'un there. The only dog, and the runt of the litter."

He points with his stick at one of the pups, who is nosing about hopelessly at the edge of the mass of milling bodies. He does look rather pathetic, about half the size of his sisters, with a sad kind of look about him, as though he's resigned himself to the leftovers of life.

"Got a bit of a weakness in a hind leg, keeps him back " says the farmer by way of explanation. "Sometimes you gets a pup with a faulty hip."

I've heard of that, and understood it to be a result of inbreeding. Graham enquires how much he's asking for the pups and we are both horrified at the price mentioned. "Pedigree animals, from good stock, I can show you all the paperwork," the farmer assures us with a touch of defensiveness.

Without a word of discussion or even a look between us, Graham and I know we wouldn't dream of paying that much for a dog, pedigree or no pedigree. Come to think of it, I don't want a dog from here at all. I find the whole set-up distasteful. The dogs seem well-fed and have clean litter in their pens, but I get the impression they don't have much of a life beyond those pens, and that they're really no more than breeding machines.

"They'll be ready in a week," says the farmer, eyeing our dubious faces. "If you'd like to pick one out, I'll make sure that's the one you gets."

"I think we'll go home, talk about it and let you know," says Graham.

"They goes very quick," warns the farmer, anxious to secure a sale.

"I'm sure they do," says my husband, and his voice is a little steely now. "As I said, we'll be in touch."

We pick our way back over the muddy yard and get into our vehicle, leaving the farmer, disgruntled, to close the gate after us.

"I didn't like that place," says Luke, voicing what we all feel.

"I liked the dogs," says Adam as we bump down the steep track. "I thought we were getting a puppy. Aren't we getting one now?"

"Not from there," I say firmly. "Those places shouldn't be allowed."

"I'm not sure they are allowed," says Graham. "And how that guy has the brass neck to ask those prices beggars belief."

"Times are hard. He's diversifying," I say, trying to be fair, and get a snort for my pains. "Make an easy bob or two, more like."

I can't help feeling that the pups were rather appealing though. And for some reason that poor little runt being kept back by his bossy older sisters has embedded himself in my mind. I say thoughtfully, as Graham eases out into the main road, "I expect he'd sell that little dog pup for a lot less than he's asking for the others, don't you think?"

Graham changes gear and gives me a warning look. "Alison, don't even think about it. We are not – repeat, not – getting ourselves lumbered with a sickly pup with a bad hip. Not even if *he* paid *us*. And didn't you just say you wouldn't buy a dog from there, not in a million years?"

"Well, I may have done. But – nobody else will want him, will they? He'll probably end up with a bullet in his brain."

I wish I hadn't said that the moment the words are out of my mouth, and expect a chorus of horror and tears from the back seat. But Adam and Luke are not listening, squabbling over some toy they both lay claim to.

Graham has that stubborn set to his jaw that forbids further argument.

"Alison, I'll say it one more time. No. Way."

*

A week later, we drive up the steep bumpy track again to collect the pup. (How Graham has been persuaded to change his mind is strictly between him and me.) The farmer seems surprised that we came back. He and Graham haggle, and both seem reasonably satisfied with the agreement they come to. We shake the dust from our feet (or wipe the mud from our wellies) and drive away with the pup on the back seat between the two boys, who seem set to kill him with kindness.

Once home, he thrives on the attention. He's a friendly little fellow, and within a few days already begins to look fatter. He has a slight limp, but it doesn't seem to bother him. Benson accepts him, rather condescendingly, though the pup is a little wary at first. Like all pups, he spends long spells fast asleep, and when he's awake, there's always someone ready to cuddle and play with him. We discuss names, and finally decide on Barney. I like his long golden velvet ears, his sad eyes, and his paws that seem too big for the rest of him. I know he'll grow into them, the way Adam is growing into his over-large front teeth.

Barney is putting on weight, but on Tuesday when the kids are in school, I suddenly notice a small bare patch among the dark gold hair of his shoulder. Come to think of it, when I really look, I'm sure his whole coat looks thinner and more sparse than it was. On the way to school, I take Barney along and stop off at Stuart's. He first gives me a serious telling-off; I'm not supposed to take Barney anywhere near other dogs until he's completed his injections, and that includes Benson too. Uh – oh, good thing they haven't been curling up together or had much to do with one another so far. Then he takes one look at Barney and says "Mange!"

That sounds ominous. "Are you sure?"

"Positive. Another day or two, and he'd start to be ill. I'll give you some stuff."

I'm grateful, and grateful also that he has the kindness not to say "I told you so!" when he learns where we got Barney. He gives me medication and instructions, and then adds "You'll have to treat Benson as well. And Ali, you and the family will need treatment too."

"What?"

"Mange mites affect humans too. They cause scabies rash. I assume you've all been touching him?"

I nod dumbly. "You'll need to see your doctor. All of you."

It's a nightmare, but it's true. That very morning I'd noticed an itchy rash on my forearm. Luke had scratched his neck as he got out of the car and I'd reminded myself to check for nits this evening.

This is worse than nits. Far worse. Scabies. All of us have to use a noxious liquid containing goodness knows what harmful chemicals, and worse, leave it on for twenty-four hours before showering. Lauren is on the verge of hysteria and refuses to go to school. Michael declines to use the stuff and say he never touched the pup. I hope he's right. The rest of us suffer, hoping nobody notices our malodorous state and praying for the time to pass. It does, and so, thankfully, do the mange mites. But I have a feeling it will take a very long time for me to live this down.

DECEMBER

Chapter Forty-Five

Each year, at the beginning of December, I begin a debate with myself; Christmas cards, to send or not to send.

One or two of my friends have made the latter decision, they make it known that they will not be sending cards, but will instead donate to some worthy cause. I admire the ethic of this and am tempted to try it – apart from bringing benefit to others, it's such a chore choosing, buying, writing and posting all those dozens of cards. And how silly is it to send a card, as many do, to people you see almost every day of your life? Surely the original idea of Christmas cards was to greet those loved ones far away who you don't often see?

So my common sense tells me. But my frivolous side loves the delivery of festive envelopes all through December (or even earlier; I had a card from a local company in November), and the colourful array of snowy scenes, fat robins, glittering fir trees – even the odd Nativity scene – that graces these seasonal missives. I love the bits of news scribbled inside some, or a fat envelope that indicates a real letter along with the card! I like the look of the cards strung up around the walls like gaily coloured bunting, or standing on the mantelpiece and sideboard. I don't even bother to do any dusting until the cards are taken down on twelfth night.

If I didn't send cards, people would soon stop sending them to me. So I guess that, once again, I'll be sending Christmas cards this year.

*

I feel a distinct twinge of apprehension whenever Caroline calls a meeting to plan the coming Christmas play, which I thought would fizzle out when she realised the enormity of what she was proposing. In fact, the plans are going forward with a velocity that I find somewhat alarming. Caroline has approached the Town Council and arranged for the lighting to be dimmed and streets closed off at the appropriate time.

She has persuaded two or three pub and B & B proprietors to take on the roles of forbidding innkeepers. Rehearsals are under way among the young people. I am impressed that my own teenagers have been drawn in, though this information came from Caroline and not from the said teenagers. Lauren is practising her carols on the flute. What Michael's part will be seems rather vague; he is not talking about it and Caroline is keeping a lot of the details very close to her chest. I am rather working behind the scenes in this production, I'm responsible for putting up posters and delivering flyers but to my relief mostly staying out of the front line.

Jacob is being drilled by Dai in the afternoons, led around the field on a halter, sometimes with Adam or Luke upon his back, and rewarded by a feed of oats. He is shaping up nicely, I'm told.

"We will need about two dozen angel costumes," Caroline informs us sweetly, bringing a slight gasp from some of us assembled in my sitting room for the latest meeting.

"Won't they be rather expensive to hire?" ventures Jo.

"I wasn't thinking of hiring," says Caroline. "Simple white robes should be quite easy to make. Old sheets would be ideal. All that's needed are rectangles stitched down the sides with openings for arms and head. Maybe a cord around the waist."

I wonder who is going to volunteer to produce a couple of dozen of these simple white robes in the run-up to Christmas. Maisie and Myra seem keen on the idea though, and offer to sort out their old sheets and make a start. Janet thinks maybe she could run up a couple, and then Jane pitches in and says she's brought her sewing machine and could do a few. I'm saying nothing. Sewing has never been my strong point.

"They'll need halos," adds Caroline. "Quite easy to do with pipe cleaners and some gold shiny material."

My own halo is slipping. Fiddling with pipe cleaners and tinsel would drive me crazy.

"I'll go and put the kettle on, " I say, and get to my feet.

The baby has accompanied Caroline and been put to sleep in our little study off the kitchen, safe from cats, dogs and loud noises. I push the kettle onto the hotplate and open the door to peep in on her. She is fast asleep in her carrier, long lashes fanned out over smooth, olive-tinted cheeks, fingers curled into little fists. Her hair is so dark and shiny that it looks as though it's painted on her scalp.

As I watch, her eyelids flutter open; she turns her head a little and looks at me with huge dark eyes. Her glance goes from my face and around the room, a little puzzled to find herself in a strange place, and then back to me again. And then her face breaks into a huge smile, as though I am the one person in the world she was hoping to see. I've read somewhere that a baby this age smiles with its whole body, and it's true – suddenly her arms are flailing and her legs kicking, her whole body is wriggling with delight at the sight of another human face. She coos softly and seems to be trying to lift her arms towards me. She wants to be picked up.

It's accepted among my circle that I don't hold babies at the moment, or cuddle them, or pick them up. Something in me holds back, I know there will be pain and I can't quite face it yet. I should let Caroline know her granddaughter is awake. But instead, I find myself reaching down and lifting her warm little body. She fits so easily into my shoulder, into the curve of my neck; it's something I remember from Luke and the others, that warm, milky, talcum–powder smell, the sweet baby–weight, the small snuffling sounds, the amazing softness of baby skin. I'm crooning the little song I used to sing to the boys, rocking her gently. She likes it, the sound and the movement and the closeness. I find there are tears on my cheeks, but there's no pain, just a sense of ease and relief and a kind of new freedom. I've forgotten the ladies in the sitting room, forgotten the coffee to be made, and it's only when the kettle whistles and Jane comes looking for me that I remember. Caroline is there too, surprised to see me with the baby, looking a little concerned. "All right, Alison?"

I hand the baby to her grandmother and smile. "Yes. Just fine."

*

Mother phones, very excited. "Ali, guess what?"

She and Dad must be taking off on one of their little jaunts again.

"You're spending Christmas in the outer Hebrides?"

"Don't be silly, dear. You know I like to be home at Christmas." She draws a deep breath and says "Mark's married!"

"What?"

"He's married! Can you believe it? Isn't it the most wonderful news?"

"But – he can't be." He was only here at Easter. There was no talk of getting married then, or of anyone special in his life.

"Well, he is. It's someone he's known for a long time, apparently. Someone he's worked with. Nikki, her name is. They had a quiet wedding, but rather romantic. On Hawaii."

To say I am gobsmacked is putting it mildly. This can't be true, surely? He wouldn't go and get married without a word, would he? Without inviting any of us? I am suddenly indignant on my mother's behalf. She

243

would have loved a wedding on Hawaii.

"Alison, are you there?"

"Yes, Mum. I'm just speechless. Whatever was he thinking?"

"You sound quite cross, dear. You dad and I are thrilled. It's something we've been praying for, for years and years."

"But you don't know anything about this – this Nikki. You've never even heard of her. You have no idea what kind of person she is."

"She must be just the right person for Mark, because that's what we've been asking the Lord for," says Mum firmly. "And anyway, I had pictures of her on email this morning. She looks just adorable."

This I have to see. "I'm coming right over, Mum."

I'd been toying with the idea of a pre–Christmas launder of the loose–covers this morning. They did look rather grubby at our last planning meeting. But they'll have to wait. Jane says she'd like to do a bit of shopping, so I drop her off in town and hot–foot it to my parents.' It's one of those short, dreary days that come in December, the afternoon will be closing in by the time I pick up the boys, and dark before the big ones get home. But Mum looks as bright as a button in her red jumper and cheerful as can be, dispelling the winter gloom. She has the computer online and clicks to show me the pictures immediately.

I see, against a backdrop of blue sky, turquoise sea and palm trees, a smiling Mark, dressed casually in a white shirt and cream chinos, and beside him a tiny Hawaiian girl, also in white, a short mini–dress with deep pink flowers in her hair. They are smiling into each other's eyes. Other pictures have other poses, the two of them holding hands and looking over their shoulders into the camera, close–ups that seem to reveal that Nikki has perfect teeth and a flawless skin – though pictures on email are not always the most accurate. There are other people in the photos, a woman who might be Nikki's mother, young people and a couple of little girls, an elderly man in a wheelchair, a little boy in white shirt and shorts.

"Isn't it wonderful – so romantic," breathes Mum.

"And very sudden."

"Yes, well, there was a reason." Mum is so excited she is almost dancing round the study. Dad is making tea in the kitchen; through the open door he looks at me and rolls up his eyes in mock despair, but he is looking quietly happy too. Whatever I might think, this turns of events is one hundred per cent agreeable to them both.

"They're coming home for Christmas!" says Mum, eyes shining. "They wanted to be married before they came, but Mark thinks maybe we could have another service and celebration here, in the New Year, for all us family and friends. Nikki's father is an invalid and unable to travel – that's him in the wheelchair in the picture – and her mother can't leave him, so they wanted a wedding ceremony there. They've been friends for a long time, and it seems that romance has blossomed in the last few months."

Dad hands me a mug of tea and winks. "The stuff of a good romantic novel, eh?"

It's all a bit much for me. I sip my tea and listen to them discussing revised plans for Christmas. I remember that we'd arranged for us all to come to mine for Christmas dinner. With Dai included, that will be ten people. Ah well, thankfully the turkey is not purchased yet. I'll have to scout round for an extra large one.

"Will twelve people fit around my table?" I wonder aloud.

"Well – er – it'll be thirteen," says Mum.

I feel my eyebrows go up. "Will it?"

"Yes. Nikki has a child. From her first marriage. That little boy in the picture. He's six and he's called Robert. Let me zoom in so you can get a closer look."

She zooms while I come to terms with this fresh shock. Nikki is a divorced woman, with a child. Mark, the confirmed bachelor, has a stepson already.

"I have a new ready–made grandson!" declares Mum in tones that leave no doubt she is delighted. "Doesn't he look a sweetie? I can't wait to meet him!"

The little boy does look rather appealing, smiling shyly at the camera, ducking his head a little. I spot him in another shot, not realising he's being photographed, helping himself to a gooey–looking cake from a loaded refreshments table set up on the beach. And there's one of him and Mark, relaxing after the wedding ceremony, kicking a ball on the sand with the sun going down.

It all looks idyllic, but surely there must be a catch somewhere. I mean – a divorced woman, a mixed marriage, a child – surely there'll be problems ahead.

Mum, as usual, is reading my thoughts.

"Look, Ali, as I said, we have prayed long and hard about a wife for Mark. Now he has a wife. And a child. We're taking them as God's gifts, to him and to us. It isn't our place to judge, or question, or worry our heads about the future. It's our place – and our joy – to be thankful for them. And to love them."

Chapter Forty-Six

With the visit of Mark and his new wife only a couple of weeks away, I feel it is time to take stock of myself. Looking at the pictures of Nikki, which Mum has printed out for me, I feel she could be described as petite, chic, sparkling and immaculate, all the things I am not. Most of my weak spots I can't do much about. I could do with losing a few pounds here and there, but a diet won't take effect in that short a time, and if I go clothes shopping it's a certainty that I will panic-buy and end up spending too much money on something horrendously unsuitable and unflattering.

But I can do something about my hair.

My hair is thick, it has a bit of a wave, quite a nice shine and is a pleasing light chestnut brown, a few shades darker than Adam's. I've always worn it longish, usually tied back in a ponytail for practicality these days, and needing only the occasional visit to the hairdresser to have the ends trimmed. Now seems to be the time for some major changes.

My hairdresser, Janine, looks a little perplexed when I mention that I'd like something different this time. Her scissors are already poised for the usual trimming of split ends.

"What exactly did we have in mind?"

Janine speaks in the plural, maybe it's something a lot of hairdressers do, but I find it rather confusing. When I enquire after her teenage daughter she tells me we should be concentrating on GCSE's but instead we're spending far too much time with our new boyfriend. Asking about her young son, I'm told we had a nasty case of chicken-pox the other week and it's been a hard struggle trying to keep from picking our scabs.

I hesitate. "We – I mean I, wondered about a bob."

"Hmm." Janine considers, holding my hair against my face at each side. "You know, I've always thought a chin-length bob would suit the shape of our face."

She goes to work with a will. I find it slightly scary when I see the amount of long brown locks that are falling to the floor and piling up around my chair. But when she has artfully shaped and shampooed and blow-dried, the transformation is amazing.

My face looks back at me from the mirror, framed by a sleek, shining fall of bobbed hair, which gleams in the overhead light and moves when I move. A soft fringe covers my worry-lines. My head feels so light and free that I'm quite giddy.

Janine looks rather smug and pleased with her handiwork, holding a hand mirror for me to view from all angles. "Well, what do we think?"

I want to give her a big hug. I'll certainly be giving her a big tip.

"We're absolutely delighted," I tell her.

At school, Luke walks right past me, looking ahead and scanning the gathered parents for his mother's face. Adam glances at me, looks away, does a double-take as realisation dawns.

"Hi there, Adam" I say breezily. "Remember me?"

"I knew it was you," he says quickly, then covers up his discomfiture by taking on an accusing note. "Your hair looks different, but you've got the same coat, so I knew."

Luke has twigged now and is frowning at me.

"Well, boys, do you like my new hairstyle?" I ask.

"I liked it before," says my youngest. "I like things to be the same."

"I quite like it," says Adam cautiously. "It's a bit like that lady on TV."

"Which lady is that?" We've reached the car and I put the key into the ignition.

"The one that does the news."

I can't recall that particular newsreader, but am flattered nonetheless.

Back home, Jane loves my hair, says it makes me look no more than nineteen. Even Michael acknowledges the change, and mutters "Nice hair, Mum."

Lauren is less forthcoming. "It's nice, but a bit last year."

"That woman on TV wears this style," I say in my own defence.

"What woman is that?"

"Er – that newsreader."

Lauren frowns, tosses her own luxuriant locks, rolls her eyes, shrugs, and goes on her way. Well, I suppose expecting a compliment from her would be asking too much.

Graham makes up for it though, when he comes in for his tea. He looks at me, blinks, and his mouth falls open.

"Wow! What's happened here?"

"New hairstyle," I say nonchalantly, making sure my hair swings and falls into place again as I turn my head to pick up a serving spoon. He doesn't say anything, and when I turn again he's still standing there staring.

"Don't you like it?"

"I love it! It's like silk. Shiny silk." He comes over and lifts up a strand, lets it run through his fingers and fall. "You know, I haven't seen the back of your neck for years. You've got a beautiful nape."

Luke and Adam are in the room, but he goes right ahead and kisses the back of my neck. Oh my! This is more than I ever hoped for. I look at him from under my lashes and casually flick back my hair as I begin to dole out the potatoes and broccoli.

*

Jane has managed to secure a six-month let for the cottage at the coast, beginning the end of the year. This means a trip there to check on everything, sort out arrangements, and make sure that personal things are locked up securely or brought away.

To my surprise, when Graham offers to go down with Jane, she says she doesn't want to go to the cottage.

"It's silly, I know, but I feel I just don't want to go there again yet. It's too soon. Maybe I'll feel differently in six months. But this is my home now. Why don't you and Graham go and sort things out? You could stay the night, make a little break of it."

Now this idea has appeal, despite the million and one things to do in the run-up to Christmas and the visit of my brother and new sister-in-law. Graham is not too busy this time of year. Jo offers to have the boys for a sleepover, and Jane assures me she can easily manage the rest at home.

We drive down on a blustery, showery morning, spells of wintry sun alternating with sharp showers that fling a cold rain hard against the windscreen. The sea is grey and choppy when we arrive, beach deserted, tall grasses in the dunes bending and swaying. The house looks sad and forlorn, windows shuttered as though it's closed its eyes for a long sleep. We hurry inside out of the wind and find a chilliness that seems to seep into the bones. The first thing we do is switch on the heating, and then Graham finds firewood and kindling and builds a fire in the sitting room grate.

We feel warmer when we've heated soup and made tea. Then we go through the house together, cleaning, putting away, packing, making notes. We'll contact the estate agent and other necessary people in the morning.

"We make a good team, don't we," I remark, as we carry out another tea chest of possessions to the Nissan, to be stored in one of the outbuildings at home.

"Yes, Mrs Harper," says Graham, touching his peaked cap. "Maybe we'll make it permanent."

It's dark by the time we've finished in the cottage. Maybe we'll manage to do a little tidying up in the garden tomorrow. I've found some old worn white sheets in the linen cupboard, as directed by Jane, which will make ideal robes for angels. All in all, it's been rather a good and satisfying day.

"Shall we see if there's a restaurant open?" asks Graham. "Or just get fish and chips?"

I opt for fish and chips, and we eat them in front of the fire, washed down with a bottle of white wine which Graham picked up from the local Spar. We're tired, but it's very restful to know that there's nothing else to do, no washing up, no homework to worry about or school lunches to prepare. We go to bed in the front bedroom, which was Molly and Jane's guest room, and from there can hear the rain drumming on the roof and the waves crashing and breaking on the shore. It's as good as a weekend break in a posh hotel. Or even better.

*

Jane has been busy for days, seated at her sewing machine and surrounded by a drift of white cotton material, the stuff of which angels' robes are made. She stitches the side seams on the machine, but carefully hems by hand the neck and sleeve openings.

"We don't want them to look like they've been thrown together any old how," she says.

I'm making a Christmas cake, and I'm afraid that description could be applied to my festive culinary efforts. Anyone else would have made their cake weeks ago, and it would be marinating, or maturing, or whatever it is cakes are meant to do. Well, tough. I'm doing the best I can. Molly always made a cake for me and this is a new venture and one I'm only intending to expend the minimum amount of time and effort on. It'll all go the same way in the end.

"Thank goodness my Little Tiddlers aren't taking a leading role in

249

the Christmas play," I say fervently, wiping a smear of flour from my nose with the back of my hand. "I'd never have time to train them."

Caroline has included the little ones in her epic production; they will sit at the front and join in the carols but will not be required to wear costume. It was mayhem a couple of years ago, when Children's Church did a Nativity play and most of my class were angels. I thought I'd managed the costumes neatly by asking each mum to make provision for her own child. Trouble was, some were obviously better seamstresses than others, or perhaps just more willing to get stuck in. Several wore shapeless garments that gaped or slipped off their shoulders or tripped up the wearer. Others had adapted party dresses which didn't quite strike the right note. One or two appeared in immaculate angel costumes with wide sleeves, flowing skirts, and one even had wings! Needless to say, this made for quite a lot of snobbery and jealousy in the angel ranks. I smile, remembering the night of the performance. My little angels had to wait with me in the wings while the opening scenes were played. Then, when it came to the shepherds in the fields, they were supposed to burst forth on the stage to a chorus of 'Glory to God in the Highest!' Unfortunately, it was a long wait. Bickering and fidgeting broke out in the ranks. The winged one managed to poke someone in the eye with her appendages. The poked one retaliated with tears and a kick to the shins. Sides were taken, names called, my frantic efforts to restore calm and tone down voices were largely ignored. By the time their cue was called, I sent forth a troop of angelic beings with tearstained cheeks, haloes badly askew, and mutinous expressions. Their promises of 'peace to all mankind' seemed a little ironic.

I smile, remembering, and begin to tell the tale to Jane. She's been a little sad for the last few days, facing up to the first Christmas without her sister, and it's good to see her smile. She actually laughs out loud when I come to the punchline.

The phone rings, my hands are sticky so Jane puts aside her angel garments and answers it. There's a short conversation, and she says "I'm sure she'll ring you back in a moment."

"Your mum," she says. "They've had a call from your brother and his wife. The flight dates have been put forward. They won't be coming next week as planned, but are leaving tonight and will be here sometime tomorrow."

Chapter Forty-Seven

I'm at Mum's, waiting for the arrival of the new family members. I think we'd be nervous if there wasn't so much to do. Dad and Graham set off for the airport before daylight, with Luke's old booster seat in place for Robert, and once the boys are in school I hurry over to my old home.

Mum is surprisingly calm in the face of all the activity and anticipation. I had difficulty sleeping last night, but she looks fresh as a daisy. We've made up beds, hoovered, and put away the huge grocery shop I did at the Co Op. A casserole is simmering in the oven; they'll be here in time for a late lunch. We pause for a cup of tea and to put our feet up for a while. I look round the bright kitchen with the Christmas cactus in bloom and bowls of hyacinths showing their colours.

"I do hope Nikki and Robert will feel at home here," says Mum, noticing my glance.

I smile, remembering last night's bedtime conversation with my boys. Luke is finding the concept of a cousin rather difficult to grasp. After all, it's something my children have never had.

"Remember he's from another country," I tell them. "So we must do all we can to make him feel welcome."

"He's only six," says Luke, with the superiority of one whose eighth birthday is not too far ahead. "I expect he'll want to play baby games."

"Don't be too sure," I say. "From what I've been told, Robert is one smart cookie."

Luke looks at me blankly. "Well, he's not as big as me. So I'll be the boss of him."

"No bossing," I tell him firmly. "Bossing not allowed, especially with visitors."

Luke looks disappointed. He'd rather looked forward to giving a few orders, and maybe having someone look up to him for once.

"You'll have fun," I assure him. "And I'm sure he'll love Fudge."

Luke brightens. "Maybe they don't have hamsters in his country.Or donkeys. I could show him how to ride Jacob. I don't fall off any more. Well, not very often."

I relate this tale to Mum and she laughs.

"I'm sure they'll love it here," I tell her. "After all, she's the one you've prayed for, for all these years."

"Yes, I must remember that," says Mum, and the furrows smooth from her brow. "Thank you, dear. You're such a comfort."

They arrive a little sooner than we'd expected, traffic having been favourable, and Graham having put his foot down on the motorway. Mark ushers in his new family as Graham and my dad attend to the luggage. I see a tiny, rather crumpled little figure in a green tracksuit, hardly reaching Mark's shoulder, smiling rather uncertainly. Mum steps forward and envelops her in a hug.

"Welcome home! It's so lovely to meet you! This is my daughter, Alison."

I hug her too; her bones feel light and fragile as a bird's. Then I step back and look into amber eyes with tired lines around them, long black hair, a sweet smile in an exquisite little face. I was right, even travel-stained as she is, she has perfect teeth and flawless skin.

"Nikki, it's good to meet you."

Mark has carried in the little boy, wrapped in a plaid rug. Robert is fast asleep and shows no sign of waking.

"He was so excited to be going on a plane," says his mother "that he didn't sleep the entire eleven hour journey, and nearly drove us crazy jumping up and down, wanting to see everything and asking questions."

"How many times did we hear "Are we nearly there yet" says Mark, and we all laugh. I've heard that query so many times, on so many trips.

"Then, the minute we were in the car, he fell fast asleep."

Mark lays him gently down on the study sofa. Robert has his mother's hair and face shape and tiny form, long dark lashes lie on his cheeks. Mark slips off his red and white trainers and removes his jacket, covers him with the rug. I'm used to seeing my brother rough-housing with my kids, but this tender side of him is new to me.

Graham and I have decided we will leave the rest to lunch together, and go home. We discuss the new additions on the way. Graham thinks Nikki is quite a looker. "Mark knew a good thing when he saw it," he remarks as we turn in at our gateway.

"She seems nice," I agree. "Mind you, looks aren't everything."

Graham grins at me. He hasn't missed the fact that I dolled

myself up to the nines this morning, best jeans, boots with heels, the cashmere sweater Molly gave me last Christmas and I've hardly worn because I'm so afraid of it shrinking in the wash. Even make-up, which I seldom use.

"No, Mrs Practical Farmer's Wife. But they sure do help."

He is still quite enamoured of my new hairstyle, so I toss my head as I get out of the car, to give him the full benefit.

*

Mark's family are badly jet-lagged. For him it's not too bad; he's crossed the Atlantic many times and knows how to cope with it.

"Don't give in to it," is his motto. "Keep the hours of the place you're in, don't be tempted to reverse day and night. Drink plenty of water."

Nikki and Robert have never travelled outside of California, and the time difference hits them hard. They are wakeful at night and want to sleep until lunchtime. Mark indulges them for a day or two, but then insists on getting them out of bed. He brings them over to us on the first Saturday so they can meet the kids. Robert and my boys regard each other curiously. Robert is tiny for six, a very beautiful child with big expressive dark eyes. Luke beside him looks positively lanky, a fact that he's taken due note of, himself. He draws himself up to his full height, and says "Would you like to play?"

Robert nods. He's still a little shy with new people. Still magnanimous, Luke says "You're a visitor, so I have to let you choose." He glances at me, acknowledging the drilling I gave him earlier. "What do you like to play?"

"I like to play chess," says Robert in a clear, polite little voice.

Luke's face falls. He hasn't yet mastered the rudiments of chess himself. "We've got tiddly winks," he offers. "Or we can play on the play station."

Robert's face brightens. The play station, it seems, crosses all barriers of race, culture, age and ability.

They go off to the sitting room, followed by a cat and a puppy or two.

"I love your home," says Nikki, who is sitting as close to the Aga as she can get. "And such a great family. I was an only child, and I always wanted to be part of a big family."

She is looking a little pinched, and smiles ruefully. "I do feel the cold though. I'd no idea it would be so cold."

Today in fact is rather mild for December, a bit grey and gloomy but dry overhead and not too muddy underfoot. Mark has gone with

Graham and Michael to walk round the fields, leaving us women and kids to get to know each other. Jane makes coffee, and Nikki takes it gratefully, wrapping her delicate little fingers around the mug.

"Didn't Mark tell you about our winters?"

"Well, maybe he did. I kind of imagined hills with snow on them and blue skies and sunshine, the way it is in the mountains back home." She takes a sip of coffee. Jane has made real coffee in the percolator, in honour of guests who know real coffee when they drink it.

"Oh, that's so good! I just can't get used to tea."

"You should try proper tea, made in a china pot and drunk in china cups," says Jane. "Earl Grey or Darjeeling. No teabags."

"I should. Mark drinks tea all the time. You must show me how to make English tea."

When she mentions Mark, she looks as though a light has been switched on inside. She mentions him a lot. Mark has always been such a good friend, even before they started dating. He's loved by everyone at work. He's amazing with Robert. Even Brad, her ex in New York, who comes to visit Robert on occasions, thinks Mark is a good guy. Brad might be the one who provides treats and expensive toys, but Mark is the one who's taught Robert to ride a two-wheeler bike, to play chess, who reads him bedtime stories and takes him swimming and helps with homework.

I can't believe this is my charming, fun-loving, slightly laddish brother she's talking about, the one we despaired of ever settling down. How things can change, almost overnight. But maybe it wasn't overnight, considering the prayers that my parents have sent up. However it happened, it's turned out well. I like Nikki a lot and little Robert is a sweetie. I send up a silent prayer of my own, of thanksgiving.

*

In moderation, I like the excitement, the razza-ma-tazz, the playing of carols and glitter of shop windows in the run up to Christmas, even though I know it's not what Christmas is all about. But enough is enough. It's not only the appearance of Christmas stuff from mid-October onward, the jolly Santas and flashing lights, the tinsel and tannoy and tawdriness that is supposed to create a festive atmosphere that I object to. It's the grab-and-get mentality, shoppers out to acquire as much as they can, buy now and pay later, and retailers scheming to make mighty profits. I'm already inclined to mutter that things weren't like this in my day.

It's true our childhood Christmases were simpler. We were often encouraged to make Christmas gifts, or grow them, or at least carefully think out what the recipient would really like. We never had the mountains of cheap plastic and trashy toys or the latest fad in technology, which my kids and their peers seem to crave.

So I try to plan my Christmas shopping, spread it over the year, buy thoughtfully and avoid the December crowds.

Yet here we are, my new sister-in-law and me, right in the middle of the city shopping mall with Christmas shoppers to right and left and garish displays in every shop window. There's a towering Christmas tree in the square, and a funfair, of all things, creating yet more noise and discord. We really came to buy warm clothes for Nikki and Robert. What my brother was thinking when they were packing I can't imagine, but they arrived far from adequately kitted out for our damp and chilly winters, with thin jersey tops and jeans and not a woolly sock between them.

We have provided Robert with outgrowns from Luke, most of which are still a bit too large and swamp his tiny figure. But at least he's warm. Today we've bought warm socks and thermal underwear for them both, some chunky sweaters and a big padded jacket, plus fur-lined boots for Nikki, purchased in the children's department of one of the big stores. Her feet are so tiny.

She opts to wear the coat and boots, and looks warmer already. We treat ourselves to coffee in the echoing mezzanine floor of the mall. Our bags flow out around our table. I've managed to get in a little shopping myself. Girly things for Lauren mostly, with advice from Nikki, to whom Lauren seems to have taken a shine.

"It's been fun, this morning," she says, pulling off her new thermal gloves. "I always wanted a sister to go shopping with. Do you and Lauren often shop together?"

I pull a wry face. "Not all that often. I daren't comment on anything – if I like something she tries on, she'll automatically rule it out. My job seems to be to wait quietly by the door and come forward with the credit card when needed."

She laughs, her perfect teeth very white against her olive skin. "She'll be okay. She's a great kid. All your kids are." She pauses reflectively. "You know, if Mark and I can create a family like yours, we'll do well. You have so much love. Just to see you and Graham, that special look you have for each other."

I put down my cup, surprised. "Do we? I know my mum and dad have that look – "

"And so do you two. As though there's something you share that just belongs to the two of you. Not even your kids – although it spreads out to them too. And to other people. I feel so welcome here – "

I have a lump in my throat, and try to make a joke to cover up. "In spite of the horrid cold weather?"

"Yeah. I love it here. But you must come to California to visit us! And to Hawaii. You'd love Hawaii."

Now there's a thought to cheer up a chilly winter's day!

Chapter Forty-Eight

It's a good thing we got that warm clothing for Nikki and Robert, because suddenly there's a change in the weather and winter is here with a vengeance. There's a drop in temperature at night and a chill in the air, the skies are gunmetal grey and full of foreboding. A thin wind seems to cut to the bone.

"A lazy wind," says Dai. "Goes right through you instead of round."

"Something coming," says Graham, scanning the sky with the keen eye of an arable farmer.

The little boys are wild with delight at the possibility of a white Christmas. They've never seen snow at Christmas, and Robert has never seen snow at all, except on Christmas cards. He has adapted to the weather, muffling up and joining in whatever the others are doing out of doors. Today Graham has taken them up into the woodland and they've chosen two Christmas trees, one for us and one for Mum and Dad. They come home triumphant, three small boys amidst a mass of greenery in the tractor box, eyes sparkling and cheeks pink from the cold. What the Health and Safety people would say I can't imagine, but they're far enough away in their centrally heated offices and not here spoiling our fun.

The boys burst in, shedding muddy boots, coats and hats and demanding hot chocolate, biscuits (or cookies as Robert calls them), and decorations for the Christmas tree. They've all shaken down very well together. Any ideas of bossing and a pecking order has vanished – if anything, although he's the youngest, Robert has acquired extra status in the eyes of Luke and Adam, for three reasons. First, he's flown on a plane, second, he plays chess, and third, he has *two dads*. They are particularly envious of the last, another dad in addition to the everyday one, a dad who visits and provides expensive toys and lavish outings, seems a very desirable accessory to their hedonistic little minds. I expect at any moment to hear a plaintive voice declaring "It isn't fair!"

Graham grins wryly when I mention this to him. "Materialistic little wretches. Makes one feel very appreciated, not!"

"Don't worry," I tell him. "I see no sign of another dad on the horizon."

"Well, that's a comfort," says Graham.

Robert has lost his shyness and, I'm afraid, picked up some bad habits. I'd hoped his exquisite manners would rub off on my own two, but, alas! I fear it's just the opposite. I see him vying with Luke for the foil-wrapped chocolate biscuit, and using his elbows to make way for himself in the crush to choose decorations when I bring out the box of Christmas tree ornaments. He shrieks with glee when the pup, Barney, grabs a long string of tinsel and runs off with it. I close the sitting room door on the melee of small boys and dogs and go to consider lunch.

*

In the afternoon, it begins to snow, beginning with a few flakes casually fluttering to earth as though they don't really mean it, but rapidly gaining momentum. By three thirty the valley is blotted out in a cloud of whirling grey dots, and what's worse, it's sticking on the hard ground. Mark phones and says he's coming to pick up Robert, which is greeted by a chorus of protest and pleading.

"Plee –eese can he sleep over?" begs Luke.

"We could build a snowman tomorrow," says Adam, and adds "Robert's never played in the snow."

Robert says nothing, but his dark pleading eyes speak volumes. I groan inwardly, thinking of the tramping in and out leaving cold draughts, frozen fingers and rows of soaked little mittens drying on the Aga rail, but I know I'll be labelled a wicked old witch if I refuse.

"Well, all right," I say, and make the arrangements with my brother, to a chorus of whoops and yells and high fives going on around me. I am a glutton for punishment, I know, but, hey, it's Christmas and it only happens once a year.

*

With time flying by, there are other worries that claim my attention. The Nativity play is scheduled for the Sunday before Christmas, which, help! is less than a week away. The snow has stopped falling but it's lying, a pristine thick covering that takes the breath away with its beauty, coating every branch, twig and stem with a pure sparkling white and crunching underfoot. I'm glad the spectacle has been provided, for Nikki and Robert's sake, but, oh, it's cold, and as always it presents problems. I speak to Caroline next day, when Michael has taken the boys sledging down our steep meadow and I have a little respite. She wonders if we should call a meeting to discuss the situation.

Now, a meeting is something I could well do without, with a trillion things to do and the minutes ticking away. I try to steer her away from this idea.

"But shouldn't we have some alternative plan," she says, sounding unlike her usual unflappable self. "I mean, the streets will be cleared, of course, but there might be patches of ice underfoot. We can't risk any accidents, with someone riding the donkey and so on. And mightn't there be travel difficulties for those out of town?"

That is a point. In fact, if more snow is on its way, our hill could become impassable, to 4 x 4s, donkeys and any other traffic. Oh dear! The whole thing could go badly pear–shaped. I'm not going to say that to Caroline though.

"Look, Caroline, there's not a lot we can do about the weather. We can pray, of course. Didn't someone in the Bible pray that there'd be no rain for forty days, and there wasn't?"

"Oh, I'm not sure that would be the right thing."

"No, I'm joking. But we can put it all in God's hands, can't we? Just pray that good comes, whether or not the play goes forward as planned. He might have something even better. We can trust him."

She sounds reassured. "Yes. You're always so sensible, Alison. So down to earth, and yet full of faith."

Now it's she who's joking, surely! I wish I was as confident as I sound. I'm beginning to have grave doubts myself about this play.

*

We needn't have worried too much about the weather. There is still snow on the fields, making a monochrome panorama with black hedges and bare trees and the silver ribbon of the river. There's been sunshine some days, bringing blue skies and a sparkle to the snow that hurts the eyes. The boys have loved it, sledging and snowballing and building a lopsided snowman on the lawn. They look like getting their white Christmas.

And now it's Sunday, morning service and dinner behind us and we're preparing for the big event. Michael and Lauren stayed in town to be handy for final rehearsals and briefings at the Vicarage, the rest of us will follow on as dusk falls. I've been alternately excited and despairing all day. This is surely the most ambitious project Caroline has ever planned. Or is it just crackbrained? We shall find out very soon.

Graham and I drop off the boys at the church where the other children are gathering, and Jane goes too. She says she would rather wait in the warm than stand about on chilly street corners. I think she's wise, it's a cold night and our breath shows as puffs of white in the street lighting. We park and walk to St John's Road, where I am amazed to see that a crowd has gathered on the pavements, muffled to the eyebrows and shuffling their feet to keep warm. There's a little muted conversation, but mainly they're quiet, waiting. Expectant. I think of all those flyers I delivered and am gratified. The whole town and district seems to have turned out.

And then, suddenly and dramatically, the street lights go out and the only light comes from some strategically placed house windows with the curtains drawn back. In the sudden hush that falls, there's a sound, the clip–clop of hooves on tarmac.

Around the corner comes a donkey, humble and plodding as though he'd never kicked up his heels and raced around a meadow. He's led by a tall sixth–former from Michael's year in school – Jason Parkinson I think he's called – and a slight cloaked figure is on his back.

I feel a lump rise in my throat. The travellers move slowly, Joseph stumbles a little as he walks and Mary sways with weariness. The donkey plods stoically. What a long hard journey this must have been. Tears come into my eyes.

They are passing us now. The gathered people seem to be holding their breaths. The travellers look to neither right nor left, they are heading for a lighted window ahead, where a sign proclaims *Red Lion Inn*. I saw a notice with 'Vacancies' in the window only this morning, but I know that when the travellers knock and ask for lodging the answer will be 'No room.'

Some of the gathered people are following, but I take Graham's arm. "Let's go to the church. I want to be there right from the start."

We take the short cut to St John's. The church has its outside lights on, haloed by frost, but inside it's dim. The only lights come from fat candles in the sconces, flickering a little and casting shadows. But the church is packed. I'd thought the whole town population was outside, watching the opening scenes, but here are more people, every seat full, even up in the balcony. We manage to squeeze in at the end of a pew, the other occupants shuffling up to make room. It's quiet, the organist is softly playing 'O little town of Bethlehem' and here again is that sense of expectancy. I peer around, trying to pick out familiar people, my own family, but it's dim and faces look veiled and shadowy. I wonder how the children are being persuaded to stay so quiet up at the front. And then, as I look, I feel my scalp prickle and my heart miss a beat. All around the nave, in the alcoves or against the walls, figures are standing, tall silent figures in white robes. They stand straight and still, hands clasped, watchful. They are waiting. I feel myself holding my breath too. At the front, the choir begins to sing, softly 'O Holy Night.'

There is a sudden commotion at the side door which opens into the vestry. People crane forward. There is movement in the shadows, then a soft light goes on at the steps to the chancel. Straw bales have been placed there, and upon them sits the tired, drooping figure of a young girl, with a young man standing by and leaning on a staff.

Suddenly, there is a blaze of brilliance as all the lights in the church go on at once. I jump, there are gasps of surprise and we're all blinking in the light. I see the watching angels come to life, lifting their heads and raising their arms. And then the door at the back of the church opens and another angel comes in, the tallest one of all, a young giant in white robes and hair like burnished gold. In his arms he holds a tiny baby. I hear more intakes of breath.

This angel strides confidently down the aisle between the rows of spellbound congregation, the infant held tenderly, and when he reaches the young girl he stoops and lays the baby gently in her arms. The girl raises her head and for just a moment they exchange a look, a look that holds trust and gratitude and something else that only the two of them share, a look that I recognise. My eyes are so full of tears that the scene is blurred. The tall angel has drawn to one side, the other angels and the choir are singing with all their might: 'Hark the herald angels sing, glory to the new born king!' The congregation is joining in now, many voices merging and swelling in the familiar words; 'With the angelic host proclaim, Christ is born in Bethlehem!'

I'm holding on to Graham's hand with all my might, my heart swelling with the wonder of it. I see Lauren's shining blonde head and hear the sweet notes of her flute. There are Mum and Dad, with Mark, Nikki and little Robert, and I pick out the heads of Luke and Adam, one fair and one tawny, among the other children. Jane is there, and Jo and Stuart and their children and there are my neighbours, Sue and Mike and their sons, and Dai. And Caroline, play producer extraordinaire, and Paul, preparing to speak. And – yes – there is Sonia, and John, with

Harry and Victoria. Little Victoria is in her daddy's arms, her head in a red fur-trimmed hat resting on his shoulder. My heart is overflowing.

The teenage mother lays her baby tenderly in the manger, which Graham spent several evenings making from pieces of oak. A little olive-tinted hand waves in the air and there's the soft coo of a baby voice. It matters not that this child is not quite newborn, and that she is the wrong sex. I feel the casting is a touch of genius. The baby is not called Bibs any more, she has a proper name and it is one perfectly suited to her first starring role, and to the part she has already played in reality in her short life. She is called Grace.

I feel my heart leap with sudden joy. God's grace and love are tangible things here, in this place, at this hour. It reaches to us all, those who know it and those who don't, and I remember again those words I heard at Molly's funeral: *'I have done all things well.'*

Tomorrow will come, and the next day, and Christmas will be here, and a new year with its struggles and sorrows and joys. But here, tonight, as Paul's strong voice begins to tell out the wonderful story of the child born for our redemption, I know that it is a time for rejoicing.